CU00829653

Heat Clinic

A HEATVERSE NOVEL

ALEXIS B. OSBORNE

Dark Moon
PUBLISHING

Copyright © 2023 by Alexis B. Osborne

All rights reserved. No part of this book may be reproduced, stored, or transmitted in any form or by any electronic or mechanical means, including information storage and retrieval systems, without express written permission from the author, except for the use of brief quotations in a book review. Purchase only authorized electronic editions via Amazon and do not participate in or encourage electronic piracy of copyrighted materials. Thank you for supporting artists. To request permissions, contact the author at alexisosborneromance@gmail.com

Editing by Lindsay York of LY Publishing

Cover © 2023 by Alexis B. Osborne

Interior art © 2023 by Alexis B. Osborne

Discrete edition cover by GetCovers

ISBN: 978-1-957341-20-0 (eBook)

ISBN: 978-1-957341-21-7 (Paperback)

ISBN: 978-1-957341-22-4 (Discrete Paperback)

The characters and events portrayed in this book are fictitious. Likewise, certain characters, places, and incidents are the product of the author's imagination, and any resemblance to actual persons, living or dead, or actual events, is entirely coincidental.

Printed in the United States of America

First printing edition 2023

Dedication

For everyone who read the tag line "it's the literary equivalent of a bunch of fetish gear tossed into a dumpster and set on fire" and 1-clicked, this one's for you. You might not want to read this one in public.

What is Omegaverse?

If you're unfamiliar with the omegaverse genre then here is a quick rundown of it's quirks and tropes. Omegaverse, sometimes called A/B/O or OV, is a sort of alternate reality where humans are divided into 3 dynamics: alphas, betas, and omegas.

Alphas are physically bigger and more muscular than betas and omegas. They're natural born leaders who fiercely protect their loved ones, but they can become aggressive at times and their jealous and possessive urges can sometimes get them into trouble. Each alpha give off a unique pheromones / scent / perfume that attracts omegas as a lure. An alpha claims another person as a packmate by biting a claiming bite into the juncture between the neck and shoulder. The base of an alpha's penis contains a knot which swells upon orgasm to stopper up an omega and tie the alpha and omega together for a short time for a higher chance of pregnancy. Alphas produce copious amounts of cum, and their cum is often highly nutritious to help feed an omega who doesn't eat during a heat. Alphas exposed to an omega in heat go into a rut and can become frenzied and combative against other alphas. Alphas purr to soothe distressed omegas, growl as a warning or threat to others, and bark to deliver a command. In heterosexual OV a female alpha often has a lock at the entrance of the vagina (the female version of a knot) that swells and locks onto a penis during her orgasm. In some LGBTQ OV a female alpha's clit swells into a pseudopenis, usually a smaller one than a male's, with a knot at the base and she can impregnate others.

Betas are the balanced citizens of the omegaverse. Their body size and shape varies from person to person. They don't experience the heats or ruts that omegas and alphas do and they don't have knots or locks. Sometimes they have pheromones like alphas and omegas do, but sometimes these are underdeveloped and faint. It varies widely from author to author. These are the average everyday regular humans of the omegaverse. Most OV books focus on alpha/omega pairings but beta packmates exist in many polyam romances too.

Omegas are the smaller and often more slender and submissive dynamic. Instead of menstruating, they experience estrous/heats. Heats range from a monthly occurrence to a few times a year depending on the author and the omega. Heats last for days to a week, similar to a period. While in heat, an omega becomes obsessed with finding a compatible alpha, nesting, and breeding. The delirium and increased libido of a heat may drive an omega to accept a strange alpha they normally wouldn't choose. Omegas produce a unique pheromone / scent / perfume like an alpha does. When in heat, this pheromone acts as a lure and becomes addicting to alphas and can send an alpha into rut. During heat, an omega produces excess lubricant called "slick" which helps ease the chaffing from a week-long sex marathon. An alpha's growl can trigger an omega to produce an extra gush of slick. Heats often make omegas physically warmer to the touch and sensitive to rough fabric. Omegas who have been bitten between the neck and shoulder by an alpha are considered claimed or mated. Mating is the OV equivalent of marriage and is usually permanent. Omegas are more fertile than betas. In some OV books, omegas are prone to having multiple babies rather than singles and sometimes the infants are called pups. While in heat, omegas usually don't eat except for an alpha's nutritive cum. In heterosexual OV, the alpha's knot lodges behind her pubic bone to tie them together and trap the pool of semen near the cervix to increase the chance of pregnancy. In some LGBTQ OV, a male omega has a self-lubricating anus and accepts an alpha's knot anally or they may have two holes plus a smaller penis. Mpreg, or male pregnancy, is a topic you'll sometimes find in gay MM OV. The male omega either gives birth through c-section or delivers anally or through their second hole. How MPreg works is author dependent and varies.

Pheromone preferences vary widely from alpha to alpha and omega to omega. The saying "one man's trash is another man's treasure" applies here. What smells amazing to one alpha/omega smells gross or bland to another. Many OV romances involve alphas and omegas looking for scent matches or their "fated mate" rather than dating. Alphas and omegas will scent mark each other through touch via pheromones, especially by rubbing their partner with their cheek or chin or touching their scent gland as a way to claim their "territory."

Nesting is something that omegas in heat and pregnant omegas do. It involves gathering lots of soft bedding and pillows and creating a small, cozy space that makes them feel safe. The nest is where omegas spend their heat and it can be where they'll give birth and raise their young, too. Think of it like the coziest adult pillow fort you've ever built. Omegas in heat like to make the nest smell like their alpha or pack through scent marking and sex. It's not unusual for an omega to drag her packmate's cast off clothes into the nest. If you've ever stollen a boyfriend's hoodie and worn it to bed because it smells like him then that's a good example of human nesting behavior.

Omegaverse books sometimes have shifters (like were-wolves) but many of them don't. Some omegaverse books even take place with orcs or elves or in space with aliens!

The Heatverse is a non-shifter contemporary OV. There are no werewolves or shifters in this series.

Content Guide

If you do not have triggers and you don't want to read potential spoilers then skip this page.

The content warnings listed below are accurate to this book but this list may not be complete. If you have questions regarding a specific trigger please contact the author at alexisosbornero mance@gmail.com

Spoiler Zone - Spoiler Zone - Spoiler Zone

Heat Clinic is a character driven cozy and steamy contemporary why choose MMMF omegaverse romance that contains mature themes of: adoption (brief mention), age gap, anal training, babies (bonus epilogue), breastfeeding (bonus epilogue), BDSM, birth control, blood, bondage, brat taming, breeding, claiming bites, deceased parents, degradation play (very mild), dogging, domestic discipline, DP/DVP/TP, erotic photography, exhibitionism, face fucking, fetish gear, free use sex, gags, glory holes, infertility (brief mention), narcissistic mother, praise kink, pregnancy (bonus epilogue), public sex, spanking, sword crossing, and toxic family dynamics.

Heat Clinic was written to be the best of both worlds for readers who enjoy the fun of breeding without the pregnancy/babies and those who like it all. For readers who prefer not to read about pregnancy or babies, the bonus epilogue can be skipped.

A HEATVERSE NOVEL

Heat Clinic

ALEXIS B. OSBORNE

Chapter One

EMILY

HOW AM I GOING TO GET THROUGH THIS HEAT CYCLE, AND WHY does my body have the worst timing ever? The double digit number of my bank account balance and the sheer number of days left on the calendar until payday mock me as another clenching spasm hits me low in my pelvis. Too many days left 'til next Thursday. Not enough money.

To be fair, there's never enough.

But my heat doesn't care about my financial situation. It always sneaks up on me. Some omegas have a regular cycle with a few days of symptoms to warn them it's coming. Hot flashes, a sore back, moodiness, a rise in their libido. Me? My body goes from *it's Tuesday* to *I need to get dicked down and knotted* in less than a day.

"Did they forget and put mustard on it again?" Lindsay asks, pulling me out of my thoughts.

I glance from my mobile banking app to my untouched cheeseburger and paper basket of fries. It's all cold. The cheese has congealed and the fries are limp. But it's not like I'm hungry anyway. Omegas don't eat during their heat. Well… not food.

"I'm not feeling well. Actually, I think I'm going to leave early and use some of my PTO," I say.

"Oh, that sucks. I hope you don't have the stomach bug that's going around. Half of my department is out right now."

"No, it's…" I look around the break room, but it's almost empty at this hour. Most people took their lunch earlier, but we got stuck in that stupid meeting that could have been an email, so it's already two in the afternoon.

I drop my voice low. "It's my cycle."

Thank goodness it's a holiday weekend and I won't have to use up too many of my hours.

Lindsay's eyes brighten as she smiles. "Ooh. Wanna go out with me tonight? My roommate's dating the bouncer at the new rut bar that opened on Cherry Street and I'm dying to see it. I hear they have champagne rooms."

I grimace at the thought of it, at the idea of wading into a noisy bar packed with horny alphas, all of their scents mingling into a nauseating potpourri as they try to pretend they're not rubbing up on me on purpose while they walk by and attempt to out-purr one another.

"Uh… no, but maybe next weekend?" I throw my napkin over the top of my uneaten meal, my stomach queasy at the sight of it. "I'm going to go check in at the free clinic. When I get home, I'll text you."

"The free-*use* clinic?" Her eyes bug out, her voice rising with each squeaked-out word.

I look around the not-quite empty break room and squirm in my seat. "Yeah. But maybe don't shout it so the entire office can hear?" Heats are a completely normal part of an omega's life. They're nothing to be ashamed of, but that doesn't mean I need the entire office in my business, either.

She presses three fingertips to her mouth. "Shit. I'm sorry.

You caught me off guard. I thought they had apps and, like, nice omega centers for that."

"Our insurance is shitty and they don't cover that. And the last alpha I hooked up with from Heat Buddy ate everything in my fridge and left me with a mountain of laundry to do when I came around. That was also the worst UTI of my fucking life."

He didn't bathe me even once during my three-day heat, and I'd woken up sticky, crusty, and reeking of sex and pheromones. The free clinic might not be glamorous, but the beta attendants make sure none of the alphas get too rough and that I won't forget to drink water or take a shower. Plus I won't have to worry about coming out of a heat with a mating bite I never consented to. It's not all that common of a problem anymore, but it happens.

"Okay, umm… be safe and have fun? Do you want me to swing by your apartment and water your plants?" she asks.

I stand and push my chair in, then toss out my untouched lunch. Another cramp hits me and I stagger a little. "That would be great, thanks. I'll leave a key under the mat and text you when I'm coming home. It'll be a few days."

My boss is less enthused for me to take the rest of the day off right before a holiday weekend, but a quick promise that I should be back when the office reopens on Tuesday lessens the sting. Traffic isn't bad at this time of day as I swing by my apartment and pack a bag with a few things. Comfy pajamas, enough under-wear to last me a month, the travel-size toiletries I keep on hand for heat emergencies, an extra long phone charger, and the soft throw blanket from my couch.

The duffel bag is near to bursting and heavy as I lug it down the stairs and throw it into the backseat of my car, stopping twice to breathe through cramps. I clench the steering wheel so tightly my knuckles turn white as I drive downtown and park in the free clinic's omega lot.

Most of the people I walk by on the street are oblivious betas, but an alpha in a suit looks up from his coffee as I pass him, his nostrils flaring as he scents me. Inside the free clinic's lobby, a half a dozen people sit, staring at their phones, while a bored receptionist taps away at her computer. I shoulder my bag higher and wait for her to make eye contact.

"How can I help you?" she asks.

"Yeah, umm, I'd like to use your omega services?"

"Do you have an appointment?"

I frown and drag the slipping duffel bag strap up again. "No. I didn't know I needed one." How does someone make an appointment for a heat?

"Fill this out."

She hands me a clipboard, so I find a seat and set my bag down in the one next to me as I go through the routine questions. There's the expected name, age, gender, dynamic, and sexual orientation questions followed by more personal ones. Last heat or menstrual period. Relationship status. I circle *single* twice. Reason for your visit today. Symptoms you're experiencing. Number of pregnancies and number of children birthed. Medication taken.

Underneath the intake paperwork, there's a discreet pamphlet about domestic abuse and how to safely ask for help. It's been laminated to the clipboard. I flip the paperwork over and continue to fill out the back.

When I bring it back to her, she doesn't even look up from her computer screen, so I set it down on the counter, then go back to my chair and wait. My foot bounces as I sit there and contemplate if this is something I really want to do.

"Emily," a nurse in faded pink scrubs calls out from the door to the back. "Hi. Follow me, please."

I rise and grab my bag and follow her in, ignoring the way my heart beats against my ribs. We go into an exam room and I sit while she takes my vital signs.

"One hundred point eight degrees. When did your heat start?" she asks.

"A few hours ago. They come on really fast. Should I have called ahead?"

"No, it's fine. We offer other routine services Monday through Saturday from six to six, but our heat and rut services are twenty-four hours. A heads up phone call that you're coming is nice. We have escorts who help omegas who need it through the parking lot. Alphas have their own parking lot and come in through the back of the clinic, but sometimes people get confused and accidental crossings happen. Here, take a card. It has our office and emergency numbers on it. Make sure you put it in your phone."

I take the business card and pocket it while she looks at my questionnaire and starts typing stuff into the computer.

"So I see you're here for heat services today. How did you want to treat that?" she asks.

Treat it? Are they really going to make me say it out loud? "Umm, I thought… Don't you…" Everyone's heard the stories. Are they exaggerated?

"We have pharmaceutical or holistic treatment options. You can either get a heat blocker shot or you can choose the room and board option until your heat has run its course."

"I don't react well to blockers or suppressors. I'd like the, um, holistic room and board option. Is that still free? I have insurance, but it's not great."

She finishes typing her note. "It's completely free. The program is paid for through government grants and private donations. All right, since this is your first time here, we have an intake video for you to watch. It's about ten minutes long, and then the doctor will come and see you and answer any questions you have. If everything is good to go, then we'll take blood samples and you'll meet your beta attendant and get your room assignment."

The video is dry and boring as a narrator moves about the screen, standing in front of anatomical models as she explains the variances in omega and alpha anatomy. It reminds me of the videos we had to watch in health class as teens. The ones that resulted in a lot of giggling as our beta softball coach tried to force us to take it seriously.

The narrator leaves the models and walks down a hallway, showing off the secure omega wing, and then she takes the viewer to the rut room.

And then it's not boring at all.

The rut room is enormous. There are rows of black vinyl padded cutouts in all of its walls. Each hole is staggered at slightly varying heights. She heads to one of these cutouts and sticks her hand through, the camera following as they show the small enclosure just beyond the wall. The tiny room is cushioned in washable vinyl and bare except for handhold straps that dangle off the walls and ceiling.

Next, she shows how stirrups unfold from the wall. A smiling, clothed actor joins her and demonstrates how the rut room is used. He enters the cubicle and lies down as the narrator helps him get his legs in the stirrups and straps him into place, then angles them until he's presented properly.

The video cuts to another room that's similar but different. The cutouts are lower, and the floor is padded. In this one, the actor slips his legs through the opening and turns, draping belly down over a padded bolster.

The demonstration ends abruptly as the credits roll. My first thought is how sticky the floor must get, and a bubble of hysterical laughter escapes me.

Am I really doing this? When I shift in my seat, the slick lips of my pussy rub and slide against one another, and my clit throbs.

I might be alarmed and nervous about the idea of being rutted raw by a room full of strange alphas, but my body is thoroughly on board. I pull at my shirt to fan my hot face.

They leave me there for what feels like way too long, and then there's a knock on the door. "Come in!" I squeak.

The doctor, an Indian woman with gray-streaked hair, opens the door and smiles at me. "Hello, Emily. Nice to meet you." She shuts the door behind her and leans against the counter. "Do you have any questions for me about what you saw?"

My mind goes blank as every question I had planned leaves my head. "I, umm… That's a lot. How many…"

"We average about two dozen omegas a day and two hundred alphas."

"Two hundred!" Oh, God. Two hundred was a lot. Every day? For three days?

The doctor smiles, the lines alongside her mouth showing that it's something she does frequently. "Yes, but remember that not all alphas will visit every station or stay for every treatment cycle. We accommodate all sexual orientations and do not discriminate, but you are encouraged to tell us your orientation, limits, and preferences in advance. Some alphas also have a weaker pheromone tolerance than others. All participants receive a color-coded arm and ankle band, and our beta attendants are trained to stop and redirect as needed. We have a strict *one-strike and you're out* policy across all facilities nationwide."

Some of my panic fades with her reassurance. "Right."

"Are you still interested in continuing, or would you like to discuss your other options?"

Another cramping spasm makes me twitch in my seat as I resist the urge to rub against the chair in front of the doctor. The slick panties I changed into will keep me from embarrassing myself as my pussy grows damp at the thought of so many alphas close by. I don't have any other choice at this point. Not really. I wasted too much time driving across town and packing. Walking out of here will end up with me latching onto the first decent-smelling alpha on the street as I try to hump their leg.

"No, I'll… I'd like to continue."

"All right." She pulls yet another form from a cubby and clips it to a clipboard, then fishes a pen from a drawer. "Fill this out and sign it. I'll send my assistant in to draw blood. We run a standard STD panel. I have your medication list from your pharmacy. Once the bloodwork comes back, we'll take over administration of your birth control and assign you a room and a beta attendant."

"Yeah, fine," I murmur as I study the three-page front-and-back document while she leaves.

A lot of it is repetitive stuff I've already answered, but some of it is new. They have me filling out an enormous preference section that asks me everything from the kinds of scents I like and what age brackets I'd like to match to. What the hell is gourmand, and are there really eighty-year-old alphas coming to the free clinic? I hesitate for a moment, then darken the bubbles for the twenty-five to forty-five brackets. Under gender and dynamic, I select all of them. The part about group activities confuses me —isn't a giant glory hole a group activity? I check the box to be safe.

The assistant comes and draws my blood, and then I wait. It feels like an eternity later when the nurse from the beginning returns and holds up a pair of white bands, then pulls some plastic charms from her pocket.

"Here's your bands, hun," she says as I hold my wrist out to her, and she snaps it into place with a bi pride flag-colored plastic triangle. The rest of the armband's holes get tagged with other colored charms I don't understand. She asks me to roll up my leggings and repeats the process with my ankle.

"Your tests came back fine. Here's your medication." She

hands me a tiny paper cup with a round pink pill inside, then fills a paper cone with water from the cooler in the hallway.

I down it and drain the cup, then hand them both back to her.

She glances at her paperwork. "Your beta attendant is Sam, and your room number is twenty-eight."

I hope she's as nice as everyone else has been. So far, I feel like I've gotten pretty lucky. This is way better than suffering through the tedium of trying to talk to a Heat Buddy match who answers every single question with a one-word answer that makes me want to rip my hair out in frustration.

"The rooms are small, but they're private. The door is keyed to your bracelet so only you and staff can enter. I wrote your room number on the inside of your band so if you forget it you can peek and check. Not that you'll be alone. One of us will always be with you, but just in case. I know that heat can make omegas confused sometimes."

That's putting it mildly.

I follow her through the maze of the back area as she leads me to a hallway filled with doors that have a room number plaque and a black badge scanner. We stop outside of room twenty-eight.

"Go ahead and try it to make sure your armband works," the nurse says.

I hold my armband up to the scanner, and a tiny LED light turns green as an electronic buzzing sound alerts that the door is unlocked. She wasn't kidding. The room is compact. It's about half the size of a standard hotel room, and the full-size mattress takes up almost the entire room. There's a narrow closet and a utilitarian bathroom.

"Your attendant will be in charge of your needs, so if there's something you want, all you have to do is ask. The attendants also bring you to and from your treatment sessions. Most sessions last about four hours and then you'll have a break to rest. As your heat reaches its peak, we'll reassess your needs and vital signs.

You'll have bloodwork done every day to make sure you're not getting malnourished or dehydrated."

That surprises me. There are so many stories, so many rumors, that it's hard to tell what's exaggeration and what's real.

"Oh, here's Sam now," she says as she glances down the hallway.

A tan man with sandy hair and warm brown eyes waves as he steps into the doorway. He's wearing green scrubs and bright blue sneakers, and his wide, friendly smile makes his eyes crinkle at the corners. A smattering of freckles cover his nose and cheeks.

Oh, shit.

Sam is a man.

And he's hot.

Chapter Two

EMILY

Sam offers to take my bag from me as I stare at him in mute embarrassment. I suppose it's silly to still feel shy. Dozens, potentially hundreds of alphas are about to see me. All of me. Naked. What's one hot beta to add to the list?

"Emily?" the nurse asks, her head cocked. "Are you okay?"

"Yeah," I croak, and let him slide the strap off my shoulder. "Just nervous. I think it's finally hitting me that this is really happening."

She nods. "Well, you can leave whenever you'd like. But only the emergency contact you listed on the forms can take custody of you while you're experiencing heat delirium."

I'm regretting listing my mother right now. But who else would I have put down? Ever since moving to Boston for college, it feels like I've lost touch with all of my old friends. And if I put Lindsay down she might try to talk me into going to that rut bar, and when I'm high on heat hormones I might go along with it.

Terrible idea.

I let out a nervous laugh. "No, that's fine. I'm fine."

"Well, I'm leaving you in excellent hands." She walks away, and it's just me and him.

"I guess I should unpack," I say as Sam stands out of the way against the wall.

The moment I unzip the bag, I remember the double-digit number of slick panties I packed because they're right on top. I blush, my face growing even hotter as I shove the stack of modest and absorbable underwear to the side.

They're just underwear. Chill. Besides, he's gonna see a lot more than that. A lot of people will when you get railed by a bunch of strangers.

My pussy throbs at the thought, a fresh gush of slick soaking into my panties, and I've never been so grateful before for a beta's poor sense of smell. The empty feeling inside of me aches, an ever-present reminder of my body's need to be filled and knotted. Instinct demands that I find the nearest compatible alpha who smells good, get down on my hands and knees, and let them breed and claim me.

I rock on my feet as the moment passes and rational thought returns. *For now.*

"There are drawers built into the walls over there by the bed," Sam says. "And you can find extra nesting material in the bottom drawer."

"Oh, that's nice." It's far kinder than I expected. I squeeze past him and look, stroking the soft blankets. They've been cleaned in null-wash so they don't smell like much of anything. I can't wait to rub my scent glands all over them.

To distract myself from what's coming, I finish unpacking. When I pull open the top drawer to put away my underwear, I stop at the sight of the hot pink vibrator lying inside. It's new and in a plastic-wrapped package, and there's a value-size pack of batteries accompanying it. The sixty-four-count box feels a little excessive.

Ignoring all of it, I throw my panties on top and slam the drawer shut with a little too much force. *Stop freaking out. You* wanted *to come here.* Knowing I can leave at any moment stops me from panicking. But knowing I'll have to call my mom to do so keeps me from chickening out. From the shortening amount of time it takes between each cramp, I know the first real wave won't be much longer.

After I put my toiletries in the bathroom and throw my blanket on the bed, I stare at Sam. "Now what?"

"Whatever you want. If you're hungry or thirsty, I can get you food or something to drink."

My nose crinkles at the thought, and Sam chuckles. It's a warm sound that makes my nipples tighten and rub against my scratchy bra.

"We have protein waters too. They have vitamins and minerals in them for when you don't feel like eating," he says. "Just let me know what you need. I'm here to take care of you."

My belly swooshes, and a fresh bead of slick is squeezed from my aching core. Damn, that sounds nice. Someone to take care of me is exactly what I want and need. Why are some alphas such knot-for-brains? Sometimes it's like they think the world ends at the tip of their dick.

I clear my throat to hide how flummoxed I feel. "Water sounds great. I don't really eat during my heats."

"Okay." He smiles wide, showing off even white teeth in a lopsided grin. "I'll be right back."

While he's gone, I toss my duffel bag into the closet and shut it, then collapse on the bed. The urge to squeeze my thighs together and rub is getting hard to ignore. Until now, I've been holding on by the skin of my teeth. The sterility of the clinic helped. Clinics aren't sexy. But this room looks more like a budget hotel.

How far away is their stock room fridge? Can I rub one out real quick while he's gone? I finger the waistband of my leggings and hesitate. With my luck, he'll come back right as I'm about to come. And he might have a blunted beta's nose, but he'll probably figure out what I was doing pretty quickly when my musk saturates this tiny closet of a room.

Should I care? Do I? It's getting harder to remember why I felt so shy earlier. My thighs squeeze together of their own accord as I rock, the movement as satisfying as it is teasing. Fuck, I want to come so badly. I'm so empty it hurts.

I'll be quick. It won't take long, not with how much my clit is throbbing. It's so swollen and taut, my slick lips sliding against it with every rock of my hips. An omega's heat is a cruel, delicious torment. It's bliss laced with agony. A craving that can't be satisfied without a fat knot and a belly full of seed.

My hand has just slipped under my waistband when the locking system beeps and the electrified handle whirrs. I pull my hand back and sit up straighter as the door opens and Sam shuts it behind him. He hands me a water.

I don't know if I should be grateful or frustrated. I'm a bit of both.

"Thank you." The plastic cracks as I unscrew the top and take a sip, pleasantly surprised at the sweet and mild taste. "Oh, it's good." My second sip is deeper, and then half the bottle is gone before I know it.

"You seemed like a vanilla girl to me."

My mouth speaks before my lust-addled brain catches up. "Oh, I'm definitely not." And then I realized what I said, and it's double entendre for those in the know. I blush so hard my ears feel hot as I think about how much I enjoy being tied down and spanked. Ridden rough until it hurts a little to sit the next day, in a pleasant reminder of the night's passion. To have my hair pulled and my nipples pinched. I'm not vanilla at all.

Sam tilts his head, his sandy hair flopping in his eyes while I avoid looking at him and pretend to be very interested in my protein water.

"Turn around on the bed and take off your shirt."

The water bottle creaks as I clench it too hard. "W-what?" My mind sputters while my body clenches with anticipation.

He goes into the bathroom and comes back with a bottle of yellow oil. "You're nervous, so you're tense. All of us are trained in massage therapy. I'll rub your shoulders and help you get loosened up."

"Oh." I can't tell if I'm more relieved or disappointed. The idea of stripping in front of him makes my stomach flip. But he's going to see me naked soon anyway, once my heat has taken over all rationality. And my black bra isn't *that* different from a swimsuit. Besides, he's a professional. It's me who's having the inappropriate thoughts here.

"Umm… okay." I screw the cap back on and put the water on the floor, then kick my flats off and get up on my knees and turn around on the bed. The cool room air is like a kiss to my heated skin as I peel myself out of my shirt and pull my long hair over one shoulder.

It's just a massage. I've had massages before. And he's a medical professional.

This is fine.

The sound of him opening the oil and slicking it between his palms is loud in the otherwise quiet room, and then Sam kicks his sneakers off and climbs onto the bed behind me as he positions his thick thighs on either side of me. He wastes no time spreading the oil along my back and shoulders, rubbing it in and moving his thumbs in circles.

Oh, fuck. The moan slips out of me before I can catch it. It's a needy sound, not quite the whine that will come when I'm in my heat for real, but close. I squirm, my thighs rubbing against his as he digs into a knot and works it free. So close.

"That's good," he says, his fingers curling around my clavicle while he massages between my shoulder and neck. "Doesn't this feel better?"

The press of his hands against my scent glands makes my clit throb and my cunt clench, the scent of my pheromones thickening the air as he expresses out some of my natural perfume. It's a struggle to keep the moans in when he touches me like that.

"So tense," he murmurs.

"Sorry. I kind of thought you'd be an older woman, not…" A guy. Young. Ridiculously hot.

"That would be Donna. She's worked here since the clinic opened, and she's about eighty years old, so she only takes emergency calls when a particularly flighty omega needs to be talked down off the ledge. She's about five foot two and maybe a hundred pounds soaking wet."

"Oh. She sounds nice." Like a grandmother figure.

"No." He laughs, and the sound makes my whole body clench tight. "She's an absolute terror. Donna used to chase the younger nurses around, barking commands at them and yelling at them to get back to work if she saw them sitting down for over two minutes, unless they were at lunch. And she still hand writes her reports in cursive. In *pencil*."

"What a monster," I agree, smiling.

Despite what he's saying, his voice is fond. It makes me wonder how long he's worked with her, and if she bosses him around, too. I can picture him answering her annoyed snaps by flirting.

His right thumb works a knot free, and I bite my lip to contain the sound of absolute pleasure it elicits. I melt under his hands, my nipples so hard they tent the molded foam of my bra and my pussy so wet that it's probably time to change my slick panties.

"That's a good girl," he says, his fingertips ghosting up the side of my neck in a move that makes the hairs on my arms stand up.

The bone-melting warmth of his praise makes my pussy flutter. I groan and rock back into his touch, my neck arching in natural submission as I give myself over to his hands. "You shouldn't say that."

"Why not?"

My body has a mind of its own as my pelvis rocks back, trying to rub against him to see if I can stir his cock to attention. "Because you're hot." And it's giving me the wrong idea. Terrible, naughty ideas that the omega side of me loves, but the woman is still scared of.

"Emily, I'm here to give you whatever you need. Not necessarily what you want. So if what you *need* is permission to shed your shyness and insecurities so you can go milk a fat knot and get some relief from this heat, then that's what we're going to do. And if you need me to give you that permission, to tell you that you're beautiful and I can't wait to watch you part those pretty pink lips and cry out as you come for those alphas, then that's what's going to happen, and I can promise you I'll enjoy every minute."

"Fuck." I shiver at the crassness of his words and the way they make me squirm as my body hunts for friction.

"Soon. Drink the rest of your water first."

I stare at him over my shoulder and try to get a read on the situation. He stares back at me, his eyes crinkling at the corners as he smiles with his easy, lopsided grin. Sam grabs my water bottle off the floor.

What a pushy, mouthy beta. "But you work here."

"Yeah," he says. "And my job is to make sure your needs are met. I read your intake paperwork. None of this violates your hard limits. Do you want me to stop?"

Yes. No. He should. I'm here to get knotted so my heat doesn't end with another UTI and a mountain of laundry. A cocky beta is not what I came here for, no matter how tightly that scrub top clings to his thick arms. The veins on his forearms stick out in sharp relief and the sight of them makes me want to trace them with my tongue. His body hair is blond and thin, and when the light hits it just right, it turns golden. He's not as large or muscular as an alpha is naturally, but his body shows he spends a good deal of time in the gym.

"Yes," I say.

He withdraws his hands and gets off the bed, and I'm hit with a disappointment that surprises me. Sam hands me the water bottle and stares at me pointedly until I finish it, his grin never wavering even after refusing him.

"What?" I ask, because this is usually the part where a male with a bruised ego gets mad and calls me an ugly bitch. Is he just waiting until I'm so far gone in my heat that I won't think to tell him no?

My horny thoughts drift to the thought of taking it back. Of leaning into his touch and letting him make me feel good. Isn't that why I'm here instead of curled up on my sofa, trying to ride this out with my favorite vibrators and knotting dildo while I swipe through hundreds of matches?

"You're cute when you pout," he says.

"I'm not pouting." I scowl at him, irritated. "Are you like this with all your clients?" A brat?

"No. Normally I leave the omegas to nest until they're ready for their first session."

Oh. "So why did you stay?"

"Because you need me to. You need someone to guide you through what to expect and tell you what to do. And because I want to. How did you put it? You're hot."

"But that's gotta be, I don't know, against the rules or something?" I try to recall if I've ever heard anyone mention the beta attendant getting involved in the heat activities, and I come up blank.

"It's not required. And I certainly wouldn't say it's encouraged. But it's also not forbidden. Sometimes the shyer omegas respond better to us betas. We're less intimidating. More familiar. Safer. Others aren't satisfied with just a good knotting in one of their sessions. They prefer to get fucked in a cuddle pile nest. And not all alphas will tolerate a second alpha in a nest, so occasionally we get asked if we want to join."

Group activities. "Oh. So you…"

"I think you're hot, Emily, and I want to make you feel good. Really good."

A shiver of pleasure courses through me all the way down to my toes. Because that is what I want. To feel good. It's what I need, and it's why I came here. For once, I want to walk away from a heat feeling great instead of tired and sticky.

"Okay."

Sam puts a finger under my chin and tips my head up so I meet his eyes as he leans down, his breath warm on my face. "Take off your pants, and lie down on your belly."

His bossiness makes my nipples tighten into such taut buds that they ache with the need to be touched and licked. More slick creeps from my core until my panties are saturated with it. He stares me down with a calm demeanor, as if he already knows I'll do exactly what I'm told.

When I dip my thumbs into the waistband of my leggings and work them down, he tips his head so he can watch. My hands tremble a little as I pull them down over the curve of my butt. I sit on one hip and pull my legs out from under me as I shove them all the way down while he watches. Once my legs are bare, he skims a finger over my ankle.

"Good girl. Now, on your belly." His warm hand splays on my lower back as he nudges me to lie down. Once I'm prone, he climbs onto the bed and straddles my thighs. There's rustling, and then the click of plastic. A moment later, warm hands covered in fragrant oil skim over my back and hips. I arch into his touch, seeking more, and he chuckles and presses me flat.

"How are the cramps?" he asks.

"Not too bad right now."

Sam massages me, moving from my shoulders to my back and then down to my hips. He tugs at the fastening of my bra and works it open, then rubs his hands over the skin he's just bared until I'm relaxed and limp underneath him.

He works on one arm, and then the other, and then his fingers graze the outside of my breast as he moves to my lower back again and kneads. Once my panties are tugged lower, his thumbs settle into the divots above my ass while he massages, and I can't hold back my groan any longer. Not when it feels so good.

"Do you like that, baby?"

"Hmm." The pet name should irritate me, but I'm too relaxed to be annoyed.

"I enjoy making you feel good. Your soft sighs, your cute little moans. How you try to hold them in until you can't. How you lift your butt in the air when I press right here."

He presses a spot on both sides of my hips that makes me buck against the mattress. If he wasn't sitting on my legs and holding me down, I'd already be in a proper omega presenting position.

"You… you're a bit of a brat. Do you know that about yourself?" I ask him, then bite my lip to hold back another moan.

"No." His kneading pauses as he leans over me and pushes me down with his body weight. His lips brush the shell of my ear as he presses his face against mine. "I'm a versatile switch who likes to service top. And I remember your preferences. I know that you like a bit of pain with your pleasure. A little humiliation with your praise. And you definitely enjoy being dominated and told what to do."

Sam sits upright, and the whoosh of air is my only warning as he brings both of his hands down on my butt. The spank is light, more sound than pain, and it draws a rush of warmth to my skin that makes my pussy tingle.

"Oh, fuck," I gasp, my hips rocking to either get away or get more. I don't know. It's confusing.

"Such a pretty ass. I can't wait to see it all pink." He spanks me again, the pain sharp and immediate, and then there's the warm, throbbing glow that follows. "You remember your safe word, right, baby?"

Red. The traffic light system is common and easy, even in the haze of a heat. "Yes."

Sam palms the globes of my panty-covered ass and squeezes, kneading them. "What is it? I want to hear you say it, so I know for sure."

"It's red."

My reward is another spank, a harder one that makes me suck in a breath and squeeze my eyes shut tight. Oh, fuck. He hits me again, five swats in rapid succession that leave me breathless and panting, my hips bucking into his grasp as he rubs the sting out.

His thumb grazes my cloth-covered mound, the slick-soaked fabric making a squelching sound that's deafening in the quiet room. "You're so wet, baby. Did you like that?"

I bite my lip and nod, squeaking when he rubs his thumb up and down my slit. God, I want him to tug that fabric aside. To stick his finger between my lips and spread that wetness around until he finds my clit and strokes it. I want him to spank me so hard I feel it for hours.

"So wet, baby. I should check to be certain. To make sure you're good and ready for all those alphas who are gonna fuck you. Knot you." He hooks a finger in my soaked panties and tugs, the fabric pulling at the top of my mound as he drags it aside and strokes me for real.

"Such a cute little pink pussy. I don't know what I like more, your ass or this pussy." He teases my seam and spreads my moisture around, then dips a finger into my channel.

The sheets twist as I clench them in my hands while he invades me with one finger and then a second, his fingers fucking into me with a wet sound as he thrusts. It doesn't take much for my pleasure to swell, for the familiar tension to coil and pull taut as he fingers me until a fresh gush of slick soaks his hand and I'm whining.

"Are you gonna come, baby?"

"Y-yes," I pant, my brow scrunched as I hold my breath and wait, balanced on the knife edge of an orgasm that my body craves more than air.

"That's good, baby. So good. Such a good girl, coming from just my fingers. I'm going to add a third one now."

My entrance stretches as he adds another finger. My drenched panties tug against my clit with every grind and thrust of my hips as I hump the mattress while my beta attendant fingerfucks me. The world narrows to the point of need between my thighs as my orgasm hits me and leaves me panting.

Sam slows his thrusting as his fingers lazily cant in and out of me. And then he spreads them, stretching my walls until they burn. Without an alpha's purr to soothe the sting, it hurts a little.

"Still too tight," he murmurs, his other hand stroking my back.

I know what he's doing. He's readying me for the blissful agony of my heat's first knot. Normally, I do it myself with a knotting dildo before the alpha I matched with arrives. With one press of the button, a toy can simulate what my body craves. What it needs.

He lifts off me, and I miss the weight of him once it's gone. "Roll onto your back, baby. We need to get you ready. Your first session's in an hour."

My throat bobs with a swallow as I go onto my back. An hour. That's not very long. "It is?"

Sam grabs my bra and slides it off me, his mouth going slack as my breasts spill out of it. "I take it back. I don't know what I like more—your round ass, your pink pussy, or these beautiful tits. Hold them for me. I want to see what they look like pressed together."

I do it. I press my breasts together and enjoy the way he looks at me. It's ravenous.

He grins that lopsided smile and hooks his fingers into my panties. I lift so he can pull them off me and unhook my legs from them. Now that they're gone, my slick creeps down my inner thighs, and it won't be long before it's puddled underneath me, the blankets of my nest soaked with them and loaded with my pheromones and the sweetness unique to an omega's heat.

When I move to drop my legs, he grabs me by the ankles and bends me, then spreads them wider as his hungry gaze devours me completely. I'm still holding my breasts and blushing as he looks up at me and smiles with a wolfish grin.

"I can't wait to see this pretty pussy dripping with cum."

"It doesn't, umm, bother you?" Some betas are insecure, as if being an alpha or an omega and having to deal with the inconvenience of ruts and heats is something to covet.

Surprise makes him raise his brows until they're swallowed by his shaggy blond hair. "No. Why would it? It means I get to lick it out of your cunt."

"Sam!" I try to snap my legs closed because nobody has ever said anything like that to me before and I don't know how to handle it.

"Emily!" He grins as he mocks me, then shoves my knees apart and falls on me like a starving man. Sam presses a kiss to the down of hair that covers my mound. "Allow me to demonstrate."

He licks me, his tongue slicking up through my folds as he works it between my labia until he's found my clit.

I let go of my breasts and grab at the bed, my nails digging into my nest as he eats me out like his life depends on it. My back arches as my hips snap up to grind against his mouth. As if there's any danger of him stopping when he tongues my hood off my clit and sucks at it.

"Fuck. Fuck. Oh, God, Sam. That's... There. Yes, right there. I'm going to…"

My orgasm leaves me shaking as I come, my walls fluttering to squeeze a nonexistent knot while slick squirts out of me, leaving Sam sticky and smiling. He looks up at me with hungry eyes as he licks his lips clean.

He presses a kiss to my mound again, then another to my thigh, and then he bites me. It's a quick nip that makes me twitch and gasp, and then he soothes it by sucking. Each tug travels straight to my clit. I just came, but I'm ready again.

Sam straightens up and uses the back of his hand to wipe my slick from his face, and then he drops over me and stares into my eyes. He's so close that we're almost kissing, and suddenly that's exactly what I want. I arch my neck and nearly close the gap, and wait, asking permission.

He leans down and closes the gap, his tongue tracing the seam of my mouth like it just did to my cunt. When I let my mouth fall open, he's there, invading it until our tongues are tangled. His kisses leave me breathless and wanting again, my need already rising once more in the exhausting clamor of want-want-want of a heat.

Our kiss breaks, and I smile at the sweetness of it.

"You'll want to shower first," he says.

Right.

"What about, umm, you?" I can see the outline of his erection through his scrub pants.

"Don't worry about me, baby. I'm fine. This is for you, remember?"

In the thick of it, I've allowed myself to forget why I'm here. For alphas and their knots. Not a cocky beta with a lopsided grin and great arms who eats pussy like he's starving. "Right. I'll just, uh…"

As I lean forward to get up, Sam gets off me. I glance at him once more while I try to figure out if he's really not jealous of the idea of me getting railed by a room full of alphas. My ankle rolls and I stumble, catching myself against the wall. Embarrassed, I hide in the bathroom and shut the door with more force than necessary.

My hair is a rat's nest, and now that I'm vertical my thighs are coated in a thick layer of sticky slick. Yikes. No wonder he told me to shower. I'm already such a mess, and it's about to get worse. That thought makes my heart race with a mix of anticipation, dread, and yearning that leaves me confused.

It's not like you're the first. Plenty of people use the free clinic.

I take a deep breath and start the shower.

Chapter Three

SAM

THE BATHROOM DOOR OPENS, AND THE STEAM FROM HER SHOWER escapes into the bedroom as Emily steps out, a towel clutched tightly around her body and her gaze shifting about the room. Her skin is flushed and pink from both the shower as well as her heat, her wet hair stuck to her shoulders and neck.

"I'm all done." She stares at the floor, her toes dug into the plush carpet.

Well, that won't do. Her first session is in twenty minutes, and she's still too self-conscious to enjoy it the way she should. The way I know she can. I have a sixth sense about these sorts of things—that's why I picked her when we were making assignments. With one look, I knew she was mine.

This is an omega who longs for all the things she wants, that her body craves, but tries to deny.

I slide off the bed and close the distance between us, cup the back of her head, and pull her up into a kiss until she's gone soft and languid again. She stops clutching her towel, her hand splayed on my chest instead as she fists my shirt and pulls me in deeper.

Oh, yes. That's good. That's what she needs.

I fuck her mouth with my tongue like I fucked her pussy. The taste of her sweet slick is still on my tongue. I don't think I'll ever tire of it. The urge to ruck the towel up and sink my fingers into her, then lick them clean, is there, but there's no time. I want to get her settled in well before the alphas come into the room. She's already nervous enough.

She moans into my mouth, and I swallow down the sound, my fingers tightening in her hair. Emily squeaks, her back arching, so her hips rub against my front. My cock twitches in my pants. It's eager to feel the heat of her, to sink into her soft omega body and fuck her until we're both sated.

Not yet.

Squeezing, I tug harder on her hair, pulling her head back as I crash my mouth down on hers and take control of the kiss. She straddles my thigh and rubs herself against me in a way I know will leave my pants stained with her arousal.

That's the key.

And now she's ready.

I hold her still as I lean back and give her lower lip a nip. "Drop the towel."

She hesitates for a moment, and then she does it. The towel puddles at her feet, and then she's bare, her nipples erect and dusky and begging to be kissed. She's sweet, soft, and perfectly bitable.

"Kneel."

A wrinkle forms between her eyebrows as she thinks.

No, this isn't the time for thinking. Not anymore. She thinks too much for an omega in heat.

"Kneel, Emily."

She does it. The sight of her at my feet, her tits on display and her face tilted up to me, makes something warm unfurl inside my chest. *Perfection.*

"On your hands and knees. That's a good girl," I say while I stroke her hair. Her eyes go half lidded, her pupils blown so wide her brown eyes look black. She nuzzles into my hand, soaking up the praise and caress in equal measures. "I'm proud of you. What a pretty, perfect omega you are. The alphas are going to be so happy."

The rosy hue of her cheeks deepens, the color swallowing up the freckles that dot the bridge of her nose. I want to kiss each one of them, along with the ones on her body. She smiles and bites her lip, her white teeth depressing that lush lower lip that begs to be sucked.

My hand slips to the hair at her nape. I card my fingers through her damp strands, then make a fist. Her mouth drops open.

"Now crawl."

I walk her toward the door, slow and steady, careful not to hurt her, as I nudge her forward. She wants to walk, but she *needs* to crawl. She has to shed all of her shame, right here and now— that way there's only pleasure left.

She deserves all the pleasure life can offer her.

"Sam?" Her voice is breathy and hesitant, not quite a whine but close.

At the door, I lean forward and open it. "Crawl into the hallway and wait for me on your hands and knees. Keep your eyes on the floor. Yes, like that. Perfect."

I close the door to her room behind me and hover over her, giving her bottom and pussy a fond stroke to reward her. She's stiff for a moment, and then she stretches into it. Emily raises her perfectly heart-shaped ass in the air. The skin's not pink anymore from her quick spanking, but I'll correct that. Later.

I slick my fingers through her wet lips and circle her clit until she's spreading her legs wide, eager, and no longer caring that we're in a hallway and that anyone passing by will see her naked and horny. She would fuck herself on my fingers and be happy to do so—if only I'd let her.

But I won't.

This omega needs a knot, and I'm going to make sure she gets it.

I pull my fingers away, and when she whines, that needy omega sound that begs for more, I swat her lightly right on her wet cunt. Emily startles and rocks forward onto her hands until her forearms are flush on the ground and her ass is up high in the air. A perfect omega position. I rub her back, caressing her from nape to rump.

"That's good, baby. Beautiful." I tap my thigh. "Come."

I walk, and she crawls beside me. Our pace is slow. To go any faster would risk the skin of her knees. But I don't mind. It gives me time to savor how everyone we pass stares at her. It lets me watch the way her ass rises and falls and her tits sway with the movements. She keeps her head down and her eyes on the floor.

At the door to the rut room, I put my hand on her shoulder to let her know it's time to stop. My badge unlocks the door, the latch buzzing, and it glides open. Good. We're not late. It's only omegas and their beta handlers here. A few are already in position, their bits on perfect display, while others are being helped through their slots. It's been freshly cleaned, the air cycled, and all surfaces treated with a sanitizer that doubles as a descenter. Soon it will be filled with the musk and perfumes of a thoroughly effective treatment cycle.

"In here, you may stand," I say. I won't have her crawling on the rut room floor. It's hard and cold no matter how hot we keep these rooms so the naked omegas are comfortable.

She stands, her knees pink despite the soft flooring and our slow pace through the hallway, and the sight of them makes my dick twitch. Emily looks around while nibbling on her lower lip, and her shoulders rise on instinct to protect her so very biteable neck.

I let her look, let her see how all the omegas are naked and displayed exactly like her, then grab her hand and squeeze it. Her face twitches in a hesitant smile, but her shoulders drop a little. Building trust is important, and I'm glad that she's already beginning to understand how well I'm going to take care of her.

Pointing, I indicate which station is hers. Her chest rises and falls faster the closer we get as I lead her to the backstage area where only omegas and betas are allowed. She presses a hand between her breasts while I badge her station open and let her explore it. It's small, little more than a box that's wide enough for her to spread both arms out and touch the walls. Stairs lead to the platform she'll lay on while she's serviced. There's no bedding or nest materials allowed for sanitary reasons, but the gel mattress is comfortable and it'll warm up quickly as she lies on it. A small view of the rut room is visible through the padded opening she'll use.

"Do I just… climb up?" she asks.

"Yes. Climb up and sit by the opening. I'll help you get into position."

Emily makes a sound I can't decipher, and I wonder if perhaps I've pushed her too far too quickly. Her chart said her cycles are rapid and brief, lasting three days total instead of the usual five, with an onset and a tail of about eight hours.

"Okay," she whispers. "Okay. Will you stay? You're staying, right?"

I pinch her chin between my thumb and finger and pull her in for a quick, chaste kiss. "I'm here for whatever you need, baby. If you need me to stay, then that's where I'll be. And if you need alone time with the alphas, that's okay too. There's no right or wrong here so long as you're happy."

Her heat-dilated eyes damn near glitter in the overhead lighting. "Okay. Good. I'm glad you're staying. I… I want you to stay with me."

I grin and plant one last kiss on her plush mouth, then let her go. "Up you go, baby."

She climbs the steps and then kneels on the platform and crawls to the opening. I can't resist taking one good, hard look at her round ass and the peek of her puffy, slick-coated sex between them.

Fuuuuck me.

Once she's settled by the opening, I close the door to her station and make sure it latches, then walk back out to the main area of the rut room. Her pinkened knees and rounded thighs block my view of the rest of her.

"When it comes to getting into proper position, the first time is the hardest," I tell her as I stop in front of her cutout. "Sit down and stick your legs out and let them dangle, then lie back. I'll do the rest."

Once she's where I need her, I pull the stirrups from their notches in the wall and adjust their angle. I lift one leg at a time into them and sink her heels into their cups. Before securing her, I stick my arms through her slot and grab her by her hips, pulling until her ass bumps against my front. She squeaks, and I smile as I tug her down so she's nearly hanging off the ledge and her pussy's opened and ready.

I buckle her in, letting my fingertips glide over her soft skin and the smooth leather of the stirrup's straps. Next, I secure her calves down so that no amount of heat delirium wiggling will let her hurt herself, and then I reach in and pull her anklet down, turning it so all her color-coded charms are visible. I tap a finger over each one. Bisexual. A white circle with a black center dot and a gray ring for her openness to betas and omegas. Solid gray for light BDSM. Fuchsia for spanking, and gold for group play.

HEAT CLINIC · 33

Squeezing the handle, I fiddle with her stirrups and the position of her legs until I'm satisfied. "How does that feel?"

"Umm… I'm not sure? I think it's fine."

I smooth over her thigh and double-check the angle of her hips and knees. "Is anything pinching or uncomfortable?"

"No."

Palming her pussy, I feel the warmth she's already giving off as her temperature climbs with her heat. The nurse will take her vital signs every day while she's here, but palming an omega's groin is a good way to tell how hot and ready they are. Her hips twitch against my hand as she grinds against it, her sigh turning into an agitated chirp when I refuse to give her the friction she craves. Her sweet slick coats my palm.

I pull my hand back and bring it down with a quick little slap to her greedy pussy. "Naughty omega."

Emily gasps, but the trickle of slick from her pussy betrays her. Splayed like this, she can't hide how much she likes this. How much she needs this.

Leaning down, I press a kiss to her inner thigh and give her a quick nip with my teeth while I breathe in her scent. God, she smells so good. Like sweet, sticky iced lemon cookies. I want to lean down and lick her cunt until she gushes down my throat. I can only imagine how feral the alphas are going to go over her.

The warning buzzer sounds. There's one minute until the alpha door opens.

I give her clit one last stroke as I look over and make eye contact with Allison who's seeing to her own omega, a slender male with olive skin and dark curls. She works his slim cock until it's hard and a drop of slick drips from his hole. We nod to one another, and then I head around to the back. I buzz myself into Emily's station and wait for the latch to engage, then test the door to make sure it's secure. Not all the beta attendants will stay, but enough of us do so it won't be seen as weird when I don't appear in the break room for dinner while all of our omegas are busy with their treatment.

Emily tilts her head back and watches me lean an elbow up on her platform while we both wait.

"Comfy?" I ask, one brow arched.

She pouts, and it makes me smile. "It's weird. I don't know if I like it yet."

"You will," I tell her, not doubting it for even one second. After so many years working here at the clinic, you just know which omegas are going to be into the group treatment sessions.

She looks up at the ceiling. "Such a brat," she mutters under her breath, but not so quiet that I don't hear her.

I squash the urge to laugh. And she thinks I'm the bratty one? All I'm doing is giving her what she needs. It's not my fault that what she needs is a spanking and some light degradation mixed with praise.

When I climb the stairs up to her platform and wedge myself into the space between her bed and the wall, her eyes widen. *Oh, yes, baby. You can't get rid of me so easily.*

"Sam?"

I love the way she says my name. Like it's a lifeline she's throwing out into a churning sea. These alphas might fuck her silly, knot her until her eyes cross, but it's me she's going to be looking at like that. Like I'm her safe space.

"I'm here," I reassure her. All I have to do is stretch and reach as I stick my arm out of her slot and tease her exposed pussy. I rub her slick labia together, then bring my hand down on it five times, one blow after the other as I spank this naughty omega's cunt and play in her slick.

"I have long arms," I tell her as I spread her lips apart and find her clit, tugging the hood back so I can circle her swollen clit. It's sticking up and begging to be touched and petted.

Emily's gaze grows unfocused as she moans and rubs herself

against my hand. The warning sound chimes overhead through the speakers. It's almost enough to drag her out of her heat haze until I rub circles around her clit and send her back down into bliss.

She doesn't even notice when the alpha door unlocks and they wander in. It's not until the first one steps up to her station and bends down to sniff her pussy that she stiffens with awareness. It's a male with dark hair that dusts his knuckles. He sticks a finger straight into her cunt and pumps twice, then pulls it out with a wet sound and rubs his thumb against them to test how sticky her slick is. A taut webbing of slick forms between his thumb and finger, drooping from gravity until it breaks.

Her thighs tremble as he sniffs his hand, then licks it clean and purrs. We're both quiet as he unzips his jeans and shoves them down, an impressive alpha cock flopping out. He pumps it twice, and that's all he needs to get hard. A room full of needy, perfuming omegas means the alphas are in a constant, almost painful state of readiness as the urge to rut consumes them.

In ancient times, there would never be so many ripe omegas in one place. Any alpha who stumbled upon them would rut them ragged until a competitor came along, and then they'd fight for winner's rights. It wasn't over 'til the omega had a claiming bite gnawed into them. We're more civilized now, but some instincts are hard to overcome, even if we've learned how to control our baser urges. Mostly.

Emily leans up on her forearms as we both watch. The alpha's cock drips with pheromone-soaked pre-cum, and he wastes no time notching himself to her entrance and sliding in to the hilt with one thrust as he bottoms out inside of her with a grunt of approval.

She yelps a little and fidgets as her body adjusts to the blunt intrusion of his broad cock and his rapid thrusting.

Fucking knot-for-brains alpha.

She whines, and the alpha purrs to soothe her omega distress signals. His purr is a rumbly sound that's ill used and out of tune. I roll my eyes and rub her clit with firm circles. He doesn't seem to mind my assistance in the matter as he fucks her with no thought for any pleasure but his own.

Her breasts bounce with the vigor of his thrusting, the leather straps of her stirrups creaking as he ruts her for a few more minutes, then comes with a grunt. He pushes his hips forward as his knot swells inside of her, locking them together. Her little belly bulges with the quantity of his emissions. He might be a lackluster fuck, but his volume is decent.

I don't like that he's not purring for her now that his enjoyment of the act is complete. It's clear from her pinched brows that Emily's found little pleasure in this joining. While they're tied, I caress her clit and trace a fingertip over her stretched inner lips where the alpha's knot has swollen and stoppered her up.

She twitches, her breathing growing deeper and faster as I circle faster, pressing harder until my hand cramps. Ignoring it, I keep going. She rocks, just a slight twitch of her hips that pulls on the alpha's knot and makes her lips part in a silent sigh.

"Oh, fuck, yeah. Make her do that again," the alpha rumbles. He grips her thighs in his large hands and rocks forward, his movements tugging on the knot swollen inside of her.

"You're so pretty, baby," I say. "You take that knot so well. What a good omega cunt, squeezing that knot. Getting stuffed with all that cum. Do you want to come on that knot, baby?"

Her eyes are squeezed shut tight, but she nods. My fingers move in a blur as I rub her clit with zero mercy until she's twitching and whining. She comes with a moan, and so does the alpha as he rocks them together, a second, smaller load of cum stuffing her full.

I withdraw my fingers after one last fond stroke and clean them with my tongue, savoring the taste of her. After a minute of rest, he pulls free with a wet pop and cum and slick gush out of her, splatting her inner thighs before dripping onto the floor.

"Such a good girl, taking that knot and coming on it," I reassure her.

She flops down and stares at the ceiling with unfocused eyes as the alpha stumbles away from her station, his cock already half hard again from the stimulation of the room. He heads left, and another quickly takes his place.

This one's dick is longer and thinner, but he pauses to run his fingers over her slick pussy. He touches and explores her, purring for her while he ruts into his own hand until his cockhead drips pre-cum down his knuckles.

When she whines, he lines them up and presses forward. His thrusts build up to the pace of the first alpha, the wet slap of their skin joining the moans and cries and chirps and grunts of the other rutting couples in the room.

Her tits bounce until I capture one, squeezing it and pinching her rosy nipple between two fingers. Emily whimpers, and she must clench down hard on the alpha cock that's working her because he purrs so loud and deep and good that it even affects *me*.

She cries out as slick coats his dick, readying her for his knot as he pounds her through the opening of her cubby in their anonymous exchange of pleasure. There are no faces, no names, only relief for everyone involved. Her hands slap at the floor and the wall as she tries to hang on while the alpha ruts her with more skill and care than the first.

"There are straps," I say, reminding her.

"Hnnng… What?"

I take her flailing hand and guide it to a strap, helping her anchor herself as she hangs onto one while this alpha fucks her dizzy. Her hand clenches the strap so tightly that her knuckles turn white, and then she comes. Her pink mouth falls open, and she makes a strangled sound.

The alpha fucks her through it, relentless, his hips battering against hers as he tries to rearrange her to fit him better. Deeper. Her belly bulges with each surge of his hips as he hits the mouth of her womb. And then they turn slower and deeper as he finds his own pleasure, his knot swelling just before he comes. His cock twitches as he pumps her full, all that good alpha seed pooling right where she needs it.

His purrs sooth her as he strokes up her thighs and rubs a hand over her belly where he's nestled deep inside of her. With a gentle touch, he rubs himself through her skin, his cock jumping with each straggling spurt of seed trapped behind that wide, swollen knot.

She moans, her head lolling to the side as she rubs her cheek against my thigh and nuzzles me, her eyes sliding closed as her entire face relaxes.

"Good girl," I say. "Such a good knot-milking omega. Did that feel good, baby?"

Emily nods and lies there in quiet contentment until the alpha's purr fades and he pulls free of her and steps away. In his absence, she whines. I'll make a note in her chart that she liked the second one. He might be worth approaching for group activities if he's open to that.

"Sam," she whispers as there's a lull in the lineup, the alphas busy with other omegas for the moment.

"Yes, baby?" I smooth a lock of hair out of her eyes.

"I want… I want you to feel good too."

Smiling, I tuck the hair behind her ear and enjoy the way she nuzzles her cheek against my hand. "I do feel good, baby. I like watching you." I caress her nipple, rolling it under my fingers. "I like touching you. I like watching you come undone when you peak. And I really like the way you taste. When we're back in your nest, I'm going to eat you out until you soak your blankets."

She groans, her lips twitching in a smile, but then she gives me a pointed stare and pouts. "You know what I mean."

It's too fun to tease her, to make her loosen up and shake off her doubts and insecurities. "Do I?"

Emily pouts harder, her eyes squinting as her mouth screws up in a way that makes me want to kiss it smooth again. "Are you really going to make me say it?"

"Say what?" I pinch her nipple and give it a tug until the purse of her mouth softens.

"Never mind." She stares at the white ceiling of her station and drapes her hands on her belly.

"Oh, do you want to suck my cock? All you have to do is ask, baby." Some of the more pack oriented omegas aren't happy until all their holes are stuffed. I lift my shirt and undo the tie on my scrub pants and shove them down along with my boxer briefs. My cock springs free, half hard and getting harder the longer she stares at it with that naked hunger on her face.

Four pumps, and it's firm in my hand. It's not as large as an alpha's and there's no knot, but all that means is I get to fuck the back of her throat and, if she's down for it, claim her ass while an alpha knots her sweet little cunt.

"Suck my cock, omega," I say as she angles her head toward me. I press my leaking tip to her mouth and spread my pre-cum over her pink lips.

Emily stares at me as she relaxes her jaw and I push inside, my head nearly dropping back with the pleasure of it as she arches and swallows me to the halfway point of my shaft.

"Oh, fuck, baby, that feels so good. You're so good at sucking cock."

I let her set the pace as she bobs her head up and down my length, her eyes going hazy and unfocused again as her heat drags her under until there's no shame, no fear, no hesitation. Only desire and hunger, sating her where the two meet.

Fisting my base, I squeeze while she pumps, my head hitting the back of her throat as she takes as much of me as she can. She doesn't know how to deepthroat, but that's okay. I'll teach her. My balls tingle with the growing urge to come, to shoot a load into her mouth and watch her throat bob as she swallows it.

An alpha steps forward and rubs her clit, making her moan around my cock. He presses inside of her and fucks her, and the sight of it is enough to make me almost lose it and come right now.

"Like that, yeah. I love fucking your mouth," I whisper, just for her. Her mouth makes an inelegant wet sound as I fuck her face while an alpha stranger stuffs her with cock and knots her. He and I come at the same time, filling her up from both ends until she's dripping. My cock twitches with each spray, and she swallows it all until she's left gasping as I pull my softening dick from her mouth and bask in our shared pleasure.

"You taste so good," she says.

I tuck myself away, then fix my clothes. "Yeah? What do I taste like, baby?"

"Like juicy oranges and french vanilla ice cream."

The way this girl makes me smile… She says such nice things to me even when she's got an alpha's knot in her pussy and a belly full of strangers' seed. The way she makes me feel is dangerous. Like maybe I can keep her. Like I want to.

I climb off her platform and work the kinks out of my body, ignoring the way she pouts when I leave her side. *Don't worry, baby. I'm not going anywhere.*

I stand over her, leaning forward until I can press an upside down kiss to her mouth. My taste is on her tongue, but I don't mind it. Not when she sticks her tongue in my mouth and tries to pull me deeper into the kiss. I don't taste any of the creamsicle she's describing, but alphas and omegas have a heightened sense of smell and taste compared to betas. Rubbing my hands over her breasts and arms and belly, I stroke her until she's purring.

Breaking the kiss, I press my lips to her ear and stare down the line of her body. "Look at how red your cunt is now that it's stretched around that knot. You're taking him so deep, pretty girl. What a good omega you are taking all these knots."

She looks and when the alpha's knot shrinks and he pulls away, she whimpers at the loss of him. Sweat dots her forehead, her shower damp hair stuck to it as she wiggles against her restraints. If she wasn't tied, she'd hurt herself by trying to crawl through that opening to get to the room full of alphas beyond her barrier.

An alpha with tan skin and a nice, thick cock steps up to her and strokes two fingers through the mess between her legs. He brushes over her clit until she grinds against him, and then he lines them up and sinks into her with a low growl that makes her whimper, her neck arching in an offering she doesn't really mean.

I nuzzle the side of her neck and lick her scent glands, then set my blunt beta teeth over them. There's no real danger here. I can't mark and mate her with my teeth. But as lost in her heat as she is, she doesn't know it. There's only the pleasure of an instinctive need being met as I nibble the place where an alpha would claim her.

The alpha rutting between her thighs groans, interrupting his low growl as he fucks her harder, each thrust shifting her up her gel mattress. She flails, and I grab her by the wrists and hold them down, using my jaws to pin her firmly into place as the alpha slams into her again and again until he grunts with his knotting and subsequent release. Her belly bulges from his fat cock and fatter knot and the pool of cum he pumps into her until her lips are slick and swollen and stretched thin around him.

This male drives a hand between her folds and finds her clit, circling it and rubbing her until she's grinding on his knot. She comes with a cry and lies there panting as I lick her through her aftershocks while the alpha plays with the mess of fluids they've made. He pulls free and gives her one last stroke.

Another takes his place.

I lick her neck, smoothing the red mark my blunt teeth have left, and swallow down her faint lemon scent lick by hungry lick.

Chapter Four

EMILY

THERE'S MORE OF THEM IN AN ENDLESS LINE OF ALPHAS. OR maybe they're coming back for seconds or thirds. I can't tell anymore. My head is fuzzy with the heat as another alpha runs his hand up my legs, stroking my ankles and calves and then my thighs as he explores me before he ruts me.

That's nice.

Feels better when they touch me before they fuck me.

It makes me feel less like meat. Like an object to be used for their pleasure as they shove their knot into me and cum, then wander off to repeat the process with another. An omega fleshlight.

Their shoved down jeans and pants rub against my sensitive skin and my inner thighs feel chafed. But the sting and stretch of their knots makes the howling need inside me dull and I find a moment of peace, of utter tranquility, when they knot me and pump me full of cum.

The shape of each one is different. The motions of their fucking too. It satisfies some unnamed, primal urge inside of me I didn't know was there. It lurks just beneath the surface of my civilized veneer.

No wonder people come here.

Come.

Cum.

I giggle. It's the heat delirium, I know that. But it amuses me all the same. Sam strokes me, his touch light and teasing one moment, then rough and needy the next. He hasn't fucked my mouth again, even though I've begged. Instead, he tenderly keeps my hair out of my face while the alphas rut me raw.

The alpha.

He snaps his hips to mine in a punishing and brutal intrusion. So thick and deep. Too deep. It's like he wants to remake me to fit him, but there's no room to stretch. I whimper as pleasure dulls with the stinging burn.

Fingers slip through my drenched folds and stroke, bringing the pleasure back.

Sam. Oh, Sam. Beautiful, sweet, bratty Sam.

My lovely beta.

I reach for him and tug him down and slant his mouth to mine. He's surprised, his fingers stilling as he struggles to keep stroking my clit while the alpha fucks me hard. His tongue slides against mine, and I'm lost in pleasure just from that.

Kissing him is divine, and I'm addicted.

Why did I ever tell him no before?

He feels good.

Right.

Like he's mine.

His lips mold to mine as he kisses me, and his fingers strain to make me come. I've lost count of which orgasm it is. Twenty? Thirty?

It hurts.

And it's wonderful.

The alpha shoves his swelling knot inside of me, forces my body to surrender or tear. He growls, and my omega cunt relaxes as another bead of slick eases the worst of his entrance. The angrier they get, the more pliant I become. A twisted trick of biology and evolution. His cock jumps, each lash of cum against my walls like a hot brand carving me up from the inside out as it paints my cervix white.

I moan into Sam's mouth and make him swallow my pleasure down as I come, the alpha's hands stroking my clit as he makes my tired cunt flutter on his knot. Milking him. He grinds us together, the push and pull and tension sucking at the pool of his seed as his cockhead tries to shoot up the neck of my womb.

To breed me.

Our bodies don't know what our minds do. All our alpha and omega brains understand is rutting and breeding.

Rut.

Cum.

Breed.

Claim.

I come again, my body squeaking out one last tiny orgasm as my walls flutter around his knot and he rewards me with one final lashing of seed. After he's done, he purrs, and my bones turn limp. Sam sticks his tongue deeper down my mouth, like he's trying to hollow a space for himself too, just like the alphas do between my legs.

The knot deflates and my pussy sighs with relief. The alpha pulls away and slaps me on the thigh with a smack that's more noise than pain.

Good job, that slap says.

They don't speak to me. Not like Sam does. Not at all sometimes, except to purr or growl or grunt or curse. Sam whispers naughty things in my ear while these alphas fuck me. He narrates it, adding teasing, bratty jabs and then praises me.

The next alpha that comes up to my station to fuck me is one I haven't smelled before. The mashup of scents in this room is confusing, but I can smell the difference so sharply. So distinctly. It clears the haze of heat from my thoughts. My sensitive nose picks out his sweet cardamom and cream scent. It's spicy, but mellowed. Like a chai latte, he reminds me of the drink I used to order whenever I spent late nights at the coffee shop while studying when I was in college.

He touches me gently, his fingers stroking me with such softness that I relax in my restraints, my thighs unclenching. Two press into me, working in and out with a steady rhythm that builds a different kind of orgasm inside of me. A deeper one. They curl and stroke against my front wall. I clench around him, my pussy squeezing like a vise.

They retreat, scooping out the lingering cum that saturates my folds, and then he leans down and presses his face to my cunt, sniffing deep before his tongue flicks out to lick me. The alpha teases my clit, retracting my hood and suckling me in his mouth.

I grind with the tiny degree of movement that my restraints allow and rub my face against his mouth. He fingers my entrance again and presses inside, curling to rub me while his tongue lashes at my sex-swollen clit.

Sam lets me break our kiss as I look down my body and watch this alpha devour my cunt like he's a starving man who's just sat down at a feast. An aquiline nose presses against my mound, and dark hair falls into his face. Blue eyes stare at me from under long, dark lashes through the small gap in the opening.

It feels different to look at him. Forbidden. But no one is stopping him and Sam is quiet, even as I fist my hand in his scrub top and squeeze.

This is supposed to be anonymous. An easy way to ease a heat or satisfy the urge to rut. But this is different in a way I can't explain.

The fingers inside of me curl and stroke, and I come with a

cry and gush on his face, more slick than he knows what to do with flooding his mouth and leaking from the corners.

Oh, God.

It's embarrassing.

And it's fucking hot.

He laps it all up, his tongue broad as he licks my folds clean and purrs against my aching cunt. It's a soothing noise that leaves me mellowed and happy, the sound of a satisfied alpha that makes all of the tension in my body unclench. This purr says *you've pleased me and I'll take care of you now.*

Yes, please.

The alpha stands and unbuckles his belt, his slick-covered fingers marking up the pristine dress fabric as he unlatches the eye hook and unzips his fly. He shoves his pants down his thighs, his painfully hard cock bobbing in the air.

My inane thought that breaks through the heat delirium is *no underwear?*

He palms his cock and taps it against my mound, his pre-cum leaking onto me as he rubs his tip through my pubic hair and folds.

He's covering me in his scent.

My pussy clenches at the thought just as he notches himself at my entrance. Large hands hold onto my hips as he rolls his pelvis, back and forth, easing his large alpha cock into me as if I need to be eased into things. As if I haven't spent the last who knows how long being fucked by a room full of alphas.

Where has this one been—and am I really his first omega of the session? None of the alphas I've seen have done up their pants after they've rutted an omega. Instead, they shuffle from station to station, their jeans or slacks sagging around their thighs or knees as they find the next omega hole to stuff with cock and knot.

His abdomen flexes with the roll of his hips as he presses a little deeper with each thrust until I've taken his entire length, my belly bulging with every canting as he seats himself to the hilt.

"F-fuck," I moan, my hips rolling with his as much as the stirrups and restraints allow while we find a rhythm together.

Sam joins us, playing with my breasts and teasing my nipples into stiff peaks as he presses a kiss to the pulse point of my throat. I arch into his touch, greedy for each gentle stroke and hard pinch or slap. All of it feels good now.

Everything becomes perfect as the alpha builds up a steady flow, each thrust getting a little faster and deeper as he hits my cervix and my belly bulges. It's mesmerizing to watch. He buries himself and grinds against me until I clench tight around him. My body wants to keep him there, buried deep and locked up tight in my cunt as he fills my womb with his seed. It needs to grind on his knot and squeeze out every last drop.

His pace quickens as if he can read my thoughts. I meet each thrust, moving with him and taking him deeper as I watch his cock spear me like a hot brand that leaves me molten with desire.

"I know how much you like that, baby," Sam whispers. "How much you like having that cock so deep. What a good girl you are. Such a pretty omega taking that big alpha cock. You're gonna milk that knot so good."

Sam is far too coherent from his sprawl on the platform next to me. He needs to feel how good this is too. I twist and grab for the ties on his pants, taking him by surprise. It's only because he's done such a sloppy job retying it that I'm able to work the knot free. I reach in and palm his dick, feeling it pulse in my hand.

It's wet. His cock's been leaking a steady bead of pre-cum this whole time, and he must be wearing special absorbent underwear like I do when I have my heat. He makes a token protest that he's fine but gives in quickly as I lap the fat droplet welling on his leaking slit.

"Oh, fuck, baby, your tongue feels so good."

That's all the permission I need as I wrap my lips around him and hollow out my cheeks and suck. Sam arches, his hips surging forward as he pumps into my mouth and spits out a stream of nonsense under his breath.

He likes to talk.

I like to make him forget how to talk.

The alpha slows his pace, pausing on each surge to grind against my clit as if he's buying time to let Sam catch up. He has to scent us and know what we're doing, has to smell this beta dripping pre-cum down my throat as I hold my breath and take him to the back of my throat until Sam's chatter turns to groans.

"God damn, that's hot," the alpha rumbles, his voice deep and gravelly.

The sound of it makes my toes curl and my pussy clench tight. This alpha leans against the barrier that divides us, his huge body blocking out the light and the crowded room behind him as he fucks into me with a roll of his hips that hits a sweet spot inside me and makes me moan around Sam's cock.

"God damn," Sam agrees.

I contort my body so I can grab the base of Sam's cock and squeeze. My tongue laps at his tip while I suck, my lips tight around his corona. The oranges and cream taste of him makes me ravenous. It makes me wonder what it would taste like mixed with chai. The thought of taking both men into my mouth one at a time, their beautiful cocks pressed together as I drag my tongue across both weeping tips, has me moaning around Sam's cockhead.

Sam's head bangs back against the wall behind him as he tries to stall his thrusting and fails. He fucks my mouth, my hand on his shaft stopping him from going too deep as he pushes in and forces me to take him.

"I'm gonna teach you how to swallow cock, baby. You're gonna be so good at it."

The alpha grunts as if in agreement, his hips jerking as he struggles to maintain his steady pace. I don't want it steady. I don't want it slow and tender anymore. I want them to fuck me, to spear me from two ends and pump me full of cum. I want this alpha to flood my womb and this beta to fill my belly until I'm spent and satisfied.

The restraints make it impossible. They stifle me and keep me from wrapping my legs around this alpha and locking him deep in my cunt where he belongs. I growl my frustration around Sam's cock.

"You want it rough, baby? Is that what my pretty omega needs?" Sam asks.

He leans over me and pulls the hair out of my face, then cups my cheek. And then his hips surge as he presses deeper into my mouth. His cock hits the back of my throat and I gag on it, my fingers useless to stop him as he fucks my face.

I'm along for the ride, my breathing at his mercy as he stuffs my mouth full of his prick, his head leaking a steady stream of pre-cum that I have to swallow constantly. Everything is a mess. My eyes leak and my nose runs as he stops letting me pretend that I'm the one in charge here and takes what he wants. Just like the alphas have taken what they want. I'm tied up, trussed like an offering, my cunt on display for easy access as they rut me one by one.

Sam lets go of my face and brings a hand down on my breast, slapping it right on the nipple. The pain is instantaneous, the throbbing in my clit a direct result. The alpha growls with displeasure until he feels how soaked I am. Growls taper off to a low rumble that has my toes curling and my thighs tense.

"You like that, baby?" Sam asks.

I can't speak with his cock in my mouth, but that doesn't stop me from trying. The sounds he fucks out of me are obscene.

Filthy and depraved.

He loves it as much as I do.

One eyebrow arches as his smile turns lazy. Arrogant. That's the word I've been looking for. But in a way that's still charming. As if he knows a secret you don't.

I give up trying to stymie Sam's thrusts and reach for his balls instead. I cup them, kneading them gently as he drags his cock over my tongue again and again. There's power here. He might be fucking my face and making me cry, but one good squeeze will put him on the floor and we both know it. People often think omegas are weak. Submissive. But we're the ones who guard the nest and our young. We can scratch back when we need to.

Sam smiles wider, his grin lopsided.

This beta's a little crazy.

But I think I like it.

He fumbles for my nipple, finding and pinching it and tugging. Each sharp pull travels straight to my clit until I'm throbbing. The alpha fucking me grunts and thrusts harder, no longer moderating his movements as he chases his own pleasure.

Sam bursts on my tongue and pumps his cum down my throat with a groan. His balls throb in my hand, two swollen, heavy globes. I swallow his seed down, losing only a little of its creamy orange flavor as it dribbles around my lips. His frantic pumps turn languid as he slicks in and out of my wet mouth. I lick him clean, chasing every last yummy drop. He uses his thumb to wipe up my face, feeding it to me. When I suck his fingers clean, he laughs.

"Fuck, baby. That was hot," Sam says. "Do you want to come now? I want to hear your moans and whimpers while you come on this nice alpha's fat cock."

"Beta," the alpha says, his first words to us.

Sam and I glance at one another, and then he looks at the wall that divides us and raises his brows. "Yes?"

"How much longer in this session?" the alpha asks.

Clothing rustles as Sam drags his phone out of his pocket and checks the time. "Twenty-three minutes."

"Okay," the alpha says, his pace slowing again. His abdominals clench and unclench, his cock jumping with each repetition. "I can manage that."

Sam chuckles. "What would you have done if it was two hours?"

The alpha grumbles. "What I fucking had to. She doesn't come until I do. Understood?"

I frown, not understanding what's happening. Coming is the entire point. It's a heat. Is this alpha crazy?

"Ooh," Sam says with way too much glee in his voice. "Edging."

The word cuts through my heat delirium like a hot knife. Struggling, I sit up on my arms and look down my body where the alpha rutting me fucks in and out of me with lazy thrusts. "Excuse me? Don't I get a say in this?"

"No," the alpha says without missing a beat. He strokes my thighs where they meet my ass, his touch gentle. Almost reverent. One large hand takes up an entire cheek.

"Use your safe word if you need to, baby," Sam says.

I cut him with a glare. "Fuck you."

Sam's cocky grin widens. "You're so cute when you pout. But that's not your safe word. Edge away, alpha. I recommend spanking. She's a lot less delicate than she looks. And don't forget her cunt."

My nostrils flare as I drag in an angry breath. "I am never sucking your cock again."

If Sam is bothered, he doesn't show it. Instead, he strokes a teasingly light touch all over me. He caresses my breasts, my belly, my hair. "You'll feel better in twenty-three minutes."

"Twenty-two," the alpha corrects.

Sam checks his phone again and grins.

The alpha's got a good sense of time. God damn, that shouldn't be hot. And yet it is.

The alpha fucks me, his pace leisurely and steady while his hands roam my lower half as if he's trying to memorize the feel of me. He bounces me on his cock, then slows it to a crawl until I'm panting with need and thinking is difficult. Fast and deep gives way to slow and easy. The constant change in pace stalls my swelling orgasm every single time until I'm ravenous for it.

"Please," I beg, no longer caring if I sound like every stereotypically whiny omega in every porno. "Please, alpha. I need to come."

Sam drags a fingertip over the bow of my upper lip. He's climbed back off the platform to hover over me. Traitor. I snap my teeth at him and almost catch the tip of his index finger.

"She's getting bitey," Sam says, talking to the alpha as if I'm not here.

"Four minutes," the alpha counters, his voice strained.

Good. I hope this hurts him as much as it hurts me. The growing, incessant, and unmet need to come is all I can think about. There's no clinic. No other alphas. It's just me and him and Sam. Sam who fucking betrayed me. I glare at him again, but all he does is smile and cock that one eyebrow.

"Is it weirdly hot how he can keep time in his head like that?" Sam whispers to me.

It is, but I'll be damned if I say so.

"Don't pout, baby girl. All those stalled orgasms are gonna hit you all at once like a freight train. You'll enjoy it."

I look away from the cocky beta, but there's only so many other places to look in this tiny cubicle. There's no bedding to fist my hands in. No nest to soak with our combined pheromones. No knot to cum on. What's even the point?

I growl and twist in my bindings, my legs going nowhere no matter how much I pull against them. Stupid leather. Stupid alpha. Stupid beta.

I need to come!

The alpha chuckles and my vision goes red. I struggle hard against the bindings, bucking until his cock's nearly unseated. A palm slaps down on my swollen, throbbing pussy, and I howl, my thighs quivering.

The alpha spanks my pussy again, the crack sharp and wet. Heat rushes to my core, and my body feels like it's on fire. He slaps it again and again, grunting when I clench around his cock.

Fuck yeah. I'm going to cum. Just a few more blows. I've never come from being spanked before, but I've also never been rutted by a room full of strange alphas. Guess today is a day for firsts.

My breath hitches as I hold still and resist the urge to buck up into his touch. He'll figure out what I'm doing and then he'll stop and then *I'll die.*

Sam leans his face down so we're cheek to cheek. "Naughty girl." *He knows.*

The alpha slaps my pussy once more, his cock kissing the entrance of my womb as he rides me deep. I'm balanced on the edge. The entire world falls away as all I care about is this pounding, pulsing need to squeeze a knot. I need it more than air.

"Omega?" the alpha growls.

Shit. He definitely knows. I'm beyond words, so all I can do at this point is make a high-pitched, needy whine.

His hips slap against me as his thumb brushes over my clit and rubs circles that make spots appear in my vision. I drag in a ragged breath and hold it, my whole body flushing with heat. Close. So close. Just a little bit…

He slams his hips home and holds it there, his knot growing and stretching me until it feels like he's on the verge of ripping me in two. "Come." His thumb strokes my clit faster and faster as hot spurts of cum coat my walls. I'm so full. So stuffed and seeded. The pressure in my belly and the stretch of my cunt around his monstrous knot is white hot.

I come with a sound that's half-groan and half-scream, my thighs trembling and my toes curled so tight they touch the soles of my feet. Slick gushes out of me like a burst damn. After I drag in a much-needed breath and sob on the exhale, my cunt flutters around his knot, milking more cum from his balls.

And then exhaustion and relief overwhelm me and blackness creeps in at the edges.

Chapter Five

SAM

THE OMEGA IS TINY AND LIGHT AS I HAUL HER OUT OF HER station and hike her up in my arms. One of the other betas, a new guy named Eric, helps me with the door.

"Damn. They really liked her. Is she okay?" he asks.

I shift her so her head lolls on my chest. "Yeah, she's fine. I checked her pulse. She just came so hard she passed out."

Eric leans on his mop handle. Since he's the new guy, it's his job to clean up the jizz. His waterproof disposable paper galoshes stick to the floor as he moves to get a new spot. Every step he takes makes a *thwock* sound.

I do *not* miss being the new guy.

"Can you imagine?" he says, his voice a little wistful as he glances at the rows of empty openings. They're spattered with so much cum and slick that everything is a sticky disaster. It always is. The real reason we do four-hour sessions with four-hour breaks is because that's how long it takes to scrub these rut rooms.

Beta attendants help their omega clients hobble from their stations, avoiding the worst of the puddles. "Why would you want to?" I ask.

Seems like it's mostly an inconvenience to me. But I'm good with being a beta. I know some people wish their dynamic had come in during puberty, but I've never been one of those people. I like my life to be uncomplicated.

"I dunno… Might be kinda nice. At least just once."

There's no point in arguing, so I make a noncommittal noise and focus on taking care of my omega instead. Her cheeks are in a permanent state of flushed now, and a fine sweat beads on her forehead. She's noticeably hot to the touch.

Time for a bath, baby.

I carry her to her room and manage to buzz the door open and kick it shut behind me. She clings to me when I lay her down in her nest, and I smile at her, my chest tight with fondness as I pry her fingers off my shirt and cover her with her fuzzy blankets. She makes a happy sigh and burrows deeper, dragging the blanket exactly where she wants it as she nuzzles it with her nose.

It's such a stark difference to the shy, insecure woman who tossed a blanket down on a bed and called it a nest. I'm gonna have fun helping her build a good nest.

And then fucking her in it.

Before I can get carried away, I go into the bathroom and draw her a tepid bath. She'll hate it. They always do. But then she'll like it. They always do.

Emily grunts as I pull her from her nest and carry her into the bathroom. I lower her into the water. Even though I'm expecting it, I still flinch when she jolts awake, her hands batting at me. It's not her fault. She's disoriented, and I don't have an alpha's purr to soothe her.

"Shh, it's okay, baby. It's just a bath. That's it. That's a good girl. Lie back and let me wash you." I talk to her like she's a frightened animal, and it's not too far from the truth. When they're in the thick of their heats and ruts, omegas and alphas get a little… animalistic. More driven by instinct than conscious thought.

When she lets me drag a soapy loofah over her body, I tell her how good she is. Her legs fall open as I rub the sponge between them, careful not to hurt her. She's gotta be raw and sensitive. She blinks heavy eyelids at me, her gaze unfocused as she lets me move her around like a doll and wash the rest of her.

I pull the stopper on the tub and wait for the water to completely drain. It's safer to be patient than to haul a fidgety, wet omega out of the bath.

"Let's get you back to your nest, baby."

She sighs and allows me to pick her up. Emily is wobbly on her feet as I wrap a big fluffy towel around her and dry her off. When she growls, her tolerance for the friction against her sensitive skin exceeded, I throw the towel aside and help her back to bed.

It's the easiest thing to convince her to climb into her makeshift nest. It's harder to convince her to drink another bottle of protein water. Once she's done, she fixes her blankets and pillows while I hand her more nesting material, ripping open the packages she ignored earlier. Once she's comfy, I grab the massage oil and coat my hands and rub her down. I start with her feet and work my way up. By the time I've reached her cunt, she's no longer twitchy at my touch. I spread the oil onto her swollen labia and gently work it around her opening. The herbs the doctors put it in will help her heal faster and relax her tired muscles.

When she grinds her pussy against my hand, even though it's half-hearted, I shush her again and tuck her in with her blankets. She disappears underneath the mound, only her nose emerging as she cocoons herself.

The faintest snores tell me she's asleep as I slip out of her room and make sure the door is latched tight behind me. I set the alarm system to ping my work phone so I'll know if she wakes up and tries to wander. And then I head to my locker and change. My scrubs are wrecked.

"Dude," Anthony says, nodding at me. "Hear you had a good time tonight. Aren't you glad you let Erin talk you into taking her shift?"

I tighten the drawstring on my new scrub pants and yank the shirt over my head, shaking out my hair. "Hmm."

"Just don't fall in love with this one. That last one wrecked you bad for like... weeks."

The last thing I need is to be reminded of Heather. I thought she really liked me, but when her heat ended, so did her interest. "I'm good, man." I slam my locker shut and head to the door that leads to our common room and then the parking lot behind it.

"Just telling it like it is!" Anthony calls out as I let the door swing shut.

I learned my lesson after Heather. I'm a beta, and I understand my place. That doesn't mean I can't be damn good at my job. The coworkers I pass exchange nods with me. Us off-shift people are close.

"Hey, Sam. We're ordering Chinese. Do you want anything?" Jane asks when I walk by.

"Sure." Chinese food is good cold. It's a solid choice for heat nanny nights, and I was too lazy to pack a meal. "I'll take the sesame chicken combo. You can just stick it in the fridge. I'll eat it when I get a chance."

"Oh." Her smile slips. "You're not gonna eat with us?"

"Nah. I have someone I've gotta talk to. Text me how much I owe you."

"Sure."

I head out the back door, the one that the smokers use to slip in a cigarette on their breaks even though this is technically a no-smoking area. Off-shift has its perks. One of those is a lack of management oversight. Dr. Sharma is cool. As long as her patients are good, she doesn't sweat the stupid shit. I enjoy working with her.

The alpha is hovering in the parking lot next to a flashy car like I knew he would be. He stands there leaning against the vehicle with his phone held to one ear. He's too far from the streetlight for me to get more than a vague impression of him, but I know it's the right one even before I hear him speak and I recognize his voice.

"Yes, I'm sure," he says to whoever he's talking to over the phone.

"Hey, man." I wave, keeping my smile friendly and my posture loose. Some alphas get real dickish about anything they consider their territory.

His head snaps up and his eyes lock onto me. "The beta."

"Sam, but… yeah." I hook my thumbs in the waistband of my fresh scrubs. "Heat minder is the actual job title if you wanna get specific. Is this a bad time?" I pointedly look at his phone.

"No, now is fine. I'm talking with my packmate."

I nod and glance at his car. It's one of those fancy new self-driving electric ones. The kind that starts at fifty grand and goes up from there. Way up. "Cool. So… she likes you."

His eyebrows climb. "She said that?"

Laughing, I cock my head and stare at him. "Naw, man. She's passed out in her nest. But I've been doing this a long time and I can tell. She likes you."

His broad chest rumbles with a deep purr.

"Marcus!" someone shouts through the phone. "I can't hear anything but your purr. You're bloody rumbling in my ear like a lorry truck."

The alpha shuts down his purr with a grimace. "Sorry. She's mine. Ours!" The voice on the other end of the line says something I can't hear from over here. "She's *ours*."

"Anyway, if you want to stick around a few more hours, the front office opens at six. You can fill out the paperwork."

He glances at his expensive watch. "Fine, I can wait five more hours. And then I can take her home?"

I blink. "Home? No. What? Naw, man. She doesn't know you. You can fill out the request for courtship paperwork, but it's up to her if she's interested." When the alpha does nothing but stare at me blankly, I cock my head. "This isn't the fourteen hundreds. You can't make off with an omega just because you like the way she smells."

He growls. He fucking growls at me! Alphas. Knotheads, each and everyone of them. I throw my hands up and start backing away slowly.

"You can stay or you can go, but taking her home is not only *so not a fucking option, dude,* it's also illegal. She's in our care and won't be released until she's legally fit to take care of herself, or her emergency contact comes to collect her. So even if I wanted to just hand her over to some random dude, which I don't, I can't. Bashing my head in isn't going to change that. You're welcome to hang out and wait. It's a free country, and I'm not the police. But do everyone a favor and wait in your car or go get a cup of coffee at the diner down the street. We're open twenty-four seven for emergency cases so you can't be hanging around in the dark parking lot like a horror movie villain. You're gonna scare the omegas."

The voice on the other end of the phone call cackles.

"I am *not* lurking," the alpha grumbles, his brows clashing in a glower that would make a weaker beta knock their knees together.

I make a big show of looking around and then glancing at my bare wrist as if I have on a watch. "Right." Because it's totally normal to hang out in the empty parking lot of a free clinic an hour after the treatment cycle ends. I walk away from him. He'll figure it out. It's not my problem.

"At least tell me her name!" the alpha calls out to me.

I freeze and spin back around. "No. That's also super fucking illegal, dude. If she wants you to know her name, she'll tell you after you fill out your courtship request form and she decides *if* she wants to contact you or not."

His face falls as if I've gut punched him, and then he recovers like it never happened. Like he has no idea how this works. "You're very protective of her."

In my head, I finish the sentence for him. *For a beta.* But he never voices it. Smart man.

"How long have you known her?" he asks.

"Like..." I do the math. "Seven hours."

That reminds me I need to sleep soon. Hopefully, she lets me curl up in her nest with her. She seems fun to cuddle. The alternative is having someone from day shift swap out with me in the morning, and that idea makes my gut clench. I don't want anyone else touching her.

"And when did you know?" he asks.

"Know what?"

"That she's yours too."

The concept he says so calmly makes me flinch. "I don't know what you're talking about. I'm a heat minder. This is my job."

He squares off at me, his shoulders straightening into a flat line that makes him look even bigger. *Damn, he's built.* It's hard to see the alphas through the slots in the stations. And after a while, all the alphas kind of blur together. Big, broad, and blunt. Even the female alphas are bigger than most betas. They're all a bygone relic from an ancient time when alphas led small clans, protecting the weaker betas and the omega breeders from rival packs. Now they tend to run companies or work in law enforcement or do skilled labor jobs. It's us betas who fill in the gaps and keep everything moving.

"You feel it in your gut," he says. "Like a pull. Looking at her makes everything brighter. Touching her makes butterflies swarm in your stomach. Fucking her… it feels like heaven."

Alphas. They love to get cuntstruck at first knot.

"Yeah. You know what I mean," he says. "I can see it in your face. Maybe you can't smell it, but on some level, you know. Come here," he barks. "I want to look at you."

I don't know why I listen to him, but my feet pull me toward him without consulting my brain. I join him under the circle of light from the streetlight he's parked under and do my best to look nonchalant. As if alphas built like brick houses tell me what to do all the time and I listen.

"Well, here I am," I snap, trying to hide my uncertainty with bluster. *What's wrong with me?*

The alpha leans down and sniffs me, his nose almost pressing right up against my neck. I freeze. It's a primordial instinct. Fight, flight, or fawn. My body screams *this is a predator, and he's at your throat.* So I freeze. *God, is this how the omegas feel?* No wonder they come to us in droves and let us lock them up in boxes where their necks are safe, even if their holes get ravaged.

He purrs, his chest rumbling so hard I can almost feel it through the vibrations of the air between us. He leans back and searches my face. Something in his rough expression softens. "We found you."

What? No. My heart jumps into my throat. The way his purr makes my body feel calmer makes my head more panicked. I'm… horny yet terrified, but hopeful too. But those childish dreams of being chosen, of being picked for a pack, died years ago. Except maybe they didn't. Or at least not completely.

Oh… no. Boy, that is a lot to unpack in therapy.

That thought is enough to break my reaction to his sniffing. I throw my hands up in the air and back away. "Gotta go." I raise my hand to my forehead in a salute that makes no sense to me. I flee, forgetting to badge into the door. It doesn't budge, and my face heats as I realize I look like a moron and… yup, he's still watching me from under the streetlight next to his fancy, expensive car.

"How soon can you get here?" the alpha, Marcus, says into his phone. "Yes, I *do* in fact know what time it is in London right now. That's not what I asked, Tom. Okay. Cancel your meetings and get on the next plane. I'll pick you up at the airport."

Fuck.

I swipe my badge against the card reader, moving it too fast for it to register and unlock the door.

"See you soon. Love you," Marcus says.

Rationally, I know that he's talking to his packmate on the phone. But the way he says those words in that rough, low purr makes my heart slam against my ribs with panic.

Fuck!

I swipe it again, slower, and this time it opens. Bolting inside, I pull the slowly closing door shut behind me so hard it slams and everyone in the break room stares at me.

"Dude, are you okay?" Diana pauses with her bitten egg roll midway to her mouth.

"Oh, awesome! Food's here. That was fast." I snag one of the greasy paper packets off the table and stuff an egg roll in my mouth, biting off a huge chunk so nobody expects me to answer any further questions I'd like to avoid.

No. I am not okay. I have not been okay since Heather made me want things that have long been buried and should stay that way. Adolescent fantasies are just that. Fantasies.

The sesame chicken goes in the fridge for later. "Let me know how much I owe you," I say around the food in my mouth as I bolt from the break room and nod to the coworkers I pass in the hall.

The egg roll is chewy and difficult to swallow without a drink. It's also ridiculously hot. I choke it down, my stomach grateful for the food even though it would be happier with a bunch of sesame chicken in it.

But there's a sleepy, cuddly omega waiting for me in her nest, and for reasons I don't want to think about too closely, I'm eager to get back to her.

It's the sleep, I tell myself. *I'm fucking beat. Just need to sleep. Everything will make sense again in the morning.*

Chapter Six

EMILY

My nest is a perfect, cozy mountain of soft blankets, and I wake up warm and content with a pleasant ache between my legs. Sam curls around me, his body fitted to mine, and he's as hot as a space heater. It makes me want to stretch against him and soak up his warmth.

Fidgeting, I rub against him, his morning erection poking into my ass, and my lips curl in a smile as moisture creeps at my cleft.

Despite being wet, now that I'm awake and remembering what I did last night, embarrassment makes me blush. I can't believe I did that—I let a whole room full of strange alphas rut me. Sam lets out a sleepy sound as he curls one of his arms around me and tugs me even closer, his hand going to my breast as he grabs it and holds it tight. His squeezing makes my sore clit throb, and it pulls me out of my inner turmoil as desire overtakes shame.

"Morning, baby," he rumbles, his voice thick with sleep. "How'd you sleep?"

"Good." My hips twitch as I grind against him. Pre-cum drips onto my ass when he rocks with me, the hand on my breast squeezing and playing with my nipple in that way that makes a bolt of lightning shoot right down to my clit.

"Sam, I want you to fuck me," I moan.

He lets go of my breast and skims his hand down my front, slipping it between my thighs and stroking it between my slippery folds. It grazes my aching clit and spreads my slick around. He teases me until my breath comes out in pants and I whine.

"So wet, baby. Your first session starts at eight."

"Nooo. That's too long." I don't know what time it is, but instinct tells me it's far too long to wait. "Fuck me now." I twitch my hips, trying to rub my clit harder and faster against his fingers. The lack of friction makes me feel like I'm going insane. Like I'll spontaneously combust if someone doesn't stick a dick in me right now. The incessant need to ride a cock grips me. "Please. Please fuck me."

He has the nerve to chuckle at me, but I forgive him when he adjusts our positions and his cock slides between my lips. Each flex of his hips pushes it through my labia, catching on my clit. It's wonderful, but not enough.

"Like this?" he asks.

What a fucking brat.

I growl to let him know I'm not amused as I reach down and run my fingers over the beautiful cockhead leaking pre-cum all over my pubic hair. It's easy to press, to nudge it where I want it until his next thrust teases my entrance. He pulls back, his hips making a lazy cant, and then the next one notches him properly inside me in a single glide.

Sam's cock sinks into me, and I sigh with relief.

He groans as he seats himself, a pleasant rumble that's all satisfied male. We rock together, my pussy stretching to take him as the river of slick my body makes eases his passage and that warm buzz builds deep in my pelvis. Our fucking is slow and languid, a stark contrast to the rough and fast poundings of last night.

Reaching back, I palm his ass and pull him in deeper until he's brushing against my cervix. But as my pleasure builds, I find it's not enough to tip me over the edge. Not deep enough. Not fast enough. It's sweet torture.

I try to take control of it, to slap my hips back against him and set the pace, but he digs his fingers into my hip and pins me where he wants me, his dick slipping in and out of me with smooth, slow thrusts. It's a reminder that I'm not in control here. The thought should make me wary. Sam is another stranger in this lineup of people I don't know fucking me raw, but it doesn't. I feel taken care of. And maybe that makes no sense to Emily, the woman, but the omega side of me is purring and content.

"Sam," I say, turning his name into a plea as I fidget.

Sam laughs and drops a kiss to the corner of my mouth, then throws the blankets of my nest off us and repositions us. He gets up on his knees and tugs me flat onto my back. One hand grips each thigh as he pulls me up onto his lap and enters me. The lazy morning fuck morphs into something rougher. This position lets me watch him fuck me, and for that reason alone, I love it. His sandy blond hair is a mess. Parts of it stick up in the air while other locks hang in his vision.

He's naked, and I eat up the sight of him. Lean. That's the best description of him. He's athletic and toned, but his body lacks the breadth and sheer intimidation and power of an alpha. Sam's abdominals flex with the work of his breathing as he ruts me into the nest. His large hands hold my pelvis on either side of me as if he's holding me tight so I won't run away. As if I'd want to get away. He pulls me deeper onto his cock with every cervix-hitting thrust.

"God, you feel so good. So hot and wet and soft." His hips

roll with each word, punctuating them, and then he goes back to pounding me.

My pussy clenches with his words, his endless praise that makes me want to duck my head in embarrassment but also preen. "So good. I love your cock."

His eyes snap up to mine with a look I can't describe. "Yeah?"

I nod, twisting my fingers in the nest. It's the perfect size. Just long and wide enough that I feel full and satisfied without the awful stretch and burn of a first knot. It takes time and patience and tons of foreplay to take some of the alphas I've fucked. But not Sam. Sam, I think I could fuck anywhere, anytime. We can be spontaneous without worrying about preparations.

The fuzzy fleece blankets rub against my skin until I'm tingling all over. With Sam, there's no endurance to this, just connection. Sometimes the alphas stretch you so badly that all you can think about is the worry that their knot's going to split you in two. There's a reason alphas purr to soothe us when we get distressed during rutting.

Sam hits the soft parts deep in me that know nothing but craving. He strokes them from the inside out until my toes curl and I'm breathing hard. His forearms tense as he holds me in place and keeps me from squirming, his forearm veins popping with the effort.

God, I want to lick them. Trace them with my tongue and cover him with kisses. Why haven't I done that yet?

"I'm close, baby. Are you ready?" he asks.

I nod, eager to take everything he gives me. All he has to do is touch my clit and I'll shatter. Each tug of his withdrawal pulls at it, and every grind of his pelvis against me rubs.

"Touch yourself, baby," he orders. "Play with that pretty clit. You're going to cum on my cock."

I do. I reach down and stroke myself, gathering up my slick

as I set two fingers over my clit and rub circles. It barely takes me any time at all to fall off that precipice, my cunt fluttering and squeezing as it tries to milk the cum right out of his balls.

Sam groans and drops his head, his gaze stuck on where we're connected as his thrusts slow. His cock pulses, jerking inside of me, and then I feel it—the first lash of hot, ropey cum. He empties inside of me, each thrust wringing a little more out of him until his breathing levels out.

He glides in and out of me a few more times, and then he pulls free and stares at my slick, glossy pussy. Fingers tease my entrance as he touches me gently.

"Push it out."

I bear down and flex, contracting my muscles until I feel the cool slide of cum trickling down the crack of my ass. Sam scoops it up and catches each drop, stroking my swollen folds as he plays with me.

"Do you want this in your nest?" he asks with zero judgment in his voice.

"Yes." I nod, and he smears our fluids on our blankets, touching each one as he spreads his cum and my slick around so that it will smell even more like us. So that it will smell *right*, instead of the scent-nullifying cleansers.

I purr, content for now until my heat ratchets up throughout the day and drives me out of my mind with lust again. Sam smiles that lopsided grin, and it makes me wonder how cute he was as a kid. How he must have had the same shaggy blond hair falling in his eyes and the same crooked smile, but with missing teeth. Is that what his children will look like?

Yearning hits me in my chest and makes me feel empty and happy and sad all at once. *It's just the heat*, I tell myself. It's biology. The evolutionary urge to pack up for safety and get pregnant fast so the alpha will want to keep and protect you.

Sam bends my legs up and folds me in half. "Hold your legs. Like that. Perfect. You're so pretty, baby."

In this position, my pussy's on display as it peeks out between my thighs. I squeeze my knees to my chest and lock my arms around my legs. Sam sticks two fingers inside of me and scoops out more cum and slick, smearing it onto our nest. Big hands rub the globes of my ass, then pull away and slap them.

I yelp and rock from the surprise.

And then he gets up and walks to the bathroom, returning a moment later with a wet towel. He cleans me first, and then himself, and then he leans down and bites my thigh, smoothing the sting with a kiss. The bed creaks as he flops down beside me.

"Can I put my legs down?" Because I need to lie on my side and cuddle again. I want to feel his thick arms wrap around me and hold me tight against his chest as he notches my head under his chin and spoons me.

"That depends. How horny are you right now?" he asks.

"Uhhh… forty percent?"

He leans on one arm and ghosts a finger over the seam of my sex, smiling at me until his cheek dimples when I twitch.

Maybe… maybe more like fifty percent. He palms my cunt and holds his hand there, cupping me.

"The alpha from last night…"

My clit throbs against the pressure of Sam's hand, and he must feel it because his eyes crinkle at the corners. Slick drips from me, but he pretends he doesn't notice even as it coats his hand and dribbles down my ass.

The alpha from last night… *God.* My core clenches at the thought of him. Of the way he mastered my pussy like he owned it. Like it was his.

"He's putting in courtship paperwork," Sam says.

"What?"

Sam hums an affirmative sound. "It's your choice if you want to consider it. Consider *him*. He's bringing his packmate into town on the chance you'll agree to meet them."

"His packmate." Of course that alpha already has a partner.

"It's up to you. Your information is confidential, of course. While you're here in the clinic's custody during a heat, you can't legally make any mating decisions. The laws are… It's complicated. He just wants to meet you. For you to meet them. No strings. No obligations. If you don't like them, we'll take care of it."

Them.

It's every omega's teenage dream. An alpha. A pack. So then why do I feel a little panicked? This is not what I came here for. I came to the free clinic to have a decent heat for once and scratch that omega itch, then go back to my life with a few stories to tell. This is… It's too much, too soon, too fast. How am I supposed to make important decisions when every single thought I have is interrupted by the need to hump something?

I let my legs fall and roll onto my side, suddenly hit with the need to burrow into my nest. To hide under the blankets where it's warm and safe and it smells right. I grab the blanket that smells the most like me and Sam and cover myself with it.

Sam rubs my arm through the blanket, his smile gone. "What's wrong, baby?"

"I don't know." My head hurts from trying to sort all of my jumbled thoughts. What would an alpha, a pack, want with me? "God, why would they want me? I'm so *old*," I say, pulling the blanket up over my head.

"What?" Sam sputters, his laughter dying when he sees my eyes are filled with unshed tears. "Oh, baby, you're only thirty-six. That hardly makes you the Crypt-Keeper." He rubs my back through the blankets and lies down so he's spooning me. It's less nice when I'm cocooned in blankets and can't feel the heat coming off his skin.

I close my eyes and pinch the bridge of my nose. "Most omegas are mated and barefoot and pregnant and in the kitchen by twenty-five." Most days, it doesn't bother me. Not even when I stopped getting wedding announcements and started getting pregnancy postcards as, one by one, all of my friends and the people I went to school with found their partners or their packs. Every year, it seems like there's more and more couples and throuples and polycules in the world than available people. But the romantic in me refused to let me settle and be happy with someone who didn't drive my omega side wild.

Sam tugs at the blankets until it's free enough that he can slip under it. He spoons against me, the press of his nudity comforting instead of sexual. He threads a hand under mine and splays it over my stomach.

"I won't lie. The idea of breeding you is hot." His cock twitches against my ass as if to prove his point. "And you're hardly retirement age. So what if it hasn't happened 'til now? I see plenty of omegas find their packs in their thirties or forties or fifties or older. And omegas are fertile for a lot longer than betas."

"Really?" Because that's not what it feels like. It feels like everyone is on the same life plan. Everyone but me. Find your pack in high school or college. Graduate, land that dream job, get married or mated, pop out two kids, adopt a dog, and move to the suburbs. All I have is an apartment that gets more expensive every year, my plants, and an office job that can replace me tomorrow.

"Really." He hauls me tighter against him and presses a kiss to the side of my throat. "Besides, I've always liked older women. You're fucking hot."

My eyes widen as my mouth drops open, and I snap my head back to scowl at him. "You're hardly *that* much younger than me."

Sam grins, his cheek dimpling as he presses a kiss to the corner of my mouth. "I'm twenty-eight."

Twenty-eight. Oh, God. I knew he was a little younger, but I didn't know there was an eight-year gap between us. I stare at the white ceiling in horror. "I'm a cradle robber," I whisper.

He snorts out a laugh and grabs the blankets, jerking them out from under me. And then he slips under them, sliding down the bed as he rolls me onto my back and settles between my legs. He nips my inner thigh, his blunt teeth pinching and I gasp.

I peel the top edge of the blanket back to scowl down at him. "What are you doing?" This conversation is important, and I only have short periods of lucidity until the cramps start again and my need builds to a point where all I can think about is sinking down on the nearest knot.

"I thought it was obvious." He pushes my legs open and dips his head between them, his tongue snaking out to lick my seam and the slick that constantly gathers there. He moans, as if it's the most delicious thing he's ever tasted. "I'm checking your pussy for a best-used-by date."

I blush, my face heating as he licks me again, my hips rising up to meet his laving tongue. "This is important. We should talk, not... hnnng. Oh, fuck."

"What do you want to talk about?" he asks, kissing my clit and coating two fingers in my slick before pressing them into me and pumping. "Don't let me stop you. Do you want to talk about IRAs? 401ks? Have you bought the black candles for your next birthday cake yet?" He sucks my clit into his mouth and runs his tongue around it, pushing my hood back for better access. "The balloons shaped like tombstones?"

"F-fuck you." *He's such a fucking brat.*

Sam lets my clit go with a wet pop and grins like an insane Cheshire Cat. "I'd rather fuck *you*. You're probably going to miss your first treatment session of the day, by the way." His fingers pump into me, and my hips move to meet him, to suck him in deeper. "That means I have to take care of you myself."

A part of me wonders if he planned for this. He seems sneaky like that. Devious. But it's hard to stay suspicious or even care at all when he eats my cunt like someone's got a gun to his head and his life depends on it.

The first orgasm hits me with a faint wash of pleasure, the swell soon rolling into another as he pulls them from me one by one with his fingers and tongue until I don't think I can take it anymore. Coming around nothing but a finger has moved beyond pleasure and into pain as the first tide of the day's heat threatens to drag me under its wave.

"It hurts," I whine when my walls flutter and clench against his knuckles.

"I know what you need," he says. He lifts off me and climbs off the bed, and my hips rock in the air of their own volition.

I need a cock. A knot. Relief.

Plastic rips, and then there's a buzzing sound. Sam returns to the bed holding up the hot pink vibrator. It's huge, nearly as big as his forearm, and the extra silicone material by the grip tells me it's the knotting kind.

He joins me on the bed again, sliding the toy up my inner thigh and teasing the seam of my sex with it as he leans over me and hovers his face next to mine, his lips as close as they can get without touching. We stay like this in our almost kiss as he presses it to my hole but doesn't sink it in no matter how I twitch or rub against it, asking for it without words.

"Tell me you'll meet them. Just a meeting, that's all," he says.

I frown. "Why do you care if I do?"

Sam presses a kiss to the corner of my mouth, the toy pressing in a little deeper. Vibrations tease my hole as arousal drips from me until I know the nest is about to be a mess of slick.

"Because you deserve all the wonderful things in life, and I think they can give those to you."

Would I be able to live with myself if I ran away like a coward and missed my chance? After a moment of hesitation, I agree. "Okay."

He sinks the toy past my public bone and I sigh as the vibrations send tremors through my pelvis.

"Will you be with me?" I ask.

The toy thrusts deeper, the silicone dragging more than skin as he slicks it with my fluids until it's gliding freely and filling me up. "If you want me to."

I sneak my arm up between us and throw it around his neck, tugging him flush against me as he fucks me slowly with the toy. The stretch and burn of it satisfies the primal side of me that craves the roughness of a huge, gruff alpha. The ripping, burning swell of a knot and the hot lash of cum.

"I want you," I tell him, sighing with relief when he fucks me harder. The buzz of the toy grows louder, the vibrations faster, and the thrusts deeper as he clicks it up, adjusting the controls on the handle without looking.

My lips press to his as I claim his mouth in a tentative kiss. *My beta*, my omega instincts purr.

Mine.

Sam fucks me until I shatter on the toy's knot, satisfying all of my cravings and squashing that roaring need that burns me up from the inside out like a living furnace. When we're done, he releases the air that inflates it, the silicone shrinking and the toy slipping out of me as my cunt flutters one last time, trying to milk the seed that isn't there. Slick flows down my thighs and ass, soaking into the bed.

But when Sam pulls me down with him and wraps me in his arms, our legs tangled together, I find I don't mind.

At some point, while I'm floating in my hazy, post-knot-drunk bliss after being fucked three more times, a nurse comes in and secures a cuff around my wrist that squeezes. She writes down notes while Sam presses a thermometer between my lips and kisses me on the nose when I pout.

The only thing that could make this better would be if he could purr. But I'm not heat delirious enough to ask and risk hurting his feelings. Betas can't purr.

He presses something to my lips, and I take it without looking. A sweet coating quickly turns to the bitter taste of medicine. Sam holds a bottle of water to my mouth next, and I obey his commands to swallow. He makes me drain it all, the water cold in my stomach, but he touches me the entire time, so I do it gladly.

Sam buries us in our nest, and I press my nose to his neck, breathing in his oranges and cream scent while I purr my dainty omega purr for us both. His fingers trace swirls on my back while my eyelids grow heavy.

Chapter Seven

MARCUS

THE WAITRESS OFFERS ME A REFILL FROM THE COFFEE POT SHE holds up, but I wave her off and stare at my mug. It's lunchtime now, and an entire diner full of people has come and gone four times over since the first morning rush for breakfast began at five. I've been here since one, more than long enough to watch the shift change as an older beta with bleached hair and graying roots and red lipstick takes over the back corner booth I'm occupying.

"You gonna order, hun?" she asks as she hovers. "I recommend the burger and fries."

The steak and eggs I let the night waitress talk me into have long since been left cold and congealing and taken away. "That sounds good, thanks."

She purses her lips, her pencil-thin waxed brows knitting together, then nods and walks away to talk to the kitchen over the opening in the counter.

I know that I'm being ridiculous. That I'm acting like a teenager who's gotten his first knot and thinks that makes him a man now. But how can I eat knowing that my omega is so close, in heat and hurting? Who will knot her? Purr for her? Some rough stranger who doesn't deserve to touch her?

The handle snaps off the mug, and I stare at the broken ceramic.

A waitress carrying two plates of breakfast combos walks by and pauses, her eyes wide at the sight of the broken coffee mug.

"I'm sorry." I brush the ceramic shards together as if that makes anything better. "Add that to my bill, please."

She walks away, carrying her food to her customers, her brown ponytail bouncing.

Get a hold of yourself. You're scaring everyone by sitting in this damn booth like a big, brooding bastard.

My phone buzzes in my pocket, and my heart leaps into my throat, racing. Is this it? Is this her? The caller ID says it's Tom. Disappointment fades to relief. I answer and press the phone to my ear. The chaos of a busy, crowded public space blasts into my ear, and then his silky British accent washes over me, soothing all of my sharp corners and making me feel less like a lunkhead about to rampage.

"Hello, darling," he says. "They just announced boarding will start. I'm about to get on the plane."

"Good. That's good."

Tom waits a beat, then speaks. "Are you okay? You're very growly today."

"They haven't called yet," I admit, feeling guilty that maybe I jumped the gun and should have been more patient, playing it by ear instead of disrupting everyone's routine, including my own. "I'm sorry. You might miss your big showing for nothing."

"It's not nothing if you need me there," Tom says, calm under pressure as always. "And I'll have more showings. Alicia can charm the buyers better than me, anyway. I'll probably sell more *because* I'm not there."

My lips twitch at his self-deprecation. If he was here, I'd slap him on the ass for saying such an unkind thing about himself. But he's not here. *Soon.* "Your work is beautiful, and anyone who doesn't see one of your photos and immediately fall in love with you is a fucking idiot."

"Don't make my head so big," Tom says. He's grinning, by the sound of his voice. "I have to fit it on this plane."

"Be safe." I hate airplanes. I loathe trusting an enormous, heavy metal contraption to stay up in the air.

"Planes fly every day. I'll be fine."

"I know. I just worry and I don't like it when you're gone for so long."

"I know." Tom sighs. "I have to go. They're calling for final boarding. I love you and I'll see you soon. Try not to scare her when she calls. You can be… intimidating when you hyper-focus."

"*If* she calls."

She might not. And somehow… I'll need to learn how to live with that. The alpha inside of me wants to storm that building and rip her out of it, to make sure she's safe and keep any other alphas from her. But the man in me knows that's only going to end up with handcuffs and fingerprint ink and the firm might get annoyed if their name gets splashed in the papers by association.

"I'll see you soon. We'll deal with it no matter what happens. Love you," Tom says.

"Love you too. No matter what."

The line goes silent, and I put my phone down on the table, my foot bouncing with restless energy. I need to punch something. Go for a jog. Maybe jerk off in the bathroom? I don't even know anymore.

I'm realizing that perhaps I was impulsive when I cleared my schedule and pissed off all my clients.

My waitress comes back and drops off my food. She says nothing about the broken coffee mug as she goes to the jingling door to greet the customers who just walked in. She grabs a handful of laminated menus from a cubby and seats them on the other side of the diner. Far away from me.

Fuuuck.

That beta was right. I'm acting like a beast and scaring everyone. Alphas are tolerated in this modern society because we're good at making quick decisions in the heat of the moment and most of us have a natural leadership quality. Unhinged alphas who scare the public are dealt with swiftly and decisively.

I pull my wallet out of my back pocket and grab a fifty, then glance at the broken coffee mug and take out a second one and tuck the cash under my untouched plate of food. Outside on the street, I take a moment to just breathe and clear my head, and then I walk back to my car.

The clinic is busy now that the sun's up, and my car is no longer one of the few in the parking lot. I unlock it and slide inside and grip the leather wrapped steering wheel until it creaks. I should go back to the hotel and shower. Change my clothes. Maybe try to take a nap until Tom gets here. If the clinic still hasn't called, then I can drive to the airport and pick him up instead of sending a car. I'll bring him flowers. Sunflowers. His favorite. I smile and press the ignition button and watch the dash light up.

With the address to the hotel keyed into the navigation software, I lean back and hook my fingers on the wheel as it makes the drive.

The call comes in five intersections later as I stop for a red light. It's unlisted. My heart leaps as I swipe the green dot to answer it.

"Hello?"

"Mr. Orello?"

"Speaking."

"Hi! This is Mary, I'm the administrative assistant for the clinic on Main Street. I'd like to talk to you about your paperwork. Is this a good time?"

The light turns green, and my car drives through it once traffic moves. "Now is fine. Is there an issue? Did I forget to fill out a section?"

"No, nothing like that," she says. "The omega you requested permission to court has accepted your request. We need you to come and fill out more forms and give a sample."

My heart nearly beats right out of my chest, and it's a good thing my car drives itself because my whole body lurches to the side as I reach for the controls and turn up the volume.

"Thank you," I say. "I can be there in five minutes."

"Oh, there's no need to rush. I'm here in the office until six tonight."

"I'll be there in five." I end the call and cancel my current route, sending my car back to the clinic as I count down each stoplight I'm forced to idle through until I pull into the now-familiar parking lot I just left. My spot is taken by an ancient Honda Civic and I have to park in the back.

The gravel crunches under my loafers as my long legs eat up the distance to the alpha entrance on the building's side. A few alphas sit there on their phones while others watch the game up on the TV mounted to the wall. The receptionist looks up from her computer behind the glass partition that separates her from the waiting room.

"Hi, I'm Marcus Orello. I just got a call from the admin assistant. She asked me to come by and fill out some more paperwork?"

"She's expecting you. I'll walk you back to her office." She presses a button on the wall, and the door buzzes as it unlatches.

She opens it and ushers me in, and I follow as she leads me to

Mary's office. Mary is sitting behind her desk, eating a sandwich, and she looks up just as she takes a bite.

"Here's your alpha," the receptionist says, then walks away.

Mary hurries to chew and swallow as she motions for me to stop hovering in the doorway and sit. "Wow, you weren't kidding. Have a seat." She tucks her sandwich into its paper wrapper and sets it down.

I sit, the plastic chair creaking ominously as I try and fold myself into it. My knees hit her desk. "I'm sorry for disturbing your lunch." This is a bad way to make a good impression on the clinic. If I'd known, I'd have waited in the parking lot. What's thirty more minutes if it gets me closer to my omega? We've already waited a lifetime.

She waves a hand in the air. "It's fine. Here's the paperwork for you to fill out. We already have a copy of your driver's license and a basic background check, but now we need you to sign off on a more in-depth one and give us permission to have your medical records released. If you can get us a record of your finances this afternoon and, pending everything coming back good, you can probably meet with the omega this evening."

"Is this… normal?" I never had to go through any of this with Tom. Perhaps it's because he's a beta?

"Since you met through the clinic, yes. If you'd had a chance encounter in public and got to know one another that way, then no. But any alpha who uses a clinic or omega center to find their packmate or mates must submit to the standards the government set. It's primarily meant to keep omegas safe and prevent any sort of human trafficking. Think of how easy it would be for an alpha to walk in, claim they've found their omega, and then walk out with them if we weren't thorough. The omega will have access to these records, but she may not even want or ask to look at them. But knowing it's been collected and added to your file… It helps.

You're a stranger to her, Mr. Orello. That's a big change to adjust to."

"I see. Can I at least know her name now?"

Mary leans back and smiles. "It's Emily."

Emily.

I choke back the purr her name summons when I think about it. It tries to rumble up through my chest anyway. I clear my throat to cover it. "Thank you."

She hands me a clipboard and pulls a stack of papers from her drawer. "Here. Fill these out."

That's a thick stack. I take the pen from my jacket pocket and click it, then get to work. Mary finishes her lunch while I fill them out, alternating between tapping on her keyboard and reading her screen. The whoosh of her emails coming in and going out is constant. When I've finished signing my life away and divulging every personal detail, from shoe size to criminal history and medical history before and after puberty, I tuck my pen away and hand the papers back to her.

I pull my phone from my pocket and start a message to my accountant. "I can have my finance summary sent over within the hour. What's easier, fax or email?"

"Either is fine. Here's my card." She grabs a business card from the holder on her desk and hands it to me, and I text both to my accountant.

"Great! I'll ask them to come and take you into the back, where you can give your sample." She picks up her phone and dials a number from memory. "Mr. Orello is ready."

A moment later, a nurse in scrubs appears in the doorway and motions for me to follow him. The hallway is quiet despite what I know is going on just a few doors away. Soundproofed. Is she being rutted by other alphas now? A spark of jealousy catches me off guard. It's not my business if she is. I mean nothing to her, even if I very much want to. But an alpha's possessiveness isn't rational. The thought of anyone but my pack touching a single hair on her head makes my fist clench until my nails press half-moons into my palm.

"In here. There are movies and magazines that you can use if you'd like. No lotion, lube, or saliva, please. It alters the quality of the sample."

The dark wooden rack of colorful printed magazines he mentions contains a plethora of pornography magazines. Slick-zone. Cumsluts. Knotty & Naughty. There's a white-topped plastic jar sitting on the counter along with an unopened, personal-size cardboard box of tissues.

It's clear they're not taking blood like they did with the STD panel. "You want a semen sample?"

"It's best if you can fill the cup with at least five milliliters. When was your last emission?"

"Thirteen and a half hours ago." When Emily squeezed my knot so tight, her beautiful pussy sucked the seed right out of my balls.

The nurse makes a mark on the chart.

"What's this for?" I ask.

"Some omegas are looking for alphas for breeding, so we run a standard semen analysis to ensure fertility. You can pay for a genetic screening if you're interested in knowing your chances of any hereditary concerns."

The idea of rutting my omega until she's pregnant almost makes me finally lose it. "Yes. Run it and send me the bill."

He makes another mark on the chart and leaves the folder on the counter, then shuts the door behind him on his way out. Once he's gone, I grab the cup and peel its wrapper open, then unscrew the lid and set it back down.

Well then.

My cock is already half hard as I undo my pants and pull it

out, giving it a stroke from root to tip before running my pinky on the sensitive underside of my crown the way I like it. I can't wait to teach her how to please me. How to jerk my cock and lick me. My hand moves, tugging, to keep pace with my thoughts.

I fantasize about her beautiful cunt and the way she dripped for me as I touched her. Her drizzly sweet lemon cookie scent. *God, I fucking love lemons.* I can never order a lemon wedge in my ice water again without thinking about sucking her perfect, juicy cunt.

Pre-cum leaks from my tip, splattering into the cup as I drip over it while I masturbate and think about her sweet little moans. The way her thighs trembled whenever she got close to coming. How she thought she could ever hide it from me. How her pheromones perfumed the room, drowning out all the other rutting, grunting alphas and creaming, whimpering omegas.

That pulsing, tugging of my loins drives an ache through me as I edge myself to the point of orgasm, drawing it out and letting it fade before building it again.

I'm going to fill this cup.

I'm going to put as many babies in my omega as she wants.

I'm going to knot her and breed her and *hnnnng.*

The orgasm makes my balls buzz as I shoot a hot load into the specimen cup, the ropes of cum painting its walls like it coated her cunt. When my knot swells, I wrap my other hand around it and squeeze rhythmically. It's not a true mimic of a clenching omega. Not close at all. But it's good enough for this.

Panting, I squeeze until there's nothing left, then shake the last drop from my head and punch the perforated top off the tissues with my thumb so I can clean up. I tuck myself away and screw the lid on the cup. It's not quite full, but it's close.

Hmm. I should probably have asked what to do with the cup once it's filled.

There's a sink cut into the counter, so I wipe the outside of the cup to make sure it's clean and wash my hands, then open the door. The nurse looks over from his computer station in the hallway and puts on a pair of blue disposable gloves, taking the cup from me.

"Great, thanks. I'll get this to the lab." He seals it in a plastic bag and tosses his gloves into the trash. And then he points to another waiting room at the end of the hall. "You can wait there."

"Sure." While he disappears to deliver my specimen, I sit in another too-tiny chair and resign myself to wait. *What's she doing right now? Who's she with? Fuck. No. It's fine. I'm fine. Is she okay? I hope Tom's flight isn't too bad. Of course he's okay. Planes fly every day as Tom likes to remind me.* My phone chirps, saving me from my thoughts.

My accountant tells me he's sent the paperwork as requested, and I make a mental note to fatten his Christmas bonus for bothering him at home on the Saturday of a holiday weekend.

My foot bounces up and down as I sit there. After what feels like an eternity, the nurse comes to collect me once more. He leads me down yet another hallway. This place is a maze. Every hallway looks the same, and I wonder if it's been designed that way on purpose.

"Everything went fine?" I ask.

"You'll have to ask the doctor, or put in a written request to the medical records department. We're going to fit you with your mouth guard."

Mouth guard? That's offensive. Like I'm some mannerless criminal who doesn't know how to keep his canines to himself. Like I can't be trusted. "Is that necessary?"

"It's protocol," he says, shrugging. The nurse stops and points into an open room with a green vinyl dental chair in the center. "They'll be with you soon."

I sit where I'm told and wait. Again. An older man, an alpha who's gone all gray and soft around the middle, comes in and takes a paper cover off the tray beside me. He rolls it over, sits on his wheeled stool, and scoots closer.

"Open. Let me take a look," he says.

I open my mouth, and he grabs me by the chin, turning my face side to side and angling my head back as he leans in and inspects me.

"You've got good teeth," he grunts and releases me. He pours powder and a liquid into a plastic cup and stirs it with a wooden stick until it turns bright purple and expands like foam. The mixture gets spooned into a curved plastic tray that he thrusts at my face. "Open. Bite. Two minutes."

He gets up and walks out, leaving me with this tray of still-expanding goo in my mouth. It overflows the edges of the tray until I worry that it's going to creep all the way into the back of my throat.

But then it rubberizes. That's the only way I can explain it. The goo stops expanding and turns firm. The old alpha takes more than two minutes to return, but I refuse to rip it out of my mouth. That might delay this process even further, and I've waited long enough to find my omega and claim them. Forty-two long fucking years.

He comes back and grabs the tray by its handle, and I open. He pulls it from my mouth, and I rub my tongue over my teeth to dislodge any gritty, rubbery remnants. Another plastic cup of powder mixes with an equal measure of water which he pours into the mold we just made and sets an alert on a portable timer.

"Thirty minutes." He leaves me again.

Fuuuuck. Thirty minutes. In thirty minutes I'll be closer to her than I have been for over forty years. It's not that bad if you really think about it.

God, it's fucking *agony*.

I want to hold her. I want to wrap her in my arms and drag her scent up into my sinuses and sink my cock and my teeth into her at the same time and… My canines ache the more I think about them, like once I've acknowledged them they won't stop.

Oh, that's actually a good call on the mouth guard.

The timer rings, and I realize I've lost track of time. The old alpha comes back and rips at the mold, tearing the purple off until there's only a white plaster cast of my teeth left.

Good God.

Is that really what they look like? My canines are pointed. All alphas are. Our bodies are weapons, designed by nature to protect those we care about. To guard them and keep them safe.

They look so much more menacing than I've ever noticed before in the mirror. The old alpha pops the lid off a tin and uses a pair of tweezers to pull out a thin, clear film of plastic. He tacks it onto the canines of my mold with a bit of dental wax and positions the film just so. And then he puts it in some sort of fancy-looking toaster oven and presses a sequence of buttons. It whirrs as a light comes on.

When it dings, he takes it out and the tooth guard is now fitted to the mold. He uses a scalpel to trim it down, then runs it under the cold tap for a bit. Once it's cool enough for him to handle it, he pops it off the mold and holds it up to the light, then hands it to me.

I take it and turn it around in my hands. It's surprisingly light.

"Go ahead and make sure they're comfortable."

Lining it up with my teeth takes a second, but they pop on and cling. I run my tongue over it, noticing how much blunter the canines are than before. It's thin and light, but I can feel it in my mouth. To make sure I can, I close my jaw. I've heard the horror stories of alphas fitted with poorly shaped caps, their mouth guard so thick they can't close their mouths completely. I bite the inside of my lip to test out how much blunter they are. He raises one eyebrow in a silent question.

"You do good work," I tell him, impressed.

He grunts and gathers up his implements, putting them away and tossing the disposables into the trash. "If you take them off while you're in this building, they'll kick you out and ban you from all government-run clinics and centers in the country." He hands the plaster cast of my teeth to me. "Don't be stupid."

"I won't."

There's a hint of a smile on his lined face as he cleans his tray with a disinfectant wipe. As he rubs it down, I see the weathered gold band on his ring finger.

My gut clenches with longing. That's what I want. A lavish mating ceremony. Two or three kids. A lake house for the summers. My mates surrounding me as we all grow old together.

"Mr. Orello?" Mary says from the doorway. "She's ready for you if you're done here."

As I follow her into the back, going through one locked door and then another, my palms sweat. *What if she's mad at me? I teased her during her heat.* Denied her an orgasm because the thought of another alpha touching her, using her, made my vision tunnel.

Mary stops in front of a plain white door and unlocks it with her badge, but steps aside. "Good luck."

I nod and grab the handle and turn it, letting the door swing open.

My omega's on a couch, her body stretched out and bare like the subject of a tasteful nude. Her beta lounges behind her, and they're both propped on a mountain of pillows and surrounded by a riot of different colored and textured blankets as he works one hand between her thighs and presses her face to his with the other. He kisses her like he's trying to suck her soul out through her mouth while his fingers make wet, sucking sounds as they ply her slick-soaked pussy.

God, she's fucking beautiful. Gorgeous. There aren't enough words to describe how she makes me hard, and my teeth ache with just one look at her. And then her pheromones hit me like a brick wall to the face, and I'm lost in her sticky lemon cookie scent.

The door shuts behind me and she breaks the kiss to whine, her hips moving in time with him as he fingerfucks her.

"Alpha," the beta says as a greeting.

I meet his gaze, noting how he looks me up and down. Sizing me up. Assessing my fitness. My shoulders square on instinct, to prove myself as a healthy, virile mate despite the grays starting at my temples. He wants to know if I'm someone who can protect her. Protect them both.

"Just Marcus is fine... unless we're fucking."

"I'm Sam."

Emily whines, her head lolling and her gaze unfocused as she stares at me from across the room and wiggles on the couch. Sam's grip on her jaw and his arm banded taut across her front keep her from falling off it. The urge to purr, to soothe her distressed cries, consumes me, and this time I don't hold back.

I purr.

"And this is Emily. She's desperate for a knot," Sam says as he nuzzles his cheek against hers. If he weren't a beta, he'd be scent marking her right now with the glands in his cheeks. "She hasn't had a real one since last night. I figured you wouldn't want any other alphas' scents on her."

She's in pain with her heat this advanced. I don't know whether to be grateful or mad. Grateful that he thought to protect her and keep her safe for me. Mad that it left her aching and unsatisfied. Maybe I'm a bit of both.

He lets go of her chin and threads his fingers into her hair, squeezing and pulling until her back arches, pushing her gorgeous breasts up in the air. "Baby, it's time to get on your hands and knees. Are you ready?"

She makes a needy sound, and tries to nod, but his hold on her hair keeps her from moving too much.

I bristle at the sight of his rough treatment of her as he takes his hand out of her cunt and he moves them both off the couch. She sinks to the floor at his feet as he leans over her.

"Careful," I tell him, threading a hint of an alpha bark into the word as he leads her to a pad on the floor in the center of the room by her hair.

The beta looks at me in surprise, his eyes widening, and then he smiles. It's such a charming, lopsided smile that's really more of a smirk. *Oh, he's trouble.* And I'm in danger.

"She likes it. I can promise you that," Sam says. And then he winks at me.

I'm a fucking goner. I love taming brats.

When she's settled on the pad, he murmurs soft words of praise to her as he positions her in a traditional omega pose. It's an antiquated gesture, but it tugs at something inside of me I didn't know cared about such things.

Sam presses her face flat on the mat, her forehead resting between the diamond her thumbs and forefingers make as she lays her head down on her hands. He strokes her back until her ass rises higher in the air, then uses his foot to kick her knees wider.

A bead of slick drips down her slit, dropping onto the mat and soaking into the fabric.

She seems to enjoy it. Her cunt glistens with unchecked desire as she kneels there and waits for a knot. My knot. Because she is mine. And I am hers.

Tom warned me to restrain myself so I don't scare her, but I don't think he expected *this*. I certainly wasn't. My self-control hangs on by a thread as I soak in the sight of her and burn it into my memory.

"Can I touch her?" I ask.

She makes a needy sound and tilts her hips, pushing her cunt out. "I hope you'll give her your knot," Sam says. Emily whines in agreement.

And I don't need to be told twice. I shrug out of my jacket and fold it, then set it in a chair by the wall. Loosening my tie, I pull it from my neck and add it and my shirt to the pile, followed by my pants and socks and shoes. Each article falls away, shedding a little of my civilized veneer with it. When I turn back around, Sam is watching me shamelessly.

But I suppose he sees a lot of nude alphas in his line of work. What's one more body? Not that I've ever been shy.

I cross to her matt and kneel behind her. She's trembling. Oh, God, I've scared her already. Can't have that. I lean in close and sniff her, dragging her lemon-sweet pheromones into my sinuses and savoring them. With her lips spread by my hand, her scent thickens in the room. I lick her, drawing my tongue up her slit and gathering up every precious drop of slick from clit to ass.

She moves, pressing into my face as I explore the shape of her inside and out, caressing her clit and plunging into her hole until she's rocking in time with each thrust. Her orgasm explodes on my tongue, and I suck down each greedy mouthful of her as she gets impossibly wetter.

My omega is so sweet. Delicious. Mine.

My cock pulses, heavy and dripping between my legs. The ache in my balls is unbearable, even though I just emptied them an hour before. She does this to me. She fills me with this undeniable need to rut. Bite. Claim. Breed. I can't do the last three so I'll settle for the rutting.

For now.

As the temporary bliss of her orgasm fades, she whines again, begging, only going silent when I palm my cock and rub my flared head across her pussy. I tap it against her clit and watch the way my pre-cum mixes with her wetness. She's going to smell like me when this is done, just as I'll smell like her. I'll coat myself in her sweet lemon perfume and savor it for later with Tom. I'll fuck her pheromones right into my beautiful beta's perfect ass.

The first press of my cock inside of her makes me close my eyes and groan, dropping my head back as the alpha rage inside of me settles. It's like stepping into the eye of a hurricane. Everything goes still and calm, but I know there are whipping winds and rain waiting for me when this delectable moment passes.

I pull back, working my cock into her by one slow press at a time as I force her channel to take me. To stretch and adjust until I'm as deep as I can get, my weeping slit notching up against her cervix as I hit the bottom of her. She swallows me to the root, and we stay like that for a glorious minute as I let her adjust to the sting and the stretch of me.

Her thighs and ass tremble again. I can feel the slight vibration where her rounded globes press against my pelvis. Is it too much? Too large? I've never fucked a cunt before last night.

It's best to let her adjust. To be patient. I reach down and stroke the taut clench of her stretched walls as her pussy grips me, the skin shiny with slick and so very pink. I rub my hands over her, memorizing the softness of her skin, the flare of her full hips, and the nip of her waist. My body covers her, and I'm careful to keep most of my weight off her slight frame as I drag my hands along her belly. Her breasts hang, just full enough to overflow my hands when I cup them. Her nipples are large, and they tighten and firm when I pinch them.

I rub down her sides, my fingers tripping over each rib. And then I curl a hand under and card my fingers through her curls until I find the round nub that makes her hips twitch against me and her channel squeeze with every caress. She whimpers, a beautiful and pitiful sound that makes me want to keep my big body curled around her and protect her from the world as a living shield.

"Alpha," Sam says. "You can tease her after you've knotted her." He stands over us in his heat minder uniform, his arms crossed as if he's just a professional. But the tenting of his pants betrays him.

I catch the beta's eyes as I pull my hips back and drive them forward, thrusting into her all the way. Her ass slaps against my thighs, and her cunt squeezes. It's like she's trying to break my cock in half.

"What did I tell you about calling me alpha?" *Such a brat. Brats get spankings.*

The beta blushes and drops his gaze as I fuck into my omega, holding her by the hips to keep her from sliding away from me on the floor as I rut her good and hard until her slick is running down her thighs and pooling between our knees.

"Aren't you joining us?" I ask, not liking the way he flinches a little. His crossed arms shift.

"I wasn't sure if you'd want me to. I have to stay for her safety, of course."

"Would it be a problem if you did?" I ask. Would the clinic mind? Although if he loses his job because I ask him to join us, I'll just find him another one. A better one. If he even wants to keep working at all.

He shakes his head, then drops his hands to the string at his waistband. He hesitates, then unties it and shoves his pants and underwear down until his cock bobs free.

It's a beautiful cock. Not too long, but thick. He lacks the breadth and extra veins of an alpha. But all that means is he's easier to blow.

"Do you fuck men, beta?"

He pauses as he's taking his shirt off, then tugs it up and tosses it aside. "I'm versatile." He kicks out of his shoes and gets naked. I don't like the way he disrespects his clothes by leaving them in a pile on the floor. I'll need to teach him to respect his things if he wants presents.

"Who do you want to suck you, beta? Me or her?"

He stops petting her hair to stare at me. "You'd…"

I get it, even if I also don't. Some alphas won't fuck betas. Some men won't fuck men. I'm a greedy son of a bitch. I want it all. "Come here, beta. I'm going to suck your pretty cock."

Sam takes a tentative step toward me. I reach up and grab him by the hip and tug him forward until his knee knocks against me. His cock wavers in the air, a pearl of pre-cum gathered at his slit. I palm his ass and guide it to my face, licking that drop of fluid up so his subtle oranges and cream taste mingles with her sweet lemon. God, they smell so good. I'm going to eat them both up.

I wrap my lips around his head and trace the rim of his corona with my tongue. He groans, his hips making a stuttered push as his hands search for somewhere to land as he rocks into my mouth.

So self-conscious. So timid, as if I'll change my mind or hurt him. But I'm even less scared of hurting him with this mouth guard in place. The thin, strong plastic smooths my canines and makes it easier to suck him. Easier to be sloppy and messy. Why did I never buy a set before?

His hands tangle in my hair, squeezing and tugging as his hips thrust in time with my bobbing. Oranges and cream runs down my throat as he leaks a steady stream of fluid that I swallow. I'm starving for him. I'm gonna eat them both up. Fill my belly with them.

Emily's cunt squeezes around me with each thrust, the wet sounds of our fucking competing with the filthy sucking noises I make as I take Sam to the back of my throat and take him to the root.

Versatile.

What an interesting choice in words. My hand strokes his ass, enjoying the fine dusting of blond hair that covers his arms and legs and butt. And then I slip my middle finger between his cheeks and stroke his asshole.

Sam groans, then swears, his fingers tightening in my hair until it hurts. Pulling back, I gulp in some air, then swallow him again. I tease his ass, stroking his opening with the tip of my finger.

And then I purr.

He pumps his cock into me, cries out, and his fingers tighten so much I think he actually rips out a few strands. His cock jerks, and oranges and cream runs down my throat, filling my belly until he softens.

I gasp in a breath when I pull off him, leaving just his tip between my lips as I lick him clean and savor every creamy bit of cum.

He pets me too, his fingers smoothing down my hair as if to say he's sorry for mussing me.

I laugh, and Emily groans. My chuckle makes my abdomen tense, and my cock bobs inside of her. Now that I'm no longer multitasking, I slam into her sweet cunt at a brutal, pounding pace that sets my balls tingling and my breath hitching. She squeaks, her fingers scraping against the waterproof mat she's kneeling on.

I don't like it. She should be in a soft nest, wrapped in the finest blankets one can buy, and surrounded by our scents in our home. Not getting fucked on the cold, hard floor of a free clinic on a scratchy mat.

"Tend to your omega," I order.

Sam walks to the couch and drags a blanket off, throwing it

on the tile before her. "Trust me, you don't wanna lie on this floor. You have no idea what it's been covered with."

I can imagine. How many people have used this room before us? Its sterile walls and easy-to-clean, utilitarian furniture disgust me. My pack deserves pampering. Not *this*. Not a free-use clinic where strange alphas use her body to rut.

Emily whines as Sam sprawls out of the floor in front of her. He strokes her hair and rubs her shoulders, then leans in and whispers things I can't hear into her ear.

Her cunt flutters, squeezing me so hard I see stars. I grab both ass cheeks and spread them wide, watching the way her pussy swallows me and her asshole tightens with every clench.

Fucking a woman is different. This tight channel squeezes me, sucking me in and pushing me away in equal measures as I try to cram all of me into her. Each jiggling slap of her ass against my thighs fills me with satisfaction. But I wish I could go deeper. The ass has a delightful way of taking even the biggest alpha cock with enough lube and foreplay and patience. But her pussy has an end to it. Her cervix stops me from staying too deep for too long. It pushes back with every insistent thrust as I try to carve a home for myself in her cunt.

It's mine.

She's mine.

They both are.

And I'm going to prove it to them.

Her moans turn to pained whimpers as I batter my cockhead at her cervix, pushing deeper as my balls tighten and the base of my cock aches. I purr, and she relaxes. She lets me rearrange her to fit me, more slick slipping around where she's stretched around me as I force her body to take me. All of me.

Sam keeps up his whispering, his gaze locking with mine as he watches me rut her until my knot swells. I surge deep, holding still, as the first wave of pleasure lashes out of me with a spray of cum. My knot swells and swells, bigger and bigger, until her cunt's stretched painfully tight. I grunt as I come for what feels like an eternity, emptying my balls into her. My seed paints her cervix, searching for fertile ground to take root in. I stroke her back and rub her as she takes it.

Good girl.

Good omega.

I can't wait to breed her.

Can't wait to see her little belly get round with our babies.

She sighs, the tension melting from her shoulders as she settles in for the wait until my knot deflates so we can untie. Sam pets her, telling her she's a good girl, and I watch them have this tender moment together with a smile on my face.

He's a good beta.

He'll make an excellent addition to our small but growing pack.

And then he looks up at me and grins, his cheek dimpling on one side as he reaches under her and strokes his fingers where we're joined.

She twitches and groans, her movements pulling on my knot in a way that tugs all the way up to my navel. And then her cunt flutters. It squeezes in a rhythmic pulsing that makes me lose all ability to think. My purr stutters, then grows deeper as Sam plays with her clit until she cries out, her walls squeezing me until I can't breathe. The tips of his fingers brush over my knot and hanging sack. Her orgasm pulls one last burst of seed up from my balls as I empty myself into her. I give her everything I have, and then I'm spitting dust, but the urge to cum is still there. It's an orgasm without the cum, and I haven't felt this way in decades, since I was a clumsy boy. Each pulse feels a little like dying.

What a fucking way to go.

When she's done squeezing my knot like it owes her money, I

collapse with her, my purr stuttering from fatigue as the urge to rut fades, leaving me mellow and pleased.

"Good girl," I tell her as I hold her to me and ease us both down onto our sides.

When the movement tugs at our tie and she whimpers, I purr until she's limp in my arms again.

Sam smirks as he gets up and fetches the rest of the soft blankets from her impromptu nest on the couch. He kneels down and covers us, tucking her in and placing a kiss on her cheek.

I reach out and grab him by his hair. Turnabout is fair play. His eyes widen with alarm as I pull him forward. He doesn't know where to put his hands as I tug him off balance, so he's forced to put those hands on me. They slap against my sweaty, hairy chest.

With my grip in his hair, I bring his face down to mine and press a kiss to his lips. They're stiff and awkward, and then he melts into it. He opens for me. I let go of his hair and cup the back of his head gently instead.

Sam kisses me back and proves he's a quick study. I purr for him too, and he smiles against my mouth as he breaks the kiss and ducks his head.

"Get in the nest, beta."

I don't need to tell him twice. He slips under the blankets and wiggles himself into place as Emily's little spoon. She nuzzles her face into his neck, and I grab the blanket that's slipped off and cover all three of us. I stay propped up on my arm so I can watch them. She wraps her arms and one leg around him, and he strokes his fingers along the curve of her arm. They thread their fingers together and hold hands, and something clenches in my chest at the sight.

This is right.

This is what it should be like.

I can't wait for Tom to join us, to tag team our omega with

Sam. My next thought pulls the floor out from under me. *God, they're all gonna drive me into an early grave.*

Sam is an imp. But Tom is a full-blown fucking brat. They're gonna run me ragged. I can already tell.

My purr stutters with a laugh that makes Sam crack an eye open and crane his head back to look at me. I bury my face in Emily's hair and breathe in her sweet lemon scent.

Everything is exactly how it should be.

Chapter Eight

EMILY

T HE SOFTENING KNOT PULLS FREE WITH A POP AND A GUSH AS
our combined fluids leak out of me, the uncomfortable pressure
in my belly easing with each trickle. *God, there's so much of it.* It
soaks our blankets and leaves me a sticky mess. Now that I've
been knotted, my thoughts are less confused and jumbled. Like a
film reel spliced out of order, missing pieces of time. Everything's been slotted back into place.

I'm so warm I'm sweating. If Sam is a furnace, then the alpha
is a volcanic eruption. His body heat radiates into me, making me
feel limp and boneless. It's hard to find the motivation to get up
and fix the nest before we get too comfortable, but the nest is all
wrong and it grates on me.

Sam is terrible at weaving the blankets together so that they
make a wall to cradle us. I move, and two looped blankets fall
apart, exposing me to the chill of the room.

"Sam," I whisper, not wanting to ruin this surprisingly sweet
moment.

"Yeah?"

"You're fired from making nests."

He makes a harrumph sound and pulls away from me, but I

move to catch him back. I was just teasing. I didn't mean to hurt his feelings. Honestly, I expected him to laugh and tease me back.

Sam rolls over so he's facing me, his lopsided smile making some of my worry unclench. The alpha rumbles, a soothing purr at my back, his large hands wandering all over me underneath the blankets. It's weird for him to be touching me so much. None of the other alphas did. Maybe that's the difference between rutting and courtship. I try to recall if the alphas I matched with ever did much more than rut me into my mattress and then eat all the food in my fridge. I come up blank. His face presses into my hair, and he inhales, the sound noisy as he sniffs me.

"I was never any good at nest building, no matter how many times Donna tried to show me. It'll be better when you're back in your own nest."

I think about my nest at home and let out a wistful sigh. The mattresses here are strange. The pillows are either too firm or too soft. I didn't think I'd miss my nest so much.

"I'll buy you all the best nesting stuff you need, sweetheart," the alpha rumbles from behind me. He lays a possessive hand on my belly and presses me against him, heedless of my mess smearing all over him. "We've got a guest bedroom that'll make the perfect nest for you."

My half-lidded eyes pop open as I give Sam a pointed look that screams *help*. Does this alpha expect me to move in with him? Is that a normal expectation of courtship when you meet at a clinic? I thought we would date first. This is all moving a little too fast for my liking.

He must smell my distress, because his purr kicks up again, rumbling through me and making everything soft around the edges until I forget why I'm worried. The alpha lifts his hand to my chin and tips my head back as he leans over me.

"Don't stress, sweetheart. Everything's going to be perfect.

We're gonna take good care of you. I've waited a long time to find you. And you were worth every second. Can I kiss you?"

It seems strange for him to ask when we've just done something far more intimate. I stare at his mouth and nibble on my lower lip. He's got a strong jawline covered in the rough stubble of a five o'clock shadow. His stormy blue eyes are just as piercing as I remembered, his brow heavy and his eyebrows thick. Dark hair that's nearly black has threads of silver at the temples. His styled hair's been messed up by Sam's hands, and it gives him a rugged look. Like he'd be more comfortable in a plaid button-up and holding an ax than in his tailored suit and fancy watch.

He's waiting for my answer. And I think... I think if I say no, he wouldn't push it. I nod, and his eyelids drift shut as he dips his face to mine and presses his lips to my mouth. His kiss is slow and sweet, a gentle brushing of mouths that makes me sigh and lean into him. And it's over too soon for my liking as it leaves my belly swooping.

"Oh, sure," Sam pouts. "She gets asked nicely while I get mauled. I see how it is."

The alpha lets out a sound that's half-laugh and half-purr. He lets go of my chin to lean over me and swats Sam on the ass until my mouthy beta yelps.

"Do you need more attention, brat?" the alpha asks. Somehow it's half-threat and half-promise. His grin borders on feral.

I can't help it—I laugh. Laughter bubbles up out of me, leaving me feeling lighter, but my amusement stutters as the bouncing of my belly works more cum and slick out of me with a wet squelch that makes my face turn red.

"Sadly, I don't think I'm the one who needs more attention right now," Sam says as he tosses the shoddy nest's blankets over his head and wiggles down and over me, elbowing me in the process as I grunt.

"What are you doing?" I ask.

Sam tugs me flat on my back and shoves my legs up to my chest. "You made me miss lunch, baby. So I'm gonna eat." His tongue glides through my messy folds, then pierces my sensitive hole as he puts his mouth on me and sucks.

"F-fuck, Sam. Oh my God." I twist my fingers in one of the nest's blankets and squeeze my eyes shut. It's more of an assault than a tongue fucking. Sam eats me out like he's been starved for a month, not half a day.

The alpha leans over me, blocking out the overhead lights as he claims my mouth in a kiss that leaves me breathless, and palms a breast, squeezing it gently.

Together, they eat me from both ends until I'm trembling and limp and the warmth and coziness of this nest, as haphazardly as it was constructed, makes my eyelids heavy.

Sam wakes me up some time later by handing me a bottle of protein water and helping me open it. He watches me drink it down as the alpha eyes us both from his seat on the couch. He's dressed again, his hair raked back into some semblance of control and his shirt tight across his shoulders.

"Can you stand, baby?"

I nod, and he helps me up, grabbing the edge of the slipping blanket to keep it from falling off me. He burritos me in it as he tells me to wait, then scoops up the rest of them and drapes them all over one arm.

"Where are we going?" I ask, rubbing my bleary eyes.

"The treatment session's over, baby. It's time for your bath."

"Oh." I glance at the dressed alpha and frown. "Already?"

"You were tired, so we mostly napped and cuddled."

I feel bad that I missed so much of it, but heats are a lot of work and my eyes still feel bruised with the need to sleep. There's a bone-deep exhaustion in me that says I still need more rest before this evening. Tonight will be the peak, my bouts of delirium longer and stronger. Still, he came all this way again to rut me through a heat spell and then I slept for most of it after.

"I'm sorry, alpha."

He stands and my neck cranes to follow it, my knees knocking together a little. *God, he's tall.* And broad-shouldered. Just… big. He walks toward me and cups my face in his large hands, his thumb brushing over my lower lip in a gentle caress.

"I'm not. And please, call me Marcus."

Unless we're fucking.

I blush as I finish the sentence for him in my head. I don't remember all of our session, just bits and pieces of moments and feelings cobbled together like a collage, but that phrase is stuck in the back of my mind. Slick trickles down my inner thigh, and it's a wonder that I have any moisture left to make it at this rate. Must be all the bottles of water that Sam forces down my throat every time I'm conscious and present.

"Marcus," I whisper, giving him a tentative smile.

"Emily." The way he says my name in that gravelly, deep voice makes my belly flutter. He leans all the way down and kisses me, our mouths melding together until he steals my breath away and makes my belly do somersaults.

I rise on my tiptoes to get more of it, my tongue pressing between his lips when it's clear he won't be the one to do it. His tongue invades my mouth, stroking me back. When I brush up against his sharp canine, I find it oddly textured. Smoother and blunter. Bite guards. My pelvis tightens, and the dribble of slick runs all the way down to the back of my knee, where it hits the crease and smears. He's thoughtful and kind and sexy as sin and more amazing than I'd ever hoped for.

"I'm sorry, but I really have to take her. Protocol," Sam says, interrupting us.

Marcus breaks the kiss, giving me one last brief peck on the lips as Sam bundles me into his side and wraps his arm around me and all but frogmarches me toward the door.

"I understand," Marcus says. "I'll see you later?"

I look over my shoulder at him and nod as Sam badges us out of the room and walks me down the hallway. I lean into his side and press my cheek to his shoulder.

"That went well," he says.

My nose scrunches up as I remember a flash of something that I'm not quite certain really happened. "Did he blow you?"

Sam is so quiet that I glance up at him and see that his face is cherry red. I gasp, then grin. "He did! How was it?"

"It was… Fuck, there are vacuum cleaners that don't suck as well as he does."

I giggle at the mental picture he paints and ignore the slick that's making a mess of my thighs. The blanket smells like the three of us as I hike it higher up my shoulders and press it to my nose. "I'm glad you had a good time."

How awkward would it have been for Sam to watch Marcus fuck me for four hours straight and have to sit on his hands on the couch and watch? That Marcus let Sam not just join but also take part makes me happy for reasons I can't describe. Some alphas are territorial and jealous, preferring monogamous pairings instead of packs. Others are possessive, but in a scary way.

We're going to take care of you.

The thought makes me tingly, but a part of me still worries it's too good to be true. That he'll change his mind. Maybe it's just because I've been on my own and struggling for so long, making ends meet while getting nowhere fast while my peers seem to pass me by.

What's the worst that can happen, though? Maybe Sam and Marcus will both lose interest in me once my heat's over. That happens a lot once an omega stops pumping out fuck-me pheromones. Then I'll… go back to my life. Nothing will be different. My plain apartment with a mold problem in the tub no matter how much I scrub and bleach the caulk will still be there. The window of plants I have because I can't afford to adopt a pet even though I'm so lonely it hurts sometimes will still be mine. My job that can replace me tomorrow will still expect me to show up on Tuesday. An app full of emotionally disconnected alphas who only want to rut and never want to stay will still happily match with me.

It's fine.

I'm fine.

My eyes sting as tears fill them and I sniff, trying to pull them back, but they bubble over and fall before I can help it.

"Baby, what's wrong?" Sam asks, stopping us in the hall.

My lip wobbles as I use the edge of the blanket to wipe my cheeks dry, but the tears won't stop. "I don't know. I'm just… sad."

He gathers me up for a hug and rubs his hands up and down my arms. "You needed more cuddles."

"But I got almost four hours of cuddles!" It's ridiculous. *I'm* being ridiculous. I hide my face in his chest and make wet spots with my tears on his scrub top.

He wraps his arms around me and squeezes me so tight it's hard to breathe, but… it helps. The tears slow down and I sniff to clear the congestion in my face. "And you need more. Everyone reacts differently when they find their pack. There's no right or wrong about it. Whatever you need is what you need."

"Do you really think he's my pack?" I whisper, scared to voice it. It seems too good to be true. Like if I get too happy about it, something will happen and take it away.

"Do you want to go back to the rut room? We have time. The next session starts in a half-hour. We can find you plenty of other alphas to rut."

"What?" I push away from him, or I try to, but he hauls me tighter against him and pets my hair.

"See? You don't want the other alphas, right? That feeling only gets stronger once you receive his mating bite, but some omegas feel it a bit before. But if you want more reassurance, I can ask for his paperwork and we can look it over together after your bath."

"Paperwork?"

Instead of answering me, Sam brings me back to my room and puts me in the bath. Since I'm lucid, he lets me bathe myself while he goes and eats something, changes his clothes, and grabs Marcus's file.

I towel off and fix the lackluster nest while Sam is gone and he can't mess it up while I'm still stabilizing the walls. The blankets smell like the three of us, and shoving my nose in the stiff, dried spots keeps me calm. I feel more settled once I'm in the center.

Sam returns and kicks off his shoes and climbs in, careful not to bring the nest down when I give him the stink eye after he's a little too rough. We end up lying down with him on his back and me spooning him from the side, our legs tangled together. One arm curls around me as he holds the manilla folder up in the air and flips through it, making humming sounds.

"Ah, here. Good. Looks like he paid for the optional analysis. I figured he would," Sam says.

"What analysis?" I take the paper from him and read it, trying to make sense of the terminology. It seems like a health workup but there are a lot of abbreviations I don't understand.

"It's his genetic profile. It says what medical conditions he'll be predisposed to. Plus anything he might give to your kids."

I drop the paper and have to pick it back up. *Kids*.

"Here's his sperm analysis. Looks like the old man's still got fast swimmers. I'm not surprised. He pumped you with bucketfuls."

My mind is still stuck on the word *kids* and *sperm* as Sam keeps flipping through papers, humming as he reads.

"I'm on birth control." Right? *Bucketfuls of sperm.*

"Yeah, baby. I gave you your pill this morning." He keeps flipping and skimming.

The relief hits me like a brick wall, but the hint of sadness underneath it feels alien. *Marcus is a stranger. I don't really know this man.* I shouldn't want this stranger to knock me up, but... a teeny, tiny foreign part of me does. *What the fuck?*

I drop the paper and struggle upright, so I'm kneeling. Sam sets the file on his belly and stares at me, his brow creased. "What's wrong? Do you not want kids?"

It's never really been something I let myself think about too intensely. I've never had a serious boyfriend who stuck around for more than a year. Most betas like the reality of dealing with a heat a lot less than the fantasy. Even with slip-on silicone knots and knotting toys, it's hard for one beta to handle how much sex an omega needs during heat. Alphas can keep up because of the rut. And most alphas are holding out for the omega their instincts say is *the one.*

I think about having a baby with Marcus's eyes, and something in my chest pinches, leaving me breathless. "I... I think I might." My head reels from how much the Earth feels like it's spinning off its axis.

"Relax, baby." Sam strokes my thigh and picks the file up. "There's plenty of time to talk about all the nitty-gritty details. You didn't sign the breeding waiver, so it's not going to happen this heat no matter what."

Being told it's not an option actually keeps me from freaking out. "Okay. Right. So what does the rest of the file say?"

"Family history of high blood pressure, diabetes, and stroke.

A predisposition to skin cancers, so make sure you put sunscreen on the small mountain of babies you guys have together."

I grab his side through his scrub top and pinch him.

"Ouch! I said *small* mountain. Put your claws away, kitten. Here are his financial documents."

I take it from him and count the number of pages stapled together. "Why is it so thick?"

"You'll see."

I have to read the number on the page four times and count the zeroes twice before it registers. There's a pie chart breakdown of his various assets, as well as a list of properties he owns. That's what takes up the bulk of the papers because there are photos.

"Is that a *fucking* castle?"

Sam glances at the one that's put my jaw on the floor. "Technically, I think it's called an *estate*."

TOM STEPS ONTO THE ESCALATOR WHILE CARRYING ONE OF HIS bags, sees me, and smiles. I hold my sunflower bouquet up for him to see. He grins the entire way down.

"Hello, darling," Tom says, taking the flowers and meeting me in a kiss.

"How many bags did you bring?" I ask, tugging him toward baggage claim. People crowd around it even though it's empty, their faces a mix of boredom, irritation, and apathy.

"Enough. You know me," he says. He takes his carry-on off his shoulder and hands it to me.

I throw it onto my shoulder and steal another kiss. "I'll go rent a luggage cart."

I feed ones into the automated machine, then take a cart and bring it back just as the first bag tumbles through the black vinyl divider. It spits them out one by one, and I grab each one of Tom's bags until the cart is stuffed with them.

"How many times a day are you going to change outfits?" I ask as I balance and stack them all like a game of Tetris.

"I was in London for two weeks, and I like to have options. That's all of them, I think."

He follows me out to the car, and I pop the trunk and start loading them, dropping each heavy bag inside and shimmying them until they fit. The small trunk closes. Barely. Tom waits for me to open his door and then he gets in. I tap in the hotel's address. The steering wheel turns as the car starts the drive.

"Any news from the clinic?" he asks.

"Yes. They called this morning, and I went to go see her this afternoon. She's perfect. I can't wait for you to meet her. To meet them, I mean."

"Them?" He turns a bit in his seat to face me.

"I wasn't sure at the time, so I didn't mention it, but there's a beta too. He's actually her heat attendant. They've already started bonding, but they both seem oblivious to it."

"It's more subtle for us betas. My, you've been busy."

I glance away from the road to study him. "Are you upset? I'm sorry. I should have mentioned the beta before anything happened."

Tom is silent for a moment as he stares out the window and thinks. It's a heavy, important silence that makes me nervous the longer it stretches on. "I didn't know you were still even looking."

My heart drops into my stomach. I grab Tom's hand and bring his knuckles to my mouth, kissing them. "You know I love you, and I always will. This doesn't change that. Not ever. And I want you to know I've never done anything with anyone before at any of the free clinics or rut bars or omega centers I've checked while I'm away on my business trips."

"I trust you," Tom says. "I suppose I am a bit jealous that you got to find our packmates and I wasn't there for it."

I smile, the heaviness inside of me lifting. "Me too. God, I wish you'd been there with me today. You're coming to the clinic with me tomorrow, right? It's too late to do your paperwork tonight, but we can go first thing in the morning. The paperwork is… a lot. It's more of an interrogation."

"Of course. It'll be one last night with just us," Tom says, his smile fond as he leans closer.

"What do you want to do? We can order in and watch a movie. The one you wanted to see last week is still on pay-per-view. My clients took me to an Italian restaurant that was—"

The sound of my zipper opening distracts me from watching the traffic flow around us. Tom fishes my soft cock out of my pants and gives it a tug. It thickens and plumps in his hand with every practiced flick of his wrist. He knows exactly how to touch me, how to drive me nuts and make me come undone.

My hips thrust into his hand as he works me, his thumb making a rough glide over my head as he spreads pre-cum to ease his tugging.

Cars drive by us. Someone might see. But all that does is make it hotter.

"Did you miss me, darling?" Tom asks.

"So fucking much," I growl, glad the car drives itself, otherwise we would have crashed by now.

"What did you miss about me?"

"Everything." I thrust into his hand as my cockhead weeps. "I missed your snark." My body rides out the post-rut state, my balls pumping out pre-cum that dribbles down his hands and soaks into my slacks. "I miss… I missed doing the crossword puzzle with you over breakfast." He jacks me faster. "I missed you hogging the blankets all night."

Tom snorts. "I do not."

My grin turns into a grimace as pressure blooms in my pelvis. "You can have all my blankets, babe. Always."

When my pulse jumps in the veins of my throat, I know I'm close. Panting, I lean into the dull ache in my pelvis. In my balls. Everywhere. I drag in a deep breath.

And then Tom stops. He lets my painfully hard dick flop and turns in his seat to look out the window. "Is that the hotel? It looks nice."

You've gotta be fucking kidding me.

I stuff my erection into my pants, shoving it all the way down my right pantleg as the car turns into the hotel's parking lot valet loop. "You did that on purpose."

Tom raises his eyebrows and feigns surprise. "Are you saying that I watched the GPS navigation and timed your handjob so perfectly that there was no way you could finish before we arrived?" He says it so deadpan that for a moment, I doubt myself and feel like an ass. And then the left side of his mouth twitches. It's his tell.

Oh, you're in trouble, brat.

"You're right." I zip my pants up and ignore the wet stain growing on the wool fabric. The dry cleaners are going to have fun with that one. "Because that would be an insane thing for the mate I haven't seen or fucked in over a week to do. His ass would really get torn up for that one." I take over the wheel and put the car into park and undo my seatbelt.

Tom grabs his bouquet and gets out of the car before me, but leans back in and says, "By the way, I prepped at the airport. Their first-class lounge has nice private bathrooms. You're welcome." He shuts the car door, nods at the valet, and wanders into the hotel.

I get out and hand my key fob to the uniformed attendant. "Have someone bring our bags up. Room three hundred and seven. On second thought... have the lobby hold them. I'll fetch them later."

I have a brat to punish.

After slipping the valet a folded tip, I go hunting for my naughty mate. I find him at the concierge desk, leaning casually on one arm as he speaks with her. She's entranced, her cheeks pink as all young women seem to get around him when they hear his British accent. As I stalk up to him, he gives me a cheeky grin.

"Ah, there he is. My mate." He leans into my embrace and slaps me on the chest. "I would appreciate it very much if you could send a bottle of champagne to our room. We're celebrating. This is a very special night for us."

My annoyance settles, and warmth pools in my belly. I tug him harder against me and nod to her.

"He's just gotten out of prison," Tom lies.

The concierge's smile turns plastic, her eyes rimmed with white. I growl softly under my breath in a warning he seems keen to ignore.

"Mafia," Tom stage-whispers.

"Excuse us." I gather up his long brown hair and wrap my fist in it and pull him back from the desk.

"Oh, someone's eager to get the celebrations going. No conjugal visits in the big house, I'm afraid. That's more of a Hollywood thing, apparently. You must be positively ready to burst, darling."

"Ignore him. He didn't take his medicine today." *His anti-brat pills.* Five minutes off the airplane and he's already giving me shit.

I drag my brat by his hair to the bank of elevators, ignoring the way people stop and stare. It's like they're afraid I've lost it and I'm about to go on a rampage. It's rare, but it happens.

Tom waves to them and chatters idly, as if being dragged into an elevator by your hair is a normal, everyday occurrence for most. The people who get out do a double-take, and nobody gets on with us. The door closes, and I select our floor. If I tug on his hair a little more than is necessary as I twist to reach it, neither of us mentions it.

"Oh!" he exclaims as the elevator rises. "We forgot to tell her the room number for the champagne."

"You won't be able to drink it anyway, with my gag in your mouth."

"You brought it?" he asks, his voice excited.

I lean in and press my lips to his ear and let my voice drop even deeper. "You think I didn't stop by a shop before I got you those flowers?"

His lips curl in a Cheshire grin. "You always buy me the nicest presents, darling. You must truly love me."

I suppress my smile. "Sucking up won't save you from that spanking you just earned. You won't be able to sit after I get done with you."

"Don't threaten me with a good time."

The elevator slows to a stop and dings its arrival. "I don't make threats." The nip to his earlobe makes him suck in a quick breath. "I make promises." I step out of the elevator and pull him with me and down the hallway to the door.

Unlocked. Lights on. Deadbolt.

I drag him over toward the king-size bed and force him down to the carpet. He kneels, spreading his legs exactly like he's been trained. The way he stares up at me, his face at the absolutely fucking perfect height and his eyes glittering with humor and lust makes my mouth water.

"Continue what you started," I command.

"I'm afraid you'll need to be more specific, darling."

"Hmm." My nostrils flare, and my eyes narrow. He's just earned twice as many swats.

"Oh! Yes. Right. *That*."

He goes for my crotch and undoes my hook and zipper, then reaches in and pulls me free from my pants. My erection is thick and veiny, swollen from his teasing and the rubbing of my suit pants. He grasps me and brings me to his lips, licking and swirling with his tongue, and then he swallows me down.

My lovely mate is at his best when his sharp tongue is kept busy, his pink lips stretched wide as I stuff his face with cock and fuck his throat. When I hit the back of him, my eyes slide shut, my grip on his hair relaxing as he bobs.

Close.

Too close.

The dull ache in my pelvis returns as everything tightens. "Stop. Get up and take off your clothes."

He pulls his mouth away, placing one last kiss on my crown, then stands and holds my gaze as he strips. Tom unbuttons his shirt, his long, thin fingers moving nimbly down the line until he can pull it open and free it from his pants. He shrugs, slipping it off his shoulders, and lets it drop to the floor in a crumble.

My jaw ticks, and I add ten more strokes for every item of his he disrespects. By the end of his undressing, he's earned fifty more. His cock is hard and heavy between his thighs as he stands there and waits for another order to defy.

So I deny him instead.

I move to the closet and make a show of taking my jacket off and hanging it up on its hanger. I take my belt off too and coil it. Best to take it off now, so I'm not tempted to use it on him later. We have a busy day tomorrow, and there will be a lot of sitting around and waiting. Once I'm bare, I dig through my suitcase and retrieve our bottle of lube and the gag.

His self-satisfied expression falls when he sees it. "Not a hollow one."

I arch a brow. "It wouldn't be much of a punishment if you liked it." His chin stubble scratches me as I pinch his jaw. "Open." He does, and I put the gag in place and buckle it behind his head, careful not to catch his long hair in the fastening.

So handsome.

I press a kiss to the gag's strap and enjoy the way his green eyes narrow. A brat to the bitter fucking end. I grab him by the back of his neck, my fingers spanning side to side, and sit on the bed, pulling him over my lap. An arm across his shoulders keeps him pinned in place and prevents him from wiggling.

A steel plug gleams from between his ass cheeks. I spread him apart and inspect it, tapping it and pressing it in to make sure it's properly seated. His ass arches into the air as I play with it until I'm satisfied.

His bottom is perfect, already healed nicely from our fun before his trip.

It's time to change that.

I rub him, warming up his skin, and when he starts to wiggle and press his ass against my hand, I bring it down sharply on one cheek in a sharp, stinging blow. The skin pinkens nicely. *Both sides should match.* I bring my hand down on the other, hitting him hard. A funishment still needs to punish unacceptable behavior—otherwise a brat would never stop bratting.

What he really needs, what Tom craves, is reassurance. That I care enough to correct him when he's bad. That I'm here and plan to stay. That I love him no matter how much of a little shit he's being.

Every loud crack of my palm against his reddening ass tells him all these things and more.

I love you.

You're mine.

We're doing this together.

Forever.

Always.

He sobs with the first breakthrough of his emotions tonight as the punishment sinks into his skin and he gives up. Surrenders to it. He goes limp on my lap, and I play with his plug to reward him. *Good boy,* this gesture says. His hips thrust, his trapped dick rubbing against my thigh, so I give him what he wants. What he needs.

"You were naughty, teasing me in the car like that. Getting me excited and leaving me hanging so I had to walk into the lobby with my cock hard and dripping."

I spank him again and again, my hand sparking heat across his ass and the backs of his thighs. He sucks in a pained breath when I catch him in the sweet spot, that little strip of skin where ass meets thigh. Such a small, sensitive area. Tender. I swat it again, one for each side. An even number.

"You've probably ruined my suit. It's wool. It's going to be a nightmare for the dry cleaner to get the stains out."

My hand lands thudding blows one after the other until his red buttocks pour off heat. We take a breather, so his lesson can sink in and he can catch his breath while I play with his skin. I draw shapes on his redness with a fingertip until he shivers. He bucks against me. This is its own sort of sweet torture.

At seventy-three swats he sobs in earnest. He sniffles, his eyes and nose running as drool drips through the open hole of his gag. The humiliation of it is the point.

"And worse than both of those things, you brought bystanders into our game."

I give him one last quick break, then finish. My hand burns and stings, and it's as red as his ass by the time I get to a hundred. The gag comes off to signal the end of the punishment and the beginning of play.

"I'm sorry," Tom gasps once his mouth is freed.

"No, you're not. But you will be when I'm done with you. I'm going to drive the lesson into you the only way you learn," I say.

I grasp the flared base of his plug and pull it with a slow, insistent tug. It pops free, and he moans at the loss of it. His hole spasms so prettily. He won't be empty for long.

He needs help to get on the bed. I lie down with him, dragging my hands down his body and brushing the tear tracks from his face as I press a kiss to his mouth and tangle our tongues together. My knee notches his leg higher as I spread him open and settle between his thighs, my cock dripping a sticky trail on his belly.

I grab the bottle of lube I tossed on the bed earlier and pour a generous coating onto my hand and spread it on the both of us. His breath hitches at the first intrusion of my finger. I work it into him and pump, slicking him up, then add a second and a third. He stretches for me, his tight hole readied by the plug that's nearly as thick as my cock.

Tom hooks his leg around my thighs, and he moans with the press of my tip against his hole. My hips cant, working it in slowly, one inch at a time, until we're rocking together and I'm fully seated.

"Do you feel how hard you make me?" I ask.

His eyes are closed as he savors each sensation, but he nods. His long brown hair tangles on the sheets.

"Harder," Tom demands. As if he's in charge here. "Fuck me harder, alpha." His cock drips pre-cum on his belly as we fuck with a sweet, slow pace that feels like coming home.

"No."

Our lovemaking is a gentle thing. A reconnection. Brutal in its denial. He didn't want sweet and slow. He wanted devastation. But my mate gets what he needs, not what he wants. I claim his mouth in a tender kiss and rub my thumb over his leaking head while we rock together. The tension that was built and stalled earlier comes back with a vengeance, and each breath gets a little deeper, a little faster as my heart races. I reach down between us and wrap my hand around his cock, working him until his chest heaves.

"I'm going to fuck you exactly how I want to fuck and you're going to take it, beta, and thank me for it after. Now, can you take my knot?"

Tom bites his lip and his brow scrunches. "I think it's been too long."

My answer is a grunt of acknowledgment. He jerks in my grip as I tug harder, faster, and pound his ass to match it. He's close. So am I. A lifetime of this, of us, has taught me how to read my mate like a book. How to edge him right up to that line and build the tension so the release is greater. But I only tease him twice.

"How badly does your ass hurt where it's rubbing against the bed?" I ask.

"It hurts so good, alpha." His voice is breathy, and his nostrils flare with every ragged gulp of air and pheromones.

We're both eager and panting and ready for it when I tip over that edge and bring him with me. His nails scrape against my shoulders as he presses his forehead against my sweat-coated chest and comes with a jerk and a cry. His cum paints his belly as I shoot ropes of mine inside of him, filling him until he's fit to burst. My knot swells, brushing up against his entrance, and he wiggles a hand down between us to squeeze it.

I grunt as he milks the seed out of me, stuffing his ass full of it. We kiss as we settle and regain our breath, and my knot slowly shrinks. Pulling out sends cum and lube running down his still red ass. We've made a mess of the bedding. But as I hold him against me, I can't find it in me to care.

"Thank you, alpha." His eyes slide shut and his lips twitch up in a smile as his cock gives one last pulse and then goes soft.

Later, when we're showered and fed and cozy in bed, only partially paying attention to the movie we rented, I glide my hand up and down his back as he cuddles against me.

"I missed you," Tom says with a sigh.

"Me too. Are you done with London for now?" My hope is

that he doesn't need to return to finish his time at the gallery. It would be nice to take everyone home and get settled. My pack.

"I can be. Alicia can run everything better than I can." He pouts a little.

"That *is* why you hired her."

"I know. But I feel useless sometimes. She's so much better at the business side of things than I will ever be."

No doubt it's his father's nagging voice in his head causing this. The man's been dead a decade, yet he still leaves wreckage in his wake. "Then I guess it's a good thing you're the one taking the photographs."

He snorts. "You would like anything I made, even if it wasn't good."

"That's true. You could start doing stick figure crayon drawings and I'd be impressed."

He slaps my chest. "Rude."

I laugh and haul him closer so he's half-lying on me. "Watch your movie, brat."

We fall asleep before we see the end, and Tom wakes me up with room service. The beta room attendant wheels a cart inside and puts a tablecloth down on the table with a bud vase and a rose. It's the smell of coffee that finally lures me out of the comforts of our bed.

He's studying the paper as he eats. "A word that means the same thing if cap- is added to the front of it."

I take a sip of coffee and rub the sleep from my eyes. "How many letters?"

"Four."

It takes me a moment, but then I have it. "Able." Tom makes a noise in the back of his throat and writes it in. "You're using a pen?" I ask.

"There's no pencil." He waits a beat, then looks at me over the edge of his paper. "Why?"

I know a trap when I hear one. I take a longer sip of coffee and throw a triangle of toast on my plate from the basket. "No reason. Just making an observation."

His eyes narrow, and he makes a show of clicking the pen and scribbling in his answer. I'm going to pay for that careless remark later. And then he'll pay for being a brat. Rinse and repeat. I take another sip of slightly too hot coffee to hide my growing smile.

Chapter Ten

EMILY

EVERYTHING HURTS AS SAM HELPS ME CLIMB ONTO THE PADDED reclined chair. He puts my arms down at my sides and fastens leather cuffs around my wrists. When he bends my legs up and sets them into stirrups, fastening those down too, I want to sob with relief. It'll be over soon. This unending, world-consuming need to fuck is exhausting. My heat has me so scattered and horny that Sam, for all that he's tried, can't meet its bottomless demands, although he makes a solid effort. Boy, did he try.

The first nudge of the silicone dildo at my entrance makes me writhe with the urge to reach down and pull it in. Anything to feel less empty. Hollow. Needy.

But the restraints keep me from doing anything but lying here and taking it, sweating and panting and crying as he gets the fucking machine into place between my legs and adjusts the angle.

I need it, I need it, need—

The machine whirs to life and makes its first rotation, the dildo pressing into me with a brief moment of white hot bliss. And then it retreats and I sob. It pierces me again, filling me up and satisfying the worst of my body's incessant demands as it fucks me, its motors making more and more noise. Faster. Deeper. Sam cranks up the dial until I go limp with relief against the padded chair.

It's not as good as being fucked in your nest by your pack. My body knows this on an instinctual level. But it satisfies enough of my omega cravings that I can stop crying and whining.

Sam kneels beside me and turns my head to the side so he can kiss me, his lips sweet and claiming. He touches me all over, weighing the heft of each breast and pinching and tugging each nipple. His hand drifts down my belly, which heaves against his palm with the way I'm breathing.

When he slides his fingers through my damp curls and caresses my clit, I'm lost. I come from just that brush, my whole body trembling as the fucking machine makes a terrible noise, its movements slowing as my cunt flutters and tries to milk a knot that's not there from a toy that can't come.

The moment I relax, it starts again, and I jerk in my restraints. The pressure builds in my pelvis, another orgasm already half-formed even though I've barely come down from the first. It goes on for what feels like forever. And then Sam leaves me.

The door opens and there's talking, but it barely registers because I'm so consumed by the fire between my legs that isn't being quenched. I need a knot. I need cum. I need to be bred. The fucking machine slows if I wiggle too much, only starting again once I'm still. It's cruel.

That now familiar scent of cardamom and spice and cream makes my mouth water and slick run down my ass crack. I whine.

"Why is she restrained?" Marcus asks.

"She'll hurt herself in her delirium if she isn't. Her heat will break soon, but right now is the worst of it. She's glad you're here."

"This is so much *more* than I ever expected," someone with a British accent says, his voice making my toes curl as the machine wrings one more orgasm from my tired body, its pace never stopping as it batters my cunt with ruthless mechanical precision. "If I'd known the heat clinics were like this, then I would have come with you all these years."

"This is my mate, Tom. *Behave*," Marcus growls the last word, and I wiggle and whine at the sound of it.

He's so close. Why isn't he fucking me? Why isn't he knotting me? I whine again, louder. Maybe he didn't hear me before over the noise of the machine.

A pair of footsteps come closer, and the scent of my alpha gets stronger, and then he's there and kneeling before me. "Emily, I'm not sure how much you can understand right now, but this is my mate, Tom."

"Hello, luv. Oh, you poor thing." He leans forward, his long brown hair slipping over his green silk shirt. He smells like buttery shortbread cookies, the kind you'd eat at Christmas at Grandma's house from the big round tin that had a fifty-fifty chance of containing sewing supplies instead of treats.

I want to lick him and see if he tastes like shortbread cookies too. The restraints hold me down as I struggle and whimper.

Tom leans forward and puts his face to my neck and sniffs. I go still, freezing instinctively, as I wait for a bite that never comes. He's a beta, and he's beautiful. He reaches a hand out to touch me, then hesitates, his palm hovering over my collarbone. "May I?"

I arch my back and push my breast into his hand. Yes, touch me. Fuck me. Seed me. Breed me. Give me some relief before I burn to a crisp from the inside out.

His large hand and long, thin fingers squeeze and caress me. Like Sam, he hefts the weight, playing with it.

"So soft," Tom says, smiling. "It's fun to play with."

Yes, play with me.

I whine, and he pinches my nipple, the tug shooting straight to my clit like the two are connected. The fucking machine pauses, its machinery whining, as I tighten down on it and squeeze.

"Oh, this is lovely." Tom reaches for my other breast, pressing them both together. He grabs both nipples and tugs on them at once and my back bows, the dildo in my cunt pausing at full thrust as I grind against it.

"Tom, don't tease her. The heat hurts if it's not fulfilled."

"Then you should fuck her, darling. I want to watch."

Yes! Fuck me.

Marcus bends down and captures Tom's pretty face by the chin, pulling him in for a kiss that makes my pussy wet with slick. And then he reaches for the buttons of his jacket and I want to cry from the relief of it.

The methodical way he undresses and folds his clothing into a neat stack that he sets aside drives me insane. It's slow torture watching him reveal each inch of hair-dusted skin. I didn't get to see him much before, so I devour the sight of him now. He's stacked with muscles upon muscles, but his broad chest tapers to a narrow waist. His arms and legs are thickly sculpted. A trail of dark hair runs down from his navel and thickens into a triangle above his crotch. It's like an arrow pointing to his cock. It's huge. His dick juts heavy and hard between his thighs, his big balls swinging low behind it as he comes closer and curves a hand around my thigh.

Sam turns the fucking machine off as Marcus pulls it from me with a wet sucking sound and slick drips onto the floor. His thumbs spread my lips wide, and then he lines us up and sinks inside of me with a single push that's neither gentle nor hesitant.

He's hot, his cock burning me like a brand as he fucks in and out of me, his hands cupping my hips as he pins me down even more, as if the four points of restraints aren't enough. As if I could go anywhere if I tried, even if I wanted to. Sam pets my hair and wipes the sweat from my brow as my pussy clenches tight, trying to keep my alpha's cock where it belongs. Inside of me.

His thrusts make my breasts bounce, much to Tom's delight. And then there's no thought. Only sensation. Only my alpha's cock battering at my womb and my betas both stroking me and everything is right now. Everything is how it should be. We aren't in my nest, but with my pack all here, that matters less. We are whole.

"Aren't you going to join in?" Marcus asks.

Tom lets go of me, ignoring my whined protest, and undresses. He's tall, so tall for a beta, and leanly muscled with a strength that's more wiry than broad. His skin is smooth, with only the faintest patch of dark hair on his chest and stomach leading down to his cock. He drops his clothes onto the floor and watches the pistoning glide of our alpha's cock in my pussy as he strokes himself until he's hard. A pearl of pre-cum gathers on his pink head.

"Fuck her mouth," Marcus growls.

Yes. Yes, please fuck my mouth. It waters at the thought.

"Can I? But I thought…"

"She's consented for it," Sam says as he slides two fingers across my mouth, then pushes them in. I suck on instinct, wrapping my lips around them.

"Well then, I wouldn't want to disappoint now, would I, luv?" Tom jerks his cock some more, then brings it to my face as Sam withdraws his fingers and turns my head to the other side.

The first taste of the beta's salty shortbread cookie pre-cum makes me groan as he feeds his cock into my mouth and glides in and out between my lips. I suck and learn the shape of him, my tongue tracing the crenelation of his domed head and the veins that jut out on his shaft. He's slimmer and longer, his cockhead more tapered.

Marcus ruts me harder, his balls slapping against my slick-coated ass while he pounds me as if the sight of me sucking on his beta's cock turns him on even more.

"Aren't you joining?" Marcus asks again, biting out his words between low growls.

Fabric rustles, and then there's more slapping noises as Sam jerks his cock until he's plumped. I pull off Tom's cock and turn my head, sucking Sam down until we find a rhythm together and I move between the both of them, both of their flavors melding on my tongue as I lap at them hungrily. It's like someone dipped a buttery shortbread cookie in orange ice cream and I want more of it.

All of it.

"Oh, fuck me, that's good," Tom says, shoving his cock to the back of my throat until I can't breathe and my eyes sting with gathered tears. I'm so full, so stretched and used, as they take their pleasure from me.

Sam undoes the binding on my wrists and guides my hand to his cock. I stroke and tug, moaning when Tom lets me up for air by rubbing his head along my lips, smearing his fluids down my chin and making a mess of me.

A hand slips between my thighs and strokes my clit and I don't know whose hand it is, who is touching me when they're all touching me. All I know is pleasure. They rub circles around my nub, my walls squeezing and pulling a moan from my alpha as he fucks me raw, his huge cock splitting me in two with every hard push and sucking pull.

Someone presses on the bulge he makes in my belly while

another rolls my clit in faster, harder circles, and I can't take it. I come, screaming, my thighs shaking in the padded stirrups. The leather creaks as I thrash against it. My alpha fucks me through each shattering spasm, merciless and demanding. There's no stopping, no pausing, no break from the sensations.

Weak, I collapse against the cushioned chair and whimper. A cock presses to my lips, and I open. They fuck me from both ends, another cock rubbing against my cheek as the betas take turns again, their cocks bumping as they compete for my mouth.

"That's so hot, babe," Marcus says, his hips rolling. The wet sounds of our fucking fill the room with filthy noises. "You're being such a good omega, taking all of us like that."

"Such a good cocksucker," Sam agrees, sliding his head through my lips.

"I think she's earned her knot," Marcus says.

Yes! Yes yes yes!

Slick squirts from me as he carves a home for himself in my cunt, his hard breathing filling the room while his cock jumps inside of me. At the first pulse of his release, I feel his knot swell. It stretches me wide in blissful agony. His splashes brand me from the inside out, painting my walls with the cum my body craves and locking it in. No competitor will pull him aside and plant their seed instead. We're tied.

Sam explores our tie, feeling how stretched I am around the alpha's huge knot, how hot and wet my folds are. He strokes my clit just how I like it. He's learned exactly how to touch me. Stuffed full and satisfied, he rubs me to orgasm until my tired cunt gives one last weak flutter around Marcus's knot.

Marcus purrs, the diesel truck sound making me calm and pleased. I have a belly full of cum and my pack is surrounding me. Everything is wonderful.

But they're not done fucking me. I'm only given a brief

reprieve to enjoy our combined pleasure and then Tom cups my face and bobs me up and down on his length, his cock hitting the back of my throat before retreating as I struggle to breathe and suck him too.

His groan warns me it's coming only a second before he explodes in my mouth, filling my belly with his seed. I swallow, drinking him down and humming happily around him as I clean him with my tongue and gather up every single drop.

Don't waste it.

Beta cum isn't as nutritious as a rutting alpha's spending, but it's still full of protein. Semen splatters between my breasts, hot against my feverish skin, as Sam comes while standing over me. He shakes out every last drop until I'm covered, then leans against the padded chair.

"Don't waste it, luv," Tom says as if he can read my thoughts, scooping two long fingers through the mess on my chest and shoving it between my lips. I suck them clean, laving them with my tongue. He repeats it twice, scraping the cum up and feeding it to me.

My belly's full in the best way, my cunt no longer cramping, and I purr while I lick his hand clean. The endless, crushing hunger of the heat eases.

For now.

Marcus's knot softens, and he tugs himself free, our fluids dripping all over the floor as it runs down my ass and makes me shiver.

Tom makes a tutting sound and reaches between my lower lips, scooping out seed and slick. "Stop wasting it, luv. It's delicious."

He shoves his slick-coated fingers in my mouth, and then my cunt. I suck his fingers clean each time. Sam undoes my restraints and rubs the circulation back into my joints, and then Marcus steps in and lifts me from the padded chair. I've already built the nest to prepare for this wave, so he sets me in the center and climbs inside. He's more careful than Sam, who knocked it down twice earlier.

I purr, and Marcus purrs back, his sound a deeper rumble that makes me calm. It feels like curling up in front of a warm fire with a cozy blanket and a chill breeze blowing through the cracked window while you read a good book and sip on hot cocoa.

He's a furnace, but I sigh in contentment when he pulls me onto his chest. I twirl my fingers in his chest hair. His creamy, spicy scent is even stronger now than before, and I drink it in and rub my cheek against his skin.

"Emily, can the betas join us in the nest?" he asks.

My answer is a purr as I nuzzle his pecs, enjoying the way our scents blend. And Tom's scent too. I can smell the beta on him, like a buttery cookie soaked in a chai latte. Sam's scent is there as well, already stuck to my skin, and combined, we smell like the bakery counter in a coffee shop.

The mattress that pads the floor nest dips as Sam and Tom climb in and get settled. I'm too tired, too content to open my eyes and check its structural integrity. It smells like pack, and that makes it perfect.

"We're going to need a bigger bed," Tom whispers.

"Good thing you always wanted a big family," Marcus answers just as softly.

Tom is curled up against Marcus's side, and his fingers trip down my spine before brushing against the curve of my butt and playing with its bounce.

I squirm, my cozy and content feelings slowly replacing with horniness as he strokes a finger across the seam of my ass and thigh and grazes my pussy in the process.

"Stop teasing her, brat, unless you want to fuck her yourself because she drained my balls and I need a minute."

Fucking?

My heavy eyelids crack open as I wiggle on top of Marcus in search of more pussy touches. He bands an arm across my upper back and keeps me in place on top of him. "See what you started?"

"Refractory period getting longer with age, old man?" Sam asks from the other side.

"Oh!" Tom cackles. "You're in for it now. He hates being teased about his age. That's why I do it so often. You especially don't want to talk about his gray hairs or sagging balls."

There's jostling and the sound of fabric sliding on fabric as Marcus works a hand free and brings his palm down on Sam's ass with a sharp crack that makes my pussy tingle from memory. I feel like Pavlov's dog. Sam yelps and scoots away, and something tells me that my beautiful nest is ruined. Sure enough, when I look, I notice that one wall of it has completely fallen. He knocked down the keystone blanket that was holding it all together.

"Why did I get spanked and not him?" Sam asks.

I growl and stretch my arm out and try to reach for it, but Marcus holds me in place and I can't.

"Oh, we've upset her," Tom says.

Sam sits up and tries to put the nest back together, but he doesn't have the instincts an omega does. He never learned how. The result is messy and jumbled, and not the smooth, pretty nest I made for us all to appreciate and then fuck in.

Rude.

"Her nesting instincts are kicking into overdrive, which means her heat has peaked. She's getting ready to breed," Sam says.

"Breed? I didn't… I mean, we haven't…" Tom stops playing with me, his hand heavy on my ass while he freezes.

"No! She's on birth control," Sam says. "But we've found

through trial and error what combination to give the omegas. If you don't satisfy the breeding urge, they're more likely to go into distress. Dr. Sharma can explain it a lot better than I can. Basically, the combination of pills I gave her today are a different formula and they make her body think she's pregnant."

"I see. Did you know this?" Tom asks.

Marcus's purring stutters, then stops. The silence is deafening. "No."

"We'll discuss this later," Tom says, his words clipped.

The beta packmate's mad.

They don't want me.

They don't want my babies.

Tears blur my vision as I whine and try to struggle off the alpha under me. He holds me tighter, which only makes me struggle harder. I scratch his chest and get ready to bite him if I have to.

They don't want me they don't want me they don't want us they don't want my babies my babies.

"Oww! Jesus Christ. Sweetheart, stop! I don't want to hurt you." His arms cage me. I growl deeper. Scratch harder.

"What the bloody hell?" The nest breaks completely as Tom scrambles upright.

Sam threads his hand through my hair and makes a fist, pulling my head back just as his hand comes down hard on my ass. It stings, then burns, then turns to warmth. He shoves two fingers roughly into my cunt and pumps.

"She thinks you're rejecting her. Calm down, hellcat."

He fingerfucks me hard and fast, his grip in my hair punishing as he overloads me with sensation until the pain and the pleasure are all I'm aware of. The wet squelch of my slick fills the room along with my pheromones.

"What do we do?" Marcus asks.

"Ideally, you fuck her. Both of you at the same time. It's not gonna be pleasant if neither of you can. She barely tolerated the fucking machine before. She's already bonding. Purr for your omega, alpha."

Marcus does. He purrs, and more of the fire leaves me as Sam curls his fingers inside of my pussy and turns my anger into lust. I grind, trying to rub my clit against my alpha's trapped cock. My grip on his chest hair slackens, and I moan.

"You're very good with her. I wouldn't have thought to be that rough with her. That she could… She's so tiny," Tom says.

Sam tugs my hair back harder and my back arches, my ass lifting. "Everyone thinks omegas are sweet and weak, but they're the ones guarding the nests and the babies. They're fierce when they need to be." He pulls my face to his and nuzzles my cheek. "You're such a good little knot-milking slut, aren't you, baby? How bad do you want a cock in you? Ride my fingers and show me. There you go. So good, such a good girl."

A cock nudges against my opening, replacing Sam's fingers as they swap out. Marcus bottoms out inside me with one thrust that knocks up against my cervix and drives the air from my lungs. My toes curl as he drives it in and out of me. I spread my legs wider and grind, meeting him.

"You're so pretty when you ride a cock, baby. Look at those gorgeous bouncy tits."

"You have a filthy mouth," Tom says, a smile in his voice.

"She likes it."

"So do I." I hear the dull thwap of Tom jerking his cock.

"That's good," Sam says. "You should fuck her together."

"I'm not sure I trust her not to bite now," Tom says.

"Well, you've got two other holes to choose from."

"Two… oh, interesting. I never would have considered it. Do you think I could?"

"It won't be any worse than a knot. She's sturdier than she looks."

Tom grabs my ass cheeks and spreads them. "Stop for a moment, darling. We're doing all sorts of *firsts* today."

Marcus stops fucking me, and I whine as my building orgasm stutters and falls flat. But then something nudges behind me. A cockhead presses to where I'm already being penetrated. It pushes and pulls and pushes again, and it burns as I stretch.

I whine, my nipples tightening and my clit throbbing as the beta forces his way into my pussy. I'm so full I can't take it. He slides in, his tapered head forcing my body to make room for him or break.

And then they move. Tom thrusts in and out of me, his cock sliding alongside Marcus's while they fuck me in tandem.

Having two cocks in my pussy is like a knot… Right. That's like comparing a tiger to a house cat.

I can't speak, can't moan, can't even breathe as they both fuck in and out of me, their cocks slipping over one another as they both fuck my pussy.

"Oh, bloody hell, that feels so fucking good," Marcus growls, his diesel truck purr rumbling through his whole body. It teases my clit where I'm sitting on him.

Sam's grip on my hair tugs each time I twitch and try to stay still. But there's no staying still. Not while they slide in and out of me, my cunt always full. Sam palms one breast and pinches the nipple, pulling on it.

My moan turns into a sob. I can't take it.

"I can… I can feel your cock twitching inside her," Tom groans. He slips in and out. In and out, as Marcus makes slow and careful thrusts. "I'm gonna come."

"Yes," Marcus says. "Come inside her, babe. We'll both fill her up."

My mouth drops open in a silent scream, my brow knitting as Tom grunts and fucks me faster, chasing his pleasure. He's going to come inside of me while Marcus is still fucking me.

Sam leans down and puts his lips to my ear as he slicks a hand between us and finds my clit and strokes. "Look at you, being such a filthy cock slut. You've got two cocks in you, baby. They're both going to come in your wet, greedy hole and then your alpha's gonna knot you and lock it all in. You're going to be leaking cum for days. Every time you sit, a bit more's gonna work its way out of you. That's how stuffed full of cream your pussy's gonna be. You like that, don't you? I knew you were a pretty little cum slut the minute I laid eyes on you."

Everything tightens, my fullness beyond the point of discomfort as pleasure and pain twine into one and my alpha and beta fuck into my cunt while Sam says such delicious, horrible things to me.

I stretch on the precipice, my belly fluttering with the gasping urge to breathe while he touches me. Strokes me. Praises and demeans me.

It hits me like a hurricane, drowning me in pulsing waves. Slick squirts and gushes, leaking through the cracks and adding to our slippery mess. My walls flutter and squeeze a groan from Tom, who comes, his cock jerking. Each pulse of hot seed threatens to spill out of me as Marcus keeps fucking me through Tom's shuddering pulses.

When Tom withdraws, I moan from the loss of him until Marcus works his cock deeper inside of me and fills me to bursting again. My belly bulges with the strength of his emissions. He pumps me full and locks it in with his knot. After being stretched with two cocks, his knot feels like relief.

I collapse, but Sam still has his hand burrowed between my ruined thighs. He pulls the hood back from my clit and exposes all of it, stroking me through my shudders and twitches as he forces another, smaller orgasm from my exhausted body.

My pussy milks my alpha's knot, draining the rest of him and soaking up his seed. Storing it behind this stoppering knot. It floods me and makes a pool for my womb to soak up.

Fatigue and contentment wash over me as my alpha strokes his big callused hands up and down my back while Sam and Tom both collapse in the nest.

"Is it always like this?" Tom asks, his voice low. "Between alphas and omegas?"

"Not always. A pack finding each other is special."

My eyelids droop again while Marcus purrs. He flinches when I put a hand to his chest and I see the scratches I made. I press a kiss to them, saying sorry, and when he strokes my hair, I know that I'm forgiven.

I fall asleep like that, only dimly aware when his softening knot unplugs and cum and slick slide out of me. Sam presses a kiss to my cheek, and I turn my head to give him my lips, purring softly as our mouths meld.

It's hours later, but it feels like minutes when Sam leans over me and pokes me awake. The fog around my thoughts is thinner.

"Can you stand?" he asks.

I roll onto my back and wince. My pussy's been ravaged. When I whimper, he gets an arm under my knees and lifts me in his arms, hitching me higher as he stands.

"I think we hurt her," Tom whispers.

"She's fine," Sam says. "We'll have a bath and she'll sleep. They always get more tired as the heat goes on. She's got one more session in her, I think, and then she goes home in the morning."

"And that's when we can pick her up?" Marcus asks.

"Speak to Mary. She'll walk you through it." Sam stops so Marcus can drape the blankets of our nest on his shoulder, then badges open the door and carries me out.

"Sam," I whisper.

"Yeah?"

I tug him closer and rub my cheek against his neck. "I'm very happy."

"I'm glad you're happy, baby. You deserve it."

I'm finally starting to believe it. To believe this is real, and let myself enjoy it. The ache between my legs is certainly real enough to convince me of it.

Chapter Eleven

TOM

Once the rut room door shuts and we're left to dress and see our way out, Marcus rounds on me while he buckles his belt. "I am so sorry. I should have asked, should have thought about it, and... I don't know what's wrong with me. It's like I can't think straight."

"It's her." The omega's heat pheromones are even affecting *me*. "Her pheromones."

I slip my arms through my jacket's sleeves and shrug it on, then run a hand through my hair to drag it out of my face. The rut room reeks of needy omega cunt and satisfied alpha and cum.

Marcus's face is crestfallen as he sits on the sofa and gathers his socks and shoes. Fondness and exasperation lead me to join him. I step between his legs and cup his face in my hands. Despite his morning shave, stubble is already scratching through.

"I know that you think your self-control is impeccable," I tell him carefully, stressing each word, "but you still have instincts. Instincts aren't rational, and you can't logic them into submission as you try to defy every alpha stereotype that exists."

Before he can interrupt me, I continue, "And I don't care that you fucked her when you found her. That you had sex with either of them. They're pack. Claimed or not, they're ours. But I will not be left out of important conversations. I will not be steamrolled by your dynamic when it comes to something as life altering as bringing a new person into this world. This isn't the Middle Ages anymore."

He nods, his face full of contrition as he bands his arms around my thighs and tugs me against his chest. "You're right, and I'm sorry. The last thing I want to do is hurt you. I love you."

Marcus is absolutely miserable through the bond and it makes it hard to stay mad at him even if I wanted to but I've never been one to hold grudges for long. I've made my point, and he's heard it.

I rake my nails through his scalp and tame his mussed hair until his eyes droop with pleasure and he purrs for me, the vibrations traveling from his body to mine wherever we touch. It shakes me, working the knot of tension around my heart free. "Oh, you're forgiven."

He'll grovel in his own way over the next few days. Little things like getting up early and fetching me a cappuccino before I'm awake, or massaging my shoulders when we cuddle. It's how he is. Always taking care of people. I can't say that I'll hate the extra pampering. He owes it to me after temporarily turning into a neanderthal.

"You agree?" he asks while he ties his shoes.

"Hmm?"

"That they're pack. Both of them."

"I think so. I'm not sure you could pry them apart even if you wanted to." Not that I would want to. They look good together. I have the mental image of dressing them both up in matching latex nun and priest costumes. *Oh, yes.* I think I'm going to like having new packmates to play with.

Dressed, we check out of the clinic and head back to the hotel. The concierge has different staff today than last night. They only cast a glance our way as we head to the elevator and then up to our room.

I blow out a breath and suppress a smile. "That was quite the adventure, huh? Who'd have thought that tiny omega could be so frightening? I'm glad Sam knows what he's doing." He knows how to wrangle a clawing, scratching demon and turn her into a purring puddle of slick. It makes me wonder what other useful skills he's got hidden underneath that eager puppy attitude. There's just something instantly likable about him. And I'm captivated with how he went from klutzy nest destroyer to omega tamer with the snap of a finger.

It would be fun to tag team her with him. Drive her wild then wrestle her back. Just as long as I'm far away from those teeth and nails. Maybe some leather cuffs? A gag? So many options. It's hard to decide where to start.

He tosses his plastic key card onto the hotel's dresser and tugs his tie loose.

"How's your chest?" I ask while I shut the door behind us. "Let me see it."

Marcus toes his shoes off and folds up his jacket, then takes off his shirt and undershirt. The pink lines have darkened, a few dark spots showing where her nails bit deeper and drew actual blood. "How does it look?" he asks, craning his head down to see.

I tut and ghost a finger near the worst one without touching it directly. "She got you good. Let's get that cleaned up. Sit."

He sits on the edge of the bed, and after I grab my travel first aid kit from my luggage, I stand between his legs. I uncap the bottle of hydrogen peroxide and open a pack of sterile gauze, wetting it and dabbing it to the deepest scratch.

Marcus winces and hisses as it makes contact. I tut at him and dab the antiseptic along the scrape. "Don't be a baby."

"That's easy to say. You're not the one bleeding. You know I don't like pain."

I roll my eyes and smile faintly. "What, you can dish it out but you can't take it?" I blot the deepest part of the scratch and revel in the way his nostrils flare and his eyes squint. "Baby," I tease him.

"Do you still want one?" he asks. "A baby."

I freeze for a moment, then set the pink-tinged gauze back in its sterile wrapper. "We haven't talked about it for so long."

His hands cup the backs of my thighs as he keeps me there between his knees like I'm at risk for running away. It's silly. There's nowhere I'd rather be than with my alpha. My packmate.

"Your shows are going well," he says. "Your prints are selling. I made partner years ago. We got a bigger place. It's all the things we said we were waiting for. What if this is it?"

My heart knocks against my ribs as I choose my words. "What if she doesn't want them? Or can't have them?"

"Infertility is so rare among omegas, but if she can't then we'll get treatment or adopt. We were going to adopt anyway. If she doesn't want them… then things aren't changing so much, I guess."

I recall the idea boards I made when I designed the nursery we never built. It's a guest bedroom now. What was supposed to be a temporary measure stuck. Now that the idea's been implanted in the back of my mind, it's all I can think of.

"Yes."

"Yeah?" he asks, his eyebrows climbing. The hope on his face makes my belly flutter. Like he's a little scared to be so happy. I feel the same way. Happy, hopeful, and terrified.

I lean down and claim his mouth in a kiss, enjoying the way his lips soften under mine. His hands slide up my thighs to cup my ass. When our kiss breaks, we're both breathing hard. Other things are hard too. I rest my forehead against his and scratch my thumbs over the stubble on his jaw.

"You wanna be a daddy?" I ask, my voice breathy.

He groans, and his fingers press divots into my buttocks as he squeezes. "You know I hate being called that."

I push him down onto the mattress, and he lets me. His hard cock knocks against mine as I hitch one of my knees up higher and grind. "Called what? Daddy?"

Despite his protests, his cock jerks against me and I grin before I claim his mouth again in a devouring kiss.

Methinks the lady doth protest too much.

When he's rocking with me and his hands wander to stroke my backside, I nip his lower lip between my teeth and let it go with a wet *pop*. "I think we should practice making a baby, Daddy."

Marcus growls and flips us, his weight heavy and solid on top of me. But I'm used to it, and now I find it comforting. One summer he was a gangly boy, and the next he was a muscled Adonis. I can't complain.

I skim my hands over his chest, enjoying the way he hisses when I touch the marks our omega scratched into his flesh.

What a fierce little omega.

She'll be a good mother.

A better one than mine.

Chapter Twelve

SAM

SHE'S NAPPING IN THE NEST AGAIN, SO I TAKE THE OPPORTUNITY to sneak out and see to a few things. I change my scrubs again, exchanging the old, slick-smeared ones for a fresh pair at the scrub exchange machine. I shovel some cold sesame chicken into my stomach and slam down two entire bottles of water, then take the longest pee of my life, before finally going to see Mary.

"Hey." I knock on the jamb of her open door, and she looks up from the briefcase she's packing as she gets ready to leave. "Glad I caught you."

"Sam! Me too. Come in. Here, I have some more paperwork for you. This patient's really keeping you busy, huh?"

I take it from her and read the top of the form. "I already have a copy of the courtship request form."

Mary shuts down her computer for the night. "Read it."

I do. "They filled it out wrong. Is this a messed-up copy? Why don't you just shred it?"

Mary sighs. "No, Sam. This one's for *you*."

"What?"

"They want to court you too. The both of you. I can't file this form, obviously. You're not a patient here or an omega, so they didn't actually need to fill this out." She grabs her bag and puts a hand on my shoulder. "But I thought you might like to see it for yourself and keep it as a memento. Congratulations. Now I need to lock up. I'll see you in the morning."

She ushers me out of her office and leaves me standing there, struck mute and dumb, as she leaves. I read the form again to make sure this is real, and it's happening.

A pack wants me.

It feels too good to be true.

My heart jumps into my throat like it does when you're strapped into a roller coaster and it drops, racing down the tracks before it levels out again. My shoulder bumps against the wall as I turn around and walk to the breakroom.

Anthony and Diana are having a conversation about an upcoming concert, and they look up when I stumble in.

"You okay, man?" Anthony asks.

"Yeah, you're pale. Sit down," Diana says.

I slump into the seat she pulls out for me and slap the form to the table.

"What's that?" Diana asks. And then she reads it. "Oh my God. Oh my God, Sam!" She pulls me into a side hug. "Sam is getting packed up!"

My face heats with embarrassment as Anthony thumps me on the back. "That's awesome, man. Good for you."

I've gotta call my mom.

"Thanks, guys. I'm gonna go call my family." I head out the back door, sobering when the cool air clears my head a little. I should call my mom, but... I should call *them* first. Make sure it's real before I get anyone too excited. That would suck to take back.

Never mind, Mom, they changed their minds. They didn't really want me after all, but they thought they had to take me too. A beta consolation prize.

I read the form and find their cell phone number and type it in, my heart beating against my ribs as I wait for them to answer.

"Hello?" Marcus's voice is deep and rumbly, and even better over the phone.

"Hey! Uh…" I clear my throat. "Hey, man. It's, umm, Sam."

"Sam," he drawls, dragging the vowel out as if he's savoring it. "I'm glad you called."

God, why does his voice have to be so husky? He makes it difficult to think straight. "I got the paperwork."

"Good. What do you think about it?"

"It's unnecessary," I say.

"I see." His voice has lost the relaxed huskiness, and then I realize how that sounded and my heart falls into my ass.

"I mean—we're not a package deal or anything. Emily's a free woman. If you, umm, just wanted her… that would be… cool."

"You think I don't want you since I haven't fucked you yet?" His voice is all gravel and grit, and it makes my belly swoop to hear it and know it's directed at me. Me.

Yet. That one word holds a lot of promise in it.

There's murmuring in the background, and then he says, "It's Sam."

It's Sam, he said. I'm not *the beta* anymore.

"That, uh… Yeah, that sounds good." I wince and rub my forehead, instantly regretting the words that just tumbled out of my mouth.

He chuckles. "Have you ever taken a cock before?"

"Ah… no. I've blown a guy and been blown before, and I've got a toy, but…"

"That's fine," he says, putting me at ease. "I'll put Tom in charge of your training."

There's rustling, and then Tom's voice is louder and clearer in the background. His voice is amused. "You always give me the *best* presents, alpha."

I'm equal parts alarmed and turned on, and it's confusing. "Well, I'm glad to hear you didn't want me only because of my omega handling skills because they have classes for that. You know... for people who didn't pay attention in health class... or for people who haven't been in school for like... thirty years."

"Hmm."

My heart races a bit when he takes the teasing in stride. "Don't worry. I know they say you can't teach an old dog new tricks, but work always makes me train the new hires, so I guess I'm pretty good at it by now."

"Mmhmm."

I bite my lip to stifle my laugh and grin like a fool. It's a good thing there's no one out here with me to witness this.

"So if you were concerned, don't be. I'll be able to catch you up on everything you've missed since the eighties."

All I hear on the other line for a moment is silence and breathing, and I worry that I've pushed it too far. But I don't think I've read the situation wrong. At least I hope I haven't. I'm pretty good at reading people.

"Oh, were you done? Please... don't let me stop you from adding to your count. It's like you think I can't spank the brat right out of you," he says.

Oh, I hope he tries.

"I have soooo much to teach you," Tom crows from the background.

"I've changed my mind," Marcus says. "You two aren't allowed to be alone in a room together for more than five minutes."

"That doesn't actually limit me as much as you'd think," Tom says.

My cheeks hurt from smiling so much as I listen to their banter and realize that I'm a part of this now. I have a pack.

"So Emily goes home in the morning and we wait for her call. Then what?" he asks.

Back to business. "My shift ends once she's released, and then I have the rest of the week off to recover. My next shift isn't until Friday. This wasn't my holiday to work, but I switched with someone." *And thank God for that.* When I think of how easily I could have missed meeting my pack, it pulls at something in my gut.

"Our schedules are flexible, so we can stay in town a few more days. Shall we plan for lunch tomorrow?" he asks.

They don't live here. I look at the courtship request paperwork and finally note something I should have seen long before now. "You live in New York City." I knew they had multiple properties, but before I knew they wanted me, I didn't pay too much attention to details like addresses.

"Yes. Is that… a problem?" he asks. "We spend most of our time in the city. Tom goes to London occasionally to deal with the gallery. I travel sometimes for business, but the city is our home."

Standing there in the paved parking lot of the free clinic, I decide. There's no way I'm missing this opportunity of a lifetime. "It's not a problem for me, but I can't speak for her. I'll talk to her about it when she's lucid."

"I'll send you the reservation information for the restaurant."

"And I'll see you there. Bye."

We hang up, and I call my mother and tell her the news. I warn her it's not a done deal yet, but she gets excited anyway, and by the end of the phone call practically my whole family is texting me their congratulations. I float back to Emily's room on cloud nine, and she's still sleeping when I creep in, but she chirps in her sleep and lets me into her nest, then snuggles against me as I lie there and stare at the ceiling in the dark.

I have a pack now. I'm going to get mated. My mates are ridiculously hot and disgustingly rich. It still feels too good to be true. I... need to figure out how to break the news to my family that I'll be moving out of state. *They'll get over it.*

Emily fidgets and fusses until she gets a hand under my scrub top and touches me skin to skin. For someone who was so initially shy about it, she's turned into quite the nudist. We nap together, and when I wake up with her climbing on top of me and grinding, I'm not even mad about how I'll need to change my scrubs yet again.

She leans down and rubs her cheeks all over me, coating me with the pheromones from her scent glands. It's not as strong of a scent as the ones on her neck. While she's dry humping me, I reach up and skim my hands over her neck and gather up the oils there, transferring them to my skin and hair. My pants are wet from her sweet slick, and my cock is rubbing against my pants in a way that's both delightful and awful.

I undo the tie of my pants and push them down, along with my underwear. "I've got what you need, baby."

She lets me lift her up long enough to bring her down on my cock, and then she's riding me for real, dropping her head to lick my neck and collarbone and the faint beta pheromones my skin secretes without the overdeveloped scent glands that alphas and omegas have. She grinds her clit against my pelvis and takes her pleasure while I palm her tits, playing with them, then trail my hands down and around to caress her ass.

"You like that, baby? Does my cock make you feel good?" She bites her lip and nods, purring as her hips rock over me.

It's a slow, sweet fucking, a delicious end to a life-shattering heat. While she gyrates above me, her brow knitting as she gets closer to coming, all I can think of is how grateful I am I switched shifts and found her. Found all of them. Now that I've met them, I can't imagine any other future.

Emily is sweet and cute. I want to cuddle and fuck her, then cuddle her some more. Tom is the best sort of trouble. I can't tell which one of us will end up topping the other, but I'm excited to figure it out. And Marcus... Marcus feels like he can wreck me and put me back together. Like I can trust him to do that.

I've met a lot of alphas in the years I've worked here. Some mistake being an asshole for being tough. But not Marcus. He's gentle when he needs to be. I can recognize a keeper when I see one.

"We're gonna be so happy, baby." I dig my fingers into her ass and help her bounce on my cock. She moans and leans against me until we're both tired and spent. My cum and her slick get added to the nest. After, she uses me as a pillow and falls back asleep, gently snoring.

Her heat breaks in the night as she sweats it out, and I bully her into the bath as she comes back to awareness and rationality. I get out the healing massage oil and rub her down, paying special attention to her sore cunt. She tolerates my ministrations with a blush, especially when I pry her labia apart to check each fold for small tears. I'm thankful there aren't any. Marcus is huge, but he's a generous alpha and that makes the world of difference. There are some things that even an alpha's growl can't magic away.

"This room reeks." She picks up one of the stained sheets and turns it over, trying to find a spot that's not crusty.

"No, baby." I kiss her nose and slap her cunt and pronounce her thoroughly tended to. "It smells like pack."

I claim her mouth in a kiss, and she's stiff for a moment before releasing a tense breath and melting into it.

"How hungry are you?" I ask.

"I'm fucking starving."

"The diner down the street makes incredible pancakes. You should take it easy today. Stick with easy-to-digest things like carbs. You can add meat back into your diet tomorrow if you eat it normally."

She gives me a funny look while she's dressing. "I think I know how to handle the post-heat phase."

I heft her bag onto my shoulder and pass her by in the cramped room, smacking her bottom as I badge open the door. I raise one brow. "Who's the expert here?"

Emily shakes her head but smiles, and I walk her up to the front of the clinic and hand her off to Amy so she can do her discharge paperwork. Before I leave, I lean down and give her one last kiss, then set her bag at her feet.

"I'll meet you in the parking lot. Wait for me."

Her eyes search mine for a moment before she nods, her ponytail bouncing.

When I go into the break room, there's a lot of cheering and backslapping and ribald comments. I wave everyone off with a grin and change into street clothes, chucking one last set of filthy scrubs down the scrub machine's dirty chute. Remembering one final detail, I grab the phone off the wall and dial housekeeping and ask them to bag and tag our nest. I can come back and grab it later after I've eaten something other than cold Chinese takeout.

Outside, I scan the parking lot. My gut tightens when I don't see her right away before I remember that she's in the omega side lot. I walk around the corner and see her standing there next to a rusty red beater, her arms folded like she's hugging herself. When she sees me she relaxes, and then she looks me up and down and for a moment, I feel like a million dollars.

Girls love the leather jacket.

I don't give her a chance to be awkward and shy. Instead, I grab her by the back of her neck and lean down and claim her mouth. I push her up against her car and kiss her until she's breathless and melts against me.

"Hey," I say, smiling as I play with some of the short strands of hair that have escaped her ponytail.

"Hey. I wasn't sure if… you know, after…"

I press my forehead to hers and breathe in her sweet scent. Lemon and sticky-sweet sugar. I don't think I'll ever tire of this smell. "You're stuck with me, baby. I'm all in. Now let's go get you fed. You earned it." A smack on her ass makes it jiggle, and my grin widens when she pouts.

I take her by the arm and lead her toward the sidewalk and down the street to the diner. A waitress seats us in a booth, and I sit next to my girl instead of across from her. I like the press of her thigh against mine, and I like being a human wall between her and the room. Alphas should be able to tell by now that she's post-heat, but I'm still not taking any chances. Crazy people do stupid things. Stupid people do crazy things. And she's too precious to risk.

The waitress hands us menus, but I already know what I want. I drop my hand to her thigh and rub it through her legging as she looks over the menu and sneaks glances at me as if she's still not sure this is for real even after everything that's happened and been said.

I lean down and whisper into her ear. "Do I need to fuck you over a sink in the bathroom or something so you know I'm not going anywhere?"

The waitress comes back to take our orders and ignores Emily's red face. "What can I get you?"

"Steak medium-rare and eggs sunny side up. Can I get an order of home fries too? And a chocolate milkshake."

"And you, hun?"

Emily nibbles on her lip and glances at the menu again. "The Belgian waffle with strawberries and a water. Thank you." When the waitress leaves, she relaxes against me, and we sit like that for a while. Not talking. Just together and present.

"So what now?" she asks, breaking the silence.

"I called Marcus. They want to meet over lunch and discuss everything. And... they requested to court me too. They asked us both to join their pack."

"Oh, Sam, that's great!"

Grinning, I duck my head and run a hand through my hair to fluff it. I'm glad that she's happy about it. A tiny sliver of me worried she might not be. She's had so many moments of hesitation and self-doubt and... I get it. I never thought I'd find a pack. It's only a fifty-fifty thing for betas. A lot of us end up in monogamous pairs, but alphas and omegas almost always end up in packs, even if maybe they take a while to get there.

That reminds me...

"Do you want a baby?"

Her eyes widen, and she glances around the restaurant to see if anyone's staring. "That's... Okay, guess we're asking the hard questions."

"They want to have lunch with us to go over details. I'm assuming whether or not you wanna get knocked up is a detail they'll wanna know. I know that in the moment during a heat you can think things that maybe you don't think normally... so you should probably think about it now. Before they ask. And they will ask."

The waitress comes by and drops off drinks, and Emily stalls for time by playing with her straw wrapper and ripping it up into a hundred tiny pieces.

I stick my straw into the milkshake and take a long pull of it, almost sighing with bliss at the first taste. And I wait. And wait.

"Do you?" she asks.

Oh, no, baby. You're not getting off that easy. "I could go either way, to be honest. I like kids. I love my little nieces and nephews. But I don't have any burning desire to have them myself. Now, Marcus, on the other hand…"

"What?" She grabs my straw wrapper and works it into a coil, winding it tighter and tighter.

"That man wants to rut you raw and breed you."

Her face turns cherry tomato red, and she sinks down in her seat a bit. "Did he say that?"

"No, but he didn't have to. That man barebacked you and forgot you were on birth control. It's pretty typical alpha behavior. Almost all of them have a breeding kink."

Her mouth flattens into a thin line as she glares at me. It's cute. It's like being mean mugged at by a hamster. "Can you possibly say that *any* louder?"

"I SAID THAT MAN BARE—"

She slaps her hand over my mouth, and I lick it. She pulls her hand away and wipes it on my leather jacket with a look of pure disgust on her face. "Gross, Sam!"

I laugh, a deep belly laugh that makes more than a few people look at us. "After all the fluids that went flying this weekend, a little saliva on your palm is what grosses you out?"

She must be remembering the many times I sucked cum right out of her pussy because she turns away from me and scowls at the table. I smirk and twist my finger in the baby hairs that dot her nape.

"All right, here we go," the waitress says, setting our food down in front of us. "Is there anything else I can get you?"

I reach over Emily and grab the ketchup for my home fries. "We're good, thank you."

"That's a lot of food," Emily says, eying my plates.

I unroll my silverware and start cutting up my steak and eggs, breaking the yolk and letting it all run together. "I did a lot of cardio this weekend." I stab a bite of steak, eggs, and home fries together and shovel it into my mouth. "I earned it," I say around my food as I chew.

She ignores me and cuts her waffle into bite-size pieces and eats it with only the strawberries and powdered sugar, no syrup.

"So," I ask between bites, "babies? Yes or no?"

Her strawberries leave pink streaks in her powdered sugar as she moves them around. "I think my mother would actually murder me if I got mated and didn't give her a grandbaby."

Oh. Oh, no. "That's not a good reason to have kids. And if your mom wants a baby so bad, she can go get one herself. Do *you* want a baby? Because Marcus is older. He's gonna wanna have them soon, if that's what we all agree to."

Emily is silent as she stares at her plate while I eat and wait for her to think it through. She's definitely a worrier, this one. "I do."

"Okay." I drop my hand to her thigh and give it a squeeze.

"Is it? Is it okay? It's not… crazy? Because we just met. Because we met at a…"

It's so easy to shift into minder mode. We deal with this type of thing a lot. Hollywood likes to paint a picture that reality doesn't always live up to. "Bonding hits everyone differently. Sometimes it's hot and fast. Other times it's a slow sizzle. Some people bond out of choice after knowing someone for years. Others find the right person or people and it's love at first sniff. That's it, no questions asked. There's no right or wrong way to do it so long as everyone is an adult and they all get a say."

She stabs a piece of waffle onto her fork, but stares at it. I don't like how little she's eaten. She did a lot of cardio too and needs to replace those calories she didn't get for three days. I scoop some of my seasoned home fries onto my fork and load them onto her plate. The salt and the grease and the herbs make her nose twitch. She pops one in her mouth and chews, then eats another. I give her the whole plate and watch them disappear one by one.

Once she's demolished them, she looks like she feels a little better. She eyes my steak as I shove the last piece in my mouth and chew. *Not a chance, baby.* The last thing we need is her getting sick in the bathroom, throwing up as her body gets used to solids again.

"Sam," she says, sitting more upright. She holds my gaze, her stare intense and a tiny bit frightening from the sudden change. "I want a baby."

"Okay, baby. We'll talk to them about it at lunch." I squeeze her thigh again, then stroke it as she eats her waffles and practically licks the plate clean. *Good girl.*

The waitress brings the check, and I fish out my wallet and pay, ignoring her offer to split it. We head back to her car and I hold her hand as we walk. When I squeeze her hand, she squeezes mine back.

"So… what are your thoughts on moving?"

Chapter Thirteen

EMILY

I PICK AT MY OUTFIT AS I STARE AT MY REFLECTION AND consider changing for the twelfth time. Sam's been flirting with me all morning by text and helping me decide. I think he just likes looking at my butt because he always asks me to text him photos of the back when I try on a skirt or dress that's fitted. My phone chirps, and I read his message.

> SAM
> That's perfect, baby. No panties.

> EMILY
> Keep wishing

I roll my eyes as I text him back, smiling down at my phone. There's zero chance of me going without a nice full-coverage pair of slick panties the day after a heat ends when gravity is still making things messy. The skirt is a fitted black pencil skirt, and I've paired it with a white satin blouse. The high neckline fastens at my throat, and the sleeves are short. I put on a pair of gold earrings and slip into my heels.

You're such a dork lol

That's hot

Wanna spank me later?

You'd like it too much

I'm ready

Are you here yet?

Your carriage awaits, baby.

I have butterflies in my stomach when I turn my lights out and head to the door, locking it behind me, and walk out to the parking lot outside of my apartment. I sling my bag across my body and put away my phone and keys.

This is a nice restaurant. Fancy. Expensive. I hope this outfit is classy enough.

Sam's chariot is a motorcycle. He sits on it, his thighs spread wide for balance, and holds a helmet out for me. He's wearing black on black with a nice dress shirt tucked into slacks and his black leather jacket on top of it.

I stop in my tracks. "You specifically told me to wear a short dress or skirt."

"Yeah, it's kind of always been a fantasy of mine to have a hot woman get on my bike and hold on to me while her tight little skirt rides up her thighs."

I take the helmet when he hands it to me and stare at it. "This is going to mess up my hair and makeup. You know that, right?"

His face falls. "Oh, shit. I'm sorry, baby. I'm an idiot. Did you want to drive? I don't have a car, only my bike. Or we can call a taxi if you think you'll want to drink."

I glance between his sleek motorcycle and my shitty, ancient commuter car. The paint is rusted and chipped, and every side's been dented over the years. There's no way I'm driving that to this restaurant. That's embarrassing. And if we wait for a taxi, we're going to be late. Plus I've never been on a motorcycle before. It's… tempting. I'm trying new things now, apparently. Maybe the new Emily rides on motorcycles with her future packmate?

"No, it's fine. Can you help me put it on and tuck my hair in, though?"

Sam helps me get the helmet on and tucks my hair up so it won't get messed up by the wind. I'll fix my makeup when we get there if we have to. He holds the bike steady as I climb on and figure out how to get my feet up out of the way. I do need to hike my skirt up a bit. I grab him around the middle and hold on to him, my fingers laced together over his stomach.

He reaches back and grabs my thigh and squeezes it, then starts his bike and kicks up the stand and zips through the parking lot toward the exit. It's thrilling. The wind whips at us as the bike rumbles underneath us. There's a spike of anxiety mixed with the hitch of anticipation and the warm glow of euphoria.

We weave through traffic and I relax into it, melding against Sam as he drives us across town. When we pull in, he drives through the valet loop and parks his bike himself. Getting off the bike is harder than getting on. He gives me a hand as I step onto the gravel and pull my skirt back down, and then he helps me take the helmet off and I check my hair and makeup in the side mirror of a black sedan.

"Ready?" He offers me his arm and we walk into the restaurant. It's stunning. A chandelier made of squiggly bits of glass stuck together in a ball hangs in the foyer. The walls and ceiling are white on white with wainscoting and trim on every panel. Glass and brass sconces drop from the high ceiling. The floor is wood with different colored woods set in a repeating pattern that looks like twelve-pointed stars.

The hostess is dressed in a tight black dress with her hair twisted in a chignon and bold, red lips. She greets us with a polite smile. "Can I help you?"

"We're meeting someone," Sam says. "I'm not sure if they're already here. The name is Orello."

She checks her list, her smile brightening. "Right this way. Would you like to use our complimentary coat check?" She brings us to a stop by the coat check kiosk, and Sam hands over his leather jacket and helmet. If they find the whole thing odd, they don't let on.

The moment I see Marcus and Tom sitting at a white tablecloth covered table and drinking a glass of wine it's like all the wind is knocked out of me at first glance. Like I can't breathe because they're so beautiful. It's the same feeling you get when you see a stunning painting or a perfect sunset.

Sam's hand at the small of my back keeps me walking forward. When they see us coming, they stand and Marcus moves to pull my chair out for me to sit.

"This restaurant is lovely," I say as the hostess leaves us. *That's a lot of forks for one setting. Are these all mine?* The menu is a single piece of printed paper set on my stack of five plates. *Why are there so many empty plates? Rich people are weird.*

"A client took me here for our meeting and I quite enjoyed the meal," Marcus says in his deep, rumbly voice.

I don't know where to look. They're all so handsome in their own way, and being surrounded by all three of them is a bit like staring into the sun. So I stare at the menu as if I need to keep re-reading the same seven main courses they offer.

"What do you do for work?" Sam asks them.

"Marcus is in finance, and I'm a photographer," Tom answers.

"I manage brokerage accounts. I followed in my father's foot-steps," Marcus adds. "That's actually how Tom and I met. My father worked for his. They were kind enough to let us use their carriage house in England for the summers when we went over to visit family. Tom and I got up to a lot of mischief in those days."

I can almost picture it. A young Marcus and Tom running about the English countryside. Probably catching frogs and sticking them in someone's bed. "That sounds lovely."

Tom snorts and adjusts his tie, leaning back in his seat. "Lovely? Hardly. He tried to drown me."

Marcus sighs. "I convinced him to help me take the old boat out onto the lake so we could stargaze and we fell asleep in it. It turns out it wasn't seaworthy anymore. It sank. While we were still in it." He turns in his seat toward Tom. "How was I supposed to know you couldn't swim?"

Their banter makes me smile. You can tell that they tell this story often. That it's a fond memory of a misbegotten youth.

"What do you do for work, Emily?" Tom asks, ignoring the question. He takes a sip of wine and sets his glass down. *God, his eyes are piercing.* They're so green they're hard to hold.

"I work in an office. It's not really exciting. I'm a member manager for an insurance company. It's mostly phone calls and paperwork. But you're a photographer? That's so cool. What kind of photos do you take?"

"Nudes."

"Umm." I busy myself with taking a sip of water while my face burns.

"Behave," Marcus growls under his breath.

The sound of his deep, rumbly voice pitching that low reminds me of our time together during my heat. I remember it in snippets that are jumbled. But I distinctly recall that voice. I fidget in my seat and find myself growing damp, and I'm grateful I ignored Sam's suggestion and wore the slick panties. I stare at the bread basket and fidget as I wonder if it's bad enough that I need to excuse myself to the ladies' room to mop it up with some toilet paper.

"I am," Tom says, sounding huffy. "I didn't tell her what *sort* of nudes."

"I definitely want to see them," Sam says, digging into the bread basket and ripping a roll open before slathering it in butter. He takes a huge bite and chews.

"I'll send you some links," Tom says.

Our waiter comes by and saves me from the discussion as he takes our order and tops off our carafe of water. The conversation stalls even after the waiter leaves to put our order in.

"Emily wants a baby," Sam says suddenly.

Marcus chokes on his wine, coughing, while my mouth drops and I stare at Sam in shock and horror with my jaw on the floor.

"Sometimes it's better to rip the bandaid off, baby. Otherwise, we were gonna dance around the elephant in the room the entire meal, and I really want to enjoy my steak."

"We've discussed it," Tom says. "First, I want to apologize for how we… handled that. We should have been more prepared. This is new to us, and we're flailing in the dark a bit, but that's no excuse."

"No, it was my fault," Marcus says. "I should have kept my wits about me better instead of getting rut for brains. I'm sorry that we initiated that conversation so tactlessly." He grabs Tom's hand, threading their fingers together. "We talked, and we decided it was something we'd like if you're open to it."

Tom puts his other hand on top of theirs and squeezes. "We almost adopted once, you know. We had the paper for the agency filled out, but… we work and travel so much. There never seemed to be a good time. But there never will be, will there? It's something you need to do and trust you'll figure it out as you go. And we'll hire a nanny, of course, to help. I know I gave you the impression this was a thing I was against, and I'm not. I needed to feel like I'm a part of the decision-making process. Especially something as important as children."

"Of course," I say. Relief washes over me, and I realize how tense I felt. How important this is to me now that I've acknowledged it. *Children*, he said. Not just one baby, but possibly more. *They want me and my babies.* "And it wouldn't be something that has to happen right away." In fact, it probably shouldn't. "We still have a lot to get to know about one another."

"And a lifetime together to learn it," Tom says.

"Well said," Marcus says. He brings their combined hand to his mouth and kisses Tom's knuckles, and warmth pools in my belly at this brief moment of open tenderness.

The waiter comes and pulls out a tray stand, setting his loaded tray on top of it. He goes around our table, taking our topmost stacks of plates away and putting our meals down. We eat and make easier conversation, and I devour every bite of my pumpkin ravioli.

Everything is pleasant until it's not. I've eaten too much, too fast, and my stomach churns. I take slow, measured breaths as I fight off the nausea and realize I'm losing the battle, so I ball my napkin up and set it on the table and stand, interrupting their side conversation. "Excuse me."

The bathrooms were by the coat check, I think. I weave around milling waiters and patrons as I try to make it before I lose it all over the lobby floor, embarrassing myself in such a nice restaurant and mortifying myself in front of Marcus and Tom. *There!* I shove the door open and push into a stall, my knees hitting the cold tile with a smack as I lean over the toilet and gag. Nothing comes up, but my stomach bounces inside of me like a beach ball as I dry heave and saliva pools in my mouth.

"Sir, that's the ladies' room!" a woman shouts.

Sam barges in, not caring one bit. He finds me hunched over and heaving. He bends over me and gathers up my hair in a fist as he hovers.

When it seems like it was a false alarm and my stomach settles, I sit on the cold bathroom floor and lean back against Sam. I keep my eyes closed and wait for the nausea to pass, as it always does once my body decides it's not going to bring everything back up after all. "I think I'll be okay in a moment if I sit here for a bit."

"It was probably the cream sauce," he says.

I groan and spit my excess saliva into the toilet, and he helps me stand. The tile is slick and my heels are high, and I'm struck by the urge to lie down and nap.

"You're still recovering. Let's get you home so you can rest."

I ruined this—we were having such a good time—but I can't find it in me to argue. Sam walks me out of the bathroom, ignoring the annoyed staff as he sets me down on a bench in the entryway and gets his helmet and jacket from the coat check lady.

Marcus and Tom see us from the other end of the restaurant and come over. "Is everything all right?" Tom asks. Marcus looks stricken, as if my dry heaving is a personal mark against his alpha scorecard.

"Yes, I'm fine. I'm sorry for ruining lunch. The food *was* excellent. I ate too much and... I'm still adjusting to solids. I'll be fine."

"I'm gonna take her home. I'll call you once she's settled in bed," Sam says.

"What is that?" Marcus asks. He's staring at the motorcycle helmet, his dark brows furrowed.

"My bike helmet."

"You drove her here on a motorcycle?" Marcus says the words so calmly, but his voice gives a dark undercurrent of menace to his words that makes my spine snap straight. His scent shifts, the spiced creamy-sweet blend of his pheromones turning spicy. It's like having to sneeze, but nothing comes out.

"Yes."

Yes is the wrong answer. Marcus grabs Sam by the elbow and pulls him outside. The door swings shut so I can't hear what they're saying, but Marcus towers over him, his face furious, and Sam's shoulders round as he takes the angry alpha's ire.

"Umm... is everything okay?" I ask, fidgeting.

Tom watches it all through the glass with his hands shoved into his pockets. He doesn't seem alarmed. "Sam is getting dressed down for endangering you."

"But he's a good driver." I have the urge to defend him because I never felt unsafe on his bike. He didn't speed or take sharp turns or drive erratically.

"We've been waiting for a long time to find you, Emily. Marcus won't do anything to risk your safety. He might be over-bearing for a bit as we all adjust. It's his nature. He's very protective of the people he considers his."

His. Theirs. My belly swoops, and this time it's not nausea causing it.

"Come. Let's get you home." Tom holds a hand out for me and pulls me to his side. We go to the hostess stand and wait for her to get off the phone. His hand settles on the small of my back, my body feeling warm where he's touching me. His faint scent is comforting. I lean against him, soaking it in, and more of my queasiness settles.

"Good afternoon. My partner needs a car to take her home. Thank you."

My partner.

While she's calling the car service, we turn and watch Marcus lecture Sam. It's like watching someone yell at a golden retriever puppy for peeing on the carpet. Sam bends his neck and takes it.

"What do you think he's saying?" I whisper.

Tom's hand slides to my hip as he pulls me against him. "How dare you endanger my precious omega, the future mother of our children? She should be wrapped in bubble wrap and fed ice cream with a golden spoon."

I snort. "Please tell me you guys don't actually own any golden spoons."

"I may have to talk Marcus out of adding a set to our registry."

I look up at him and study Tom's profile. He's a handsome man. As tall as an alpha, but lean and with a quiet strength instead of brawn and bite. He keeps his jawline more clean shaven than Marcus, who seems to always sport some degree of stubble. Long, dark eyelashes frame his piercing green eyes. *Why do men always have the prettiest eyelashes? It is seriously not fair.*

"We have a registry?"

"Oops. Let that slip, did I?" He looks at me and grins, then winks, and I forget how to breathe. "It's mostly for the family. So they have something to spoil us with. Everyone is excited. They can't wait to meet you both."

Oh, God. They've told everyone already. The idea of being

swarmed by so many new family members makes my neck itch. I'm not just adding one set of in-laws, but three. It's daunting.

"Do you both have large families?" I ask. There's still so much we have to learn about each other.

"Marcus has a sister who owns a bakery in the city. I'm an only child, but I have many cousins. We see them once every few years, sometimes at Christmas and other times in the summer. I think this coming Christmas is supposed to be in England. Marcus would know for certain. He's the one who keeps track of those details. Have you ever been?"

"To England?" I've never left the state let alone the country. "No."

"We'll rectify that then. You'll love it during Christmas. And we'll do all the terrible tourist things that are absolutely mandatory for someone to do on their first trip to London. If you're very good, and by that I mean incredibly naughty, you might even convince me to go down to Bath and see Stonehenge and the Roman baths. They have a Christmas market and these sweet buns that are sort of like a brioche and… Well, you'll have to try one and tell me what you think."

I try to imagine what that sort of life will be like. Living in New York City. Taking Christmas trips to London. It's exciting and terrifying. Marcus pulls Sam into a bear hug and pats his back.

"Looks like they're done."

Marcus holds the door open as Sam ducks inside.

Sorry, I mouth at him. He rubs his hand through his hair, messing it up, and shrugs, looking sheepish.

"I've called her a car," Tom says. "Oh, I think that's it."

A sleek black Town Car pulls up to the valet stand and idles. Sam presses a kiss to my cheek and whispers for me to text him when I'm safe at home, and then Marcus comes up next and holds out his hand for me to take. Tom takes his arm from around my waist and ghosts it down my ass, giving a cheek a squeeze before he lets me go.

Marcus curls his fingers around my hand and leads me to the door, holding it open. The driver gets out and comes around to get the car door for me. When I'm settled on the seat, Marcus shoos the driver off and leans in. His enormous body fills the whole doorway as he presses a kiss to my forehead.

"I hope you feel better soon. If there's anything you need, let me know and you'll have it."

"I will." He shuts the door and stands there while I give the driver my address and he pulls away. Tom and Sam come up and join him as they all see me off, and I spend the entire ride home wishing I hadn't gotten sick and ruined it because there's so much I want to learn about them.

At home, my key sticks in the lock until I shimmy it and push at the same time so it opens. I lock it behind me and drop my purse on the coffee table and collapse on my sofa, kicking my heels off and lying down as I get a pillow into place. My stomach settles once I'm horizontal for a bit and I debate what I want to watch as I fish my phone out of my purse and text Sam that I'm home. Marcus and Tom will want a text too, but I realize that I don't have their phone number. *Wasn't it on the paperwork?*

The folder's on my coffee table, unopened since I got home. It feels invasive and weird to read it now that I know they're not kidnapping murderers. Like an invasion of privacy. But if they're my packmates then it's stuff I should know, right? Even if we haven't had a ceremony or marked each other. Deep inside of me, I know they're mine. The feeling scares me. Like looking down at the drop before you let go of the rope swing and let yourself fall into the lake. You know you're going to fall, and you know the water will catch you, but your heart still races when gravity takes control.

I'm overthinking things again. Exactly like I did when it took me four terrible heats to work up the courage to go to the free clinic instead of roughing it at home.

Plenty of people jump all in when they find their packmates. But I've never been an impulsive person, and it's difficult to break old habits even if everything inside of me is screaming to let go and enjoy it. Let them spoil me if they have the money for it. Let them take me on fancy vacations abroad. But I draw the line at the golden spoons. That's absolutely ridiculous.

At the very least I need to thank them for lunch. I find Marcus's number on the form and send him a text. Should I mention the end? Maybe apologize for ruining things? But I don't want him to think about how mad he got at Sam. I decide not to bring it up at all.

EMILY

> Hi. It's Emily. Thank you for lunch. The restaurant was lovely.

MARCUS

It was wonderful to see you again, sweetheart.
How are you feeling?

> A lot better

> The first day back to normal is always the worst

> I'll be fine tomorrow

Good to hear. When do you go back to work?

> Tomorrow. I work until five thirty.

We can stay until Wednesday, but then we have to return home.

Wednesday. But that's so soon. It's hardly any time at all. Rationally, I know they have lives to return to. Their home is in New York. They have careers, friends, and family. Marcus was only here on a business trip. Of course they have to go home. But I didn't realize it would be so soon. I've never been in a long-distance relationship before, and the idea of being so far apart so early makes my chest pinch.

> We'd both love it if you came out to stay with us. See the city and spend time together. Both of you. As soon as you can.

I have to return to work. At least long enough to turn in my paperwork to take some FMLA for pack bonding. Twelve weeks should give us plenty of time to decide if this is working.

> How soon is soon?

> I can put in the paperwork tomorrow to take some time off from work

> Start packing.

I send him a heart emoji. Pink, not red. Because I'm not sure if we're at red heart emoji level yet, but fuck… I think we'll get there, and I'm happy and nervous and horny as hell about it.

But what about my plants?

I can't ask Lindsay to water them for potentially three months straight. And what if she kills them by overwatering them? I'm already worried that my monstera is getting root rot.

> I have plants. I'm not sure what to do about them.

> I've never been gone for a long time before.

> Bring them.

I hope you have a truck.

I don't, but I can hire one or we can hire you a
house sitter. Up to you, sweetheart.

I don't really like the idea of moving them recklessly. Moves
are stressful and my fittonia is a huge overly dramatic baby that
plays dead if you so much as look at her wrong. And a house
sitter will keep my place from getting broken into while I'm
gone, and keep spiders from moving in.

House sitter, please.

Give me your address. I'll handle it.

My belly flutters. I send Marcus my information, then switch
texts to Sam to share the news.

I'm going with them to NYC on Wednesday.
Say you're coming too.

SAM

Yessssss

Wanna help me pack?

I'm on my way

It only takes him twenty minutes to get to my place. I open
the door wide and tuck my hair behind my ear. He leans down
and presses a kiss to my lips and pushes around me.

Sam studies the plant wall in my living room, as everyone always does when they come over for the first time. "Wow, you've got a lot of plants. I can't even keep a cactus alive. My mom says I have a black thumb. Every plant I touch dies."

I shut the door and set the chain. "That's good to know." That means he's never, ever allowed to touch them. These plants are my babies. The thought of babies makes me hesitate as I realize that's something that is very much in my future now.

And that thought brings another realization with it. "Oh my God."

He backs away from my jade pothos whose leafy vines grow down my bookcase. "I didn't touch it, I swear."

"No, it's not that. Well, yes, don't touch my plants. *Ever.* But I just realized I never called my family." And I'm leaving town on Wednesday for weeks if everything goes well. They're gonna kill me.

"So call them now."

I'm dreading it, but I know it's the right thing to do. Delaying it only makes it worse. I call my mother, and she picks up on the fifth ring.

"Hey, honey. What's wrong?" she asks.

"Hi, Mom. Nothing's wrong."

"Really? You only call me when something's wrong, or you need something. Is it money? I told you that Boston is too expensive to live in with this economy. You should move back home. You know your dad and I are only getting older. It's hard to keep up with the yard work and snow. You could help us around the house, and then you wouldn't have to worry about money. Maybe you could save enough and get a house out here in Marlborough. You barely see Gabbi or your sister anymore, and she's starting preschool next month and—"

"Mom!"

"Well, don't shout at me, honey."

"I found my pack."

"You found your… Oh, honey, that's wonderful! Who is he? Or she. You know we don't judge. What's their name? What do they do for a living? We didn't know you were seeing anyone."

I roll my eyes and shove a hand through my hair. I can already feel the headache forming after two minutes of conversation with her. "There are three of them. Marcus and Tom and Sam."

"Three! Well… you always were oddly competitive with your sister. I'm so happy for you, honey. When do we get to meet them? Oh! Kevin, get in here! Emily found her pack! There's three of them! Three! THREE! Turn your hearing aids up! OUR DAUGHTER EMILY FOUN—"

I hold the phone away from my ear until she's done shouting at me. I don't know how she's never figured out that dad turns his hearing aids off when he wants a break from her. "MOM!"

"Don't shout at me, honey. I can hear you just fine. It's your father who keeps forgetting to change his battery. So when do we get to meet them?"

"That's why I called. I'm not sure. I'm going to take FMLA from work so we can spend some time bonding. We met, uh, *recently,* so everything is still new."

She heaves a wistful sigh in my ear. "I remember those early days. Enjoy them, honey. Why don't you guys plan to come over one of these weekends? We'll get the whole family together and celebrate. We can have a cookout! They eat meat, right? Because your father got a new smoker and he's been smoking everything that used to walk or swim or fly. Although I suppose if they're vegetarians he can smoke some eggplants or mushrooms or something. We'll figure it out. I can find a recipe online. Of course I'll make my—"

"They live in New York!" I blurt out.

The phone goes dead silent, and I jump at the chance to get

this all out before she can go off on another tangent. I'd email her instead, except she always forgets to check it. "They live in New York City. So I'm going to spend a few weeks with them while we get to know one another and bond, and then I'll let you know what we're doing."

"Well, I'm glad to hear that my daughter intends to keep me in the loop while she goes gallivanting off to another state for weeks at a time with three strange men she just met while your father can't even push the snow blower up the driveway anymore."

I rub my forehead as my headache pounds behind my eyes. It's like I'm being stabbed in the head with an icepick. "Olivia lives two blocks away from you. If you need help around the house, Mom, call her."

My mother sniffs. "Your sister's busy. She's a mom."

"And she has two mates. One of them should be able to push the snow blower for you. Or maybe you can hire a company to do it."

"Your father would never agree. He has his pride, you know. Well… I won't try to talk you out of it. Not even if you're going to be very far away and almost never see us again and probably get mugged on a subway. God knows, you're an adult and you have your own life to lead. Are you going to have kids?"

Sam goes into my kitchen and pulls open my fridge. He ducks his head inside and looks around, then pulls out two of my hard ciders. I watch him through the opening between the cabinets and barstool counter as he lifts his shirt up, exposing his abs, and uses it as a cushion while he twists the lids off. He brings them into the living room and hands me one, and we both take long pulls. Either he's read my mind or he can hear every word she says since she's used to talking loudly for my hard-of-hearing father.

"We are, actually. But I'm not sure when. We're figuring things out."

She sighs, which confuses me because she's always harping about how old I am and how it's harder to get pregnant for the first time at my age, even as a hyper-fertile omega.

"New York is an expensive place to live, especially when you have kids. The public schools are terrible so you're going to want to put them in private school. Is your pack going to be able to handle that? Maybe you should all think about moving up here. You'll need help once the baby's born. It's a lot harder than you think."

The idea of moving anywhere within a thirty-mile radius of my mother fills me with dread. The only saving grace I have is that she gets horribly car sick if she's in a car or on a train for over fifteen minutes and is terrified of planes.

I love her. But I love her like chocolate cake. It's wonderful when you want it. It's great when you have a bad day and need it or it's Christmas. But you wouldn't want to eat it every day for the rest of your life.

"They can afford it," I tell her. Oh, boy, can they afford it. But I am *not* telling my mother about the castle. Estate. Whatever the fuck it's called.

"Well, what do they do? I know nothing about them, and I'm just supposed to hand my baby girl over to them?"

I take another long pull of my cider until it's halfway gone. "Marcus works in finance. He's a brokerage account manager. Tom is a fine arts photographer. He does… portraits. And Sam is in healthcare."

"Emily," my mother says, her voice dropping so low I can hardly hear it.

"What?" Okay, now she's got me scared. My mother hasn't talked below a soft scream for at least ten years.

"Get pregnant right away. At your age, you can't afford to put it off too much longer anyway. Trust me. You never really have a man hooked until you're carrying his baby."

"Oh, God, Mom! I am not going to have a trap baby."

She sighs and goes back to her normal voice. "I can't believe my little girl is getting bonded! You know, you always were late to everything your entire life. I was in labor with you for twenty-three hours, and you came a week past my due date."

When my mother tells birthing stories, it's time to get off the phone. "I love you, Mom. Don't worry about me. I am *not* going to get mugged. I'll talk to you later. Bye!" I have the phone up before she can think of five million other things to tell me and toss it onto the sofa so I don't have to look at it.

Sam's eyes are wide. I have no doubt he heard all of that.

My jaw works side to side as I try to ease the tension from clenching my teeth. "You know… moving a five-hour car ride away from my mother is looking like a fantastic idea."

"YEAH. OKAY, SO LET'S GET YOU PACKED."

Sam helps me go through my outfit. He makes me model a few for him, mostly so he can grope me in them. The pencil skirts are his favorite and I work in an office, so I own a lot of them. He rifles through my underwear drawer and manages to find every single thong in my cluttered drawer with some sort of supernatural thong hunting instinct.

"Give me that!" I yank the black lace thong out of his grasp and shove it into my suitcase with the rest he's snuck in there.

"Are you wearing one right now? I should check." He grabs me around the waist and hauls me to him, one arm banding across the small of my back as he pulls my skirt up my thighs and fondles my ass.

"No, I'm not, and you know why."

"Hmm." He rubs the crack of my ass through my slick panties. "Because you're still leaking our cum? Let me check."

Sam tugs my panties to the side and slips a finger between my cheeks, stroking lower as he finds my slit and rubs. I'm wet, my slick still producing at a heightened level as my body works all the cum I've been soaked with for the last three days out of me.

He grazes my clit as I arch against him and moan, pressing my pussy against his hand as I push my ass out in search of more. He dips a finger into my hole and fucks it in and out of me.

"Put your heels back on. And can you put your hair up in a bun really quick?" he asks.

"What?"

Sam stops fingering me and disappears into the living room. He comes back with my heels and slips them onto my feet, then grabs a hair tie off my nightstand.

I take it and throw my hair up in a messy bun. "Satisfied?"

"Do you have any glasses?" When I shake my head no, he hooks my panties and tugs them down, then helps me step out of them and tugs my skirt back down into place.

"Miss Thorne, I am very disappointed with your typing this week."

I blink at him until it registers that he's slipping into a role-play scenario. Oh. Oh! "I'm sorry, sir. What seems to be the problem?"

"There were six misplaced commas and four typos. You're clearly not paying attention when you work. I'm afraid I'll need to enact a correction."

"I see. What sort of punishment did you have in mind?"

He grabs me by the hips and spins me around, then presses a hand down between my shoulders as he bends me over the edge of the bed. "The corporal kind, Miss Thorne. Lift your skirt and take it with grace. Ten strikes. One for each mistake. That seems fair, doesn't it?"

"My skirt, sir?" I look over my shoulder at him, a strand of hair falling out of my messy bun. I need to buy a pair of fake glasses pronto.

"Yes. It's not a punishment if it doesn't hurt. I'll deliver the blows to your bare bottom for maximum impact. Maybe in the future you won't be so careless about your typing."

I bite my lip, his eyes tracking the movement, as I wiggle my tight pencil skirt up until my wet cleft and ass are exposed.

"Miss Thorne, why aren't you wearing any panties? Is this why you've been so distracted lately during our meetings?" He grabs my cheeks and pries them apart, the air cool on my wet slit as he exposes it. "Oh, look at how wet you are. Clearly you're enjoying this. Spanking you won't be much of a punishment if you're enjoying it."

"It's not my fault, sir. I can't help it. The truth is... I find you very handsome."

"Hmm."

"Can I make a confession, sir?"

"This is the best time for it, Miss Thorne, since you're already going to be punished."

"Sometimes at lunch after we've spent all morning together, I touch myself in the bathroom."

"Where do you touch yourself? Show me so I know how bad your behavior has been."

I reach a hand between my legs and find my clit, getting my fingers wet with slick as I rub and roll it until I'm fidgeting and pleasure tightens into need in my belly.

"Such vulgar sounds you make, Miss Thorne. It's very unbecoming behavior for my secretary. That type of wantonness deserves to be punished."

"Please punish me, sir." I stroke my clit faster and harder and let out a filthy moan. He's hard, his dress slacks tented with the state of his erection, and all I can think about is him fucking me.

It doesn't matter that we've been going at it nearly nonstop. Finding my mates has lit a fire in me that threatens to consume me. Their pheromones have dumped gasoline on this heat's cinders.

"Hands flat on the bed, Miss Thorne. Get ready to receive your correction."

Biting my lip to hold back my grin, I put my hands flat on my bed and push my ass out.

The first smack to my bottom is light, but the second one stings, and when it fades it leaves heat behind. He spanks the other with two strokes to match, then slaps them both at the same time. I cry out, the force of his last blow making my knees hit the edge of the bed.

"This is for your own benefit, Miss Thorne."

"Thank you, sir."

He spanks me again, his palm leaving heat and warmth and pleasure as he strikes the shape of his hand into my flesh.

"How many strikes was that, Miss Thorne? I hope you've been paying attention."

I struggle to count them. "Five… no, six, sir."

"Very good, Miss Thorne. It appears you can pay attention when you're properly motivated. Perhaps there's some hope for you as my secretary yet. Four more strokes for your grammar, and then we'll attend to your wantonness."

"Thank you, sir."

His palm hits me, harder than he has before, then follows it with another blow until all I can feel is the sting and the heat. He lights a fire inside me with every smack.

Nine.

Ten.

When it's done, he drags his trimmed nails over my sensitive skin until I wiggle and gasp. "Here is your last punishment, Miss Thorne."

The sound of his zipper sliding open is loud. The blunt tip of his cock slicks through my folds twice, then notches at my entrance and thrusts to the hilt. It's a hard entry that knocks the air out of me, my knees hitting the bed as he fucks into me. The metal teeth of his zipper scratch at the sensitive reddened skin of my ass. My body clenches tight around him as if to trap him there. To hold him there, deep in my pussy, rutting up against my womb where he belongs.

"Miss Thorne, do you still feel the urge to touch yourself between the legs?"

Fuck. God, yes. I want to come. "I do, sir. I want to touch myself and come on your cock."

He leans back and slaps my ass. "Such filthy language, Miss Thorne. It's not befitting my secretary. Perhaps you need to work this naughtiness from your system so you can behave and be a good girl again."

"I think you're right, sir." I reach between my legs and pull my skirt up higher, then sink my hand between my folds and stroke my clit. It's too much. Too much sensation, too much pain, too much pleasure, too perfect. His dress pants rub against my chaffed bottom as he fucks me over my bed and then I'm coming, my pleasure taut and coiling before it snaps.

I cry out, my walls fluttering as I come on his cock and he fucks me, still going, heedless of how sensitive I am now as he takes what he wants from me and seeks his own pleasure. Using my cunt like it's his. Like he owns it.

"Are you ready for your last punishment?" he asks, his breathing hard and his pace battering.

"Yes, sir. Punish me. I deserve it. I've been a very naughty girl."

Sam comes with a grunt, his pace slowing as he fucks me deeper, shoving his way to the end of me as his cock juts and spasms with each hot pulse of seed. He drags his cock in and out of me, using my pussy to stroke the last pump of cum from his balls until there's nothing left and he groans, as satisfied as I am.

He glides a hand over my reddened ass and back, petting me. "Fuck, baby, you're so goddamn hot. I love you."

My eyes pop open as I struggle to process what he just said and if he meant it. It's early. Too early. Right?

Sam hisses in a breath and gives one last pump into me, then withdraws. He spreads my cheeks apart to watch me contract my muscles and push our mixed cum and slick from inside me.

"Stay right there," he says, and then he walks away. The tap runs for a moment and then he comes back with a damp towel and wipes me down.

I pull my skirt down and sit on the bed as he takes the messy towel to the laundry hamper in the bathroom. When he comes back, he cups my face in his hands and kisses me, then asks if I want to finish packing.

When my bags are bursting with clothes and necessities, I change into pajamas and he takes his dress shirt and pants off and borrows one of my old oversized band tees and wears it with his boxer briefs. We lie down together on the sofa and cuddle and watch bad TV.

"Chinese or Thai?" he asks during a commercial.

"Hmm?"

"For dinner." He plays with my hair, pulling it from its messy bun so he can run his fingers through it and bring it to his nose to smell. "I figured pizza's out since you didn't react well to dairy. Chinese or Thai should be pretty safe. Are you okay? You seem a bit distracted. Are you still thinking about how your mom reacted?"

"Either is fine. I'm just thinking about something you said while we were…"

His hand stops carding through my hair. "Did I take it too far?"

"No, it's… I liked all of that, the roleplaying and the spanking, but at the end you said you loved me. And I know sometimes in the heat of the moment people say things, so—"

"I do love you, Emily."

My heart flutters against my ribs like a songbird beating at its cage. His eyes are warm, and his expression is serious. He means it. "Even though it's only been a few days?" Not to mention that I've spent half that time delirious from my heat.

"I don't hold back my feelings, Emily. My dad died when I was nine. He went out for a jog and it was hot, so he jumped into our pool to cool off. He dropped dead at thirty-four of a heart attack from the shock. After that, it was me and my mom and her sister. Growing up without him was hard. I learned not to hold back my feelings or not say I love you because you never know when it might be your last day. If there's something I want to do, I do it. If there's something I want to say, I say it. So when I tell you I love you, I fucking love you with every single part of me. We don't live and love on anyone else's timeline but our own."

The pain of what he must have gone through rips me up. "I'm so sorry about your dad. It sounds like that was really hard."

He presses a kiss to my forehead and goes back to playing with my hair. "It was. It's okay if you can't say it back yet. I'll say it for the both of us. When you're ready, I'll be there. I love you, baby. I love how kind and sweet and caring you are. How you nibble on your lip when you want to say something but think you shouldn't, and how you get that little crease between your eyebrows. How you eat my food—"

"That was one time!"

"Is it, though? You strike me as a food thief. It's okay. I don't mind. I'll just order enough for both of us and you can have half. Oooh, right there. That face. I love it when you pout. I think I love your pouty face almost as much as I love your orgasm face. And your boobs. And your butt."

Twisting, I give him a light slap to the stomach. He grabs my hand and drags it to his mouth, pressing a kiss to the heel of my hand. "I love you, baby. And I love that I'll get to prove it to you every single day. I'm going to love our baby... and I'm *really* going to love practicing making that baby until you're ready to get knocked up."

My face and ears grow hot. "You're terrible."

He tucks my head under his chin and hugs me tighter to his chest as we both ignore the movie we're not watching. "I'm a terrible, horrible brat. Do you have a ruler? You should punish me."

I laugh until my eyes water.

His next words are soft, and he rubs my back as he says them. "I'm sorry that your mom doesn't seem to think about your feelings. I know she probably loves you in her own way, but... that still sucks. I'll give you a fifty percent stake in my mom if you want. She's awesome, and you know she really likes you when she bakes you snickerdoodles."

"That sounds really nice. I like cookies."

He leans down and presses a kiss into my hair, inhaling deeply. "So... we never decided. Chinese or Thai?"

Chapter Fourteen

EMILY

I'm late to work because Sam wouldn't let me leave bed until he'd *eaten breakfast* before leaving to get his own packing done. I slip into my cubicle and throw my purse into the filing cabinet and boot up my computer. People walk by sipping their coffee or running papers around, and it seems like they all stop and say hello and wish me a good morning, and I keep thinking *they know*.

That they know I spent the whole holiday weekend getting railed by *strangers*. That I've had more dicks inside of me in the last four days than I have all year. That I found my pack. But none of them say anything—and of course they don't because that's crazy, and I need to stop imagining that every single person who asks how my holiday weekend was isn't secretly fishing for details on the dicks. Quantity, size, and shape.

At lunch, Lindsay corners me, but the break room is crowded because we're eating at a reasonable hour for once and we have to talk in girl code.

"How'd it go?" she asks.

"Great. Really great, actually." I take a bite of my sandwich, glad that my stomach is finally feeling back to normal.

"Everything you thought it would be?"

I think of the rut room with the padded stocks and the stirrups and the endless line of anonymous alphas. I think of Marcus finding me, then fucking me until I passed out so nobody else could visit my station. I think of Tom, who made me take both him and Marcus. At the same time. In my pussy. I think of Sam, who makes my heart race when he grins and that dimple forms and he says he loves me, even though it's only been a few days and that's crazy. My instincts are on overdrive, telling me to stay with them so they can keep me safe. I think that I'm quickly on my way to falling in love with them, and it's scary and thrilling. They're strangers. But I don't want them to be.

"Yeah? Girl, it must have been life-altering because you're glowing. That's good. You'll have to tell me all about it later. Oh! I went to that bar with a friend from college. Maybe we can all go together on Saturday."

Next weekend. The rut bar. *Shit.* "I can't."

"Okay," she shrugs and stabs her fork in her salad. "Maybe next weekend? We'll find a day when we're all free."

"No, I can't." I lower my voice since I haven't turned in my paperwork yet and I don't want it getting around before I talk to HR. "Because I found my pack."

"You… Oh my God, girl!" She hits me on the arm, and I wince and rub the spot. "Way to bury the lead! Next time you start with that, okay?"

"Shh." I glance around the breakroom. A few people looked over at us, but most have their noses buried in their phones. "I haven't gotten to go to HR yet because I was late this morning. I'm going to take FMLA and spend some time with them."

"Them?" She arches one brow and chomps on a slice of cucumber. "Spill it."

"Uh, yeah. There are three of them. Marcus, Tom, and Sam."

Her other eyebrow rises, and she eats the rest of her cucumber slice and then a cherry tomato. "Wow. When you finally do something, you go hard. Good for you."

When she smiles, some of my tension uncoils in my stomach. "Thanks. It's new and scary, but exciting and I'm happy."

"I want to meet them. We should all hang out together. I'm thinking about getting back with my ex. We could double date!"

"I thought you were going to that bar?"

She shrugs. "I could go either way. So this weekend? Or do you guys have plans?"

"Uh… so, funny story, actually. They aren't from here. Two of them aren't, anyway. Sam is. He was my… attendant. We're leaving for New York tomorrow."

She slaps me lightly on the arm again in the same spot.

"Oww!"

"You are the *worst* storyteller," she says.

"Fine. So Sam was my… spa attendant. And we… enjoyed the sauna together. And then Marcus came—"

"Yeah," she interrupts, snorting with amusement. "I'll bet he did."

I glare at her as she sips on her iced tea. "Anyway… Marcus came to the spa, and he realized we, uh… I'm running out of metaphors here."

"He planted his flag?"

I sigh. "Flags don't really have anything to do with spas, but right. He planted his flag, and we both felt like it was the right flag, so he called his partner Tom who flew in and… he planted his flag too." I leave out the part where they *planted their flags* in the same hole.

"That's a lot of flags in your golf course."

I level a look at her because she's far too amused by all of this. "It's a spa, not a country club."

"Some country clubs have spas in them."

I stand and push my chair in and grab my trash so I can toss it out. "I have to go to HR and fill out those forms. Do you want to hang out tonight before I go?"

"Yeah! Let's do that. Do you want to stay in or go out?" she asks.

"I want to pick up a new book for the trip. Want to go to the bookstore with me?"

She agrees and we set a time and location, and I walk to HR feeling lighter and happier. The woman in HR offers me congratulations and helps me fill out the forms. The paid leave is only a percentage of my salary, but it's enough to cover my rent and utilities while I'm gone, since I assume I won't be buying groceries or gas.

That night when I'm back home with three books shoved into my luggage, I take a moment to look around my apartment and make sure everything is in order. I clean out the old takeout and leftovers from my fridge so they don't spoil, and then I take out the trash before I dust and vacuum.

The house sitter will come over after I leave in the morning, so I write out detailed notes with phone numbers and the day that recycling comes, and then I look at my plant babies and write notes on post-its and stick them on each pot. I'll put a key under the mat in the morning. I almost don't care if she thinks I'm insane for giving her watering, feeding, and sunlight instructions for each plant. How else is she going to know that some of them get balcony time on the weekends? And I've had some of these plants since I was a teenager.

I am showered. My outfit for tomorrow is laid out. Sam helped me pick it and has forbidden me from changing it. Again. I am packed… and I can't sleep.

I'm too nervous about tomorrow. What if they change their minds? They're not gonna change their minds. What if I sleep through my alarm and I'm not ready when they come to pick me up? I set five more alarms spaced at various intervals ranging from three minutes to ten and give each one a different ring tone. There's no way I can sleep through that many. *Maybe I should start one of my books.*

My mind races too much to stay focused for more than a few paragraphs at a time, and when I realize I've read a few pages while absorbing nothing, I give up. I shove it back into my bag's exterior pouch.

My phone chirps with a text. "Oh, thank God." *Wait, what if they're canceling?*

SAM

Stop panicking

EMILY

It's who I am

Don't judge me

You need to relax

Wanna know what's very relaxing?

Orgasms?

I was going to say cookies you naughty girl but I like your idea better

Come outside and you can have both

He's here? I slip my feet into my ratty house slippers and head outside, not caring that I'm braless and wearing old, mismatched pajamas. My neighbors have seen worse.

Sam leans against his bike, and he's holding his helmet in one hand and a giant boxed cookie cake in the other. He grins when he sees me in my ratty band tee with holes and faded pajama bottoms with tiny penguins on them. He looks at me like I'm the most beautiful woman in the world, and it makes my pulse race.

"How did you drive your bike here with that?" The cookie cake is at least a foot in diameter.

"Carefully. I am a master of balance. Read it."

My brow wrinkles as I try to make out the icing writing. "Wanna puck?" It's hard to tell because the icing is written in cursive, and some of it's been smeared.

"The people at the cookie place weren't very amused by my request. And it turns out red icing stains, so swiping some of it off doesn't really work either."

He shows me his red stained finger, and I see where it looks like he tried to turn the P into an F. I burst out laughing, then kiss him. *What a dork.*

I take the cookie cake from him and we head inside. For the rest of the night, I'm not nervous at all.

"GOOD MORNING, LUV." TOM LEANS DOWN AND KISSES ME AS Marcus grabs my bags and hauls them to the car. If Marcus and Tom find it odd that Sam is with me at six in the morning instead of at his place, they say nothing.

I'm still not really certain how this pack thing works. Is there a schedule? Do I go down the line? Are we all supposed to be there? What if someone is out of town? It's one more thing to stress about.

By some miracle, Marcus manages to play car tetris and fits both of our overstuffed bags into his already very full trunk. It's impressive. Both in that Tom can pack so much for what they said was his two-week stint abroad, and that the trunk fits every-thing and still latches.

Sam leans into the front of the car through the open window. "Wow! It's so fucking cool. I've never seen one up close. Is this the XS or the XL model?"

"Touring," Marcus says as he puts my smaller car bag into the back seat. The back middle seat is the safest place according to crash test dummy experiments, he explains, and that's my designated seat. Tom wasn't kidding. I'm surprised there's no roll of bubble wrap waiting for me.

"Can I drive?" Sam asks.

Marcus snaps upright so fast he hits his head on the door-frame with a *thunk* that makes me cringe. "Not today."

"Fine. But someday, right? Hey, Tom, can I ride in the front?"

"Of course. If that's okay with Emily," Tom says.

Am I in charge of the seating assignment? "Yeah, that's fine." I hand my fluffiest pillow to Marcus, who puts it in the back for me. I fully intend to read, but car rides put me to sleep.

"Excellent," Tom says, sounding a little too pleased to be giving up the coveted front passenger seat. "Shall we?"

"Uh-huh." I narrow my eyes at him, but he only smiles wider. Somehow I feel like he's outmaneuvered us and we've already lost—and I didn't even know we were playing.

"Is that everything?" Marcus asks as he scans the sidewalk for more bags, as if the car could possibly fit anything else.

"Yeah, I think so." I tuck my hair behind my ear and take one last look at my apartment.

Tom and Sam both climb into their seats as Marcus cups my face and pulls me in for a kiss before he watches me get into the car and buckle my seatbelt. It's only when it's clicked that he shuts my door and gets into the driver's seat.

"Do you have enough leg room?" Marcus asks as he presses the ignition button and the dash lights up. The car is sleek and modern, and its engine doesn't rumble to life so much as purr.

My eyebrows climb my forehead because it's like he's forgotten how short I am compared to the rest of them. "Yeah, plenty of room."

As if that was what he was waiting for, he plugs our destination into the computer in the dash and the car drives itself while Sam oohs and aahs over it, and Marcus gives him a tour of the car's features while he keeps one eye on the road.

I wedge my pillow between me and the door and dig my book out of my bag. Tom appears content to watch the scenery through the window as we get onto the highway and merge into traffic. The car ride is smooth, and despite how early it is and how tired I am since Sam kept me *relaxed* until late last night, my book's able to keep my attention and I finally get past the first ten pages. There's music on low while Marcus and Sam bond over their love of cars, and it makes me happy to eavesdrop on their conversation until my book absorbs my full attention.

The heroine and her love interest have just discovered Mr. Pemberton's body in the secret tunnel connecting the manor's bedrooms when Tom's hand lands on my thigh and rests there with a comforting weight.

I peek at him from over my pages. He's still looking out the window and watching the scenery. I go back to reading for a few more moments. My plucky heroine and her scandalous rake have decided to investigate and solve the murder themselves.

Tom's hand rubs my thigh distractedly, and I'm reading the same sentences on repeat. *Is he…* His hand rolls inward and strokes my inner thigh, but he's still pretending to watch the tree line outside as he pulls my leg toward him on the backseat, spreading me.

When I don't protest or brush him off, he grows bolder. He strokes up my leg from knee to inner thigh, then drops the pretense all together as he rucks up the edge of my short dress until my panties are exposed.

I should put a stop to this.

My knees seem to fall open of their own accord as my book drifts toward my chest and his hand caresses my fabric-covered cleft. He strokes, teasing my slit until I get wet and soak through the thin material.

Marcus and Sam are still engrossed in their conversation as I slouch in my seat, giving Tom better access. He takes immediate advantage, his hand creeping inside my panties as he fingers me and spreads my wetness along my cleft. The first glide over my clit makes me whimper, and the game is up.

Sam glances back and does a double-take. "Hey, I didn't know car sex was an option or I wouldn't have given up the back."

"Car sex is always an option," Tom says, smug as he rubs me faster and harder until I'm wetter and the noises we make are louder, the need for staying quiet no longer necessary.

He presses one of his long fingers inside of me, and I rock my hips to meet him as much as my seatbelt allows. I moan and throw my head back against the edge of the seat as he fucks his finger in and out of me. The wet sounds I make grow louder than the low music playing in the background.

"God, that's so hot, baby. Put your leg up. If I have to watch instead of joining in, then let me watch for real."

My toes curl inside of my shoes as I wiggle against Tom's hand and spread my legs wider. Sam digs his phone out of his pocket and snaps a photo. "Get her panties out of the way. Let's see that pretty pussy."

Tom pauses his fingering of me, ignoring my moan of protest, to hook my underwear to the side. And then he goes back to stroking me, his long fingers making swirls around my clit as he rubs faster. Firmer. Tension pulls tight inside of me. I hold my breath as the moment stretches. My legs go so taut they risk cramping.

The shutter snaps and I come, moaning through my release as I unravel. Tom sticks two fingers inside of my cunt and I spasm around him, trying to milk a cock or a knot that isn't there. When I'm limp and sated, he pulls them out of me and leans forward so he can feed the taste of me to Marcus.

The sound of Marcus licking Tom's fingers clean and purring makes me even wetter, and I whimper as I sit more upright, my panties still askew. A passing motorist could see us. They could look in and see my lewd display. It's broad daylight, and I just got fingerfucked in a moving car.

But I can't bring myself to care when it feels so good.

"Find somewhere to pull over," Tom says, stroking my thigh again.

"There's a rest stop in three miles," Marcus answers.

"Perfect."

Good. I'll be able to use the bathroom and get cleaned up, otherwise there's a serious risk that the leather's going to get wrecked and Marcus probably loves this car. I tug my panties into place to stem the flow of my arousal and sit up, squeezing my legs together.

Where's my book? I pick it up off the floor and sigh. "You made me lose my place." I think I was somewhere around chapter eleven.

"I'll happily keep you entertained until we get home, luv."

I snort and instantly regret it, because my panties are soaked. I have an idea of what he'd find entertaining. Squirming, I end up sitting on one hip and crossing my legs. "I don't think this sedan is big enough."

He's undeterred from groping me as his hand settles on my thigh once more. I flip through my book until I find my place and slip the bookmark in, then tuck it safely away in the seat pocket.

"You'd be surprised what I can accomplish when I'm properly motivated," Tom says. He's grinning and no longer hiding his mischievousness. With a smile like that and his accent, it's clear he's used to getting away with absolute murder.

I side-eye him. "I'm not sure you need much outside motivation at all."

His grin widens, and then a few miles later we veer off to the right and head down the ramp to the rest area. It's a grassy, shaded area, but there are indoor bathrooms with vending

202 · ALEXIS B. OSBORNE

machines out front. Picnic tables and metal grills dot the land-
scape under shade trees. It extends further back then it appears at
first glance with an area off to the side for trucks and oversized
vehicles to park. It's there that Marcus pulls over and parks in the
back corner of the lot by an enormous maple. We pull off the
paved area and go onto gravel.

"We're parking pretty far away from the bathrooms," I say as
I sit up and look out the back window. There are a few people
around using the facilities or stretching their legs. An older
couple at the opposite end walks their small poodle mix as it tugs
at the leash and barks at the cars zipping by on the highway.

"Did you need to use the bathroom?" Marcus asks.

"Yeah, I need to get cleaned up unless you want a wet spot on
the leather."

"Wash up? Whatever for?" Tom asks.

Sam glances between them both as if he's not quite understanding what's up either.

"You want to wash up after I spent all that time so nicely
preparing you?" Tom asks.

My nipples harden and scratch against my lace bra.
Preparing. Preparing for what?

"It was thrilling, wasn't it, luv?" Tom undoes his seatbelt and
leans over me. "The rush of being naughty. Of doing something a
little forbidden and a whole lot of fun. Of taking pleasure when
you want it wherever you want."

I hesitate, knowing this is a trap, a game I don't fully grasp
the rules to, but also don't want to stop either. I remember how he
groped me in the restaurant as I was leaving, and my pulse quickens. It would be pointless to lie. I came hard and fast just now,
my panties wet with the evidence of exactly how much I
enjoyed it.

"It was."

He kisses me and strokes a hand over my collarbone, his

fingers dipping into the top of my dress to touch the swell of my breast. "You could have closed your legs. Taken my hand off your thigh. Told me to stop. But you didn't."

Tom takes my hand and guides it to his crotch while his lips tell me what he means without words. He doesn't just kiss me—he consumes me. His cock is already hard inside his pants. I trace the edge of his head, my thumb sinking into the divot of his slit.

He bites my lip, a light nip that makes me gasp, then takes my mouth like plundered conquest as he deepens our kiss. He could have slid his tongue against my lips and asked me to open for him. Instead, he took it.

His hand on mine falls away as I stroke him on my own, feeling him get impossibly harder and longer as his dick strains against his pants.

He breaks our kiss to drag his mouth down my jaw, my collarbone, my neck. He finds my scent gland and licks it, and I whimper. Blunt beta teeth scrape over the sensitive area, and then he sucks. Each pull of his mouth throbs between my legs until my clit pulses with each sucking tug and tongue stroke.

He grabs my knee and pries my legs apart, unhooking them, then sinks his hand between my thighs again to tease my soaked slit. I rock against him, grinding my cunt into my palm as he rubs me and kisses me until I'm breathing hard and ready to come again.

And then he stops, ignoring my whimper, and unfastens my seatbelt. Tom gives me a feral grin and opens the door, then steps out of the car.

"Where are you going?" *Why did you stop?*

He leans back in and grabs me by the hips, tugging me toward him until I'm halfway down the seat. Unbalanced, I fall back a bit. He presses a hand to my sternum and pushes, guiding me flat on my back so I'm lying down across the back seat, my legs bent and propped on it as I try to fit in the cramped quarters.

"Only making room, luv." Tom pulls me by my hips again until my butt hangs at the edge of the back seat, my heels pressed against my ass at the risk of dropping them to the rough ground below.

"You know you could have asked me to lie down," I say. When he strokes my damp panties again, my protests fade. He can toss me around like a rag doll all he wants as long as he doesn't *stop*.

"This is more fun." He unbuckles his belt and unzips his pants, then shoves them down his thighs. He lifts the edge of his shirt out of the way and strokes his cock. "Have you ever heard of dogging, luv?"

I lean up on my elbows on the narrow seat and watch how he touches himself. How he rolls his wrist when he gets to his tip. I study the motions so I can mimic them later. "No."

"I'm not surprised. It's more common in the UK than in America. I've never done it before, but it's always been a fantasy of mine. It's something you need more than one person to do properly. And I enjoy doing things properly or not at all."

He stops jerking himself and hooks his fingers into my panties and drags them down the curve of my ass. My thighs. My knees. He guides my feet through the holes and tosses them onto the floor of the car.

I'm bare, the open air cool on my wet slit as he traces his thumb over my seam the same way he thumbed his own dripping slit.

We're in public. Anyone walking this far out who looks will see what we're doing. They'll see Tom standing in the open doorway with his pants shoved down to his knees, his hard cock bobbing in the air as he spreads my slick along my lips and teases my clit.

Somehow, that only makes it hotter. The thrill of being watched, of being caught, makes my pussy ache to be filled.

He lines us up, and then he sinks into me with two insistent thrusts. His head drops forward, and he sighs as he does it again. He rolls his hips, thrusting faster and deeper as he fucks me where anyone might drive past and see.

I bite my lip to hold back my noisy moans and whimpers as he sets his pace and hits the mouth of my womb with each deep thrust.

"Fuck," Sam groans. "I can't see anything good."

"You weren't listening," Marcus says, chuckling. "Go wait for your turn."

"Oh, hell yeah," Sam says. His seatbelt is off, and he's out his door and then he slams it shut. He leans over Tom's shoulder to watch, one arm resting on the curve of the door frame as he grins down at me until his cheek dimples.

Tom pumps in and out of me, our wet, filthy fucking noises interspersed with the sound of birds chirping in the tree above us and car doors closing. The dog's no longer barking, but people are talking to one another from across the parking lot as they go on about their life a hundred feet away from where Tom's fucking me.

"I love watching you try to be quiet." Tom finds my clit and strokes, my body clenching around him as everything tightens.

"You're so hot, baby. Is he making you feel good?" Sam asks over Tom's shoulder.

I nod, not trusting myself to speak. As if letting the first sound out will release all of them like a pent up dam. My heart pounds in my temples as my breathing hitches.

Tom rubs my clit with rapid circles until I'm panting from the strain of holding still, staying quiet. "It makes me wonder what it will take to break you. Did you like being watched at the clinic? To have all those hungry eyes on you, eating up the sight of your slick-drenched hole as all those alphas took their turns rutting you until we found you?"

Oh, fuck, fuck, fuck.

My body clenches tight, and then the tight spring snaps and I come, my walls fluttering as Tom groans, heedless of the noise he's making or simply not caring as my release triggers his own. His cock jumps inside of me as he pulses, his seed drenching me as he pumps all of it deep inside and slows his pace, dragging it out. He digs his fingers into my hips and gives one last thrust, then withdraws and tugs his pants up as he steps back.

I lie there panting and dripping while Sam unzips his jeans and shoves them down to his knees. He gives his cock two tugs, and then he's ready and sinking into me, pushing his way in. He's careless of my aftershocks, of the way my body twitches as he hits my cervix and pulls out and thrusts again until he finds his rhythm.

I'm barely coming down from the first release when he starts to pound into me, to thrust the way he's learned I like as his balls slap against my ass. He's thicker, a little shorter, and he lacks the slight leftward curve Tom has. I think I'd know them all apart from one another, even in the dark. They leave their brand on me, inside of me, one by one.

Tom leans over Sam's shoulder and tuts. "She should have her tits out so we can watch them bounce. Darling? You haven't taken part in our little dogging adventure so far."

"You're right. Let's fix that." Marcus reaches into the back-seat and grabs the top edge of my dress, tugging and hooking the stretchy material under my breasts.

"Fuck, baby, you wore the lacy one?" Sam stops and pulls my breasts over the cups of my bra and pinches my stiff nipples, then goes back to fucking me. "God, you're so pretty," Sam groans. "I want everyone to look at you and see how pretty you are when you come and drench my cock with your slick."

"That's much better," Tom says. "It occurs to me that perhaps we should have access to all of her at all times. Maybe forbid her from wearing panties altogether?"

They wouldn't dare. I make a rough sound of protest.

Marcus rumbles, but his voice is so deep I can't tell if it's a low growl or a deep purr. A trickle of slick rolls down the crack of my ass at the sound of him, and I whimper as Sam plays with me, toying with my overly sensitive clit.

"I'll consider it," Marcus says. "It would be nice to bend her over and take her whenever and wherever we want."

It's too much. Too much sensation. Too much work trying to stay quiet. My toes curl in my shoes as I squirm, trying to get comfortable in the back of this car. It's awkward. There's nowhere to put my legs. Nothing to grab and squeeze and hold onto while they drag me under and drown me in pleasure. My shoe falls off and lands somewhere in the gravel—I don't know where. I don't care. An entire marching band could walk by, and I'm not sure I would notice.

Tom reaches between me and Sam and works my clit until it feels so good it hurts, and I don't think I can take it anymore without bursting. I press my face into the backseat of the car and use it to muffle my whimpers as I come.

Sam doesn't stop. He doesn't give me mercy and pause to let me come down or find a break to breathe. He fucks me until my legs are shaking and he pants with his efforts.

"Not all of them, though," he says. "She's got a crotchless one with a sequined heart that sits above the crack of her ass. Fuck, just thinking about it's enough to make me fucking *hnnng*—"

He comes, flooding me, and leans against the roof of the car until his cock stops twitching with each pump of cum he empties inside me. After he's caught his breath, he pulls out and spreads my labia apart to see their handiwork.

"Very nice," Tom says, dipping a finger into me. I clench

around the intrusion, more of their cum and my slick sliding down my ass to make a puddle underneath me.

They've wrecked me.

My chest heaves, I've bitten my lip a little too hard, my breasts are spilled out of my bra, I've lost a shoe, the cops are probably on their way by now for our lewd act of public indecency, and I'm wet and dripping with the cum of two men.

Fuck the upholstery.

They deserve to have stained leather for torturing me like this.

Marcus shifts in the driver's seat, opening his door and getting out. It slams shut, and my heart thumps in my chest, my breath hitching as he walks around to the open doorway I'm partially hanging out of. They move, making room for him, as he stops between my spread thighs. He fills the entire space, his broad frame blocking everything out.

Fuck, the way he drags his fingertips around the outsides of my thighs makes something tight clench tighter inside of me. Like he's proud. Like he's happy they've rutted and wrecked me on the side of the road for anyone passing by to see. Tom and Sam shift so they can watch from the sidelines.

His thumb slicks through my soaked folds and teases me until my hips rock against his touch, seeking more. I'm close again, impossibly hungry for it even without the haze of a heat to explain this raging desire that won't quench. It's them. Their pheromones. They've triggered this latent urge to bond. I whine when he stops, my lips pressed into a thin line to dampen the sound. To not get caught.

Marcus unzips his jeans, the metal zipper loud among the birdsong and dull roar of passing motorists, and shoves them down. He's hard, his big alpha cock getting thicker in his hand with every tug he makes, and then he notches himself at my entrance. His thrust is slow. Controlled. He hits the end of me and pushes, forcing me to stretch, to take him. It's a pleasure that straddles the line of pain without the heat delirium to soften its edges. If Tom and Sam hadn't warmed me up, it would hurt.

"You're so wet, sweetheart," Marcus says. "They prepared you so well for me."

From this angle, I can see each moment he seats himself completely. His huge cock makes my lower belly bulge as he fucks me gently with deep thrusts that nudge at my womb and fill me 'til I'm aching with him.

"You like being used like this, don't you? Like a good omega pleasing her pack?" Marcus asks.

I whine and nod, and he purrs as he fucks me, my other shoe dangling off my foot and threatening to fall with each jarring thrust. *Don't stop, don't stop, don't stop.*

"You take us so perfectly. Are you gonna take my knot, sweetheart?"

It's a terrible idea. We'll be tied for several minutes until he softens. Exposed. My body squeezes him as if it can clench his knot to life on demand from pure wanting. I need it in a way I've never needed anything more.

I nod again, a whimper leaking through my fingers, and my nails dig into the leather seat.

He plays with me while he fucks me, thumbs my clit until everything tightens and I have to slap a hand over my mouth to contain my moans. It's too much. Too much cock. Too many orgasms. I'm achy and tense, my legs trembling as his pace quickens. As his balls slap against my ass, he bends his knees to get a better angle. Marcus wraps his rough hands around my hips and tugs me to meet him, my butt hanging off the seat as he pulls me onto each thrust and holds me so tight his fingers make divots in my skin.

His pace changes, turning rough and steady, and then he groans and I feel the nudge of his growing knot against my entrance. It's a blunt, wide intrusion, and he presses it deep, the fat head of his cock making my belly bulge as he forces it in and locks it up tight against my cervix with his knot. He swells, my walls stretching to take the crushing width of him. To keep him there where he belongs as his cock pulses and he fills me with the first pump of cum.

Marcus drops his head and grunts as he empties himself into me, his eyes locked onto where my pink lips stretch wide around his flared base. How did I ever take two of them at once? I thought I was wrecked before, but I was wrong. Taken and filled by all three of them here on the side of the road, their cum running down my ass, I'm ruined for any others.

When he reaches down to thumb my cunt, teasing my tautly wrapped lips and playing with my clit, I pant against my hand. Aching and exhausted, he wrestles one last orgasm from me. It's a shuddering, weak thing, more of an aftershock, as my tired walls struggle to milk his knot. His grunt turns into a purr as his cock gives one last pulse.

"Wrap your legs around me and hold on," Marcus says before he leans into the car and pulls me out. I dig my heels into his ass and cling to him, hissing a breath between my clenched teeth as each slow step he makes toward the grassy wooded area tugs at where we're locked together. I wrap my arms around his neck and hold on tight.

He carries me over to one of the picnic tables and sits, arranging us carefully so I'm straddling his lap. My dress falls and covers our tie. I bury my face in his neck, breathing in his spicy, sweet scent. His rumbling purr vibrates his entire chest as he smooths his hands up and down my back and bottom.

Tom and Sam join us and stroke me too, petting my hair and pulling wayward strands out of my face. They rub their hands down my arms and thighs, rubbing all of our scents together. The only thing that could make this better is having a nest to curl into. I want us all to sprawl out and tangle together, all naked limbs and wandering hands. When I press my ear to his chest, his heart-beat makes a pleasant *thump* that floods me with calmness.

"How are you feeling?" Marcus asks.

"Mmm." I'm too spent for words. I settle for a gentle purr.

"Use my handkerchief," Tom says.

"Ready, sweetheart?" Marcus doesn't wait for my answer. He lifts me by my hips, his softening knot tugging deep inside me until he pops free with a gush.

I whimper at the loss of him as one of them presses a cloth to my leaking, dripping cunt. They soak it all up, capturing the cum and slick that runs out of me now that its stoppering dam is pulled out.

"That's so fucking hot," Sam says. "Push, baby."

I flex my tired muscles and work their cum out of me, and they pat me dry with the handkerchief until it's soaked. Tom reaches between us and adjusts my breasts back into my bra, giving each nipple a pinch first, and then he tugs my top into place so I'm covered.

"Do you think you can walk?" Marcus asks as someone slides my forgotten shoes onto my feet. I'm not sure when the second one fell off.

"I think so."

He helps me slide off his lap and stand, his big hands almost circling my waist as he makes sure I'm steady before he gets up too and uses the handkerchief to wipe himself down. Marcus tucks his soft cock away, and everyone rights themselves, adjusting clothing, while I make certain I'm decent. It doesn't escape my notice that they never gave me back my panties.

Fluids creep and shift with gravity, so I press my legs together to stem the flow. "All right. *Now* that you're all done rutting me like beasts, can I go wash up?"

Marcus grins and pulls me into a kiss, bending down to claim my mouth as I lift onto my tiptoes to meet him. I stroke his chest, marveling at the sheer power of him, at how gentle he always is despite his scary size. He palms my ass and tugs me up higher before finally letting me go, then swats me once. I yelp and dance away from him, rubbing the sting out.

"What was that for?" I ask.

"I already have two brats to deal with. You're not allowed to get mouthy too." Marcus smiles wider, the sight of his sharp alpha teeth turning my insides molten. He grabs me by the back of my neck and tugs me against his chest again, holding me there, his other hand rubbing my ass. "Be our good girl."

My heart stops and starts again at his words, and I bite my lip as I smile and press my face into him, hiding.

"Scared you'll get outnumbered?" Sam asks.

"Careful," Marcus growls. "Don't let your mouth write a check your ass can't cash."

Sam sputters. "What does *that* mean?"

I turn my head and watch their antics, my cheeks hurting from how much I'm smiling.

Tom throws an arm around Sam's shoulders and knocks into him. "That means when we get home, you're mine."

"Oh, fuck."

"Indeed." Tom's tone is thoroughly pleased.

I'm glad it's not directed at me. I'm not sure I could take many more surprises. I roll my eyes and tip my head back to look at Marcus, who is watching them with such a fond expression on his face. "Alpha, may I go get washed up now?"

It should chafe at me to ask. I'm a grown woman. I've never had a lover who demanded control outside of the bedroom. But I'm not scared. Full of anticipation, yes. But I know Marcus won't hurt me. I can feel it in my bones. I remember turning into an angry, feral thing, and how carefully he held me despite how I fought him. He's patient and caring.

Marcus presses a kiss to my forehead and releases me. "Yes, you may."

Sam stares at me with pink cheeks and a dimpled grin while Tom holds him in a headlock and ruffles his hair. Idiots, both of them. I smile and shake my head and make my way to the bathroom, scanning the faces of the people I see milling about when I get close. None of them pay any attention to me, and the worry knotted in my stomach loosens. Maybe we're not about to get arrested after all.

Yes, officers. This one right here. She's terminally horny and the men are perverts.

In the bathroom, I wet a couple of paper towels and bring them into the stall with me, wiping my thighs and between my legs before I pee. I gently pat dry because everything is getting a bit chafed without the clinic's healing oil or the barrels of slick my heat makes me produce.

I wash my hands and do my best to smooth my sex-rumpled hair with damp hands so it looks a little less like I just got fucked in a car—even though that's exactly what happened. Once it's as good as it's going to get without a brushing and a shower, I head back.

Tom holds up two cold bottles of different chilled drinks and lets me pick, taking the other one. I unscrew the lid and take a deep pull of it as I watch Sam clean the car. It looks like he's on detail duty, but he doesn't seem to mind. He scrubs a leather cleaner onto the seat with a soft cloth, and he talks to the car the whole time while he does it.

Marcus and Tom watch the whole thing with an air of amusement passing between them. I walk around to my side, and my heart clenches at the sight of my folded blanket lying there. Someone must have dug it out of the trunk while I was in the bathroom. I sit and buckle in, then get cozy.

The car reeks of us, despite the scented leather cleaner, but then again, so does my blanket. It's the one Sam saved from my heat, and it makes me calm and sleepy. His thoughtfulness makes my heart feel too big for my chest.

When Sam is done and the leather care kit is tucked away, they all climb in and Marcus resumes our route on the dashboard computer. We pull away and get back on the highway. I drag my pillow down from where it got lodged between my headrest and the back glass and jam it into place so I can lean against the door, my capped drink cradled in my elbow.

Tom goes back to staring out the window, and his hand goes back onto my thigh, but all it does is lie there with a comfortable and comforting weight. *He's so pretty it hurts.*

"Was it everything you'd thought it would be?" I ask, my voice low. Just for him.

He meets my eyes, his thumb rubbing up and down my leg through the fuzzy blanket that smells like all of us. "Everything and more."

There's a seriousness about his gaze that makes me wonder if we're talking about the same thing.

Am I everything you thought I'd be?

Maybe that's the real question here. Or maybe that's my constant need for reassurance. This is wonderful. It's fun. It's sexy as hell. But is it really forever, or is it more like a vacation? An enjoyable adventure, but then one day you're ready to go home and let your life return to normal.

No one has ever liked me enough to keep me before. Part of me still worries this is too good to be true.

Tom goes back to watching the countryside pass, but his hand never leaves me, not even when the soft music and the comforting smell of pack and the rumble of the road underneath the tires makes me doze.

Chapter Sixteen

TOM

SAM AND EMILY HAVE SUCH DIFFERENT REACTIONS TO OUR arrival in the city. Both are fun to see in their own way. Emily watches the city line quietly through the window as we weave our way toward home on the West Side of Manhattan. Sam gawks like an eager puppy, asking question after question and barely waiting for the answer to the first before moving onto the next.

And then we're home at last. Marcus pulls up to the front of our building and idles in the marked delivery area. We pile out, and I help him pull the suitcases and bags from the trunk as our doorman Bobbie brings out a brass luggage cart around and helps us load everything.

"See you upstairs," Marcus says as he leans down and kisses me before getting back in the car to go park it in our spot.

"Welcome back, Mr. Orello," the doorman says after he's loaded the last of our mountain of luggage. "You have some packages at the front desk when you're ready to collect your mail."

"Thank you." I gesture to Emily and Sam and introduce them. "They'll be staying with us for some time. This is Emily, and that's Sam." Bobbie pushes the heavy cart inside and summons the elevator, and we wait for its wrought iron door to open. It creaks and squeals as it descends to the lobby.

"Is this thing safe?" Emily leans closer and asks in a low voice.

"It's existed since nineteen-oh-one when the building was finished," I say. And then I lean down so my mouth is by her ear. "What if today is the day its chain snaps?"

She narrows her eyes and pokes me in the ribs, and it bloody hurts. "Mean."

Perhaps I was teasing her a little too much if she's actually afraid of it. It's hard to reign in the sarcastic brat side of me that comes so naturally after spending the last two decades with just Marcus. We're still getting to know one another. It's going to take some time for everyone to adjust.

"We could take the stairs if you prefer, although I warn you it's seventeen stories," I say.

Emily glances at the iron railed stairs at the end of the marble hallway. "Rickety death trap it is."

"It passed its inspection this spring. If that makes you feel better, miss," the doorman says.

She smiles at him, then glances at his nametag. "It does. Thank you, Robert. The building is beautiful. I don't think I've ever seen anything quite like it. How long have you worked here?"

He enjoys her attention, his round cheeks pinkening as he adjusts his black cap on his balding head. "Call me Bobbie, miss. I've been a doorman here since I was sixteen, and my father before me. Here we are. Let me settle this first, and then I'll hold the doors for you."

When the door opens, he loads the cart inside, then holds it for us and selects our floor. It creaks and squeals as it climbs, slower than a modern elevator but a hundred times prettier and authentic to such a grand old building.

I'm glad the co-op board opted to repair instead of replacing it.

It stops and opens onto our floor, and Bobbie helps us get the overloaded luggage cart to our door. I pull my keys from my pocket and unlock it and promptly put Sam to work, moving everything into the foyer.

"Oh, wow, this is quite the place," Sam says once he's moved the last of it and the doorman leaves us.

"Let me give you a tour," I say and lead them into the living room, then show them the formal dining room, Marcus's study, and the library.

Emily runs her hands over the books and walks around the room, and I make a mental note that she loves reading. I know the perfect place to take her on our first outing. They follow me to the kitchen, and I show them which door is the pantry and which is the wine closet.

"Our bedroom is on this floor. The guest rooms are upstairs." They climb the stairs with me, and we pause in the den for a bit as I point out the laundry room and then finally the guest bedrooms that we'll need to convert for them.

I lean in the doorway while they inspect the first one. "These rooms don't get used often, but they should have everything you need for now, and then we can get whatever else you need later. I'm sure Marcus is already planning the new decor, so if you have anything specific in mind, you should mention it sooner rather than later. He has a tendency to run full-steam ahead and assume everyone else is on board."

Emily's eyes are wide, her shoulders stiff, while Sam pokes and prods at some knick knacks I've never noticed before. The front door slams, and Marcus shouts, asking where we are.

"Upstairs!" I yell back. His loud steps echo on the creaky stairs, and then he comes into view. I go to his side and lean into him, curling my arm around his waist.

"Have you decided which rooms you'd each like?" he asks.

I pat him on the chest. "Let them settle, darling. Let's go unpack while they discuss it."

"Right," he says, his smile falling for a second before he catches it. "We'll just be downstairs then. Come down when you're ready. I'll bring your things up in the meantime while you're getting sorted."

We head back downstairs, and I supervise while Marcus divvies up the luggage, putting our bags in our room and bringing theirs upstairs to leave in the den.

"Her scent is stressed," he says as he drops the last bag by our bed. "She was fine in the car. Did something happen?"

I pause in my unfolding and think. "She was nervous about the elevator—it's antique and it creaked—but... I think it's more that she walked into an alpha's den."

He sits down hard on the bed and his shoulders slump. "You think I scared her? Was today too much? We should have waited before doing something like that. God, we shouldn't have pushed her too fast. What if she wants to leave already? We only have three months to court her."

I put the shirt down and stand between his legs, my hands on his shoulders as he stares up at me, miserable and frightened. "If you couldn't tell by how wet she was, let me say it. She liked what we did. And like you said, she was fine until we came inside. I think there have been a lot of changes one after another for her, and the reality of walking into an alpha's den, being in an unfamiliar place surrounded by our scents, is finally hitting her. Give her time. Let her adjust."

"Right." He stares straight ahead at my middle and nods, his brow creased. "Of course. We should give her some time and space to realize she's safe here, even from us. The last thing I want is for her to feel unsafe in our home. I want her to feel like it's her home too."

"What?" I cup his face and tilt him so he's looking at me. "No. We should not *give her space.* We should bend her over every piece of furniture all over the apartment and rut her brains out. Sam said she's overthinking everything. That she doesn't trust her omega instincts. So we need to short circuit her mind so her hind brain can take over. We have to trust the rest of her will follow."

"You... want to fuck her into loving us?"

"Well, it worked for me." He acts like he'd forgotten how disastrously horny we were as young men fucking all summer long, cramming an entire year's worth of togetherness into two short months.

Marcus narrows his eyes at me. "That is *not* why you fell in love with me."

"No." I brush his hair out of his face. He needs a haircut. I'll make him an appointment tomorrow. "I love you because you're kind. Because you take care of everyone who you consider yours. Because you are loyal and thoughtful. But it certainly didn't hurt that you have a massive cock, a talented tongue, and an arse to die for."

His lips twitch in an almost smile, which was my aim. "Let's go over the plan again." I hold up my hand and make a fist, putting up one finger at a time. "One, make their spaces comfortable for them. Two, get to know one another and go on lots of dates. And three, the most important rule?" I wiggle my three fingers in the air.

"Fuck her over every piece of furniture in the house?" he asks.

"Precisely. Fuck her over every single piece of furniture we own, and quite a few we don't. Don't forget the terrace. And let's also not overlook Sam. He needs his own sort of reassurance that he's wanted here."

I remember what Marcus said, how Sam insisted they weren't

a package deal. As if he expected an extraneous beta to be some sort of consolation prize. I understand the thought, even if it hurts to know our packmate feels that way. Sam is a natural. He knows exactly how to handle our omega, and he's slotting in perfectly between us. His carefree nature makes him easy to like.

"I have a plan for Sam. Do you want to see it?" Marcus asks. His eyes light up with excitement.

"Does it involve a gimp mask shaped like a dog's muzzle?" I hope we haven't bought him the same present. Mine is custom-made and not returnable. The express rush cost a fortune. I ordered it last night when I was too eager to sleep.

"What?" Marcus laughs, his deep belly laugh that makes me melt when I hear it because I know it's real. Visceral. "No. Why would you ask that?" He shakes his head.

"What is it then?" I answer without answering. "I want to see it."

"It's in the basement. One of my clients owed me a favor, and I called it in. They dropped it off this morning."

He stands and I follow him out. We call out that we'll be right back in case they come downstairs, looking for us while we're gone. Marcus leads me to the storage area in the basement. There, sitting in the center of our designated storage cage, is a rusted motorcycle with a big red bow attached to it. Its paint is chipped, and the swoopy piece of metal that covers half the back wheel has a dent.

"Umm…"

"It's a 1955 Triumph T110 in shell blue," Marcus says, as if that explains everything.

"Is that supposed to mean something to me?" I ask and walk around the bike, looking at it from every angle. The headlight is yellowed and fogged with age, and the leather seat is cracked. It's a wreck.

Marcus sighs. "It's one of James Dean's favorite bikes. Sam

told me that when he was little, he used to watch his dad fix up an old Chevy Bel Air. He'd hand his father tools and hold the light. And then his dad died when he was a kid and the car sat there untouched under a tarp in their garage until he took auto shop in high school and finished restoring it."

I touch the bike, dragging my hand over the curves of its mechanicals. "And it's going to take months for him to restore this one so he'll know we mean to keep him. Good job, darling." I press a kiss to his lips and settle into his side.

"Exactly."

"I'm afraid he thinks we don't really want *him*," Marcus says after a pause.

I'm not shocked to hear it. Even the most well-adjusted beta can struggle to accept the uniqueness of the alpha-omega dynamic. For betas who want a pack rather than a single partner, it can sometimes be hurtful.

"Let's give him my present tonight," I say. "The tracking information says it was delivered this morning."

"Do I even want to know?" Marcus asks.

He locks the storage cage behind us, and we walk to the lobby. There's a thick stack of mail in our mail slot and a half-dozen packages. I'm not the only one who's been buying presents.

"You'll find out soon enough." I search through the plain brown boxes until I find the one I'm looking for. *Perfect.*

Chapter Seventeen

EMILY

Falling asleep in a strange bed, no matter how comfortable, has always been a challenge for me. The mattress is too soft, the pillows too firm, the sheets too slippery. I think they're silk. Sitting up in bed, I click the lamp on and look around the room. Part of me still can't believe I'm really here.

The bedroom is beautiful. Their entire house is stunning, and it looks like something straight out of a magazine spread. It has crown molding and wainscoting, and even the ceilings are decorated. Everything is painted a warm white or covered in patterned wallpaper. I didn't know people still used wallpaper at all. Oriental rugs that are probably older than me crisscross one another in the enormous downstairs living room and upstairs den, and all I can think of is how all that velvet seating is going to get absolutely wrecked. Like the car.

I'm terrified to touch a single thing. Everything looks delicate and breakable and either antique or very fucking expensive. Priceless knickknacks litter every horizontal surface. This house is a gorgeous landmine waiting to explode from a single bump against the furniture.

I don't want to be by myself right now. Maybe Sam will

cuddle me to sleep? I've never had a problem living or sleeping alone, but in the last week it seems I've already gotten used to having someone there with me. I don't want to give that up.

I slide out of bed and slip my feet into my slippers and go to his room, knocking on his door.

"Sam? It's me. Can I come in?"

There's a muffled thump and then the sound of boards squeaking as someone walks over and then the door opens, but it's Marcus standing there, not Sam.

I look past him and see Sam kneeling on the floor, his bare ass in the air, and Tom positioned behind him. They're fucking. And that's not what's strange—it's the outfit Sam's dressed in.

What the fuck is he wearing?

A leather harness with silver O-rings crisscross Sam's body, and there's a strap for gripping between his shoulders. A strappy black leather half-mask that looks like a dog's muzzle covers his lower face. Buckled straps secure it around his head. A pair of leather dog ears decorate the top strap. All of it connects to a thick leather collar around his neck that's been stamped with his name in it and painted red. A metal milk bone shaped tag dangles from the collar, jingling with every slap of Tom's hips against Sam's ass while they fuck on the floor.

"I... I didn't mean to interrupt," I stammer, the hand I knocked with dropping to my side.

"You're not interrupting at all," Marcus says. "Sam said you could watch. Didn't you, Sam?"

Sam stares at me and nods, the dog ears flopping with every bucking movement. Tom thrusts hard, and Sam's eyes close. He drops his head down and moans, the sound muffled by the mask.

Marcus steps aside so I can enter, and after a moment's hesitation I do. It's part curiosity and part voyeurism. My sore clit gives a weak throb at the sight of them and the sounds they make. This isn't my sort of thing, but Sam and Tom seem happy enough with the roleplay and it's their enthusiasm I respond to. I'm riveted by the picture they make together. Is this how they feel when they watch each other fuck me? Marcus shuts the door behind me and pulls me over to the armchair positioned across from them. He sits and pats his lap, and I climb up, letting him arrange me while I watch Tom and Sam keep going.

"Isn't he beautiful?" Marcus whispers against my ear.

Which one? They both are in their own way. Sam is light where Tom is dark. Broader and shorter versus taller and leaner. Enthusiastic and freckled against maturity and elegance. They make a handsome pairing. A study of contrasts.

"Yes, they're perfect together."

Tom grips Sam's harness handle and pulls, bringing the younger beta up on his knees until his back arches.

There's a matching silver O-ring around Sam's cock. He's swollen and red. A steady stream of pre-cum leaks from his fat head and splatters onto the glossy hardwood as Tom pounds into his ass with hard, smacking thrusts that make Sam whimper. He's gagged. I couldn't see it before with him on his knees and his head down, but there's a hole cut into the boxy muzzle of his dog-shaped half mask and through the opening I see the red rubber ball gag stuffed in his mouth. It's a dog's ball. His lips wrap around it, his jaw forced open wide to take it.

"Naughty puppies get taught their lessons," Tom says, reaching one hand around to stroke Sam's dripping cock. He squeezes it and tugs, his thumb rubbing over the sensitive head.

I shift on Marcus's lap and realize I'm wet, my folds slick and rubbing against each other as I get more comfortable for our show. I understand why they enjoy watching me get fucked now. Why they're happy to wait for their turn on the sidelines. I can't look away.

"What did he do?" I whisper, not wanting to interrupt, but needing to know.

"Our Sam has a bit of a bratty mouth on him, and now he's learning there are consequences. That his ability to speak is a privilege. One that can be taken away."

Fuck. I vow to never be mouthy again. Although Sam seems to enjoy it from the way he thrusts into Tom's hand, his hips slamming back down on the cock buried in his ass. He whimpers around his gag.

Marcus trails his fingertips along my arm and shoulder, the barely there tickling sensation making me squirm on his lap. *God, I'm so wet.* I came how many times in the car? An impossible number. Yet my body craves more, as if I'm still stuck in the peak of my heat, my carnal appetite endless. What are they doing to me? It's like I'm addicted to them, their scents, their touch, their praise.

"Sweetheart, I can smell you." Marcus inhales, his chest rumbling as he sniffs the air.

"I can't help it. They're so pretty together."

Tom looks at us and grins, his green eyes full of dark promises. "Good boy, puppy. You take my cock so well. Don't come until I say you can or you'll be punished." His hand tugs harder, faster, and Sam shudders and groans as fluid dribbles down flexing knuckles.

"I thought you'd be tired," Marcus says, trailing his fingers down my body. He touches my thigh, then grabs one knee and pulls my legs apart, rucking my oversized sleep shirt up in the process. He hits the seam of my sex and slicks through my wetness, spreading it while he teases me. "No panties, sweetheart?"

"No." I don't wear underwear to bed. I bite my lip and sigh around it when he strokes my clit, his touches gentle, until my hips thrust to meet him. To urge him on. Why can't I get enough of them?

"Look at what you've done, naughty puppy," Tom says, his hips slowing until he stops. "You've made a mess in this house."

I've been distracted from the show. Sam's cum is splattered on the floor in front of him. The milky white droplets starkly contrast against the dark, gleaming wood.

Tom pulls out and slaps him on the ass, then fiddles with the mask. He unhooks and pulls the ball gag out of the opening in the muzzle. "Clean up your mess." Tom grabs a fist full of Sam's hair and pushes his face to the floor.

Sam's pink tongue flicks through the opening of the mask to lap it up. His reward is the pump of two fingers in his ass. Marcus fingers me too, the two of them pleasuring the both of us in tandem as if they're trying to match one another or compete.

"Good boy," Tom says. "Now clean your Mistress. You've made a mess of her too."

His Mistress? My lips curl with a barely suppressed grin. *Interesting.*

Marcus lifts my legs so I'm perched on him, his hard cock grinding into my ass while I balance with my heels on his knees. I'm spread open wide for easy access and he plays with my clit until I'm dripping. Our alpha rolls my clit in circles that make me gasp and groan and twitch against him.

Sam crawls forward on his hands and knees and shoves his face between my thighs. Marcus drags my night shirt all the way up and toys with my breasts, pinching and pulling them. The leather of Sam's mask is cool and sleek against my skin, but his tongue is hot. He licks it through my folds and laps at me, drinking down my arousal and thrusting his tongue inside for more.

Tom walks over and kneels behind Sam again, stroking his own cock as he pumps two fingers into Sam's hole, then positions himself at that entrance again. He sinks in with a single thrust, Sam's mouth tonguing me deeper as we all rock together.

"Oh, fuck." I drop my head back against Marcus's chest and close my eyes, breathing harder while we move as one.

"Good boy," Tom says, the slap of skin against skin filling the room once more, that tongue deep inside me pressing even deeper with each thrust. "You're licking your Mistress so well. What an obedient puppy you are."

Marcus pinches my nipples harder, the feeling traveling straight to my clit. Sam's mask rubs against me as he tonguefucks me and I grind against his face, seeking more. Everything pulls tight inside of me, and I hold my breath as the moment stretches. Warm breath teases my ear and the nape of my neck as Marcus nuzzles against me. He presses a kiss to the side of my throat and tugs the collar of my sleep shirt to the side for better access.

His tongue licks across my skin, dragging hard over my scent gland at the base. My perfume fills the room as he mouths it, his teeth grazing the sensitive skin and making my cunt tighten on Sam's tongue.

Is he going to bite me? The thought should terrify me. An alpha has so much power, so much control once they've claimed you. I wait for the panic to come, but it never does. Instead, I'm strung taut with anticipation. His lips close around my scent gland, and he sucks. There's so much trust here. He could bite me, claim me, and there's nothing I could do to stop him. Not even if I wanted to. His teeth lightly graze my skin.

I squeeze my eyes shut tight. "F-fuck, I'm gonna...."

I come against Sam's face with a ragged moan, my hips moving on their own as my body tightens down in rolling waves. Sam licks me through my aftershocks, his broad tongue lapping all my wetness up as he laves me clean and gives my clit one last flick that makes me twitch and recoil.

"Too much," I protest, wiggling out of his reach.

Marcus is hard as a rock underneath me and he grunts as I rub against him while I evade Sam's touch. I'm too sensitive. Too well used after the earlier antics of the day.

"Get ready, puppy," Tom says, never stopping. "I'm going to come in your ass and watch it drip out of your hole, and then you'll clean up your mess, you naughty, dirty boy."

Sam presses his face against my inner thigh and moans. On impulse, I reach down and stroke him, ruffling his shaggy hair and making those leather ears flop.

"What a messy puppy," I say, grinning even though I know I'll likely pay for it later. Sam's big brown eyes look up at me, and my heart clenches in my chest. His pupils are blown wide and dark with lust. There's something nice about the sight of him on his knees at my feet. He really looks like a cute little puppy.

All he needs is a... "Is there a matching tail?"

"Bloody hell," Tom curses, his back arching as he grunts and comes, his hips swiveling to pump his seed deep into Sam's ass. When he stops and he's regained his breath, he looks over my head at Marcus. "We've made a little monster."

Are they talking about me? I twist to look up at Marcus and see that he's got a hand pressed to his mouth like he's holding in laughter.

"What?" I ask.

Marcus shakes his head and grips my chin, tugging me up for a kiss. He whispers against my lips. "You're perfect. You both are."

Oh. I'm content as he presses his mouth to mine and traces the seam of my lips, asking for entry. I open for him, sliding my tongue against his as he explores my mouth and leaves me breathless. His cock twitches against my bare ass. Everyone but him has come, and that isn't fair. I break our kiss and put my feet down on the floor, lifting enough to grind against him, stroking him with each swivel of my hips.

"Good boy," Tom says to Sam. "Lick it all up. Clean up your mess."

I watch Sam suck Tom's soft cock into his mouth and lick it clean. That long pink length disappearing between the opening of the black leather mask is obscene.

"Good. Now the floor. I want it spotless." Tom pulls Sam off his cock and points him to the cum that's splattered on the floorboards.

Marcus rumbles with a purr at the sight as I rub my ass against his clothed cock and tease him while Sam licks up Tom's cum.

Tom grabs him by the handle on his harness and drags him up. "Good boy. Now tend to your Master."

Marcus taps me on the thigh and I take my cue, climbing off him and letting my sleep shirt fall back down to cover me as I step aside so Sam can crawl between the alpha's legs. Sam goes for his pants, unbuckling the belt and then unhooking the latch and tugging the zipper down.

Our alpha's cock spills out, painfully hard with a bead of pre-cum gathered at his slitted tip. Sam bends his head down and feeds it through the opening of his mask, swallowing it down and bobbing on its length. Wet sucking noises and heavy breathing fill the room. Marcus pumps his cock into the beta's eager mouth.

"Here," Tom says, handing something to me. I take it without looking. I'm so engrossed in the sight of them. It's a matching leather tail attached to a steel butt plug. *Oh, it's perfect.* The tail is curled, the tip narrowing into a point that will stick up in the air as Sam sucks our alpha's cock. He hands me a bottle of lube next. It's creamsicle-flavored, and I smile as I read the label. Where did they find it?

I take both and come up behind Sam and kneel, setting everything down so I can run my hands down his back and over his ass, then down his thighs. "Sam, can I put something in your ass?"

He lifts his butt up higher in the air without stopping his work on Marcus, and I take that for consent. I've never touched someone here before. I spread his cheeks apart and look at him first. His hole is puffy and wet from being so well used.

I pour lube on two fingers and spread it around, then stroke his hole and gently work them in. He's warm and clean inside as I apply lube inside him, then add more to the plug. It's a blunted cone shape with a wide, flared base and then the tail. I press it to his hole and push. He stretches, taking it, and when the thickest part is inside, he closes up tight to keep it snug there.

The leather tail curls up in the air, and I swat it, enjoying the way Sam moans around his mouthful of cock. His dick and balls hang down between his thighs, his tip leaking even more pre-cum as the tight cock ring keeps him stiff without direct stimulation.

I've never seen it from this angle, and I take my time exploring him. I rub the skin between his ass and balls, then cup their weight and roll his sack in my hand. He shudders and groans when I palm his engorged cock, teasing his head and fingering his weeping slit. I curl my hand around him and stroke.

"What a good puppy you are, sucking our alpha's cock," I say. His cock jumps in my hand as I tug him. Sam loves a fun little fantasy. He loves playing and pretending and dress-up. I work him in my hand as I kneel beside him on the floor and stare up at Marcus. His expression is intense. Focused. He drops a large hand onto Sam's head and just holds it there between those flopping ears.

Tom joins us on the floor, grabbing Sam by his tail and tugging on it before pressing it in, working that thick plug in deeper only to do it all over again. And again. "Good boy."

Sam humps my hand as I tug and pull, and then he comes and I get to watch from my new vantage point. I see what happens to them when they orgasm. The bulging stretch of skin between his balls and ass pulses, his balls rising and falling as the first spurt of cum shoots out and strikes the floor. I milk him with my hand, wringing every drop and lash of seed from his sack until it goes still. When his cock stops twitching, I press the tip of my finger into his slit and gather the last drop, bringing it up to Tom's lips. He slides his mouth over my finger and sucks, his tongue licking me clean. I giggle, and he lets me go with a wet pop.

"Are you ready?" Marcus asks, his voice all growl. His chest heaves and his nostrils flare as he cants his hips into Sam's mouth.

Sam's answer is to reach up and wrap a hand around the base of our alpha's cock. It's swelling, pushing at Sam's fingers as Marcus drops his head back and comes. He shoots his seed down Sam's throat as the beta squeezes that knot, searching out every drop of creamy cum as he noisily sucks it down and makes a satisfied sound around his mouthful.

"Fuck," Marcus groans as they sit there and both catch their breath. "That was so good, Sam."

Tom grabs me by the arm and tugs as he stands and we get on the bed and cuddle one another while we give Marcus and Sam their moment. Tom's hand glides up and down my back as I press my face to his chest and listen to his heartbeat.

After a few more minutes, they untangle, and Sam sinks onto the floor between Marcus's legs as the alpha leans down and unbuckles the harness from his head. He pulls it free, smoothing the beta's hair, then reaches down and brings Sam up with him.

Marcus works the cock ring off Sam's length. He takes the harness off next, then undresses himself, and they join us on the tiny bed as we all try to figure out how to fold ourselves up small enough to fit on the queen-size mattress. The bed creaks ominously.

It's a disaster.

I end up laying half on top of Tom as Sam spoons me and Marcus stays on his side behind him.

"We need to go bed shopping," Tom says, breaking the silence.

Marcus purrs and rubs everyone he can reach with soothing caresses that speak of an alpha well satisfied. "Told you."

"Well, you don't have to gloat about it," Tom says.

I smile and bury my face against Tom's smooth chest. We are a tangled pile of limbs and I fall asleep, waking only when Marcus and Tom both slip from the bed. Marcus moves to scoop me up, but I roll over and wrap my limbs around Sam like an octopus. I don't want to sleep alone in a cold, unfamiliar bed that doesn't smell right. I want the comfort of pack. Of a warm body that holds me tight and smells right.

"Leave her," Tom says softly. "I think she needs him."

There's a tug and then a blanket settles over us, and Sam and I cuddle all night.

Chapter Eighteen

EMILY

By the time Sam and I both stumble out of bed in the morning, Marcus is already gone. Back to work, Tom explains. The house feels emptier without him. We eat breakfast while Tom goes over the day's agenda. We're going shopping, but from the way he discusses it, it's more like he's planning a battle.

"That sounds like a lot of stores," I say between bites of jam-smothered toast.

"Eat." Tom uses tongs to put a couple of strips of bacon on my plate, then cuts up an orange and divides it between us. "You'll need your energy."

Sam shrugs and grins. "You don't have to twist my arm."

Tom smiles and loads extra bacon onto Sam's plate. "That's the spirit. And after, I have a surprise."

A surprise? We eat and get showered and dressed, and Tom calls for a Town Car to take us to Fifth Avenue. I stare out the window as we pass by Central Park and turn onto the street with all the shops.

I try on clothing until I'm numb and exhausted. Why do I need so many evening dresses, and where the fuck am I going to wear opera-length gloves? I've never been to an opera before.

After the first five minor heart attacks, I stop looking at the price tags and remind myself they have a castle and can clearly afford it, even though that one dress alone cost more than a month's rent for my apartment in Boston.

I'm grateful that I get to sit and watch when we go to the men's department for Sam. They measure him for suits, and he tries on several styles until he settles on a designer and cut that makes him look so fucking handsome that I can hardly stand to look at him without dragging him into the fitting room and getting us all kicked out. Maybe arrested.

My libido's never been this high before outside of a heat. It's like the more I have of them, the more I want. Like there's no quenching this thirst they've created.

While he's trying on casual outfits, I pull out my phone and investigate. The internet says what I expected but still can't quite believe. Forming packs often go through a period of hormone fluctuations that encourage bonding, mating, and breeding. The longer the claiming bite is delayed, the stronger the urges become. If we're a week into this and I already feel like tossing Sam down on this tufted ottoman poof and riding his cock right here in the middle of the fitting area, then how bad is it going to get in a month? In three months when I have my next heat?

I need to get a hold of myself. I can't mate with three people I still barely know, no matter how much I want their teeth and their cocks in me. We need to do this right. Get to know each other. Go on dates. Meet each other's families. I grimace at the thought.

"Everything all right?" Tom asks, hovering like he's been doing all morning.

"Fine." I put my phone to sleep and slip it into my purse.

He shoves his hands into his pockets and tilts his head, staring at me in that way that feels like he's looking right into my messy, anxious head. Sam says I need to be more honest with myself and everyone else about what I'm feeling or thinking. About what I want.

What I want more than anything is for this crushing anxiety to leave me alone so I can enjoy myself. I sigh. "Can I be honest?"

He goes still, then sits in one smooth movement. "Please."

"I don't know how to let myself enjoy all of this because I keep thinking you'll realize I don't fit. What the fuck do I know about opera? Puccini. That's the beginning and end of my knowledge about the opera, and I don't even know why or how I know that. What do I have in common with people who own a fucking castle?"

What if they regret me in a year when I'm not what they thought they wanted?

"A castle?" Tom's brow wrinkles as he thinks for a moment. "Do you mean Hardcastle Hall? I can see why you thought that, but it's a house, not a castle. Castles were built for defense. Hardcastle was built as the country seat for my ancestors."

See? I don't even know the difference between a house and a castle, but Sam did.

"Hardcastle Hall is hardly a prize, although I suppose it looks grand in photos. Only half of it is livable. The rest is too damp and full of rot from a roof leak that wasn't repaired properly by my great-grandfather. The electrical's been upgraded so many times over the years and it's still a mess. If you run the microwave and the electric kettle at the same time, you'll blow the entire kitchen's fuse. We only use it at Christmas and special occasions like weddings or funerals when the whole family gathers.

"It costs an absolute fortune to run, so we let it out as a museum and sometimes we rent it out to film production companies. That covers most of the house's expenses. When Marcus and I formalized our mating, my father was enraged. Even though our fathers were lifelong friends, he was still seen as the help.

Marcus was considered beneath me. It didn't matter that he worked and he's successful. That he had money of his own. My father told everyone I'd been cut from the will, only he never actually changed the papers the lawyer drafted. And then he died. I inherited it." He takes a deep breath and goes silent as he stares off into the middle space, lost in thought.

"I'm sorry," I say, putting a hand on his knee. "That must have been so hard. You never reconciled before he passed?"

"No, my father wasn't the forgiving type. Now Hardcastle hangs around my neck like an albatross. If I sell it, my family loses a part of their history. I can't do that to them. So we shut up the West wing and rent out the rest of it and every couple of years we all gather for Christmas for a week and then I don't have to think about it again for two or three years except to sign the occasional contract or cut a repair check."

He takes my hand and threads our fingers together, and I squeeze, offering him what comfort I can. I have my own issues with my family. But as much as my mother can drive me insane, I know she loves me the best she can. And I can't ever imagine abandoning my child or making them feel like my love is conditional.

"I hate the opera," he says after some time. "Always have. They used to take us on field trips in school and I never liked it. But Marcus enjoys all sorts of theater shows, so every once in a while he convinces me to go." He shudders in an exaggerated movement, as if the very thought fills him with dread, and it makes me smile.

"And I think you fit." Tom bumps his shoulder against mine and grins. "I think you fit quite nicely. But if you're not sure about the fit, I can think of a few creative positions for us to try to see if you fit better."

I roll my eyes, but I can't keep the smile off my face. "You're incorrigible."

"No, luv, I'm persistent. The key is knowing who to direct your attention to and when to adjust tactics. One is a virtue, the other a vice."

I side-eye him as he strokes his thumb against the back of my hand. "I think you and vice are well acquainted."

Tom pretends to look offended. "Ask any of my classmates at boarding school. I was an apt pupil."

"Except when it comes to the opera."

"We can't all be perfect."

"No? With your wonderful, handsome partner and your jet set life and artistic career and leaky castles and beautiful, perfect house full of beautiful, perfect knick knacks that absolutely fucking terrify me?"

"Our knickknacks terrify you?" He's amused, his face lighting up. His green eyes catch the light and glimmer.

"I feel like I'm going to bump into a table and send your grandmother's priceless heirloom to the floor to shatter. I honestly don't know how you live with that constant threat looming over you."

Tom's eyes widen, and then he drops his head back and laughs. We earn a few curious glances as other shoppers look at our loud display. "What?" Clearly, I should have kept it to myself instead of confiding in him.

When he stops laughing long enough to know that I'm both serious and annoyed, he throws his arm around my shoulders and pulls me against him. He wraps me in a tight hug that squeezes the last of my anxiety out of me along with my breath.

"Luv, most of that stuff was picked out by a designer. I couldn't even begin to tell you what some of it is, let alone where it came from."

Oh. Oh, I feel stupid, yet relieved. It's a weird combination.

"How about this," he says. "I'll move any priceless family

heirlooms we own onto a higher shelf. Will that set you more at ease?"

It actually would. "Sure." My belly swoops at his thoughtfulness.

"I feel like I missed something," Sam says. He's standing in the dressing room doorway with a dozen articles of clothing draped over one arm.

"Just some redecorating plans," Tom says. "Are you finished?"

"Yeah. I left the ones I didn't like in the fitting room," Sam says.

Tom lets go of me and waves our personal shopper over, and she takes Sam's choices from him and brings them to the register with the rest of our purchases. We're shooed out to wait on the sidewalk when I choke over the rising total on the register's display.

"And that's just one store," Sam says in awe.

"I don't want to think about it."

Tom joins us and when we ask him where the bags are, he looks at us oddly and explains they're being delivered to the apartment. "You'll like this next one," Tom says, smiling in a way that doesn't at all put me at ease. Is it another lingerie store? We've already been to three. I'm not sure how many crotchless panties one woman needs.

We follow him and cross five crowded blocks and then I see it. "Is that a Nested?" I've only seen them in glossy magazine ads and movies. Through the enormous window display, I see the variety of different omega nests they sell and the walls and racks of pillows, blankets, and other accessories.

I go for the door and rip my way inside, pausing to enjoy the way the store smells like warm cashmere and happiness. The store clerks are all omegas, and one comes up to greet me.

"Welcome to Nested. Have you shopped with us before?" he asks.

"No." I look around, taking it all in. All the nests are set up in staged sets as if two dozen complete bedrooms have been plopped down in the middle of the store. The walls are lined with cubbies stuffed with soft goods in every color and texture and fabric.

I have died and gone to omega heaven.

"What are you looking to do today?" he asks. The name Jamie is written on his black nametag in white script.

"We're doing a complete redecoration," Tom says, him and Sam catching up behind me. "Whatever she wants."

Jamie nods and pulls me deeper into the store, explaining the pros and cons of each style. Some are simple and not much different from a regular mattress with only a slight rolled lip around three of the four edges. Others are round, and a few are half-circles that dip down like a cup. I frown at those. They look super cozy to nest in, but how would you get fucked in them? I shake my head, and we pass them by. He leads me to the nests with canopies, some metal, others wooden or upholstered, and I forget how to breathe.

It's perfect. I reach out and touch it to make sure it's real. It's rectangular like a standard bed, with a high padded wall on three sides. A wrought iron canopy frames it, and white fabric covers the sides, back, and top so it's closed up like a box. Inside it, someone's hung soft white string lights back and forth. The blankets and pillows inside are all white on white, but each item has a different texture.

"Can I climb in?" I ask.

Jamie nods. "How else will you know if it's right?"

I kick my shoes off and hop up, settling in the middle on my back and stare at the ceiling. I sigh, all of my tension leaving me as something tight in my chest unclenches for the first time in forever. The blankets and pillows are wrong, but I'll fix that. I close my eyes and imagine all of this but in soft, dreamy blues and grays. The string lights will be little stars. I'll find a pillow shaped like a cute little cloud. There's gotta be one in here somewhere. Nested has *everything*.

I sit up and grab fistfuls of the blankets underneath me and twist them like someone's going to attempt to pry me out of it by force. "I want this one."

"Wonderful." Jaime grabs a paper slip from the clear plastic holder hanging off the bed and hands it to Tom. "What size? It comes in twin, full, queen, king, and Alaska king."

"The Alaska king would fit our pack best, but I'm not sure it would fit in the room," Tom says as he studies the card and flips it over to check the dimensions.

I see its quadruple-digit price point and decide I don't care. *Worth it.*

"I have an idea," Sam says. "Put a door up between the den and the staircase landing and turn that into her room. The room she's using now can be a nursery."

Oh, hell yes. That's what I want. I want it more than anything I've ever wanted before in my life. One giant nest to cuddle and sleep and fuck in and then later, to have our babies in. It's perfect.

Tom considers it, and I hold my breath. That's a big change to ask them to make. A pretty permanent one. I'm not sure if framing out walls and adding doors is what Tom and Marcus had in mind when they mentioned redecorating.

And then Tom smiles and talks to Jamie about delivery dates, and my pulse quickens and I know this is real. Really real and permanent, and it's scary and wonderful and I want it so badly my chest aches. And I no longer care if it's only been a week and they were strangers, because they're mine and I'm theirs and this nest feels right. They'd have to pry me out of it with force.

Sam climbs into the nest and flops on his side, grinning at me, and I'm too happy to bother scolding him about wearing his shoes on the model bed. I lean down and press a quick kiss to his lips as a thank you for making the suggestion.

When Tom and Jamie have hashed out the details, the omega takes the paper to the register for them to start the ordering process. Grudgingly, I clamber out, and we head to the walls to pick out bedding and decorations. They let me take my time, feeling each one and showing them the ones I like so they can appreciate my choices even if they don't understand them. When I've picked through the entire store, ignoring my growling stomach as we push past a late lunch and edge into dinner time, we walk to the register.

The cashier taps my long list of specifics into the computer. If she thinks my nit picky attention to detail is odd, she doesn't show it. Maybe it is normal, and I've just never had the luxury to really care before. She rings everything up and sets the delivery window. A month seems like forever away, but also a short amount of time. Don't home renovations usually take several months? I've watched enough home repair reality TV shows to know that's true.

Outside, I continue to float in my bubble of happiness as I cling to Tom while we walk and Sam carries my cloud pillow for me. I wouldn't let them bag it with the rest of our order. It has a smiling face embroidered on the front and a sad face on the back. Stuffed felt raindrops hang from it on braided string.

Tom bundles us into the Town Car he ordered then slips in with us. "Are you ready for your surprise?"

Sam and I exchange looks. "That wasn't it?" I ask.

"No. That was all the necessary stuff that had to get done. This next one's for fun."

I'm not sure what could top a wild spending spree in Nested, but if anyone could do it, it would be Tom. We travel across town until the car finally stops, and we all file out. The surprise is a used bookstore. A fat and obscenely fluffy orange cat sits in the store window, watching the pedestrians walk by, and a bell tinkles overhead as we push the door open and step inside.

The shop smells like old books and coffee. Shelves line the walls with carts and tables making up the middle, and it seems to go on and on. The store is impossibly large on the inside. The further back we go, the more we find. Rooms have been devoted to entire subjects. Natural history, women's studies, poetry. It keeps going.

While Tom and I browse, Sam gets us drinks and brings them to us. I sip my cappuccino and pull out one book after another, flipping through them.

"Hey, look at this one," Sam says.

I look over and see he's holding up an old leather-bound book with a plate-printed image of a Japanese woman being fucked by an octopus. Her head is thrown back in ecstasy as its tentacles writhe inside her while waves crash behind them. *Of course he found porn.* I shake my head and bury my smile in my coffee cup as I search for my own rare finds. One by one, I pull them out and make a stack that continues to grow.

"Find anything good?" Tom asks, coming back over with his own selection in his hand.

"A bunch of them." I point to my stack. "What about you?"

He holds it up for us to see. "It's a first edition of Beatrix Potter. I figured... for the baby."

My heart clenches as he opens the aged volume, turning the pages so we can see the drawings of bunnies and mice and geese. He stops on a page with a hedgehog wife hanging up her family's laundry on a clothesline staked out on tiny twigs. It's precious and perfect, and it fills me with longing.

"I love it," I say as I lean up and kiss him.

He adds it to our towering stack, and we shop until hunger finally drives us out into the rapidly cooling afternoon air. We've shopped all day, and I'm tired and happy and hungry for something other than food, so when Tom asks where we should go for dinner I say *home*.

I'm good in the Town Car and all the way home until we get into the elevator, and Tom's hand settles on my ass and then I can't take it anymore. My desire is a fire that's been fed and stoked all day with every compliment, every shy smile and brush of hands. I grab him by the shirt and pull him down for a kiss that's anything but chaste.

Sorry, Bobbie.

The doorman pretends he sees nothing as I hook my arm around Tom's shoulders and swallow his tongue. It only takes a moment for his surprise to mellow and for his hand to grab my ass for real. He slips it into the back pocket of my jeans and rocks me back against the elevator wall, the old thing squeaking and squealing in protest.

Sam drags us both out when neither of us notice we've arrived at our floor. Bobbie leaves us with the brass luggage cart loaded with packages and plastic-wrapped clothes, and Tom barely gets the door open and everything inside the foyer before he's on me again, kissing and groping me.

He walks me back until my ass hits something solid, then sweeps his arm out and knocks the stuff on top aside. At least one delicate trinket shatters against the floor. And then he grabs me by the hips and spins me around, pushing me down so I'm bent over it.

The button pops off my jeans as he yanks them open and unzips them, shoving them and my panties down to my knees. The first touch of his finger on my wet, needy slit makes me moan. Tom doesn't waste time. He probes me enough to make sure I'm slick and ready, and then he's pushing inside of me and I didn't even register him undoing his own pants.

He sinks in deep and takes me hard, the force of his thrusts driving me up the table. Another knickknack falls and cracks against the hardwood floor. I push back against him, urging him to go deeper.

"Fuck, that's hot," Sam says as he flicks his jeans open and drags his zipper down. "Hold her down and pull her hair. She'll like it."

I whine at the thought of it. Tom grabs one wrist at a time and pulls them to the small of my back, pinning them there, and then he tugs my ponytail holder out of my hair and grabs a fistful by my nape. Restrained, he holds me in place as he pounds into me, the table groaning with each surge of his hips.

Sam shoves his jeans and underwear down his thighs and strokes his cock, then presses it against my cheek. It slips over my skin, leaving a wet trail of pre-cum behind.

Tom pulls me by my hair, tilting my head to the perfect angle. "Suck his cock, omega."

I wrap my lips around Sam's head and hollow my cheeks as he feeds his cock into my mouth. He hits the back of my throat and pauses for a moment before retreating and then doing it all over again.

Held down, pinned, I can't do anything but take them and obey as Tom fucks me so hard over this table that I'll leave with its impressions bruised into my hips. Sam gags me on his length until my eyes water.

That's how Marcus finds us when he opens the front door and calls out that he's home.

"In the living room!" Tom yells, his hips never stopping. His balls slap against the apex of my cunt, the sensation enough to tease my clit but not enough to let me come.

We make filthy wet sounds as Marcus sees us and pauses, his footsteps stopping before continuing again. He walks over to the sofa and sits, unbuttoning his suit jacket and loosening his tie. *Oh, fuck, he looks so good in his gray suit. So fucking handsome with his dark hair that's gone silver at the edges and his black and silver tie.*

Tom hits a spot inside of me that makes me lose my focus, and Sam takes advantage of it. He rips the control away from me, and I moan around Sam's plunging cock with every rub against that special place.

"Oh, fuck, baby. That's good. You're so good at sucking cock. Make her do that again."

He fucks my face until the room fades away and all I know is the two men wrecking me and the bite of the table's edge.

It's rough. Claiming. Desperate. Like they need to take, to leave their mark, to know I'm theirs. Pinned down and fucked from both ends, there's no running away. Not even if I wanted to.

The last thing I want to do is run.

We have plans. I have a nest coming. A proper one. And they're going to fuck me in it and breed me. We'll raise our beautiful babies together, and they'll be safe and cared for and loved.

Tom's cock pulses as he groans and cums, his pace slowing as he uses my pussy to stroke the seed from his balls. He fills me until I'm dripping, and his cum runs out of me as he fucks me with languid thrusts throughout his release. His hands never ease, never let go of his hold on my wrists or his grip in my hair. All he does is step aside.

The couch groans as Marcus stands, the floorboards creaking with each heavy step that brings him closer. Sam pauses, only his tip on my tongue, which I suck, as our alpha undoes his pants and notches himself into place.

He sinks into me with one insistent thrust, his path made easier by their work and Tom's wet seed. I am desperate for release, for any stimulation on my clit to satisfy this burning urge inside me. They both move, no hurry to their pace, as they take turns stroking in and out of me, and all I can do is lie here and take it while Tom pins me down and the others rut me from both ends.

I slide my tongue on Sam's slit and savor the taste of him until he moves, using my face for his own pleasure as he chases his release and comes with a groan and a flood of semen. Ropes hit the roof of my mouth and tongue, and I swallow it down, drinking him up, and lave him clean until he pulls free with a grunt. He caresses my face, brushing my hair out of my eyes as I whimper with each cant of Marcus's hips.

"Please," I beg. "I want to come, I wanna… hnng."

"No."

Marcus slaps forward, his big swinging balls striking the top of my mound in an almost-right way. He fucks me deeper, harder, rearranging my body to suit his needs. His cockhead hits my cervix and presses, making room.

"You aren't allowed to come until I do," Marcus says.

"F-fuck," I whine, squeezing my eyes shut tight. *It's not fair.*

"Such a naughty mouth our pretty girl has," Tom says.

Tom's grip on my hair tightens as he tugs my head back, arching my throat and lifting my breasts into the air. Sam gropes them, pinching my nipples and holding their heavy weight as they swing with each thrust as Marcus fucks me over this table.

"She was behaving better when she had a cock in her mouth," Sam says. He presses two fingers to my mouth and slides them in, trapping my tongue against the floor of my mouth. In and out, he slicks them with my saliva and works them like they're a cock.

The tease of Marcus's sack against my clit works me up twice, but each time I get close, he changes his pace. He goes back to slow, steady thrusts that steal my momentum and leave me panting and begging incoherent nonsense around Sam's fingers. Marcus's edging is merciless. He torments me until I can't take it anymore.

"Is that right?" Marcus asks. "Do you need a cock in all of your holes to behave like a good omega for her pack?"

When Sam pulls his wet fingers from my mouth and sets them on my throat, his thumb and middle finger pressing on the pulse points there just enough to stem the flow of blood and make my head foggy, I can't think about anything but the slick slide of the cock shunting in and out of me.

"She needs to start her training so we can take her ass too," Tom says.

"Tomorrow," Marcus agrees.

What?

Sam relaxes his grip, letting me catch my breath for a moment, and then he does it again. And again. My pulse pounds against his fingertips and throbs in my cunt, like all that stoppered blood is being shunted down to my clit. To the empty womb that Marcus batters as his hips snap faster. Harder. His balls swing, heavy and full, with dull smacks to my juncture.

"Don't come," Sam says. "Not yet. Not until you're knotted like a proper omega. Fuck, I can't wait until all of us can fuck you at the same time, filling all three of your cute little holes."

Everything pulls taut and slows, winding tight, and words and whines are beyond me. There's only stillness. Tension. I hold my breath through the throb between my legs and the grip on my wrists, the burn at my nape and the hands on my neck, the cock carving itself a home inside of me. Remaking me just for them.

Marcus groans. "She's squeezing me like a… Fuck."

The stretching burn of Marcus's knot brushing at the root of my clit from the inside as he swells makes my control snap. I come with a ragged cry, my walls clenching down on him as he stripes my walls with ropey spurts of seed, and I flutter, milking him.

All of it. All of them. That's what I want. They're mine.

Those holding, pinching, squeezing hands soften. Sam's grip

on my neck eases, and I gulp in a cleansing breath. They rub me, stroking the circulation back into my skin and caressing my face, my neck, the curve of my back while Marcus's knot swells and ties us together.

"You okay, baby?" Sam asks when I collapse against the table and press my flushed face to its smooth surface. It's cool relief is heavenly on my heated skin.

I make a satisfied sound and focus on my breathing until the dizziness fades. "I'm goooood."

Marcus chuckles, his locked cock jumping inside me with the pull of his abdominals, and I whine at the stinging tug on my cunt. "Not that I'm complaining about the results, but what happened here?" he asks.

Sam pulls his jeans up and buttons them. "We went shopping."

"We went to Nested," I say, sighing as my body gives one last squeezing aftershock around my alpha's cock.

Tom kicks the worst of the shattered knickknacks into a growing pile. "The contractors will be here on Friday."

"Contractors?" Marcus stops rubbing me.

"We're turning the upstairs den into her nest," Tom says. "Her room will become the nursery. Do you mind? You're the one who said we need a bigger bed."

Should we have asked first? Maybe… maybe we were a tad bit impulsive.

Marcus purrs, and the tension in my shoulders relaxes as he goes back to stroking me with his fingertips in soft circles along my back. "I think that sounds perfect."

He leans over my prostrate body, the movement tugging at our tie, and he presses a kiss to the side of my neck. My scent gland. The thought of him sinking those sharp alpha teeth into my tender omega skin sends a pulse through my body. My cunt squeezes, trying to milk one last spurt of seed from him as if I'm fertile now and it can take root. As if right now, he's breeding me.

Not today. Not today, but... soon.

After a little while, his knot shrinks and his soft cock slips from me along with a deluge of seed and slick that runs down my thighs and soaks into the panties still shoved down around my knees. Marcus bands an arm across my middle and tugs me back, bending down for a kiss until I forget all about it and forget why I ever cared when everything is right.

This is perfect.

Chapter Nineteen

SAM

EMILY IS FAR TOO ADORABLE WHEN SHE POUTS. IT MAKES ME want to spank the expression right off her face. She takes the steel butt plug from my hand and stares at it, then gives a wary glance at the special bidet attachment on the toilet.

"Do you want some help the first time?" I ask.

She blushes, her cheeks turning bright red, and she all but shoves me out of the room. "You just want to watch, you pervert."

Well... yeah. Obviously.

I want to see that little wrinkle form between her brows when she's concentrating while she lubes up the small plug and works it into her tight little ass for the first time. She's had nothing in there before, she confessed last night after Tom brought home a brand new set of crystal-studded plugs for our pretty girl.

Emily shoves me out of the bathroom and slams the door shut, and then the water runs as she heats up the attachment. They've got a fancy model with all the bells and whistles. She'll be fine.

"I'm going down to the basement if you need me," I call through the door.

There. I head out and take the elevator down. Now she can't accuse me of lurking to take advantage of her since Marcus ordered her to wear only skirts or dresses and forbade panties all together whenever she's at home. With Tom busy supervising the contractors and Marcus off to work, if I'm eighteen stories downstairs maybe I won't be tempted to flip her skirt up and take her, heedless of the strangers tromping through her sacred space and making her all antsy and irritated.

Omegas hate having intruders in their nest.

The basement is empty and quiet. I flip on the lights and pull out the key Marcus gave me over dinner. I still can't believe it. A 1955 Triumph T110. She's the second prettiest girl I've ever seen.

I stroke my fingers over her handles and inspect her closer, making a list in my phone of the parts I'll need and browsing the auction and hobby sites for suitable replacements. It'll take some research, but I think I'll be able to do everything but paint her. Some jobs are better outsourced to professionals.

My hands are covered in grease and I've got the rusted carburetor out when Emily joins me. "So this is it?" she asks.

"Yeah. She's going to be gorgeous once I've got her restored."

Emily looks at all the pieces lined up on the workbench for inspection and cleaning or replacement. "Wow, it looks like you really know what you're doing."

"I used to hand my dad tools when we worked on his dream car. A 1957 Chevy Bel Air in surf green. She was beautiful. He never got to see her finished, but I took auto shop in school and learned how to fix her up. My instructor helped me with the harder stuff."

She smiles, her eyes softening the longer she looks at me. "I'm sure your dad would have been proud of you for finishing his dream."

My throat gets thick with emotion. "Hand me that wrench?" I

nod to the one I need, and she does, then watches me work. I spray it down with carb cleaner and get all the tiny pieces apart, then put everything in a big bucket to soak in cleanser until tomorrow when I can really start cleaning the rust off.

"How's your ass?" I grab a rag and wipe the worst of the grease and mess off my hands.

"It's… It was weird at first. The prepping part wasn't fun, but…"

"But the plug being in your ass feels good once it's in?" I finish for her.

She bites her lip and nods. God, she's so cute.

"I wanna see."

Emily looks around the basement, checking that it's empty. Not that it would probably deter either of us if it weren't. She enjoys being watched. Being coveted from afar. And I enjoy showing her off. I think we all do. *Look, don't touch. Isn't she gorgeous? Watch us fuck her. Aren't you jealous? You should be. She's ours.*

She turns around and lifts up her skirt, bending over a little so I can see the round, clear crystal peeking out between her butt cheeks. The thatch of dark hair on her pussy is glossy and damp. She likes it a lot more than she wants to admit.

"Baby, can you do me a favor?"

She looks over her shoulder.

"Can you sit on my bike? No, straddle it. Just like that. Now lean over and grab the handlebars. Lift one of your legs up higher. Fuck, that's perfect. Keep your skirt up."

I dig my phone out and take a photo. Her shiny jewel gleams between her cheeks in the light, and the seam of her wet pussy below makes me so hard. As she straddles my bike with her skirt up around her waist, all the blood rushes from my head and goes straight to my cock. Getting closer and dropping my phone low, I take another photo of her perfect cunt and pretty ass.

How the fuck did I get so lucky?

I toss my greasy rag to the floor and tap a fingertip against that gem, enjoying the way her pussy and ass clench as it shifts inside her. I do it again, teasing her with just a nudge on the end of that plug until she moans.

"You're so pretty with that toy inside you, baby. Do you want to know how good it feels when both holes are stuffed?"

She nods. "Yes."

"Get up and lean over the bike."

When she's in place, I grab her by the hips and tug her back a little more so her tight, stuffed ass is higher. God, she's so perfect. I unzip my jeans and shove them down and then my underwear, my half-hard cock bobbing as it swells. I tug it until it's rock hard and that low pulse of pleasure forms at my base.

Emily's cunt is so wet as I sink into her, and her ass so full. My cock knocks against the big, flared plug buried deep inside her through the thin wall that separates us. I fill her cunt and rub against it with every rocking thrust. Is this what it'll feel like when two of us are in her at the same time? It's so good it's obscene.

"Fuck, baby. You're so wet. Do you like being stuffed full? You like having that toy in your ass while I fuck you?"

"You feel so fucking good," she moans and moves with me, pushing her hips back for more as I build a rhythm until my gut tightens and that first clench hits me at the base of my cock.

"I can't wait to fuck your tight little ass while our alpha knots your pussy." Reaching around, I find her clit and play with it, pulling her hood back and rolling that firm nub in circles until she clenches around my cock and her plug and her hips take on a mind of her own.

The squeeze of her cunt makes me lose it as she comes, and I join her, my cock jumping and pulsing with each shoot of seed as I fill her pussy and spread her cheeks so I can watch the shiny little gem twitch inside her ass with every clench and spasm.

"Oh, fuck." I sigh and work my cock in and out of her a few more times, using her fluttering to work the last shot of seed from my balls. When she's filled and I'm emptied, I pull out and tap on that gem.

She moans and arches her back, lifting her ass up higher in the air. Her cunt pulses, and the first dribble of cum drips out of her.

"That's good, baby. Push it all out so I can see. You know how much I like to watch."

Emily hangs her head and pushes the rest of my cum from her wet hole while the butt plug winks in her ass, and I spread her wide so I can see everything. Cum drips out of her and falls to the floor. I'll clean it up later.

"Are you ready?" I ask.

"Hmm?"

I grab her plug by the flared base and pull, and she cries out as I pull it free. Her hole is puffy and wet, and it tightens up now that it's empty. She flexes her muscles, and another bead of cum works its way free, sliding down her swollen clit and splattering on the cement floor.

"Feels even better coming out, doesn't it?" I ask and pull my jeans up, shoving the toy into my pocket and tucking my cock away.

"Mmm." She breathes hard as she stands and smooths her skirt down until she's covered.

Grinning, I spin her around and claim her mouth, kissing her until she's mellowed against me. I nip her lush bottom lip and smile against her mouth. "I fucking love you, baby."

She kisses me back, and I don't mind that she doesn't answer in kind. I know she loves me even if she can't say the words back yet. She says it with every lingering glance, every soft sigh when

I bottom out inside her. She tells me every time she reaches for me in her sleep and holds me tight.

Emily pulls back and stares at me, her thumbs sweeping along my jawline. Her eyes go soft. "I love you too."

My heart trips into a gallop as I pull her in for a hug and drop a kiss into her hair.

"Oh, I'm still dripping." She makes an unhappy, pouty sound. "This no panties thing isn't working."

I grab a handful of ass and squeeze it, ignoring the way she wiggles against me. "Oh, I don't know. I think it's working out great."

"Of course you do. You're the one benefitting from it. Meanwhile, I'm dripping, and it is *running* down my leg."

She turns in my arms so her back's flush against me, and I lean down and lick the side of her neck, teasing her scent gland and taming her until she's arching against me once more. Her ass rubs against my front. I bite down lightly, just enough to make her gasp and squirm some more. The more she moves, the more my cum's gonna drip out of her, and the more she's gonna smell like me when we go back upstairs and she checks on the progress of her nest that's currently infiltrated by so many unfamiliar alpha contractors.

"I don't see the problem," I say, enjoying her low growl of irritation and holding her tighter. I suck on her scent gland, lapping up her sweet lemon scent.

She stops fighting me and goes still. "Fine. Then you can join me. No underwear, and when they pound your ass and fill you up, you get to drip everywhere too."

I bite her a little harder and slide a hand up to her breast and squeeze. She says it as if I wouldn't enjoy it. "Deal."

"Oh, you're such a pervert." She wiggles free, and I let her go this time, mostly because it gives me a chance to spank her on her naughty ass. I get one good smack in before she dances away from me, out of reach.

"Yes, but I'm *your* pervert," I clarify.

Emily grins and shakes her head, backs away slowly, then turns and runs to the elevator.

Fuck it. I'll clean up our mess later. I'm still pulling up and zipping my jeans when I chase her and jam my hands into the closing elevator doors and force my way inside before she can leave me behind. I pull the lever that closes the door and hit the button for our floor. I've been watching Bobbie work the ancient thing.

As the elevator lifts, I back her into a corner and cup her face in my hands, lifting her up for a kiss while I bend down to meet her. My mouth claims hers, and I fuck it with my tongue like I just fucked her downstairs. The elevator rattles as we arrive.

I follow her inside, and we go upstairs and stop at the top to peek at the renovations and see how they're going. Putting in a door isn't as simple as I thought. They've taken the walls down to the studs, and they're reframing things. The end result will be a pair of French doors with stained glass insets to match the fancy windows in the dining room downstairs.

The alpha contractors glance up and then ignore us, going back to work as their tools whirr and sawdust flies onto the tarps they've laid down to protect everything from the mess.

"Come on, let's go eat lunch. I'm starving." I worked up quite the appetite this morning.

Tom heats up the leftovers from dinner last night, and we sit in the kitchen while he throws it all into the hot oven. I'd have used the microwave. He's fancier than me. I'm sure his way tastes better, and it makes me glad he knows this kind of shit so he can help us take care of our girl the way she deserves.

I sniff the air, my stomach growling. "That already smells good."

He smiles and jabs the corkscrew into a bottle of wine he pulled from their fancy ass wine pantry. His hand twists as he works it in, then pulls it out with a pop and leaves the bottle to breathe, whatever *that* means.

"I guess we can't leave while they're here working," Emily says.

"Where did you want to go?" Tom asks. He pulls out three glasses and sets them in front of us.

"We still haven't gone to the park. The weather's supposed to be nice for a while," she says.

"Yeah, what do you do all day when you're here?" I ask. Marcus has to leave to go to his office, but Tom explained he sets his own schedule and he's taking time off to help us settle in.

He pours the wine for us. "Deal with the gallery, read, do yoga, watch a movie, or go shopping. Occasionally, Marcus drags me to Broadway for a show. There are a few restaurants we like that we'll take you to once he catches up on the clients he rescheduled. And of course I take photos. Sometimes I take videos too." He takes a sip of his wine and holds my gaze. "Just like what you did this morning."

Oops.

We've been caught.

Wait, how the fuck does he know that? The smug, smart bastard smirks while Emily glances between us. I swear, occasionally I think he can read my mind. Tom pulls his phone from his pocket, taps at it, and sets it on the counter. It's security camera footage of me fucking Emily over the bike, my bare ass pumping into her.

"What... Where is there a camera down in the basement? I don't remember seeing one. Oh my God." Emily freezes as she watches it with her wine glass stopped halfway to her mouth. She looks at me, and something about my expression must give me away. "You knew about this?" She slaps me on the arm and gives me an adorably grumpy face.

I scrub a hand through my hair as Tom lets the video play. "The owner had the super put in cameras a few years ago. There's a security guard and an entire wall of screens showing the feeds that cover the common areas of the building. I explained that we're newly bonding. Many of them are mated, so they know how it is. They deleted the feed as a courtesy. I would recommend, however, that you refrain from any further adventures unless you want a room full of security guards watching you."

I don't mind, but Emily's got her hand pressed to her mouth, so I guess that basement and elevator shenanigans are off the table now. Tom peeks in the oven to check on our food. "You know, if you want to join me on a photoshoot, I wouldn't mind. Have you ever used a real camera before, Sam?"

No. But now I fucking want to. Emily's draining her wine glass and holding it out for a top up.

"Wanna be my model, baby?" I ask her, petting her hair.

"I was wondering the same thing," Tom says, shoving his hands in his pockets all casually.

Suspiciously casual.

"Umm, sure. Wait. What kind of modeling?" She narrows her eyes, as if she's suspicious too. *Smart girl.*

"I'll show you. Our food has some time before it's ready." He adds more time on the oven timer and leads us into the bedroom he shares with Marcus. Up on the walls, large prints have been hung up in thick, black frames.

They're mostly closeups of intimate moments or a backlit model showing off the curve of their anatomy printed in black and white. Not all of them are explicit, although all of it is erotic. Some focus on the play of shadows across the model's ribs, or the way clawing fingers leave shallow divots as they grasp a thigh. Each one is beautiful in a raw, distinctly primal human way.

The largest one hangs over their bed, and it shows the closeup of a man's throat as an alpha bites his claiming mark into flesh, sharp canines sinking deep until a small trickle of blood runs down the other male's lightly muscled chest. I know that chest. Those hands. That small scar on the bicep.

"That's you guys. You photographed your mating," I say, staring at it. The alpha's face is shadowed in the dim lighting, his hair hanging down, so all the viewer's attention is focused on the flash of white teeth that bite into tender skin.

"I did. And I'd like to photograph yours too." Tom smiles and stares up at the pictures with fondness. "When you're ready."

I reach and grab Emily's hand, threading our fingers together and squeezing. She squeezes me back. "I'd like that."

"Me too," she says.

The timer's beeping draws us back into the kitchen, and we eat and make plans and wait for Marcus to come home tonight and the contractors to leave so we can speak freely.

We'll decide to wait for our nest to be done. For it to be special.

But that doesn't mean we can't practice until then. I blow on my pasta to cool it enough so I can eat it, and I grin as I chew.

Lots of practicing.

Chapter Twenty

MARCUS

WE'VE SETTLED INTO A NICE ROUTINE THAT LEAVES ME SATISFIED on a visceral level. Early morning sex with Tom, sometimes in the shower, before I head to work. Group play with anyone who wants to join in when I get home. Sam is a voyeur who enjoys watching as much as he likes to take part. Now that Tom's put a camera in his hands, the boy's incorrigible.

Naughty puppy.

Tom thinks it's hilarious until he has to teach the eager beta the next stage of being a photographer, post processing. They've disappeared into the office and left me and Emily on the couch. It's a fifty-fifty chance if they're working right now or fooling around.

I don't know what I love more, the sound of our turning pages as we both read, the crackling fire that wards off the early autumn chill coming through the open window, or the warm press of her small body against mine underneath our oversized blanket.

I hold my book open with one hand, flipping the page with my thumb by leaning its weight against my knee because I won't stop carding my fingers through her hair for anything in the world, not even for reading.

"Marcus," she says, her voice soft.

"Hmm?"

"When will the work upstairs be done?"

"Early next week. Tuesday, I think. And then the housekeeper comes to do a deep clean. The delivery is scheduled for Friday. Why?"

"Did you talk to Sam yet?" she asks.

Ah.

I close my book around my thumb to mark my place and look down at her, brushing her hair from her pretty face so I can see her better. "I did. He wants to be mated in the nest when it's finished. How do you feel about that?"

The skin between her brow creases as she thinks. "I want to wait for mine until my next heat. Is that okay?"

"Of course it is. But I meant about him using the nest for his mating. Are you sure it's still okay with you?" I ask.

She frowns and presses her book to her chest as she tips her head back to get a better look at me from her spot on my lap. "Where else would we do it?"

Emily doesn't know how precious she is. How big her heart and her capacity to love are. Some omegas are so territorial they won't allow anyone but the children in the nest except during a heat. But she's already planning movie nights, and she's talked Tom into mounting a video projector to her ceiling. Not that he needed much convincing. I'm sure he'll hook it up to porn at his first opportunity. Anything to earn a good spanking.

"You're right. It's the perfect place." This is what's perfect. Our pack. It's how it should be, and maybe it took a while to find them all, but they were worth waiting for.

"I've been thinking about something else I wanted to ask about," she says. "Why did you come by the clinic that night?"

"I didn't tell you that story?"

"You were in Boston for a business meeting," she says.

I watch the fire flicker and pop while I rub a strand of her hair between my fingers. "I've always known I'd have a pack. Some alphas don't feel it, or don't care, but it was something I knew about myself. Tom and I found each other early. And it happens like that for some. Sometimes the personal bond or emotion is so strong the pack bond forms over time. Other times, it's more of an instinctual reaction. A whiff of pheromones that triggers the urge. Tom and I had the first. We bonded in our early twenties, much to his family's horror. Their ambitions for him were shattered when he announced we were mated and he was moving to America with me. After a few years, most of them learned to live with it."

"Except for his father."

I nod. "Except for him. But after he passed away in a car accident, the rest of the family slowly came around one by one. They'd already lost one family member. There wasn't any sense in willfully losing another who was right there if only they'd pick up the phone. So they did. The betrayal was deep and it took him a long time to forgive them. Over the years, we talked about expanding the pack. We dated a little. We went to clubs and parties and met as many people as we could. And when that failed, we joined matching service after matching service. We did too many pheromone swabs for me to count. And… nothing. We thought maybe our pack was in England. That's where Tom and I had bonded and where my great-grandfather was born. So for a year we lived there in a tiny flat in London. We went on a lot of first dates. Filled out profiles. Went to clubs. Did even more pheromone swabs. Nothing. We never found anyone else who triggered my nose.

"So that's when we talked about adopting. We looked at a dozen websites and filled out an application. We thought that maybe if we weren't finding our pack with lovers, perhaps our pack was supposed to be with our children. And then Tom got his big break. He got a deal for his first show in a tiny gallery in London. We put the adoption application in a drawer. We focused on work. There'd be time later, we thought. What was the rush? We were still young. And then... we never did it. We moved back to New York. I got a promotion. His first show was a hit. He sold eight pieces his first night. The orders for custom photo shoots came pouring in. We both started traveling for work. He was booking sessions all over Europe and North America, even Tokyo once. I was flying out to sign new clients and meet with other firms. So I started going to clubs whenever I was out of town. Rut bars. Speed date rings. Free heat clinics. Omega centers. In whatever new city I went to, I went looking. And then I found you."

"How did you know?" she asks.

"Meeting you and Sam felt like coming home. Like I was whole now. It only took one sniff."

She sits up, and I let her go, her hair slipping through my fingers. Emily sits beside me on the sofa and stares into the flames. "I never believed in the fated mate stuff like some omegas do. My parents are betas. They fell in love and chose to be together. I thought that's what it would be like for me too. That I'd have what they had. But all the alphas I ever dated wanted more. They wanted me to feel something I didn't know how to give them. So they left. And I tried dating a couple of betas for a while but... there was always a fear that eventually I'd meet an alpha and leave them, so they left me first before they could get hurt."

"Good."

She turns on the sofa to face me, her eyes wide with surprise as the blanket slips off her shoulders. "What?"

I grab her by the arm to keep her from getting up and drag her closer until she has to either choose to settle on my lap or push off the couch. "I would have waited my whole life to find you, Emily. But I'm glad I didn't have to. I'm happy that we get to form our pack and make babies and have a whole life together, and it's fine if you don't believe in fate because I believe enough for the both of us. You were made for us, and I can't wait to make you ours because now that I know you, I can't imagine going back to a life without you."

Her arms go around my neck as she sits on my thigh, and I loop an arm around her hips to steady her. "Oh, that's actually very sweet."

I chuckle, my hand sliding down to cup her ass. "There's nothing I want to do to you that's sweet."

She fists her hands on my shoulders and arches back so she can see me better. "All three of you are huge perverts." She smiles as she says it.

"Oh, sweetheart, you have no idea." If she'd only seen some of the outfits Tom's got bookmarked for her.

She wiggles on my lap, her knee dangerously close to sensitive parts. "I'm pretty sure I got a good idea of it this morning."

"Oh? What'd you do this morning?"

Her cheeks pinken. "You'll find out. It's a surprise."

"A surprise?" I arch one brow and consider it for all of two seconds before I decide it's time to play dirty. "Is my pack keeping secrets from their alpha?" My hands drift higher up her back, moving to her ribs. "Do I need to torture it out of you?"

The first barely-there graze on her ribs makes her twitch. The second sets her squirming. When she finally realizes I'm tickling her, it's too late for her to stop me.

"Stop! St—stop it." She giggles and shrieks and pants, her hair whipping me in the face as she tries to clamber off and almost falls off my lap. But I keep her where I want her. I keep her safe. By the end, she can barely catch her breath as I stroke my hands over her back, soothing her.

"Are you ready to be a good girl and give into your alpha?" I growl.

Emily rocks against me, her skirt riding up her smooth thighs. She bites her lip and moans, her pupils wide and her eyes dark with pooled desire. It's amazing what simple little things make my pretty little omega want to submit to me. Grabbing a slim wrist and pinning it to her back makes her breath hitch. A tug on the hair at her nape makes her mouth drop open. A slap to her heart-shaped bottom makes her wiggle. Tickling her until she's panting leaves her pliant in my arms. Such simple things that trigger this exchange of power between us. A power I'm all too eager to take whenever she's willing to give it. A power I covet. After all, I'm a greedy bastard and I want all of her. I want everything.

"Only naughty omegas keep secrets from their alphas. You've been a bad girl. How are you going to make it up to me?"

She hesitates, then goes for my belt, working it open and undoing the fastener and zipper. I'm hard already as she pulls me free and slides her hand up and down my shaft. Her fingers barely wrap halfway around the thickest part of my girth as she strokes.

I let her take her time, let her explore me and play while I gather up her long hair and bring it to my nose to sniff. So fucking mouthwatering. Her sugary sweet lemon scent is bright and juicy. My teeth ache with the urge to bite into her soft skin. To mark her as mine. Claim her as ours.

Emily teases my crown, dips a fingertip into my slit and smears the pearl of pre-cum already gathering there. When she brings that drop of fluid to her mouth, her little pink tongue darting out to taste it, I can't hold back my groan. She makes me want to do such filthy things to her.

I pull her higher onto my lap and notch myself into place. With no panties to stop me, there's nothing keeping me from sinking inside her as I bring her down on my cock and slowly feed it into her. She closes her eyes and moans, throwing her arms around my neck as she helps work herself onto my cock and sinks down until I'm buried deep. I never want to leave. Her tight, wet heat is like a homecoming.

We move together like a wave, her hips rising as she rides my lap and presses her forehead against mine, and I surge into her. It's a slow, sweet torture, the way her pussy clenches on my cock and she sighs. I capture her mouth with mine and swallow down her little noises and sighs as she grinds. It's a claiming, both body and soul. *Mine*, each press of my hips says. *I'm yours*, her body answers.

She shudders and breaks the kiss to drop her head back, her back arching as she rides my cock and takes her pleasure. I wrap my arms tighter around her waist to keep her there and lean down to kiss and lick her neck. She trusts me enough to let go and let me take her weight.

I curl around her and drag my tongue up the side of her neck, licking over her scent gland and sucking it. Each pull of my mouth makes her pussy quiver. She squeezes me tight when I scratch my teeth over it.

I don't know who I'm teasing more, her or me.

The urge to bite, to mark and claim, comes from a deep, dark place.

It speaks of possession. Of jealous guarding. Of taking.

And I ignore it, pushing it down, licking and sucking and kissing her instead until she's ready. She is mine. Ours. And that's enough for now. She has no chance of escaping us now that we're inside her heart. Her soul. We are her pack, and she's our omega, and in her next heat I'm going to bite our claim so deep into her neck that she'll wear my scars forever.

I nibble at her, choosing the precise area I'll one day sink my teeth into, and Emily comes undone with a moan and a shudder. Her sweet little pussy squeezes me, tipping me over that edge. Pulsing and groaning against her neck, I empty inside her and fill her to bursting, my knot swelling past the curve of her pubic bone to lock us together as my body practices breeding her.

One day.

Soon.

We have time.

Now that we've found each other, we have the rest of our lives. She goes limp on my lap as her aftershocks squeeze my knot, milking the dregs of my seed. I press a kiss to her mouth, her forehead, her hair, and tuck her into the hollow places of my body where she fits perfectly. I stroke her back, smoothing my hands over her as we wait for our tie to fade.

"I love you, sweetheart." I kiss her temple and drag her scent even deeper into my head until it's etched into me.

Her arms squeeze tighter around my neck. "I love you too."

My entire being bursts with happiness with those four simple words that mean everything.

I purr for her and hold her until my knot releases, then abandon my book and carry her into my bedroom. Sam and Tom look up from their cuddling on the bed as I set her down with them and go into the bathroom to draw her a bath. While the water's heating, I lean against the open doorway and watch them lie together with a deep sense of rightness in my bones.

My pack.

Mine.

Chapter Twenty-One

TOM

It's almost too cold to continue doing yoga on the terrace, but I'm loath to give up this view. From up here, I can see everything. The people walking at a steady clip on the sidewalk. The cars and yellow taxis weaving around them. All of the leaves have turned. Central Park is bathed in shades of green, yellow, and orange. It's a chilly, overcast day that reminds me of England.

With my headphones in, I miss Emily coming out onto the terrace while I finish out my session with one last stretch. When she leans against the railing and looks out, I fish the earbuds from my ears and tap my music off.

"It's so pretty up here," she says.

"It's my favorite place."

"I didn't mean to interrupt." She wraps her cardigan tighter around herself and tucks her hands. "I just wanted to watch the sunset. It gets dark so early now."

"You're cold. Here." I grab the hem of my hoodie and peel it off. The crisp autumn air is downright arctic where it blows against my sweat covered skin. The short-sleeve shirt I wore underneath is useless at keeping me warm, but I don't mind. This is the first time she's sought me out alone.

She nibbles her bottom lip and takes the hoodie, then gives me a shy smile and slips into it. I don't miss how she gives it a little sniff. It's pleasing to know she genuinely likes the way I smell. That she's accepting me as pack. Marcus and I bonded slowly after years of knowing one another. I wasn't completely sure what that might mean for her and Sam. Would they feel the same sort of biological imperative, or would that also take them years?

The hoodie swallows her to mid-thigh and hangs over her fingers. She's adorable. "Thanks."

Before it can blow away, I grab my yoga mat from the rough floor and roll it up, then stick it in the lidded box that stays out on the terrace. "I've been thinking of places that you might want to see. I know Sam's busy. How do you feel about a little outing? Just us?" I ask.

Her face brightens. "Oh! Sure. What did you have in mind?"

"I would be a terrible secret keeper if I told you." I throw one side of the French door open and follow her in.

Emily gives me a suspicious, assessing glance. "How will I know how to dress if I don't know where we're going or what we're doing?"

Nice try. I lean down, letting my lips slide along her cheek as I whisper against her ear. "I think you look perfect as you are." Everyone we come across will scent me all over her. There won't be any question of who she's with and if she's taken if she smells like me and wears my clothes. I'm beginning to understand why Marcus has such a brutish possessive streak he tries to keep hidden. I'm wondering if I'm not more similar to the alpha than I thought.

Her cheeks pinken as I pull away and head into the bedroom so I can grab a sweater from the closet. I leave my joggers and trainers on so she won't feel so out of place with her casual outfit. She's wearing her coat, a puffy ballet slipper pink thing that swallows her up, and everytime I see her in it, I grin. She looks like a marshmallow. A lemon candy-flavored treat. Biteable.

I grab my wool trench coat from its peg and slip into it, then make sure I have my wallet and grab the keys from the bowl by the door. We both chat with Bobbie as we spill out onto the street.

"It isn't far if you don't mind walking."

"Sure." She falls into step beside me and we head east.

"Autumn is my favorite time of year in the city." It smells less like hot, stinking garbage and piss. "Feels a little more like home. Doesn't seem to matter how many years I live here, I can't quite get used to the heat of summer. I'm glad you're seeing the city before the winter when everything looks sad. With all the traffic, any snow that falls turns gray pretty fast."

"It's like that in Boston too. Do you miss England?"

I shake my head, and we stop at a crosswalk and wait for the signal to turn. While we stand there, I put my hand to the small of her back and she inches just a little bit closer until her coat brushes mine. "I miss some things. The tea. American tea isn't really tea at all. And iced? I'm not sure why you'd ruin a perfectly good cuppa with ice. Chips with malt vinegar. Popping out with friends to the pub. Taking a train to another country for a quick getaway. But I wouldn't trade my life to go back there. What about you? Will you miss Boston if you move here?"

She was silent as she thought about it and we waited for the cars to pass. "There are things I'll miss. Boston is a weird town. I moved there for college. There's a sort of speakeasy in the basement of an Italian restaurant. And the entrance to the best shopping is hidden behind a vending machine. There's a lot of museums and art exhibits and festivals. It's close enough to visit my parents without them expecting me to be over there constantly. But I wouldn't call it home. I think I stayed because it was easier than thinking of what I really wanted to do."

This is a difficult subject to bring up, but it's an important one. One I can sympathize with. "Sam mentioned there was tension with your parents." I leave the statement open-ended so she can pick it up if it's something she wants to talk about. I don't want to push her too fast. None of us do. But I want to get to know her too. It's a tricky balance. One that I'm not used to. I've never really seriously dated anyone other than Marcus before.

When the pedestrian light turns green, I urge her forward until I see our destination just up ahead. The building is plain, yet imposing. Easy to miss. Not something you'd ever look at and wonder about. Square and made of rows upon rows of huge glass window panes, it's a typical New York City building. Unless you know what's inside.

Emily tucks a strand of windblown hair behind her ear. "I love them, but... they're both betas and so is my sister. I'm the only omega in my whole family and they don't really understand it. They certainly didn't know how to handle it.

"I was in school when my first heat started. With my cycles, I don't get a lot of warning time. It was even worse when I was a teenager. I sent half the football team into a rut. It was chaos. The omega center had to come and pull me out and take me home. My mom was mortified. They weren't ready to deal with it. Didn't know how to handle that sort of thing. Nobody suspected I was going to present as an omega, not even the doctors. So they locked me in my room.

"It hurt so bad I thought I was dying. You learn about heats and ruts in health class, but it's not the same as living through it. I didn't have a phone in my room, so I tried to climb out through my second-story window, but the plastic rose trellis broke and I fell. Broke my ankle and ended up needing surgery. They were just relieved the hospital put me out for my whole heat and didn't wake me up until it was over."

I steer us out of the flow of foot traffic and stop, and she follows my lead. "Bloody hell. They sound even worse than my parents and I didn't know that was possible. My father never quite forgave me for not turning out to be an alpha like him. It's draining trying to live up to someone's unrealistic expectations of you. I'm sorry you went through your first heat alone. Your parents sound like a couple of muppets."

"Muppets?" She looks at me with wide eyes, then bursts into laughter. It's an honest laugh full of belly breathing and a dainty snort. It's cute. The wind catches her hair again, and she turns into it so it blows the strands out of her face. "I'm not laughing at you, I promise. I'm sorry. I was just imagining my parents as muppets." After a little more giggling, she pulls herself together. "I'm sorry about your shitty parents. Your dad sounds like an ass if he thinks you being a beta means you're not as good as an alpha."

"He was," I agree.

The wind blows again and Emily shivers from the cold. "All right. So where are we going? Will you tell me now?"

"We're here." I jerk my chin over her head to point, and she turns around to get an eyeful of the nondescript building. "Come on."

I pull the door open, and she stands as still as a statue in the doorway as she cranes her head back and looks up. "What… How…"

My hand at the small of her back propels her in, and I follow her deeper into the lobby. "It's the headquarters for a landscaping company."

She spins in a slow circle. "It's beautiful. These trees have to be really old to be so tall."

"Come on." I take her hand and lead her to the stairs that go down to a small, rectangular pool of water. With our backs to the street on the other side of the wall of glass, it's easy to pretend you're in a park in the springtime. "They stay green because of all the glass and the lights. It acts like a greenhouse."

We sit on the bottom steps. It's like being in a park. From the outside, you'd never know it's here. From the inside, you'd never know you were in one of the most densely populated cities in the world. The soft music piped in through hidden speakers adds to the magical feeling of the place.

"This is so much better than I thought my surprise was going to be," she says, her voice breathy and full of wonder. "It even smells good." She reaches over and strokes the tip of a fern, then digs her fingers into the soil. "They're real."

"Look up."

She does, and I enjoy the sight of her pale white throat as she tips her head back and looks at the stacked balconies of the tower's interior. It's a high-rise building. That's a lot of floors. And each balcony is trimmed in plants, their vines cascading over the side like a green waterfall of leaves.

"Wow. It's so beautiful."

I wish I had my camera. Marcus would love this moment. He'd be jealous he didn't get to share it. But a small part of me likes that it's just us right now. I don't mind sharing. I like to watch. But this moment is mine. "It is. It's very beautiful."

Emily looks at me and blushes, her cheeks and the tip of her ears turning pink. Making her blush has quickly become one of my favorite things. She's so easy to tease. Her eyes soften and her shoulder bumps against me. "Thank you."

"You're welcome."

Pointing, she tells me the names of all the plants she knows. All of them look pretty much the same to me. I'm not a plebian. I can tell the difference between a rose bush and a dahlia. But her knowledge about plants is extensive. It's clearly one of her passions.

"That's a Prince of Orange Philodendron. I'm surprised they have it planted here. It's fairly rare. See how some of the leaves are yellowish or even peach? That's where it gets its name from."

"It's pretty. Is it your favorite?"

She shrugs, but smiles. "Sure. I have a lot of favorites, though. It's hard to pick just one."

"Do you miss your plants? I saw your collection. It's massive."

Emily nods and leans more against me. "I do, but the house sitter sends me photos every few days. She's doing a good job, so I'm not too worried about them."

We sit like that until a cloud of people walk through, edging past us on the stairs as they make their way to the bank of elevators beyond the trees. Dressed in suits and dark coats, they're ready for a meeting. Her stomach growls, and I glance at my watch. Marcus and Sam will be home soon.

"We should head back." A very bad idea forms in the back of my mind. It's the best sort of bad idea one can have. An impulsive one. "Ready for your surprise?" I stand, and she blinks up at me before taking my hand. I pull her up and glance around the emptier lobby. The group of people who came through have gotten into their elevator. There's only a few lingering, talking on phones or chatting with one another.

"This wasn't it?"

I jump down those last two stairs and step into the dirt, digging my hands into the soil. It's cold and damp against my skin, and it's getting embedded underneath my short nails, but the look on Emily's face is worth it. Her expression is a mix of baffled amusement and horror. That's my favorite kind.

"What are you doing?" she whispers, glancing around.

I rip a few roots as I tug it free, scooping the small plant from the ground. "I would think that was obvious. All right, luv, time to go."

The pilfered plant drops soil onto the smooth concrete floor as I hold it to my chest. I grab her hand with my filthy one, smearing her with dirt, and lead her up the stairs at a brisk pace. You can't run. That attracts too much attention. But we definitely hurry.

We hit the glass door and push it open, cold air smacking me in the face as we spill out onto the street.

"Hey!" someone shouts as the door swings shut behind us.

I've changed my mind. Running is definitely a good idea. I squeeze Emily's hand in mine. "Run, luv!"

And we do. A few people glance at us, but most New Yorkers know how to mind their own business. We dash down the street and run a few blocks, getting lucky with the crosswalks. Outside of our building, we stop to breathe.

The plant's lost most of its dirt, and my coat is filthy. The dry cleaner's going to have a hell of a time cleaning it. But Emily's wide smile and laugh make it worth it. Her smile is radiant. It lights up her eyes and makes them crinkle a bit at the corners. I've always been slightly more partial to men than women, but she captivates me. Completes us.

She holds my gaze, and something passes unspoken between us.

Something soft and warm.

I lean down and claim her mouth with a kiss, a tender brushing of lips, and I'm careful not to crush the delicate plant in my grip. She has no such qualms. Emily throws her arms around my neck and curls me down to deepen it. My tongue slips into her mouth, stroking against hers. Tasting her. Marking territory.

When we break for air, she rests her forehead against mine. "You're crazy." She says it with fondness. "And that's why I love you. And for the record, I think you're perfect exactly as you are."

My heart squeezes, my chest too tight to contain it. I didn't realize how much I wanted—needed—her to desire me as much as her dynamic makes her crave our alpha.

"I love you too. And I prefer to call it being creative. But I just realized… we don't have a pot to put this in."

"Come on," she says, grabbing my empty hand and leading me past Bobbie and into the creaking elevator. "I have an idea."

A few moments later, I cross my dirt-stained hands over my chest and look down at our handiwork. "I like it."

"I'll need to get some potting soil to fill it in, but it'll work for tonight."

"I'm home!" Sam calls from the doorway. "I brought pizza."

"In the library!" I call back.

Sam pokes his head in the doorway and looks between us, then glances down. "Cool plant. Hungry?"

"Starving."

We wash up and eat, and my phone dings with a text from Marcus saying his meeting is running late. I put a few slices in the toaster oven so he can heat it up when he gets home, and we settle on the sofa in the living room and eat.

"Wanna play Mario Kart?" Sam asks when we've finished, grabbing the remote and switching the input.

"Only if you want to lose," I answer, throwing down the gauntlet.

He gives me an appraising look, then grins, his cheek dimpling. "Game on. Be prepared to eat those words. I'm the King of the Kart."

"Care to make it interesting?" I ask, arching a brow and glancing over Emily's head.

"What'd you have in mind?" Sam selects the game from the

options on the console and then gets up and grabs the controllers from their charging stand.

"Hmm… How about… Loser has to say yes to everything the winner asks of them for an entire day?"

Sam licks his lips and grins wider. "Deal."

"Can I play Yoshi?" Emily asks, taking one of the controllers.

"Of course, baby." Sam drops a kiss into her hair and chooses his character. I pick mine, and then we select a track.

After five rounds, you'd think I wouldn't be surprised when Emily comes out of nowhere, her green dinosaur character tossing a turtle shell at me and knocking my cart over before flying past and nailing a boost that sends her way out in front of Sam.

"How the bloody hell are you so good at this?" I ask, a little baffled and slightly aroused.

She retakes first place in the final lap and drives over the finish line before Sam can catch up to her. I'm still spinning in the back when the screen cuts to our final score. She shrugs. "It's all about the way you drift. Does this mean you *both* have to say yes to everything I tell you to do for an entire day?"

"I'm home!" Marcus calls from the doorway.

"In the living room!" we shout in unison.

"You're food's in the toaster. I already timed it. Just hit start," I tell him.

He stands in the doorway and loosens his tie, flexing his neck from side to side as he tugs it down. "Thanks, babe. You guys look like you're having fun. Let me just set this down and grab my food and then I'll join you.

Marcus picks his briefcase back up and disappears. He's only gone for a minute or two before he returns without the briefcase or his jacket or tie. The top button of his shirt is undone, a hint of chest hair peeking out. "Why is there a plant in my mini bar globe?" He undoes the buttons on his sleeves and rolls them up, baring his muscled forearms.

Sam hits the control to select our next track. Rainbow Road. Everyone's favorite. I can't wait to get slaughtered on it.

"Because it looks good there," Emily says, glancing up from the screen.

Marcus frowns and opens his mouth to say something, then shuts it again without speaking. *Smart man.* He makes a noncommittal noise, then turns around and heads into the kitchen.

Emily and I share a loaded glance and growing smiles. She snuggles deeper into my side until she's half laying on me. Not to feel left out, Sam picks her feet up from the seat and sets them in his lap, rubbing the sole of one.

"You guys ready to lose again?" she asks.

Chapter Twenty-Two

EMILY

It's coming, it's coming, it's coming! I glance at the Nested app for the hundredth time as I watch the green dot make slow progress around the city.

"There it is!" Sam calls from the window.

"What?" The app says they're still blocks away. And then it refreshes, and the dot moves at an impossible diagonal through buildings and stops on our street. I run to the window and look out, following Sam's pointing finger. There it is. Nested's delivery truck.

The truck pulls up to the unloading area and idles. Two big alphas jump out and tug the back open, and then they pull the plastic-wrapped nest out in pieces. Even the pieces are huge.

Oh, shit. How are they going to get it up here in the tiny elevator?

I call down to the lobby and ask the front desk person to let Bobbie know we're expecting a delivery, and then I pace. Twenty minutes later, there's a heavy knock on the front door and Sam throws it open.

"We got a delivery," the alpha says. "Where do you want it?"

"Upstairs."

If the delivery men are mad about having to bring the heavy nest pieces up a flight of stairs, they don't show it. They lift the furniture pieces up like it's nothing and Sam and I hug the wall upstairs as they set the parts down one by one and go back and forth for the rest.

They take less than an hour to haul everything in, unwrap it, and put it together. He does a final inspection to check for damage, then hands me a tablet to sign for receipt of delivery. Sam shows them out while I pet the nest with reverent strokes.

It. Is. Enormous!

Oh. My. God.

The bed is twice the width of a king, and the canopy almost touches the high ceilings. It's perfect. I jump into it through the opening and shove my face into the mattress, sniffing the awful factory smell that I can't wait to replace. Sitting up, I glance at Sam, who's giving me a goofy smile.

"Get naked," I say.

He raises his eyebrows but tugs up the hem of his T-shirt without question or comment. His muscled torso flexes as he undresses. I shuck out of my clothes, throwing them in the huge nest to help us cover more ground faster, and then I flop down onto my back and rub all over the mattress. Sam sees what I'm doing and follows suit without prompting, diving onto the other end of the nest and rubbing and rolling all over as he works his scent into the fibers.

It won't be enough. If it was a normal bed, then sure. But this mattress is orgy size. It would take us days to cover all of it and we don't have days because it needs to be perfect for tonight, since this is the night Marcus claims Sam.

"Do we still have the laundry, or is it in the wash?" I ask.

"I think we still have it," Sam says. "I'll check."

I stretch and rub, trying to work my scent into every square inch I can reach. Sam comes back and upends the laundry bag, dumping it all out onto the bed. Perfect. Tom did a yoga session yesterday on the terrace, so his workout clothes are extra scented. I find his gray sweats and sniff them, satisfied with how strong his buttery shortbread cookie scent is, and then I rub it all over the mattress until the notes begin to layer one on top of one another.

"Wanna fuck?" Sam asks as he takes one of Marcus's under-shirts and drags it over the curved upholstered sides that form the nest's high lip. "That'll help."

It would, but while I want the scent of us embedded in the mattress, I don't want it stained. "I've got a better idea. Lie back."

Sam lies down and I hand him a pillow to rub against himself as I shimmy down his body and settle between his thighs. His cock is still in that in-between state of soft and hard and it fits all the way in my mouth as I envelop him to the base.

He groans, his cock twitching as it hardens on my tongue, and I lose some length as he fills my mouth. I suck, bobbing on his cock as he drops the pillow and reaches for another.

"I'm home!" Tom calls from downstairs. The front door slams shut.

"Upstairs!" Sam calls back. "Oh, fuck, baby. That's good." He runs his fingers through my hair and pushes it back so he can see the way my cheeks hollow as I suck on his tip while my hand squeezes and pumps his shaft.

"Oh, it's huge," Tom says, walking closer. "I like it. Why is there laundry everywhere?"

"We're making it smell like pack so *hnnng*—oh, God, baby, that's soooo fucking good. Don't stop."

Salty, musky, creamsicle pre-cum fills my mouth as I take Sam's cock into the back of my throat and swallow again like he's been teaching me. I press my nose to the thatch of hair at the base of his cock and hold him there until the urge to breathe can't be ignored. Sam's hips thrust, trying to follow me as I pull back and lave his head with my tongue, lapping up every drop.

"Get in here, man," Sam says between groans. "Fuck, baby. You're so good at sucking cock."

Clothes hit the floor and then the bed dips as Tom climbs on. He palms my sex, pulling my checks apart and prodding at my folds. He dips a finger in and adds another, fucking them into me as he tests how wet and ready I am. I pull off Sam's cock and look behind me. "No fluids on the bed until we've got the water-proof mattress cover on it."

"Yes, ma'am," Tom says, being a smart ass.

Omegas may tend to be naturally submissive, but our nests are our territory and betas and alphas come in by our invitation. Here, in this sacred space, I am its queen.

His fingers never stop as he fucks them in and out of me while I go back to sucking Sam's cock, working him exactly like he likes it. Quick pumps of his shaft. Lots of attention to his slit and the sensitive underside where his shaft meets the crown. I trace my tongue over the veins of his cock and take him to the back of my throat, swallowing him down until his breathing gets ragged and I'm starved for air.

His abdomen tenses and flexes. I palm the heavy weight of his sack and press a knuckle into the bulging underside. It pulses against my knuckle, his cock jumping in my mouth, and he cries out a warning as he shoots his first pump of seed into my belly. I swallow all of him down. After he's spent, I lick him clean, purring with happiness.

I take the scented pillow from his weak grip and hand him another to nuzzle as he lies there, basking in the endorphins of his blowjob.

"I have an idea," Tom says, slipping his fingers from my pussy. "Sam, turn around so she can straddle your face."

Sam flips around, and Tom nudges us into position, my pussy

hovering over Sam's mouth as I look down at his body and Tom settles behind me. The nest is so big it accommodates us easily, and I'm so grateful we waited a month, no matter that it felt like an eternity, and did the renovations. It was worth the wait.

He bends me over Sam, and his searching tip finds my entrance, sinking in with a stretch and a sigh as he works his way in deep. "Lap at your Mistress, puppy."

Sam nuzzles against my thigh, then tips his head back and slips his tongue through my folds. He licks through my labia, finds my clit, and rolls it in circles while Tom fucks me from behind, pushing me harder onto Sam's mouth with each thrust.

Can Sam breathe?

Tom grabs my hips and tilts them, hitting a spot inside me that makes my toes curl and my pussy push down on Sam's mouth.

Oh, fuck. Sam will figure it out.

Tom ruts into me, his thighs slapping against my ass, and each thrust rubs my clit on Sam's frantic tongue. Tension coils tight inside of me, a dull ache that begs for release. I forget my concern. Forget everything but the dick rearranging me to fit him better and the tongue swiping between my folds.

"You're soaked, luv. Is your puppy being a good boy? Is he keeping your cunt nice and wet for me?"

"So good." I pant and claw at the mattress, wishing there was a sheet to twist my fingers in as I ride Sam's face while Tom fucks me harder against that beautiful mouth. "He's such a good boy."

"He is. What a good, smart puppy we have. Now he's going to clean up this mess and lick up every drop." Tom's cock jerks deep inside of me with the first pulse of his release, his thrusts slowing as he works it deeper and comes.

Tom hisses out a breath and thrusts into me twice more before pulling free and moving back. I glance over my shoulder and see him watching us as I clench and release, working his cum from me. Sam's swiping tongue goes still and ready as he waits for it to drip into his mouth. Squeezing, I push out another bead, feeling it dribble from me.

Sam's cheeks brush against my inner thighs as he leans up and laps at it, licking at my folds before pushing inside me to get at every last drop.

Fuck, that's good. His soft cock twitches against his thigh, so I stroke it, rewarding him for being such a good boy. For licking me clean and not wasting a single drop of Tom's cum. He sucks at me, circling my clit, until I'm lost. I pant and ride his face, all thoughts and concerns gone until there's only pleasure left.

I sit up tall and grind against his face, taking my pleasure as he sucks every bit of seed from my pussy and laps at my clit again.

That tension snaps taut, then rips free as my walls clench around nothing, aching and empty, and I come on his face. He licks me through it, swallowing down my slick and Tom's seed and licking me clean until I'm spent and can't stand another ounce of sensation.

Unhooking my legs from his head, I fall onto my side and throw an arm across his body as Tom settles in at my back, and we cuddle, letting our sex and satisfaction pheromones soak into the mattress until we're recovered enough that we can get back to work.

We pass the pillows around like an assembly line as we all take turns rubbing against them while we wait for Marcus to get home.

"Let me show you what I bought," Tom says once all the pillows are scented. He gets up from the bed and gathers his cast-off clothes from the floor, throwing them down to the other end of the mattress we haven't gotten to yet.

It's gonna be a busy afternoon.

He pulls a box of string lights shaped like stars and crescent moons from a bag he dropped by the stairs. "These are what you wanted, right?"

They're precious and perfect. I rip the plastic box open and unwind the lights from the packaging inside. "I love them." I press a kiss to his mouth and tug him in for a deeper kiss. "Thank you."

Tom pushes my hair back and tucks it behind my ear. "Anything you want, luv."

"Will you help me hang them?"

He's tall, and he has the longest arms of the three of us. Tom stands on the mattress and wraps them around the canopy's poles, hanging them where I tell him to. It takes eight of the ten boxes he bought to get them just right.

I pull the enormous bag of nesting blankets and bedding from my old room while Sam rolls around on the bed and itches his back on the mattress while Tom shakes his head. "Let's get the waterproof cover and sheets on."

Getting it all on the mattress is harder than I thought it would be, but eventually we manage it. We all give the pillows one last rub, and then they hand them to me while I fit them into place, finding the perfect space for each one. My cute cloud pillow is last, and I set it in the middle of the pillow mountain in its place of honor.

Tired and finished and deliriously happy, I climb in and settle down for a nap with the both of them. The nest is cozy and warm, and it smells like us. That's how Marcus finds us later when he comes home, shrugging out of his jacket and draping it on the edge of the nest as I blink up at him through bleary eyes. He takes his clothes off and hesitates at the foot.

"May I enter the nest, omega?"

I smile and reach for him. "Always."

Marcus grins, showing off one sharp alpha canine as he puts a knee on the bed and climbs into the nest to settle down and join us. I hand him a pillow to scent, and he tells me about tonight's plans.

Tonight, we mark Sam.

Marcus will bite his claim into Sam and make the beta pack.

Chapter Twenty-Three

SAM

MY BELLY IS ALL FLUTTERY NERVES, AND IT'S NOT BECAUSE OF the prep—it's for what comes next. I pull the plug from my ass and drop it in the sink, shuddering as the sensation travels straight to my cock. The final one in the lineup is huge. It's over two inches wide at the flare. I haven't been able to take it yet, but now there's no choice. Marcus is finally going to fuck me tonight, and I need to be ready because he might be even bigger than this toy.

I flip the cap off the lube and pour a generous amount onto the blunted steel toy, slicking it well. I lift my leg up and perch it on the bathroom counter and reach back, pressing it to my hole and relaxing as I push. The stretch is intense, and I take deep breaths, doing my best to stay relaxed because tensing up undoes all my careful work today.

It takes an extra squirt of lube and three more attempts to get it in past the flared head, and then my hole tightens around it, snugging it up between my cheeks as my body locks onto it.

A little pre-cum drips onto the edge of the sink as I play with the plug a bit, making sure it's seated properly, and the stretch turns into pleasure.

Hands off now. I've been ordered not to touch myself

anymore than is necessary. I wash the smaller plug and my hands and go out to my bedroom, where Tom's waiting for me to finish.

"All done?" he asks, his legs crossed as he lounges in my armchair and flips the pages of his photography magazine. All he's wearing is a black and green-edged leather collar with a big silver D-ring in the front. He appears unfazed by his nudity, and even naked, he has a refined air about him. Maybe it's the accent. Or the hair. *God, he has gorgeous hair.*

"Done. I got it in."

Tom grins and uncrosses his legs. "Good boy."

Warmth curls in my belly at the praise, and I'm glad he's here. I'd be a nervous wreck without him guiding me through this.

"Are you ready?" he asks.

When I nod, he stands and crosses the room, his chest pressing to mine as he reaches around me and a hand slides between my cheeks to press on the flared steel base of the plug. He tugs on it, plays with it, and it's so deep inside of me I swear I can feel my belly bulge with every press and pull of it. My cock twitches against his hip, and I moan as my head rubs against him.

"You're not ready, silly puppy. You need your ring."

He steps away and pulls my cock ring from the porcelain bowl I've been keeping it in. His grip on my cock is unyielding as he works it over my head and down my half-swollen shaft. He fists me, tugging and working me until I'm breathing hard and pumping into his hand. "Now you're ready." He lets go of my cock and slaps me on the ass, the plug shifting and tugging at my hole.

I rock with it and gasp, a drop of pre-cum dripping onto the floor as my hard cock weeps and my ass aches. "Fuck," I grunt, wanting to take myself in my fist and pump until I find release, but knowing that I can't. It's forbidden. Tonight, the only way

I'm allowed to come is with my alpha's cock deep in my ass and his seed in my belly.

Tom sets a teasing finger to my leaking tip and rubs, spreading the moisture and dragging his nail on the sensitive underside until I'm shivering from the force it takes to hold still. To not rock against him. To not seek friction or the release I so desperately want.

"What a good boy you're being. I'll stop teasing you."

He doesn't. It's a lie. He plays with my sack instead, rolling my balls in his palm.

A knock jars the door.

"Come!" Tom says over his shoulder. He winks at me. "Not you."

Emily opens the door and stands there, and I groan at the sight of her, my cock bobbing against Tom. She's wearing a leather collar, but hers is baby pink and white. The D-ring at the center of her throat is gold. Her hair flows free and brushes the tops of her breasts, and she has a gold chain connecting them together with little pink hearts dangling from the wire ring that tightens around her erect nipples. Peeking out from the hair that covers her sex, there's a flash of metal down there too as she fidgets in the doorway.

"Are you ready?" she asks.

Fuck yes. Yes, I am. But speech is beyond me right now as she floats across the room like a naughty cupid and goes up on her tiptoes to kiss me. Tom stops teasing me, and she grabs his arm, hooking him to her side.

"We'll be waiting for you," she says. "Come out when you're ready."

I wait until they disappear into the nest and count to a hundred. There's a formality to this I wasn't expecting, and it makes me glad we practiced it this afternoon after Marcus came home.

It's time.

I walk out, and my heart trips against my ribs when I see them, lined up and waiting. Emily smiles reassuringly at me while Tom takes the lens cap off his camera. But it's Marcus I can't stop staring at. He stands there, nude and confident, in front of the nest's opening. In his hand, he's holding a black and red-edged leather collar with a black D-ring, and as I step before him and wait, he holds it before me.

"Samuel, I come to you as an alpha seeking pack. Will you submit?"

I sink to the ground and put my hands on my knees. "I do." The camera shutter snaps as I stare up at him. My alpha.

Marcus unbuckles the collar. "A beta's role is to accept an alpha's command. To guard the nest, and protect the omega and the young when the alpha is not present. To deliver discipline and maintain order. Will you pledge this service to your pack?"

"I do." He wraps the collar around my throat, and I lean my head down to give him the back of my neck as he buckles it into place. Wetness gathers in my eyes when it latches. It's snug. A physical reminder of his claim.

Marcus strokes a hand over my shoulder and steps closer. "Will you take as much pleasure as you give?" he asks. His thick, hard cock bobs at the side of my face.

"I will, alpha."

"Then give so you may receive."

To answer him, I lean up and take the rounded head of his cock into my mouth, wrapping my lips around it and sucking. I lave him with my tongue, gathering up the creamy pre-cum pearling at his tip with greedy swipes of my tongue. I swallow him down, taking him to the back of my throat and gagging myself on his length. He's girthy and large, too much to handle, and the need for air and relief from the burning stretch of my jaw drives me back.

"Pack, will you accept this beta?" Marcus asks.

"We will, alpha," Emily and Tom both answer.

"Then join us. Give and take, but do not let him come. That pleasure is mine."

"Yes, alpha."

Emily sinks onto the floor behind me and kisses my shoulder, her breasts and the cold chain connecting them pressing against my back as she reaches around to slide her hand down my stomach. She plays with the snug ring fitted around the base of my swollen cock. Her small hand gathers up the fluid leaking from my tip and spreads it over my sensitive head.

I moan around my mouthful of cock as she tugs me with teasing, playful movements, and Tom takes photos, memorializing this moment for eternity.

Marcus reaches for the ring on my collar and tugs, pulling me down on his cock and gagging me as he fucks into my throat and presses past the tight ring of leather. My cock jumps in Emily's hand and then she abandons it, her hand reaching underneath between my cheeks to check the plug fitted there. Her light taps and tugs on it make me groan around the cock choking me, and then Marcus pulls out and I can finally breathe. I suck in greedy gulps of air, saliva and tears leaking down my face.

"Are you ready to take my knot, beta?"

I shiver and nod, my hole clenching around my toy as if the knot's already there and ready to squeeze. "Yes, alpha."

Marcus sits on the edge of the nest, his cock jutting into the air. My mouth waters at the sight of it, of knowing that this monstrous thing is about to be inside me. All of this training, all of this prep has been for this moment.

I'm ready to be claimed.

Emily wraps her fingers around the base of the toy and pulls, and I moan at its loss until her fingers replace it, slicking my hole up with more lube and pushing it in deep.

296 · ALEXIS B. OSBORNE

"Then come and take your place." Marcus holds his cock up, pumping it lazily.

I stand up and step between his thighs, turning around and throwing one of my legs over his as he helps me get into position. He notches his head against my hole and pushes until the tip sinks in.

Rising and sinking, I work myself onto him, taking a little more at a time as my body works to adjust. To take him until there's no more to take. He's seated deep, his cock filling me up and stuffing me full, and then, when he's buried to the hilt, he moves. He thrusts, bouncing me on his length as I lean back against him and surrender. I give myself over to him completely, and it's like falling and knowing he'll be there to catch me. Marcus wraps his arms around me and holds me still, controlling our movements.

Hands on my cock make my head drop back on my alpha's shoulder as Emily kneels between my legs again and takes me into her mouth. She palms me and sucks. It's like this morning, but so different. There's a weight in the air, as if our energy charges this nest. Now there's no rush to chase pleasure. No steady sucking or squeezing to push me off the cliff. She teases me, bringing me to the edge of release before abandoning me there.

She does this five times until my cock is so swollen with need that it hurts. The tight ring squeezes the base of my shaft while she tongues my balls, licking them and sucking the skin into her mouth.

"Will you take my mark, beta?" Marcus growls.

"Yes." It's delicious agony, this waiting. My breath stutters as she sucks me into her mouth again and purrs while he fucks my ass, pounding deep and fast.

"Will you take my knot?" he asks.

"Yes!"

Hot breath puffs over the skin between my neck and shoulder. He nuzzles it with his nose, finding the right spot, and sucks the skin into his mouth. Skin slaps together as he ruts me hard, and then the burning stretch of his swelling knot makes me cry out. His teeth slam down, biting deep and ripping flesh, and I'm not sure which hurts worse, my neck or my ass.

Emily swallows my cock down and kneads my balls, and I come, pumping seed into her belly like my own is filling with our alpha's cum.

There's a horrible, wonderful soreness as he laps at the punctures he's made, a trickle of blood rolling down my chest while his cock jumps and pulses inside of me. He fills me with cum while he licks me, his tongue making soothing swipes at his bite mark as he cleans it and keeps it from clotting so it scars deeper.

So it's permanent.

He purrs, and the feeling of pack slams into my head in a dizzying rush that leaves me breathless. I've been claimed, marked, and now I feel whole. Like a door I didn't know was shut is opened. Through the bond, I can feel Marcus and an echo of Tom inside of me, and my heart aches at the spot where I know Emily will go when she's ready. Tears well in my eyes and threaten to spill, and the sound of the shutter makes me look up at Tom as I lose the fight and weep.

"Sam, are you okay?" Emily asks, stroking my thighs.

I don't have the words to explain it. To say how wonderful it is, how bittersweet knowing that I'm pack but we're not fully whole yet.

"He's fine, luv. Just overwhelmed. Having other people in your soul is a lot to adjust to." Tom puts the camera down and rubs my chest, some of the incomplete pack bond easing with his nearness and touch.

Marcus stops licking my bite mark when his knot shrinks, cum and lube making a mess between us as he helps me climb off his cock. Before he lets me go, he pulls me down to his face, the iron taste of my blood in his mouth sweet as he kisses me.

"Cuddle pile time?" Emily asks, rising off the floor. She grabs the cock ring from my shaft and gently twists it off, setting it aside to deal with later.

"Cuddle pile time," Marcus agrees, dragging me into the nest and spooning me. He tangles his legs with mine as if to trap me there. As if there's anywhere I'd rather be but in this nest, in the arms of my alpha and the comfort of my packmates.

I sigh as we settle, and Tom and Emily climb in with us. She kneels on the bed and grabs one of her fluffy blankets and wraps it around her shoulders, then fingers the chain between her breasts.

"What's wrong?" I ask. She's usually lying against me now. She likes to be the big spoon, even though she's barely over five feet tall.

"I'm dreading taking these off. They hurt at first and now they're numb, but I think they're going to hurt like a bitch again as soon as I undo them."

"It's not that bad," Tom says, reaching for the one between her legs. Before she can stop him, he plucks it free and she screams, slamming her legs closed and trapping his hand there.

"Yes, it fucking is!" she growls. "Oww!"

His hand moves, slurping between her thighs as he shoves his fingers inside her and pumps despite her squeezing. "And yet you're soaking wet, luv. I can feel your clit pulsing. Does it hurt? Want me to rub it better?"

She scowls at him, but spreads her legs to give him better access as he rubs the sting from her tortured clit. Marcus and I both chuckle as we lie there and watch them bicker and fight, and then fuck. Tom lies down and pulls her onto his cock, fucking up into her as he twists her nipple chain in his fingers and tugs it. Her breasts sway with her movements until she's flushed and panting. When she comes, he rips them off her. Her moans turn into whimpers as she collapses on top of him. When they're done, he drags her fuzzy blanket over her and holds her.

Marcus rubs soothing circles against my back and thighs, grabbing my chin between his fingers to turn my head and check the marks.

"How's the pain?" he asks.

My throat and my ass ache, but the deep satisfaction in my soul soothes any discomfort. "The pain is good." It's a reminder that it's real. That it happened. I was claimed, and now I have a pack.

I cup his face and stare up at him, wondering how I ever got so damn lucky. "I love you." The burst of warmth from his side of the bond makes me smile.

Marcus dips his head down and presses a gentle kiss to my lips. "I love you too."

Chapter Twenty-Four

EMILY

MARCUS AND TOM BOTH DROP US OFF AT THE TRAIN STATION, BUT it's clear our alpha's not happy about it. His wide arms cross over his chest, and his biceps threaten to rip a seam in his tailored suit jacket.

"We'll be fine," I say. "We're just going to pack up our apartments, and then we'll be back in three days."

"I know. But I hate being separated," Marcus says. "I'll worry every minute until you're back. Why can't the movers we hired manage everything?"

I rub his arms and do my best to soothe him while passengers waiting to get onto the platform make a wide berth around my seething alpha who's pumping out *I'm upset* pheromones by the bucketful. His scent is so spicy that he almost makes me sneeze.

"Because some of my plants are very particular and they'll try to die on me if they aren't moved properly. It's cold out, and I'll have to wrap them. They'll already be under a lot of stress from the move. Besides, we both have to break our leases and sign a bunch of paperwork and then quit our jobs and—"

"Right." He sighs and rakes his hand through his hair. "I know I'm being irrational."

302 · ALEXIS B. OSBORNE

"For the record, I already quit my job," Sam says. He hikes his duffel bag up higher on his shoulder.

"You did?" I ask. "When?"

Sam shrugs. "Before we left. You didn't?"

"No. I took FMLA, and my twelve weeks are up tomorrow. That's why I have to go back and work at least one day or I'll have to pay the benefit back."

"You know we wouldn't mind paying it for you," Tom says.

I shake my head. It's not about the money. It's about saying goodbye. "No, I appreciate it but I want to do this. I need to sort through and label my stuff and take care of my plants and quit and say goodbye to my friends."

"I can't wait to meet your family next month," Marcus says.

Sam and I share a loaded look. I sigh, deflating more and more the longer I think about it.

Marcus misreads my hesitance. "Mothers love me. I do very well with meeting mothers."

"That's true," Tom says. "I think my mother loves Marcus more than me."

We're going to miss our train if they keep stalling us. That might actually be their goal. Marcus wanted to drive us back to Boston, but he has meetings he can't rearrange and I can't keep putting this off. It has to get done.

"All right," I say, pulling my hands free and patting him on the chest. "The train's about to leave, so we need to go. I'll text you when we get there. I love you both."

I kiss him and then Tom and grab my bag. Sam and I hop on the train and wave from the open doorway, then grab seats in a quiet car and lift our bags up into the luggage rack.

My phone chirps, and I tug it out of my back pocket as we sit.

MARCUS

I miss you already. Love you.

EMILY

I love you too

💚

Sam rubs his chest as he stares out the window, and after a few minutes the train pulls out and picks up speed. He's still rubbing his chest when I look up from my book a few chapters later.

"Are you okay?" I ask.

"Fine, but he's sad. It's weird to sense someone else through the pack bond. It's like the impression your pen leaves on the sheets underneath the paper you've written on. I'm not sure if I'll ever get used to it."

I can't imagine what that's like, but I won't have to guess for much longer. My heat is due in a week if the dynamic specialist who Marcus is making me go see is correct.

In a few days, I'll be claimed, and our pack will be complete.

I lean against Sam and drop my head onto his shoulder, savoring his creamsicle scent. He stops rubbing the ache in his chest and strokes my hair instead. Trees in shades of yellow, orange, and red whip by as the train takes us out of the state, and I marvel at the scenery that always feels a little magical. They're losing their leaves, and it won't be long before we have the first snow of the year.

When we get to Boston, I send Marcus and Tom a text while Sam stuffs our luggage into a taxi. My apartment is smaller and shabbier than I remember, but none of my plants are dead. I read the note the house sitter left behind detailing when she last fertilized and watered all of them.

"Looks like the movers have already started. There are extra boxes and cling wrap. What do you want to work on first?" Sam asks.

"Books, clothes, and plants. Everything else is getting

donated. Hand me that box?" We spend the afternoon wrapping and packing, the permanent marker squeaking as I label each box.

It's odd seeing my things lined up in brown boxes stacked against one wall. The apartment looks strange. Like it already isn't mine anymore. And it's not, or at least it won't be in a few days. We order takeout and eat out of the cartons so there are no dishes to wash.

Even my bed feels wrong. Small and empty. It smells like laundry detergent and a faint whiff of the house sitter's powdery lilac scent. My sleep is fitful, and the blaring alarm makes me wake with an irritated groan. It's so fucking early. Sam's arms try to keep me in bed with him as I pull myself from its warmth and stumble into the bathroom, brushing my teeth and getting ready for my last day of work.

Driving through morning commuter traffic is harrowing. It's only been twelve weeks since I left. How have I already forgotten what it's like to drive at this time?

I've also forgotten my work password, and I spend the first half hour of the day on the phone with IT as they reset it and then finally I'm logged in. I count the hours down until it's lunchtime. The work is even more mind numbing than I remember. At lunch, Lindsay is eating with someone I don't know, but her eyes light up when she sees me and she hugs me so tight I can't breathe.

I pat her on the back and smile. "I missed you too."

"Sit with us! Dawn, this is Emily. She's been out on leave." She swings her head to me. "Dawn works in accounting with me. So how have you been? How did it go?" Her eyes flick to my neck where my sweater doesn't cover. She's looking for a bite mark. Her smile falls when she doesn't find one.

I rub the empty spot on my right side where we've decided it will go. "It went really well. We're waiting until my next cycle to make it official."

Lindsay grins and knocks her shoulder into mine. "Told you it would." She leans over toward Dawn. "Emily won the lottery. She found a pack, and they're loaded and live in some fancy high-rise apartment in New York."

I scrub a hand over my face. "Oh my God, don't say it like that. That sounds like the only reason I'm packing up with them is because they're well off." She would understand why I love them if she'd gotten to meet them. Marcus is so protective, caring, and sweet. Tom is an imp, keeping things interesting and Marcus from brooding. And Sam is so naughty and fun. He makes me smile until my cheeks hurt.

Lindsay arches a brow. "Marilyn said it best. A man being rich is like a girl being pretty. You don't marry a girl just because she's pretty, but boy, it sure helps. Besides, I'm hoping they have some single friends."

I shake my head and grin. "You should come and stay with us sometime. We'll show you around. The museums are really interesting." I stand and nod to Dawn. "It was nice to meet you. I have to go talk to my boss and hand in my resignation."

My manager reads my printed letter of resignation. My stomach is in knots while he reads it. He gives me grief over the lack of two weeks' notice after coming back from leave, then asks for my badge and calls security to have me escorted out before the day is even over. They offer me a box, but there's nothing at my desk that I need other than the family vacation photo I hold to my chest as I leave the job I've worked at for years. It's bittersweet, and I'm strangely sentimental about a job I never really liked.

For a moment, I sit in my car in the parking lot and remind myself to breathe, and then I call Sam.

"Hey," he answers.

"I'm done early. They walked me out like I was going to trash the place. What are you up to?"

"Packing your summer clothes." Something heavy thuds in the background as he keeps working while we're talking.

My stomach flips, feeling too light for my body. He could have been watching TV or grabbing his own stuff from his apartment. Instead, he's taking care of me. How did I get this lucky? I grin. "You just wanted an excuse to go through my panty drawer again."

"You do have a very sexy blue and yellow polka dotted one."

Blue and yellow polka... "My slick panties? Those are *not* hot." They're as full coverage as it gets, going from the tops of my thighs up to my waist. My face heats at the thought of him looking at my ratty old slick panties.

"Baby, I can assure you they're very fucking hot," he says, his voice getting husky. "Because it makes me remember our time together at the free clinic, and then all I can think of is what's gonna happen with your next heat. I've had a boner all morning."

I tuck my lips and bite them to keep from laughing. "You're terrible."

"And you love me anyway. Are you coming home now? If not, then I can't make any promises regarding the state of cleanliness your panties might be in when you get home."

I slot my keys into the opening and turn, starting my car. "I'm coming home. Do *not* use my panties to jerk off." I hang up before he can think of a smartass reply. The commute back to the apartment is faster, and when I get there, he opens the door before I can get my key into the lock. He greets me with a kiss, tugging my hand between his legs to feel how hard he is. We make out all the way to the bedroom where he shows me exactly how excited those panties got him, and we make the bed that's strange to me now smell a little more like pack.

We lie together afterward, and I stare at the blank white wall as Sam draws circles on my back. I rest my head over his heartbeat and play with the faint smattering of hair on his chest. *I don't want to sleep here*, I realize. Not for one more night. Why did I ever think coming back here was so important when half of my heart is two hundred miles away?

My plants are packaged and ready for the movers. They already know what to move and what to donate. The charity is coming to pick up the donations and my car in a few days. None of my few friends can hang out on a Thursday afternoon.

"I want to go home," I say.

"Yeah? Didn't you want to stop in and see your family before heading back?"

It takes two seconds for me to think about it and chicken out. "I'll see them next month." Future me will probably regret it but that's her problem. I prop my chin on his chest and look up at him through my eyelashes. "Let's go home. Unless you have stuff to do at your place?"

He pulls his other arm from behind his head and plays with my hair. "I'm good. Marcus had it all taken care of. We can go if you really want to. I'll text them and let them know we're coming."

I pull out of Sam's arms and get dressed, throwing on my wrinkly clothes and hopping into my pants. He's ready before I am and waiting at the door as I run a brush through my hair and throw all of my stuff into my bag and zip it shut.

"I called a taxi and texted them," Sam says.

On the train, I stare out the window and look at the passing countryside until darkness settles and there's nothing to see. I curl into Sam's side and watch him play a game on his phone, and then he's shaking me awake, telling me we're home. Rubbing the sleep from my eyes, I take my bag when he hands it down and follow him onto the platform.

Despite the late hour, Marcus and Tom are standing there with an enormous bouquet of red roses, and we hurry down the long platform. I drop my bag and throw my arms around Marcus's neck, breathing him in deep and savoring his spicy-sweet scent. He nuzzles my hair, his hands on my back in an almost hug and everything feels right again.

Pulling away, I reach for Tom and hug him too. He's less chaste, his hands drifting down to grab my ass and squeeze, and I laugh.

"Did something happen?" Marcus asks.

"No, we just finished early and wanted to come home," Sam answers. He takes the bouquet and a kiss from Marcus.

I press my nose to Tom's throat and inhale deeply. "I couldn't stand the thought of spending another night out of my nest."

"How do you like that, darling? We rank second below her nest." Tom clicks his tongue. "I think our omega has gotten spoiled. Perhaps a spanking is in order?

Sliding a hand under his jacket, I grab a bit of skin through his shirt and pinch. "That's not what I said!"

Tom pulls a hand away and brings it down sharply on my rear. "And she's wearing panties. A clear rule violation."

I dance away from him before he can spank me again because Tom doesn't know when to stop unless you make him.

"It's thirty degrees outside and we're not at home. I'm allowed to wear panties!" I say the last bit louder than necessary, and a few bedraggled passengers walking by turn their heads and stare at us before continuing to their trains. My face heats, and he grins.

Marcus pulls me into his arms as if he's shielding me from Tom's incessant teasing. "Behave, or I'll make you."

Tom's grin widens. "That's not much incentive to stop, I'm afraid."

"Save it for tomorrow. It's late, and I have a meeting at eight." There's a note of finality in Marcus's voice. A thread of alpha bark woven into the words that makes my knees weak and my panties damp.

"Yes, alpha," we all say in unison.

Marcus takes my bag from my shoulder, and we head home where everything is right. It smells like all of us. My nest is heavenly. From inside it, all I see when I look out is a jungle of greenery as my new plants line the triple set of windows on the opposite side of the room. I can't wait to add the rest of them to my rapidly growing collection. Tom rigged the sun lamps so they get enough light since it's a west-facing window.

And that night we all sleep in it in a tangled pile of limbs, and in the morning Marcus presses a kiss to my temple before he climbs out to go to work. I roll over and cuddle into Sam.

Everything is perfect.

Chapter Twenty-Five

EMILY

EVERYTHING IS ALL WRONG. *THIS CAN'T BE HAPPENING.*

Once again, my heat starts at the worst possible time, and it hits me with such sudden forcefulness that I end up doubled over and clutching my cramping belly as I breathe through the pain and grunt.

Sam is in the basement working on his bike, but there's no cell service down there. Tom is across the city picking up our surprise bonding gift. Marcus is at work with an important client his firm is trying to land. There is a strange alpha in the apartment fixing the broken dishwasher, and I left my phone on the coffee table when I went to the bathroom. That's when the cramps started.

I sink down to the floor and curl up in a ball on the cold tile, hugging my knees to my chest as I wait for the latest cramp to let me out of its grip. I'm two days early for once instead of late and it couldn't be worse timing. The pain eases with a gush of slick that soaks through my underwear and leggings. I'm not even wearing slick panties because I'm never early. Never. I gulp in a shuddering breath and unclench my teeth.

Boots make loud steps as the repair guy leaves the kitchen.

"Ma'am? I'm all finished. I just need you to sign the work order and then I'll be out of your hair."

"I'm in the bathroom! Umm... Can you... can you slip it under the door?"

There's a heavy silence and then the sound of him coming closer. "Slip it under the door? I can wait if you'll only be a few minutes. I'll go pack up my things."

"No." The last thing I need is the temptation of some random alpha when all my hindbrain wants is a knot. Any knot. "I'm going to be here a while. Slip it under the door, please."

He huffs, and then a moment later he shoves a work order under the door. *Fuck. A pen. Is there a pen in the bathroom?* I don't know why there would be, but boy, I hope there is.

I slap the paper onto the floor and rifle through the drawers I can reach, gritting my teeth and breathing through a cramp, and another rush of slick soaks into stretchy spandex. My fingers hit something in the back of a drawer that rolls, and I grab it. Eyeliner. It'll work. I sign the paper and slide it back under the door. The alpha takes it, his boots creaking as he stands, and then I hear him sniff it.

Fuck.

"Are you okay, ma'am? Do you need me to help you call someone?"

The last thing I need is for him to know I'm stuck in here alone without my phone. Maybe he's the nicest guy in the world and I'm judging him solely on his dynamic, but with enough time and exposure, my heat will trigger his rut and reduce us to little more than animals.

So I lie. "I already did, but thank you. You can show yourself out. My alpha will be home soon, and he won't like it if you're still here."

I hear him shift on his feet, and I look at the door again to make sure the locked knob hasn't somehow come unlocked. Not that something as flimsy as a door will stop a determined alpha in full rut.

"All right," he says. "I'll leave your copy on the counter. Have a good day."

Another cramp squeezes me, and my leggings grow damper as I lie there on the floor and strain to hear him through the door. Is he gone? Did he really leave, or is he waiting for me to open the door? This is the fastest oncoming heat I've had since my dynamic developed as a teen. Each one is a little different from the next, but this is bad. It's all wrong. We had plans. It wasn't supposed to happen this way.

So I do the safest thing I can. I wait. Curled up and whimpering, I lie there and wait for someone to come home. There's no clock to tell me how much time passes, but the sun is setting when I hear footsteps outside the door and it was a little after lunchtime when the repairman came.

"I'm home!" Tom calls out. "Sam? Come help me bring everything in."

I drag in a breath to answer him when another cramp hits me, and all that comes out is an agonized whimper.

"Sam? Emily?"

"In the bathroom!" Straining, I reach for the knob and turn it. The door creaks open, narrowly avoiding hitting my head.

"I got the prints back from the framer, too. You're going to die when you see them, they're—Emily!" He rushes to my side. "Are you hurt? What happened? Where's Sam?"

"He's in the basement. I left my phone on the coffee table and the dishwasher broke and—*hnnnng*." I pant as another cramp crushes me in its grip. It's never been this hard, this fast and painful before.

"What's wrong? Did you fall? Should I call an ambulance?" Tom kneels and puts his cool hand over my sweat-beaded brow. My hair sticks to my face, and he brushes it away.

"No, it's my heat. It's bad." I whimper again, trying to curl up tighter. "Can you help me into the nest?"

"Of course, luv." Tom steps around me, then gets his arms under me and hoists me up. Despite his lean frame, he's strong. He walks us sideways through the door and helps me upstairs. The nest is deliciously soft and full of pack scents as he sets me down in the center. "I'm going to get the others."

"Don't leave me," I say, not above begging. I'll do anything, say anything, as long as someone puts a cock in me and ruts this pain right out of me.

He unbuttons his jacket and tosses it to the floor, then pulls his phone from his pocket. "Of course not." He dials and puts the phone between his ear and shoulder, then undoes the buttons on his sleeves. "It's time," he says into the phone. "No, I'm not teasing you." He sighs and grabs the phone, holding it out toward me as another cramp hits me, and I whimper, rolling onto my side and hugging my knees to my chest.

"I'm on my way," Marcus growls over the line.

Tom pulls his shirt off and tosses it to the floor, then dials again. When it doesn't connect and gives him Sam's voicemail, he makes an irritated sound and rips his belt open, and then his pants, and shoves it all down.

The dark trail of hair leading down to his cock makes my mouth water and the cramps less important as he finishes undressing. I wiggle against my fuzzy blankets, hooking my thumbs in my stretchy waistband as I rip them down my hips.

Tom helps me, taking over as I lift my bottom and he undresses me. He's gentle, and that irritates me. I want to be stripped. Flipped over, rutted, bred. Desire and pain crush me in a vise as he shoves my sweater up and reaches under me to find the hook on my bra.

I hook my legs around him and try to pull him closer. To line his cock up with me and work myself onto him. He lets out a surprised breath, then chuckles and claims my mouth with a kiss, distracting me as he finishes working it open. He lets my mouth go, and I try to follow him until he pulls my sweater up and I'm trapped in it for a moment as he tugs it over my head and tosses it aside. I throw the bra off, grateful to be rid of it. Now I'm free. I'm naked in my nest where I belong, with my packmate between my thighs where *he* belongs.

I reach for him and tug him into another kiss, pulling him closer with my legs. I set my heels into his ass and trap him there. Why isn't he in me yet? I rub my wet slit against his front, searching for his cock. It's soft against my inner thigh. Frustrating. I make a sound of displeasure.

"Sorry, luv. Turns out I'm not into weeping. Give me a moment." He reaches a hand down between us and grabs his soft cock, stroking it.

Weeping? I press my fingers to my cheeks and they come away wet. I've been crying this whole time. His arm rubs against my belly as he tries to bring it to life. If he can't fuck me, then I'll take my comfort another way. Getting more of that buttery cookie scent in my sinuses will help. Leaning up, I trail kisses along his neck and lick over his healed mating bite, setting my teeth over it and sucking. It tastes faintly of his pheromones, his beta scent gland so underdeveloped it's flat, but it's there if you know where it should be. I bite him lightly to make it perfume.

"Blimey. That'll do it."

He groans and stops stroking his cock hard as he drags it over my inner thigh. Tom guides it to my center while I suck on his mating bite so hard it'll bruise. He sinks into me with a hard thrust and no foreplay, his cock carving a path through my squeezing walls. I don't need the prep. I'm soaked with slick and aroused from the heat. The first hit of his head against my cervix makes the cramping stop, and I sigh through my mouthful of skin and rock against him, asking for more without words.

He delivers. Tom pistons into me, hitting the mouth of my womb and pressing onward, forcing my body to shift and make room and give until my belly bulges with each deep thrust. The hard stretch satisfies some primal urge and leaves me purring as I clutch him to me, my heels locked against his ass and my hands curved into claws at his back. My teeth are still at his throat, as if to keep him from pulling out and leaving me before I've been properly seeded.

"Stop biting me so I can fuck you properly, omega," he says, sliding a hand into my hair and squeezing. He pries my teeth from his throat and ignores my whimpers of loss, and then he moves and I forget why any of that mattered when he's reshaping me, forming my body to fit him better. Tom fucks me into the nest with punishing thrusts that smack our skin together.

"You are a feral little thing sometimes," he says, squeezing that hand at my nape and tugging. Each slap of his hips against mine pulls at his hold and makes my eyes roll back in my head. He takes his pleasure, using my body and pinning me under him as he fucks me until he's as sweaty and panting and desperate as I am.

"You want this, luv? You want me to fill up this pretty pink cunt?"

I whimper and nod, ignoring the dull ache in my scalp. His rhythm changes, those thrusts coming deep and slow, and then his cock pulses and I know he's close. And I want it. I want him to come inside me, to fill me with seed and satisfy this unquenchable hunger, even if it's only for a moment.

"Here's your cum, luv. Be a good little cum slut and don't lose a single drop."

The first hot pulse of his release lashes at my walls and leaves me purring as he pumps me full, his hold in my hair never slackening as he rolls his hips, using my channel to milk his cock. When I'm filled, he pulls off me and squeezes my legs together, pushing my knees to my chest as he teases the seam of my sex, sliding a finger through my wet folds and toying with my clit.

"Hold your legs up, omega, and don't waste my seed. I was kind enough to give it to you, so now you have to keep it right where it belongs. In this greedy fuckhole."

Tom rolls my clit in circles until I'm panting and wiggling with the impossible struggle of holding still as he rubs me 'til I'm clenching, my pleasure pulled taut and low in my belly. He tuts and swipes two fingers lower to gather up the cum trickling out of me as he brings me close to orgasm.

"Bad girl, losing precious seed. Let's put this back where it belongs." He sticks those fingers in, working his semen into me. On the withdrawal, he drags his fingers over my front wall and tuts again when I clench, more seed and slick dribbling out.

"What a naughty thing you are, losing my cum when I told you to hold it. Maybe a spanking will help you listen better."

Tom brings his hand down on my ass and thighs, catching my pussy in his path as he spanks me again and again. I gasp and jerk, trying to put my legs down. He grabs my wrist and holds it tight, shoving my legs up higher so he has a better view. I'm exposed. Vulnerable. And my bratty beta has no mercy.

He smacks me hard and fast until my cheeks glow red and hot. The fall of his hand is careless, spanking my pussy as much as my ass or thighs, and tears well in my eyes until he stops abruptly and rubs the sting out, turning it to liquid pleasure until I'm clenching and desperate.

Slick and seed run out of me as he palms my throbbing, wrecked sex and glides a finger between my swollen folds in search of my clit. He finds it. Oh, does he find it. That long, thin finger strokes me until I'm rocking against him, my fingers digging into my thighs as I take the pleasure he's giving me as payment for the pain. Panting, I cry out as the tension pulls taut and I come, my core squeezing around nothing as it tries to milk a cock that isn't there.

"So wasteful even after you've been punished so beautifully," he chides me, scooping up the leaking cum and slick and working it back into me. The tip of his middle finger hits my cervix, and I twitch as he adds a third finger inside me, stretching me wide. Readying me for what's coming once the others come home.

"Did you know we discussed who gets to take your ass's virginity tonight?" He pulls his fingers from my pussy and drops them lower, teasing my tight hole. "Sam and I flipped a coin, actually."

Tom leans over me, his weight pushing my legs into my chest and crushing the air from my lungs. "Guess who won?" His grin is full of a feral delight.

I whimper, a strangled sound, and his grin widens, showing off white teeth. He's as beautiful as he is frightening when his bright green eyes take on this manic gleam. His weight disappears as he gets up and grabs me by my wrist, pulling me from the nest. "Get up, luv. It's time to prepare you."

Tom bullies me into the bathroom, then sets me down on the toilet and warms up the bidet and its special attachment. "You will be done by the time I return, or I'll do it for you."

He leaves, and I do it, going through the now familiar routine despite this first hazy wave of my heat making my thoughts slow. My whole abdomen cramps as slick creeps out of me while I make myself clean, getting my ass ready for a cock when it's only had fingers and plugs until now. Under normal circumstances, I'd be more scared than I am right now, but the heat makes me bold. It makes me ravenous for more. And more is what my pack will give me.

Through the crack in the door, I hear him talking. He's on the phone. I dry myself off and finish and hover in the doorway for a moment. He didn't tell me I couldn't leave the bathroom, or that I had to wait for him.

The sight of my beautiful, perfect nest fills me with intense longing. I go and climb into it, shoving my face in the soft, fuzzy blankets that smell like us. The fake fur rubs against my heat sensitive skin, and something tight inside me relaxes. This is better. This is where I belong.

Tom comes back and walks over. He strokes a hand over my back and ass. "Are you ready, luv?"

I get to my knees and turn my head so I can watch him and I nod. "Mmhmm."

He pushes two fingers into my pussy, working them in and out until my eyes slide shut and I sigh and then he pulls them free and presses one into my tight hole, easing it in. "Your slick is so convenient. All I have to do to make you drip with desire is rub you a little. Your pretty cunt is so greedy. Tell me, is your ass this eager too? Are you impatient to have us fill all your perfect holes?"

I moan as a second slick-coated finger joins the first, stretching me wider, and pumps until I'm rocking back on each knuckle until it's fully seated. "Slick this for me," he says as something nudges against my pussy. He presses it in, and cold metal steals my warmth. It's one of my plugs.

He works it in and out in teasing thrusts that aren't enough. Once it's warm and coated, he pulls it free and presses it to my other hole, pushing it in. My ass stretches around it, taking it, until it's seated. I groan once it's settled, my backside stuffed full. He taps on the gem, checking its seating or teasing me. Probably both, knowing him.

"Perfect. Don't move."

Tom leaves my side, and I groan as I wait there, ass up and stuffed with an empty, slick dripping pussy. The sound of a shutter snapping lets me know he's returned. Tom holds his camera up and lines up his next shot. He shifts around the room, then comes over and pushes me down onto my side, arranging my legs so they're bent. I'm a doll, his little fuck toy, and he poses me how he wants me, taking photos and stroking my clit to tease me until I'm dripping. The dripping is his favorite, he says. As if the empty agony of my unfulfilled heat is some shiny new toy for him to play with as he pleases. And it does. It pleases him greatly. So he plays with me.

"Stand with your legs together. Just a little apart. Perfect." He sits on the floor and brings his camera low, pointing it right between my legs. He swipes his thumb over my clit until I clench. Slick drips, splattering on my knee and calf. He pulls his hand back, and the shutter snaps repeatedly as he captures the shot.

"Tom," I whine, so needy and empty except for the toy that teases me with every shift and fidget.

"What is it, luv?"

I grab him by his long hair and drag his face between my legs. "*Pleeeeaase.*"

He chuckles, puffs of his breath teasing my inner thighs. "Is this what you want?" He shoves his chin between my thighs and drags his tongue over my slit, lapping up my slick and humming as he swipes again, seeking more. "So sweet. I could eat you up."

Yes. That's the entire fucking point. I rock my pelvis against his face, my head falling back when his tongue probes between my folds and finds my clit. He rubs it until I'm panting and that familiar tension coils low in my pelvis again.

"Hmm." I ride his face, staring down at him as he looks up at me from under long black lashes from his place on the floor. Everything pulls tight, and I hold my breath as I shatter apart and come undone, slick gushing out of me and soaking his face as he laps me through my orgasm and licks me clean. He pulls his face from between my legs and wipes his mouth and chin with the back of his hand.

Tired and satisfied, I let him maneuver me to the nest, let him position me however he wants as he takes his dirty photos. He cards his fingers through my hair, draping it over my breast as he goes low and takes an upward angle shot.

The door opens downstairs. "Emily? Tom? Are you guys okay? I have a dozen missed calls and texts."

Tom sets his camera down and leaves me in the nest. I hug myself around a pillow and resist the urge to press it between my legs and rub. Why isn't one of them fucking me? Instead of fucking me, they're bickering. I shove a hand between my thighs and rub, seeking the friction that the slick makes challenging to find.

"Bad puppy, leaving your Mistress alone so close to her heat," Tom chides as they come up the stairs.

"It's early? Shit. She's not due for two or three days. I've been tracking her cycle." He sighs. "Probably because she's resisted the mating bite for so long. Her body's pressing the issue."

"Hmm. We'll deal with this oversight later. For now, fuck her, please. I have preparations to make."

I stop eying my cute little cloud pillow while thinking dirty thoughts when footsteps come closer. Sam gives me a sheepish grin when he spots me lying there in the nest, rubbing between my legs and panting. I whine with need.

He undresses and climbs in, pulling me against him. "Sorry, baby. Didn't mean to leave you alone for so long. I lost track of time."

I'll forgive him as soon as he puts his cock in me. Tipping my chin up, I kiss him and sigh with relief when he palms my breast and squeezes. He slots a knee between my legs, knocking my hand aside as he rubs. I throw my arms around his neck, holding him close as he grinds against me until I'm clenching and whimpering with the need to come, to squeeze a cock until I'm soaked with seed.

"Don't pout, baby. I've got what you need." His cock rubs against my belly, leaving my skin damp with pre-cum as he nips my lower lip.

"It hurts. Please, Sam. It hurts so bad."

He kisses the corner of my mouth and pinches my nipple. I gasp and arch against him, grinding my cunt on his leg as he rocks with me. "I told you it would be bad if you waited so long between bonding and claiming, but you insisted. Said this was what you wanted."

I was wrong. So fucking wrong. This is agony.

My hands curve into claws as I dig my nails into Sam's back and try to force him to move faster, to grind harder, for him to lift my leg up and slip inside me and make this stop hurting.

I whimper instead of answering because words are difficult when I'm stuck in this limbo of pleasure and pain.

"Are we breeding you, baby?"

My pussy clenches at the thought and I moan, squeezing my eyes shut and rubbing my clit against his firm thigh. "I… I'm not…" What if I'm wrong about waiting for that too? My body knows what it wants, even if my mind sometimes struggles with it. What do urges know of time? Of bonding and intimacy and planning. All my hindbrain knows is rutting and seed. "I don't…"

"Be right back." Sam extricates himself from me and leaves me with a kiss to the top of my head and an unfulfilled orgasm. I can't fight it anymore. I grab one of the pillows and shove it between my legs, pressing the seam between my lips until it hits my clit and then I grind.

He finds me like that a few moments later when he returns with a cardboard and foil pill packet and a bottle of protein water.

He pops a pill free and sets it on my tongue, then uncaps the bottle and holds it to my mouth so I can drink.

Sam makes me drink the entire bottle before he agrees to get back into the nest. He tosses the pillow aside and rolls me onto my belly, pulling me up on my knees as he settles behind me. His thick cock presses against my opening and he pushes inside, seating himself before pulling out and thrusting again.

I press my face into the sheets and bask in the smell of us, in the stretch and glide of him in my pussy as he holds me by my hips and tugs me onto his cock with every surge. The drowning need of the heat abates a little until I can think again. "Will they be disappointed?" I ask, softly, in case Tom is closer than I think.

"Disappointed?" Sam pauses, then chuckles when I whine and try to push back to work myself on his cock. He fucks me again, his thrusts knocking me out of my movements, and I give myself over to it, letting him set the pace and our rhythm as I lie there and take it.

"Why would we be disappointed about getting to practice breeding you?"

He grabs fistfuls of my ass and spreads my cheeks apart, then tugs on the plug in my rear. The feel of it sliding against my wall as he's fucking me leaves me panting and desperate to come. He curves his body on top of mine, pinning me against the bed as he fucks into me and presses his mouth closer to my ear. "One day we'll fill this cunt so full of cum we'll breed you. We'll pump a baby into your belly and watch you get big and round. I bet pregnancy's gonna make your tits huge."

I moan from his words, from the picture he paints and the slap of his hips against my ass. From the slide of the plug in my ass and the shunting of his cock in my pussy. Stuffed full and fucked face first into my nest, my pleasure swells as he whispers filthy things to me about cunts and seed and breeding, and when I come on his cock, milking and squeezing, he joins me.

Sam moves upright and spreads my cheeks apart as he fucks his cum into me and leaves me dripping and spent. Satisfied. For now. We settle on our sides with him spooning my back, and he tugs a blanket over the both of us as we rest and recover.

Tom sets a big black case down and clicks it open, pulling out photography equipment as he sets up around the room.

"Sleep, baby," Sam whispers against my hair as I fight the closing of my eyelids so I can watch Tom make everything perfect. "You're gonna need the rest. Marcus is on his way, and we have a busy night ahead of us."

My alpha. My betas. My nest. I snuggle into the safety and comfort of Sam's arms and close my eyes, drifting off almost instantly.

The bed dipping stirs me awake, and I sigh as I crack my eyes open. Tom settles in behind me and moves my leg up higher where it's hooked over Sam. He presses something into my pussy, and it slides right in until I'm full on both sides. He grasps the plug in my ass and plays with it before pulling it free.

It slides free from my body, and I whimper at its loss, the pleasure of its withdrawal making me clench around the larger one in my pussy.

"Ready, love?"

I nod and breathe as he pulls the plug from my pussy and notches it lower, pressing its slicked, blunt taper to my hole. I stretch around its flare, but it's too wide. Too large.

"Relax, love. Let go. Trust us. It will fit."

I can't do this, I can't... He doesn't stop until I'm stretched taut and gripping, and then it's past the ring and everything in me relaxes as my body tightens around it and holds it in place.

"Shh, don't whimper, luv. You break my heart. This is for your own good." He drops a kiss to my thigh and rubs the seam of my sex until I'm aching and needy.

It's the strangest thing to be so full, yet so empty. He dips a finger inside me and presses against the back wall where the larger plug is nestled. When he replaces his fingers with the head of his cock, I could cry. He bottoms out inside me, and the relief is nearly instant as he moves, his head sliding against the big plug in my rear with every thrust.

Sam works his hand between my thighs and finds my clit as his tongue licks across my throat, his face buried in the crook of my neck. He laps at my scent gland and hums, a happy sound, and bites me for more pheromones. My back arches, pulling Tom in deeper as they drive me to wicked heights and drop me off that ledge until I'm gasping and flushed. The scent of icing-drizzled lemons fill the nest.

Tom comes with a grunt, pumping me full, and Sam reaches lower still and wrings out the last drop with fingers circled around his base.

The front door slams shut, and we all go still. It's Marcus. Our alpha is home. My body burns with need, and now that he's here, I'm desperate for his knot. I wiggle in their grip, but powerful arms pin me down and hold me tight. Their cruelty makes me whimper. Why won't they let me up?

I feel my alpha from across the room, his energy pulsing like a dark living thing between us as Marcus stops at the top of the stairs and waits. All I can see are our tangled limbs and the line of pillows that border the rimmed nest, the soft white canopy lit up by the twinkling stars and moons we've hung from the frame.

Fabric rustles as Marcus undresses, saying nothing. I can picture it so clearly. The careful, methodical way he slides his arms out of his sleeves. How he folds and stacks his things into a neat pile that he sets down somewhere safe. He purrs as he undresses, that low, deep rumble soothing me as I stop struggling against my betas. I wait.

He comes around the corner and drops a hand on my ankle, his fingers circling it completely. That simple, chaste contact makes my pussy weep slick down my thighs as my body tightens with need. All I am is need and wanting.

"Emily," he says, his voice rumbling and low. "I come to you as an alpha seeking pack. Will you submit?"

Sam and Tom let me go, sliding from the nest as I get up onto my knees and press my chest to the bed, presenting myself to him for mounting. I stick my ass up in the air, a bead of slick sliding down my folds and dripping off me. It's so hard to remember the words through this haze. "I do."

He touches me, his hand sliding up the outside of my leg, and I quiver, eager for him to touch me for real. For him to slick his hand between my thighs and caress me where I need him most.

"An omega's role is to accept the command of her alpha and betas. To keep the nest and whelp its young. To guard them and guide them. Will you pledge this service to your pack?"

The thought of letting them breed me, of holding our baby in our arms in the safety and comfort of our nest, fills me with such longing. I want this more than anything. One day. Maybe soon. "I do."

The camera shutter snaps. He smooths a hand over my backside, his fingers ghosting over the crystal ended plug before dipping lower and pushing into my hot, wet core. "You've been well prepared by your pack. I'm satisfied. Will you take as much pleasure as you give?"

"I will, alpha." His finger withdraws, and I whine from the emptiness.

He grips my hips and tugs me back, the blunt head of his cock nudging at my pussy. "Then take it." He pushes in, quick thrusts working his thick cock into me with careful movements that make me rabid from the urge to sink back and impale myself on him. To bury him to the root until my belly bulges as he ruts a place deeper inside of me and squishes my guts.

"Pack, will you accept this omega?" Marcus asks.

"We will, alpha," Sam and Tom both answer.

"Then join us as you wish."

Tom and Sam climb back into the nest, but they don't join. They watch. And they wait.

He slides deep, pulling out only to do it all over again as he knocks at the entrance of my womb and I sigh in relief. The sting of his wide entry fades into pleasure as he fucks me face down into the mattress, his cock sliding against the plug with every bottoming thrust.

My alpha is rutting me. Our nest smells like pack, and I have a belly full of seed. Everything is right again.

"Are you ready?" he asks, but he doesn't wait for my answer. Marcus works an arm under my chest and hauls me upright. I sit on his lap and he bounces me on his cock.

"Turn her around. I have the lighting set for this side," Tom says, holding his camera up and pointing.

Marcus bands me to his chest with thick arms and turns us until Tom's happy. And then he thrusts, driving his cock deeper as he trails a hand down my front and slips it between my labia. He finds my clit and rolls it, and I whine, my hips stuttering and trying to move. But I'm trapped. He's bigger and stronger, his grip unbreakable, as he works my clit until I'm panting but leaves me hanging and unfulfilled. Three times he works me up, higher and higher, only to let the buzz fade as he stops us and holds me until I'm wiggling against him, annoyed and desperate.

"Alpha," I wine, batting as the arm locked firmly under my breasts tenses. I try to roll my hips, to work my cunt onto him, but the angle's impossible. There's no traction, no friction, unless he gives it to me. And he seems keener on teasing me than pleasing me.

"Yes, omega?"

Tom's shutter snaps as he moves about the nest while Sam

lounges in front of us, his hand alternating between tugging his cock or teasing my slicked up thighs.

"*Please*," I whine, begging. The plug shifts in my ass with each wiggling movement as I try to slide up and down his buried cock. My belly cramps, and more slick runs down his length. Tom leans in low and bends over Sam to take a closeup shot.

"Please... what?"

I growl, a low, threatening noise that sets him laughing. It's a good thing he's got me trapped against his front because his laughing makes me want to bite him. I sink my nails into his banding forearm and dig.

He bounces me on his cock, heedless of the crescent moons I'm digging into his skin as he jerks me up and down, using me for his own pleasure as he edges me once more until my teeth ache for his blood.

"Is this what you want, baby?" Sam rubs his thumb through my lips and finds my clit, stroking it and rubbing it in circles, and I go limp, letting my head fall back onto my alpha's shoulder.

"There you go, good girl," Marcus says. He lifts me up and drops me down, working me on his shaft while Sam brings me once more to that familiar ledge. Warmth unfurls in my chest as I go limp and they let me rise higher. Higher still. Everything pulls taut, and I hold my breath as all of my focus narrows. Is this what they wanted? My absolute surrender? For me to go limp like a rag doll as they use me? Rutting me like I'm their fuck toy?

Marcus's head dips down between my neck and shoulder. His hand settles between my breasts, over my heart. He nuzzles me with his nose, inhaling deeply and rumbling with that purr that makes my toes curl. He presses a kiss to my scent gland, licks it, then sucks it into his mouth. His canines scrape over the skin, and everything snaps taut as I come with a moan, my walls fluttering on his cock.

He bites, and agony rips through me. Teeth cut, pain mingling with pleasure as my pussy squeezes his buried cock and his teeth scissor down deep, biting his bond into me until something in my chest cracks and he sneaks in, his soul melding with mine. Beyond the blunt intrusion of him, I feel the whisper of Sam and Tom as well.

And then it's nothing but pleasure. Marcus's pleasure. His feelings, his elation and triumph. Those foreign feelings flood me and drown me, and I come again, but it's not my release I'm feeling. It's his. His knot swells inside me, and I sense it through our new bond. His cock jerks, pumping seed deep, and a wash of euphoria floods the both of us as he ties me to him, his teeth still buried in my neck as deeply as his cock is locked in my cunt.

Sam reaches up and rubs Marcus's cockhead through my belly, and I stretch and stretch and stretch as Marcus fills me to bursting and pulls his teeth from my skin. He laps at my neck, his wide tongue licking up the blood and pheromones in equal measure. My pussy squeezes his fat knot, pulling the dregs of seed from his balls, and the only reason I'm still upright is because he keeps me hauled against his chest. Marcus's rumbling purr and feelings of primal satisfaction drown out my own quieter thoughts and emotions.

"Fuck, baby. That was hot," Sam whispers.

Sam teases me, his fingers occasionally brushing against my overly sensitive clit as he explores our tie, feeling the way my pussy stretches thin around that knot that locks us together. I twitch and groan and try to move away, to beg him to stop, but I'm trapped and too heat drunk to find my words.

Sheer pleasure purrs through my soul, and it's foreign. It's my alpha's. And it's mine. Because we're bonded and I'm his. Theirs.

My eyes slide shut as I struggle to process it, to come to terms with all these feelings in my chest as Marcus laps at the bite mark, cleaning the wound and keeping it from clotting so it scars deeper. So it's permanent. A tongue on my breast makes me jerk back to awareness.

Tom's set his camera down, and he's leaning over Sam again, his tongue dragging up my breast as he licks at the droplet of blood that rolled down my front. Marcus purrs, satisfied and proud within our bond.

"Fuck yeah. Let's all lick her." Sam wiggles into place between my thighs, his head tipped back.

He licks the slick from my lips and runs his tongue up through my folds, swiping me from clit to knot. He licks at our tie, and I clamp down, squeezing one last shot of semen from Marcus as Sam tongues me to orgasm. With Marcus at my throat and Tom at my breast and Sam between my thighs and the mating bond ripped into my heart, there's not an inch of me that isn't reeling with sensation.

The room spins, and the next thing I know I'm opening my eyes to the light-strewn canopy. Marcus cuddles me against him, his enormous body curled around me, and Sam and Tom are playing. Sam sucks Tom's cock while Tom takes photos, his camera shutter snapping as he photographs the blowjob.

Such perverts. I smile, and Marcus's hand stops stroking my hair. "How are you feeling?" he asks.

He already knows the answer. He can feel it through our bond, but I like that he asks me. Now that the worst of the first heat wave has passed, my brain can string more than four words together.

"Like I got fucked unconscious." I roll onto my side and throw my leg over his and run my hand through his chest hair, stopping when I see the ring on my fourth finger. It glints in the light, the large oval diamond glittering with the smaller ones that halo it. The band is rose gold, the prongs white. Or maybe platinum. It's heavy, the center stone nearly the width of my finger. "What is this?"

"Your mating day present. Do you like it?"

My throat is thick with emotion. He remembered. I told him my parents were betas, and he remembered and bought me a ring. It's exactly like the kind that betas exchange when they get married. "It's beautiful." Everything blurs as my eyes fill with tears. It's so sweet. So thoughtful. Completely unnecessary by alpha and omega standards, but deeply appreciated all the same. He kisses the top of my head, and that's all it takes for the damn to break and for me to sob as wetness coats my cheeks.

Sam and Tom look up from their antics. Marcus hauls me up onto his chest so I'm lying on top of him and his hands skim all over my back.

I throw my arms around his neck and bury my face in his throat, breathing in his spice and sweetness scent. He purrs and strokes me, the others joining us as they pet me while I cry. I wipe my hand across my face, knowing that I'm being ridiculous but not knowing how to stop.

"I just… I love you guys so much." I drag in a shaky breath and fight past these tears that choke me.

"I love you, sweetheart," Marcus says, his purr rumbling like a Mack truck. He cups my face in his hands and pulls me in for a kiss.

"I love you, baby," Sam says, rubbing soothing circles on my back.

"I love you, luv," Tom says, leaning over and pressing a kiss to the dimples above my ass. He slips a hand between my cheeks and prods at the plug still nestled there. "And since my fun was interrupted, I think I'll claim my mating day present now."

He tugs on the plug, not enough to dislodge it, but enough for me to feel it as I hiccup and my tears dry. Tension coils low in my belly again as he toys with it.

"Why do *you* get a present on *my* mating day?" That's not how this works.

"Shh." Tom bends my legs so I'm kneeling over Marcus, my cheeks spreading. "Alpha?"

Marcus grunts, and his cock bobs against my juncture. Someone reaches between us and presses its tip to my pussy. He shifts me, sinking into me in one smooth thrust. Slick flows freely at his blunt intrusion, and I gasp, my hand tightening into his chest hair as I hold on to him while he fucks up into me from underneath. His cock slides against my back wall and the plug there.

"What about me?" Sam asks. "Do I get a present too?"

"You can have her mouth, puppy," Tom says.

I'm about to snap at them that it's a bit heavy-handed to decide which of my holes they all get to fill when Tom grabs the plug and pulls it free. *Fuck!* My pussy spasms around Marcus's cock as pleasure ripples through me. I close my eyes and arch my back.

"Let me get slicked up," Tom says, a hand on my hips tilting my pelvis. His cock prods my hole, but it's not the one I expect. He notches it alongside Marcus's, and my alpha holds still as Tom pushes his way in, making my pussy stretch wide to take them both. It's as devastating as I remember. He scoops slick from my thighs and folds and smears it on his length, working his way past the tip until it's like being split in two.

I tremble, trying to hold still. "I can't, it's too much, it's—"

"You will," Marcus says with enough alpha bark threaded into his voice that there's no arguing.

"We did this last time. You can take it, luv. You'll take all of us tonight. One in every hole. Now give me this pretty ass. It's mine."

Tom slides in and out of my pussy, and when he pulls free I sigh in relief, but then he notches his cock at my ass and pushes. "Relax, luv. Let me in. Shhh, don't whimper. It's halfway in now. You're doing so well. Such a good girl, taking both of us. That's right. Push back, take me all the way. God, you're so tight. There. That's it. That's all of it. Not so bad, right? And now it'll feel good. You'll see."

They move, one sliding out and the other in as they fuck me slowly. They move as opposites, one filling me as the other leaves, and then when the fullness turns into pleasure, they change it all over again. They fuck me together, working in sync to stuff both of my holes full as Marcus hits the mouth of my womb and Tom buries his cock in my ass.

Sam settles on his knees by my head. His cock thickens in his fist as he pumps it slowly, a bead of pre-cum leaking from his tip. He drags his thumb over my mouth, pulling my lower lip down.

"Open wide, baby."

The moment I relax my jaw, he pushes his way in, pinning my tongue down as he pumps it in and out. Saliva floods my mouth as he hits the back of my throat and pauses, pulling back to let me breathe before doing it again. They use me, filling all my holes as they work their cocks into me. There's a certain level of trust here, in knowing that they only want what's best for me and what's best is all of them. At once. This full of them, there's no room for me to over think or worry.

Sam hits the back of my throat and pushes and I open, swallowing him down until he's past the tight ring there and my throat bulges around him. His head rolls back, and he groans as he holds there for a bit, and then retreats. I drag in a breath, whimpering as Tom fucks faster into my ass while Marcus keeps up his slow and steady pace. He's relentless but endlessly patient, and he's a stark contrast to our pushy betas. Dependable where they test the limits.

Again, Sam pushes into the back of my throat. They fill me to bursting and take their pleasure one after the other. Trapped between them, all I can do is take it.

Sam pulls back, and I suck his head, laving him with my

tongue and tracing the veins on his shaft and the sensitive under-side where his corona flares. He groans and surges forward, choking me for even longer.

Skin slaps against skin, the filthy sounds of our fucking filling the room as Tom slams into my ass and comes with a grunt, his cock jumping as he shoots his seed deep in my belly. When he's spent, his cock emptied, he pulls free and rubs a thumb across my puffy hole.

"Push it out, luv. Let me watch you drip with me."

I push, Marcus's cock meeting resistance, but he only fucks me harder as my ass drips. Tom's cum runs down the curve of my sex to pool on our alpha's cock.

"Such a beautiful sight. Thank you, luv. I'll cherish knowing I was your first there."

Choke. Breathe. Lick. Suck. Choke. Sam uses me. He fucks my mouth, a hand tangled in my hair as he presses my nose to his groin and stays buried in the back of my throat. "Fuck, baby. Almost there. Almost. One more."

He pulls back and strokes his shaft, his fingers squeezing tight. Hips pressing, he pulls my head down on his cock as he feeds me his length, his hand still stroking. He cums, his cock jerking against my tongue as he pumps his seed down my throat and fills my belly another way.

"Fuck, that's good." He pulls out of my throat but leaves his tip in my mouth to lick clean.

God, he tastes so good. Like hot summer days at the pool and sticky popsicles. I suck his softening head and clean under his crown.

"You're such a good cocksucker, baby." He gathers my hair back from my face so he can watch how my cheeks hollow as I swallow the last of his cum.

Now that they've both pulled free, Marcus grabs my hips and bucks up into me, hitting my cervix and shoving around it as he hollows me out, my full belly sloshing with all of them. He ruts me, and it doesn't matter that he's the one underneath me. There's not even the illusion of me being in control here just because I'm on top. I hold on through this ride as he buries himself to the root and makes my belly bulge with every pounding thrust.

I work a hand between us to stroke my clit, to find my pleasure, but Marcus grabs it and hauls it to the small of my back. He pins it there, his grip strong and unwavering. Controlling.

"No." His voice is deep and dark, nearly a growl. "You don't come until I've knotted you."

A shiver rolls through me, and my clit throbs from where it rubs against him as he fucks me. I tilt my pelvis, letting him hit that spot over and over again. Need tightens in my core, turning my insides liquid gold. All I can think about is coming, finding that release that makes the heat stop crushing me from every direction. My toes curl, the hand pinned to my back squeezing into a fist as I balance on that edge.

Tom chuckles, and I know I'm caught, but I'm almost there. Just a few more thrusts. A few more rubs against his pelvic bone and he can knot me as many times as he wants.

Marcus stops. Just stops completely, his hard dick sitting in my entrance as he waits. His message is obvious. He is the one in control here, and he can be patient or he can be cruel.

I moan in stuttered agony as my orgasm stalls out. *I was so close!* Why is it right for them to use me like a toy? To stuff all my holes full and leave me still wanting? If he knew how much it hurt… How agonizing it was… Can't he feel through the bond how much these denials pain me?

I struggle against him, trying to sit up so I can ride him, but all that earns me is my other arm being pinned behind my back to join the first. Marcus chuckles when I let out an annoyed whine.

If he only knew…

But why shouldn't he?

I go still, dropping my head to his neck. I slide my nose across the stretch of skin there and find the source of his scent. Creamy, spicy sweetness. I lick his scent gland, enjoying the way he moans and his cock twitches inside me.

"It's cute watching her struggle for dominance. Like watching a hamster try to fight a bear," Tom says.

Hamster?

I suck Marcus's scent gland into my mouth and graze him with my teeth. My canines aren't as sharp as an alpha's. They're not as long and pointed. But they're less blunt than a beta's.

Don't they know even hamsters can bite?

Before they know what I'm really doing, I've already broken skin. I bite down hard, savoring the way Marcus gasps underneath me. I clamp my jaw down tight, scissoring deeper. His cock twitches inside me.

"Fuck!" Marcus curses. The cords of his neck pull taut, and I tighten my jaw to pin him there, to keep him under me.

"Oh, shit. Quick, give me my camera."

"Daaaamn, baby."

The shutter snaps as I gnash my jaw, cutting deeper. Blood wells in my mouth, the coppery tang of it spiced with sweet pheromones that make me groan as I try to lick it all up without letting him go. I won't let him go. He's mine. They all are. And it's time they know exactly what they do to me when they tease me like this.

The bond rips again, but this time it's me worming my way into Marcus. I sink deep inside him, curling up in his heart. His soul. Inside him, I can feel the others even stronger than before. The imprint of them sharpens, getting clearer. They wrap around me like one of my fluffy blankets. Their surprise, their shock, their amusement, I feel all of it. They watch me claim my alpha, my big beautiful brute, and mark him as mine.

Mine.

My jaw cramps, but I ignore it. I bite my claim deeper around his scent gland until the slick taste of spicy chai and blood flood my mouth.

Marcus lets go of my wrists and cups my head, the gesture gentle as he urges me to bite deeper still. To mark my claim for good so there's no chance of it fading as it heals. His fingers tangle in my hair as I ignore the ache in my jaw and rip. There's nothing delicate about it. There is no gentle breaking of skin with long, sharp canines made for just that purpose. This is grinding teeth and instinct. Instead of pulling me off him, he cups me gently and pulls me deeper.

Marcus grunts. My teeth carve deeper.

When I'm certain it's taken root, I release his scent gland and lick it clean, purring as I lap up his pheromone-soaked blood. I grind and rub against him, the friction on my clit making the crushing pain and need of my heat ease as pleasure chases it away like light cutting through a fog. The agony lessens a little.

"I'm sorry," he says, still stroking my hair. "I'm sorry. I didn't know, but now I do. Take, and I'll give."

Satisfied, I sit up, and he lets me. I roll my hips and work myself on his cock. The angle lets him hit a spot inside me that makes my toes curl, and I don't even need to touch my clit to come as I ride him, using him to quench my raging desire. I put my hands on his chest to get leverage, and my bonding ring glints in the twinkle light. Warmth and love make my belly flip flop, and I drop my head back as my pleasure builds. It winds tight, and everything is right again.

He grabs me by the hips and rolls up into me, and we find our rhythm until we both come, fluttering and pumping, and his knot swells inside me. It stretches me wide and plugs up my hole, trapping his cum deep inside me where it belongs.

I collapse against his chest and duck my head to his throat to lick at his mating bite, licking up the trails of blood that have rolled down his front. We're both purring by the time his knot shrinks and cum and slick slide out of me, soaking into the bedding underneath us. Someone throws a blanket over the both of us, and I sigh, content. At least for a few hours.

"Fuck, that was hot," Sam says.

Tom grunts in agreement, his camera clicking again as he takes a few more photos. "I'm going to transfer these to my computer. Let's have dinner while they rest."

Sam and Tom both press a kiss to my cheek before slipping out of the nest and wandering downstairs.

I'm sorry, Marcus's soul says through our bond. It doesn't use words. In the bond, there's no need for them. I hear him all the same.

Forgiven, mine answers.

He holds me tight and wraps his arms around me, and I'm happy beyond belief.

Chapter Twenty-Six

EMILY

Three days later, when we all emerge from our sticky, messy nest, we take a group shower, washing one another as we savor the intimacy of nonsexual touch. Even Tom manages to behave himself. His balls are spent, he says. Sam laughs and offers him a vitamin combination that can help increase semen production.

"Don't worry," I say, rinsing the shampoo out of my hair. "I've hit my dick quota for the week."

Everything is chafed. I wash between my legs with a gentle swipe of a sudsy hand. After we're clean, Sam massages me down there with a bottle of that healing oil he says he took from the clinic on his way out.

"I still have to send the photos to the printer, but do you guys want to see the ones I think are the best?" Tom asks.

I'm dying of curiosity. The pictures from Sam's mating are gorgeous. They're not just sensual and sexual—they're visceral and raw. "Yes! Oh, that reminds me." I turn to Marcus. "We never gave you your mating present. Everything got kind of crazy in there."

"It shouldn't be that bad next time, now that you're mated,"

Sam says. "You had three months of bonding chemicals bottled up and ready to explode."

Marcus leans down and kisses me, then wraps me in my fluffy robe. "Is this the secret you were keeping from me?"

I belt the waist and nod, his smile making me weak in the knees. *Nope*, I tell my battered pussy when it gives a half-hearted attempt to boot and rally. *We are closed for business for at least a week.* Wet clumps of dark hair threaded with silver hang in his face, and he brushes them to the side, a bead of water rolling down his stubble. *At least three days.*

"I hid it in the office," Tom says. "I'll grab it."

We all end up piled on the sofa in the living room while the nest bedding runs through the wash cycle. Marcus pops open the bottle of wine he's been chilling in the fridge all week for this very moment and pours us all a glass. Tom comes back with a large leather album in his hands. The cover is stamped with black on black designs that swirl together. He hands it to Marcus, takes his glass, and joins us on the couch.

"You made this?" Marcus asks, trailing a finger down the edge of the leather-bound book.

"We all did," Tom says.

He cracks it open, and the stiff spine creaks before giving. The title page is our family name embossed in shiny black on the matte black page, and my stomach swarms with butterflies as I realize that's my name now too. He flips the page, and we see the first image. It's a self portrait of the three of us lying in the nest, our limbs pretzeled together with the sheets twisted all around us. It's more intimate than scandalous. Only knees and thighs and a foot are visible.

Marcus turns the page, flipping through the book. It's a shot of my torso with Sam's hands gripping my breasts like a bra as I ride him backward. The room is dark, the shape of us only lit in contrast with a white rim light that shows the curve of my breast and rib cage and the rough texture of his hands. He's gotten callused while working on the bike.

The next one is a flash of Sam's throat with Tom's hand cupping his jaw and forcing his head up. Fingers dig into skin, pressing on the pulse point. Sam's lips are wet and swollen from being kissed.

On the next page is the curve of my back and the top of my ass, a hand splayed across it so the pinky settles in the twin divots above my crack. The Venus dimples, Tom had said. I'm not even certain whose hand it is in the photo. It doesn't matter.

In the next one I'm standing in front of the window wearing Tom's shirt, the sleeves rolled up because they're too long on me. The light shines through it, turning the fabric sheer. You can see the curve of my body, the dark thatch of hair between my legs, the jut of my nipples. I've piled my hair on my head, my fingers tangled in the locks as sun highlights the strands.

Sam reclines in bed in the next photo, his cock soft against his thigh. A trail of cum is splattered across his abs. On the next page, Tom takes Sam from behind, their hands tangled together on top of the desk and Sam's mouth rounding as he comes. Sam kneels on the floor in the next one, his collar a stark contrast against his throat. A leash disappears out of view as its holder tugs his head up.

Marcus flips the page, and we see Tom leaning against the wall, his jacket and shirt unbuttoned and open and his pants gaping as he dips a hand inside. Only the trail of hair leading down is visible, but his hips pump into the air and the fabric is strained, the edge of his hard erection barely visible with the dark lighting.

The book gets more risque the deeper it goes. As if the viewer is being asked to join us. And they are, because this is a gift for Marcus's eyes only. It's a celebration of our love, our bond.

Our pack.

Marcus flips through it, studying each page with equal attention. There's a closeup of my pussy wrapped around Sam's girth, my lips shiny and stretched thin as my sex grips him as if it doesn't want to ever let him go. Then Sam's ass, red and striped from the lashing of a belt, his hole puffy and used with a trickle of cum that curves down its slope.

Me laying on my side, my legs pressed together and showing only the seam of my sex and the gleam of my jeweled plug peeking out through my cheeks. Cum drips down my sex, following the curve of my body as it trickles down my lips and over that spot where the thigh meets ass before beading in a fat drop.

Tom's long cock rising from his thatch of dark hair with my face pressed against Sam's as I lick the shaft and he licks the balls. A pearl of pre-cum gathers at the slitted tip, balanced precariously and suspended forever in this captured moment.

It continues to Sam's mating ceremony. It shows Sam kneeling at Marcus's feet, his silver plug catching the light as he looks up at the imposing, naked alpha. Marcus looks larger than life from the low angle, like a statue of a Greek god. His broad shoulders taper to a narrow waist. He's stacked with muscles and almost twice the size of Sam.

In the next one, Sam's lips wrap around that cock and they're shiny with spit, his cheek pouching out where Marcus's head presses against the skin from inside. Then, in the next one, Sam is held to Marcus's chest, thick arms caging him in. There's a closeup of their bite, Sam's head rolling to the side as teeth rip into the patch of skin between neck and shoulder. A thin rivulet of blood escapes the alpha's blood-stained teeth.

Then there's me, kneeling in the nest, my hands on my thighs in proper submissive posture and the nipple and clit clamps dangling and gleaming. Next Sam is underneath Marcus, a closeup of their grinding hips as the alpha takes him for the first time, the edge of Sam's ringed cock barely visible from the way they're turned. Now it's me riding Tom, my collar around my throat and my breasts swaying and blurry with movement. The gold chain that connects the nipple clamps catches the light where it's twisted up in his long fingers.

And that's the end.

For now.

There's plenty of room in the back of the album for more pages to be added.

"That was beautiful," Marcus says, his voice gravelly and thick with emotion. He closes the book and rubs his hand over the cover lovingly.

"The printer can add to it as soon as I get these new images processed," Tom says. "Sam helped me with these. He has a good eye for this."

Sam blushes. "I'm only doing what you tell me to."

"I love it," Marcus says, putting the book down on the coffee table. He leans over and kisses Tom. "Thank you."

Through our bond, I feel how happy our alpha is, and through his bond I catch an echo of the others. It's comforting knowing they're there. That they always will be and I'll never be alone again.

Marcus turns to me and kisses me, his lips gentle. "Thank you." He reaches across me and grab's Sam's hand, pulling it to his mouth and kissing the knuckles. "Thank you."

I clutch my wineglass to my chest and slump against Marcus, cuddling against him. Sam sits on the other side of me on the couch and presses his weight against me. Tom leans his head on Marcus's shoulder, and we all stay like that, piled up and happy and basking until the dryer buzzes and we head to bed with freshly laundered sheets.

We make the bed and settle into the nest, none of us ready to leave it yet even though my heat's over and we're all exhausted.

The wine goes straight to my head, my stomach empty these last three days except for the flavors of my mates, and I curl up between them, sandwiched and warm while someone draws swirls onto my back.

It's bliss.

"We should have a big ceremony," Marcus says after a while, pulling me awake from the half-asleep state I was resting in. "Have all our family and friends come and celebrate."

"A big ceremony?" I crack my heavy eyelids open and stare at the twinkle lights.

"Mmhmm. Won't your mom be disappointed if we don't?" he asks. His breath fans my forehead as he nuzzles into my hair. "I know she expected you to stay a beta and get married. She probably expected you to have a wedding."

Fuck. I hadn't even thought of that. The notion that I'll have to live with a lifetime of *my other daughter didn't even have a ceremony* makes me want to hide in my nest and never come out. She would never let that go. It would get brought up at every single Thanksgiving and Christmas. "Uh… sure."

He kisses my hair and hugs me tighter. But I stay awake for a while, even when they're all snoring.

Fuck.

Okay, I can do this.

Chapter Twenty-Seven

EMILY

I CAN'T DO THIS. THE EVENT PLANNER HUNTS ME DOWN LIKE A big game shooter on safari, even though I'm hiding in the bathroom. Her heels click on the tile, and I lift my feet up onto the seat. Maybe she didn't see my legs?

I don't know what to tell this woman. She keeps asking me to pick things and make decisions, and then I have to admit I don't know the difference between dining à la russe and à la française. I can't do this. They'll know that I'm a fraud. That I'm not some sophisticated woman who knows how to throw a lavish party. I thought it was just going to be friends and family celebrating our mating. I didn't know that almost half of New York City and London would be here. The ballroom holds five hundred, she told me proudly. Five hundred! I don't even know five hundred people.

"Mrs. Orello? I'm so sorry to disturb you but it's been half an hour, and the kitchen needs an answer because they'll need to plan if we want to get the best choices when they go shopping first thing in the morning. And if you're dining à la russe, we'll need to arrange for more centerpieces with the florist."

"That, uh, sounds fine. Let's do that." I put my feet down and stand, unlocking the bathroom door and facing the music. To her credit, the woman doesn't gawk at me. Instead, she scribbles on her clipboard.

"Lovely. We'll dine à la russe, and from the guest list your mate gave me... you'll need twenty tables. Each rectangular table seats twenty-four. Unless you'd prefer round tables?" She looks up at me expectantly.

"Uh... rectangular is fine."

That crease is back between her brow and I break out in a sweat. Did I pick wrong? Are round tables better than rectangular ones? Does it matter as long as people have somewhere to sit so they can eat? She clicks her pen and presses the clipboard to her chest.

Shit. I definitely chose wrong.

"Either option is fine, Mrs. Orello. We have eight-foot round tables that can seat ten guests, so we'd simply need to sacrifice the dance floor if you'd prefer round tables."

Dancing. Oh, God. I don't know how to dance unless looping your arms around your partner's neck and swaying counts, which I have a feeling it won't. "You know, maybe round tables would be best." If the room is jam packed with tables, surely nobody can expect me to know how to waltz.

She clicks her pen again and scribbles on her clipboard. "Very good. Your mates asked me to make sure you have anything and everything you want." She sighs, her look dreamy, and then she snaps back into her professional face. "Shall we go over floral arrangement options? I have some preserved samples for you to look at unless you have something specific in mind."

"Yes, flowers. Good." I follow her out, and she makes me sit, then wheels in a cart loaded with different floral arrangements of varying heights and styles. There are short, round ones stuffed with white roses, and dramatic sprays of greenery and pastel blooms. There's a bright one with tropical flowers in hot pink and yellow, and a dark one with blood red flowers and stabby-looking thistles. I point to the pastel one set in the gold vase. "These?"

"Those are my favorite."

I sigh with relief.

"Do you like it as is, or would you like to substitute any of the flowers?"

God, why are there fifty choices within a single choice? I've never been the omega who thought about her dream mating celebration. Many don't even have one. I don't enjoy being the center of attention. And I definitely don't find party planning exciting or fun. It's exhausting. Tom dragged us to over thirty venues all over the five boroughs and a few upstate before I made him pick one.

"Now for the tablecloths." She reaches under the floral arrangements and pulls out a swatch ring and flips through them. "We have bright white, soft white, champagne, blush, silver, ecru, eggshell…"

My eyes glaze over, and I pick one called candlelight. She recommends antique gold sashes to complement them, confiding in me she thinks they look better than the standard gold. I didn't know white and gold came in so many shades.

"Now, have you chosen your own bakery, or will you be using our kitchen for the cake?"

My phone chirps, and I latch onto the excuse to walk away.

SAM

How's it going?

EMILY

Save me

That bad?

You have no idea

I'm not kidding

> Please come save me. I can't take it anymore. Do you have any idea how many shades of white there are?

I'm outside

I head back over to the coordinator and grab my bag off the chair, slinging it onto my shoulder. "I'm so sorry, but my mate is outside, and he needs me. Can you forward any other questions you have to my mate, Tom?"

Her eye twitches, but she gives me her customer service smile and offers me her card. "Of course. I'll have my secretary type up a list of the remaining details that need to be settled and have her send it to Mr. Orello."

I run out of there, my shoes clicking against the tile as I button up my coat and step out into the cold, avoiding a pile of dirty slush as I spot Sam and throw myself into his arms. He hugs me, squeezing me tight underneath my jacket.

"Where's Tom?" he asks.

"He got a call about picking someone up from the airport. I guess a few of his people flew in early from England and forgot to tell anyone, and they didn't know how to get to their hotel."

I pull out my phone and start texting.

EMILY

> I'm tapping out and leaving the venue with Sam. I will owe you a favor if you finish party planning for me so I don't have to think about any of it again except to show up on time.

TOM

Anything?

Deal.

I shiver, knowing that I've just given him carte blanche to do who knows what to me. Whatever it is he wants, I'm fairly certain I'll enjoy it. He sends me an emoji of a grinning devil.

"Better?" Sam asks.

"All good now." My chest no longer feels pinched, and now I can breathe.

He tugs me to the curb and hails us a taxi, and we head home. Bobbie smiles at us and holds the door, and I murmur our thanks. The elevator carries us up, and when we're inside I shuck out of my coat and boots, toss my purse onto its hook, and collapse face first onto the sofa. Sam sits on the coffee table and rubs my back, petting me. He digs his thumbs into the knot in my shoulders, and I groan.

"It can't really be that bad." He laughs at me.

Sitting up, I glare at him. "You wanna do it?"

He looks away.

"I didn't think so. Why is this my job?"

"Because omegas usually go nuts over this kind of stuff?"

All I can hear is my mother's nagging voice in my head telling me I've done everything wrong, then acting confused when I get mad at her for yelling at me. "That's a stereotype." I flop back down and shove my face into the sofa and wiggle my shoulders, and he goes back to rubbing, his thumbs digging into exactly the right spot.

"I guess you don't want to hear that your dress came back from getting altered and steamed. It's hanging upstairs in your closet."

I gasp and wiggle out from under Sam's hands and run up the stairs. He follows behind me, laughing under his breath. The dress is the only part of this whole thing I've enjoyed. Trying dozens of them on and standing up on that pedestal in front of the bank of mirrors in the dress shop made me feel like a princess, and I can't wait to feel like that again when I wear it while

Marcus, Tom, and Sam introduce me to their family and friends. I drag the zipper down and run a hand over the delicate fabric. The beaded lace flowers hang heavy on the layers upon layers of sheer tulle. Seeing it again makes me begrudge the event planning a little less.

The front door slams shut, and I yelp, carefully shoving the dress's fluff back in its bag and zipping it shut.

"I'm home," Marcus calls up. His keys clink as he sets them down in the key bowl by the door.

"Coming!" I call down. We both head downstairs and take turns kissing him. "You're home early."

Marcus arches one brown and checks his watch. "So are you. I thought you'd be at the venue all day. My last appointment was canceled. I can finish everything else from home."

"Nope," I say, avoiding that conversation. "Are you hungry? I have soup in the crock pot."

He loosens his tie and bends down. "Starving." He kisses me slower, deeper. "But not for food." He nips my lower lip between his teeth, and he cups my ass, tugging me up. I wrap my arms around his neck and let him lift me, squeezing my legs around his hips.

"You're incorrigible," I say, giggling.

"You like it." His fingers tighten against my butt as he carries me up the stairs.

I do. He's warm and happy and full of lust, and I feel all of it through the bond. It makes me ache between my legs when he thinks like that.

"Are you joining us, Sam?"

Sam hurries after us, and we fall into the nest together, and when Tom gets home, we pull him in, too.

It's the big day, and my stomach feels like it's full of writhing snakes. I've met everyone important. We did Marcus's family on Tuesday. Sam's on Wednesday. Mine on Thursday. And Tom's on Friday after the last one landed from England. The hardest part is over. So why do I still feel like throwing up?

"Here." Sam shoves a glass of champagne into my hand, and I down it like a shot. The bubbles fizz in my nose and make me want to sneeze. "Hmm." He hands me his too, and I swallow it in two gulps. "Nervous?"

I pat my mouth with my fingers, careful not to smudge my makeup. "How can you tell?" I ask, my question dripping with sarcasm.

There's a knock at the dressing room door, but they don't wait to be told to enter. The door opens, and my parents step in, not bothering to close the door behind them as they gape at the room. "Mom! Shut the door."

She huffs and rolls her eyes, then smiles as she looks me up and down. "Relax, honey. It's fine."

It's not fine. Nobody else is supposed to see me before my father walks me in. Sam is only allowed because I'd probably be collapsed in a puddle of skirts in the corner if he weren't, and Marcus understands even if he doesn't get it. Social anxiety isn't something you can really explain to someone who doesn't have it.

"Oh, sweetheart, you look so beautiful," my dad says as he comes over and grabs my hands, holding them. His eyes grow damp and glassy as he makes me twirl for him. "My little girl's all grown up."

"That dress is gorgeous," my mother says. "It's very flattering. You can't even tell you're wearing shapewear underneath. Is the waist a little too tight, maybe? Any big news to share?"

I bite back a scream, my nostrils flaring as I keep a smile plastered to my face. "It's just the style, Mom. It's supposed to be fitted."

She grabs my hand from my father's grip. "Let me see that ring again. It's huge! I don't know how you get anything done with that heavy thing on your hand. What do you do all day?"

"Mrs. Thorne," Sam says, stepping in. "You look stunning in blue. Did you know that? It makes your red hair look absolutely vibrant. May I show you to your seat? It's about to start."

My mother pats her dyed hair and blushes, giving Sam a coy smile. "Oh, you're so sweet. Of course you may." She takes his arm, and he walks her out.

Sam looks over his shoulder, and I mouth *I love you* to him. He winks and shuts the door behind them.

"Are you happy, sweetheart?" my dad asks.

"I am. I really love them." I touch the bite mark, still healing at the base of my neck. It barely shows through the lace neckline of my dress.

He nods and holds his arm out. "Then chin up because that's all that matters. Come on now. Every journey starts with one step."

I glance at my reflection in the large gold-framed mirror and smooth a nonexistent wrinkle from my skirt and take his arm. He leads me into the hallway, and the coordinator spots me, running ahead as fast as her heels let her. We walk slowly to give her time and to keep my train from catching on anything. Right as we turn the corner to the entryway, the music starts.

My heart slams against my ribs, the snakes in my belly wrestling with the butterflies as my hand goes clammy in my dad's soft grip. The attendant throws the door open, and my dad walks me in.

"Please stand," the officiant says.

All eyes turn as we enter the crowded ballroom and everyone rises. Marcus, Tom, and Sam all stand in a row at the front of the room. They're so handsome in their matching black tuxes, a pink bud pinned in each of their buttonholes.

There's a floral arrangement suspended from the high ceilings to mark the spot, as if I could miss it when my mates stand there, beaming at me like I'm the most beautiful creature they've ever seen. Marcus's face crumples as he tries to hold it together, the love he's pouring through our bond so strong I forget to breathe. Tom reaches up and rubs his back, and Sam grins like he finds this all very amusing.

My dad stops us right in front of them.

"Who gives away this omega?" The officiant asks.

"I do," my father says. He kisses me on the cheek and goes to his table, taking his seat next to my mother.

"Who receives her?"

"We do," Marcus, Tom, and Sam answer in unison.

"Take each other's hands and form a ring. A ring is a symbol of eternity, for it has no beginning and no end, just as the love you four have has no end. Together, you will share your sorrows. Your joys. Your burdens and your dreams. Together, you are stronger than you ever were apart. You may kiss your omega."

Marcus tugs me in first, his kiss sweet and the bond full of love. He puts a hand on the small of my back and cradles me to his chest. When he lets me go, Tom grabs me next. He drops me into a dip, his lips capturing mine as I squeak. He takes advantage of my parted lips by sliding his tongue against mine as he deepens the kiss until I'm breathless. The room bursts into cheers, and my face is hot when he spins me upright and passes me to Sam. Sam catches me with both arms around my waist and kisses me until the room stops spinning, his forehead pressed to mine when we part.

"Ladies and gentlemen, I have the honor of introducing the Misters and Missus Orello."

The room fills with applause, and I take refuge in the arms of my pack as I avoid looking at the crowded room.

"Please be seated," the officiant says as we head to our small table at the head of the room. "Dinner will now be served."

Waiters circle, bringing out the first course as the quartet in the corner plays, and the murmur of conversation fills the room. I'm starving. I've had more champagne than food today. The manicurist, pedicurist, masseuse, hair stylist, makeup artist, and the photographer Tom hired have kept me running since dawn. We eat and drink and bask in our happiness until dinner is finished, and then we mingle, walking around and talking to everyone. Sam bustles my train so it doesn't get stepped on before he's pulled away by his cousins.

They've all left me, tugged in one direction or another as they talk with friends and family, some of whom they haven't seen in years. I spot Lindsay at the singles table. She's flirting with the handsome man sitting next to her, and I hesitate to interrupt them until she spots me and stands, her hands waving with excitement. I walk into her hug and grip her back.

"Oh. My. God! You look so hot," she squeals into my ear over the noise.

"I'm so glad you came. I think I know about fifteen people here."

"Girl, I wouldn't have missed this for the world. Your mates are so handsome. It's ridiculous. And the food was fantastic. Don't tell anyone, but I've been visiting all the different waiters and stealing hors d'oeuvres. I have a whole purse full of fried shrimp."

I wrinkle my nose and laugh. "You don't have to steal them. I'll ask the kitchen to make you a to-go box if you want."

She shakes her head, her curls bouncing over her shoulders.

"That defeats the entire purpose. It's the stealing that makes the food taste better."

I'm not sure that I agree with Lindsay about purse shrimp, but she's happy, and that's what matters. I glance over at the man seated next to her at the table and send a silent *thank you* to the coordinator. "Who's your friend?"

"Oh, you're not gonna believe it. He's an accountant too, and he told me the funniest joke that I'm absolutely going to steal about taxes and fines and—"

"Emily," my mother hisses, cutting into the conversation. "I need to borrow you."

"Mom, I'm in the middle of—"

She grabs me by the wrist and tugs me toward her, and it's either give in or stumble, so I let her pull me away. Lindsay and I share mutual horrified looks, and I glance around to see if anyone else has noticed. But they're all absorbed in their own conversations or dinner or drinks.

My mother drags me over to the back of the room where the venue has set up a signing station. There's a leather-bound blank book for people to write in best wishes and congratulations and a sign asking people to donate to a local charity we chose instead of giving us gifts. There, above the table, are three black and white copies of Tom's prints displayed on easels. It's our mating bites. Tom's, Sam's, and mine all lined up together.

"Did you know that someone put up pornography? Your grandmother is here! What will people think? I told them to take it down, but that nitwit coordinator of yours won't listen to me."

Thank God for small favors.

I make a mental note to have Marcus give the coordinator a bonus. She's done a remarkable job.

"Mom, it's not pornography, it's art. And they're Tom's photographs. That's what he does. Remember? I told you he's a fine arts photographer."

"I thought he took normal portraits, not... not *this*. It's obscene."

I could smooth things over. Ask the coordinator to have the portraits moved. Tom would understand. He knows what difficult families are like. My mother will pretend this never happened until later. In private. When she drags it out as yet another reason for why I'm worse at everything than my perfect sister. That's what she does. My mother nags and snipes and coerces, but only when nobody else can see it. Can't have anyone see the cracks in the facade of our perfect family. Sometimes, when she insists that something upsetting never actually happened and I'm misremembering things, she makes me feel crazy.

I'm tired of feeling crazy.

I'm tired of pretending everything is fine.

I'm tired of her making me feel ashamed of what I am. An omega. But there's nothing wrong with being an omega and I'm done with this endless cycle of misery.

I'm done with her. The moment I think those words I know they're true. The sudden clarity makes me calm.

The prints are sensual, they're intimate, but there's nothing really showing, and it's not my fault if she can't tell the difference. And I'm not a little girl anymore. I'm thirty-six, and these are my mates. I refuse to be ashamed of my dynamic anymore because it's inconvenient to her sense of propriety.

I jerk my wrist out of her grip. "They're staying. If you hate them so much, then *leave*."

She rears back like I've slapped her. "Emily Marie Thorne!"

Now people are staring. They look over, and my face grows hot with embarrassment and shame. Not at my mates, not with myself or our portraits, and certainly not for the bond we created through love. But shame that she's never accepted this part of me and that I've internalized it too, hiding from it like it's something dirty.

But there's nothing dirty or shameful about being an omega.

I ball my hands into fists until my freshly manicured nails bite into my palm. "It's Orello, not Thorne. And if you're so ashamed of me for being an omega, then I *want* you to leave. Go."

Someone I don't know takes a step forward to intervene, and I lose my nerve, giving into the impulse to run. I push through the crowd and duck into the hallway, my heart pounding in my throat as I flee. There's nowhere to go. We're dozens of stories up, and I don't actually want to leave. I just need a minute. I need a moment where I can sit and calm myself. Where people aren't staring at me.

Someone is coming down the hallway from the other end. I duck into the nearest room and realize it's the coat check. The attendant's gone, probably on her break, and I decide this'll work. I shove through the racks of winter coats until I hit the back, and then I sit. My dress puffs up around me, billowing with air. I grab fistfuls of the coats hanging before me and tug them together on their rack to hide me from view.

The tears fall, probably ruining my carefully applied makeup, and I press my forehead to my knees and cry. Why does she always ruin everything? Why can't she just be happy for me? She'll never be what I want her to be, and wishing she were is an exercise in frustration for both of us. My mother genuinely doesn't understand why our relationship is strained, and it doesn't matter how I explain it. She consistently twists herself into the victim.

Someone grabs the coats shielding me and pulls them apart. It's Tom. He looks down at me sitting there on the dirty floor in my expensive white dress.

"I just needed a minute." I pat my damp cheeks, trying not to disturb the makeup more than it already is. "I'll come back once I've pulled myself together."

Tom frowns, his lips thinning into a flat line, and then the expression smooths out. He holds up a bottle of champagne. "I nicked this. Want some?"

"God, yes."

He sits down on the floor next to me, his long legs poking out beyond the next track as he hands me the bottle and adjusts the coats, covering us so nobody walking down the hallway will see us through the coat check's opening.

I wrap my lips around the opening and drink until the bubbles make me want to sneeze. "How'd you find me?" I hand it to him.

"Hmm. When the bride runs away from her own ceremony, people tend to notice. I caught an echo of your distress through the bond." He lifts the bottle to his mouth and drinks, his throat bobbing as he swallows.

"Sorry." I've made a mess of things. I shouldn't have yelled at her, then run off crying to throw myself a pity party. People flew in for this from across the ocean, and I'm making things awkward and weird.

"You didn't want this party," Tom says. He closes his eyes and shakes his head. "I tried to tell him, but he thought you were just being shy. That you didn't want to ask. You don't like to ask for the things you want."

My throat feels like an apple's lodged in it. "I'm sorry." The words are barely more than a whisper, but he hears them and looks at me, his eyes wide with surprise.

"Sorry for what? I didn't want this either. I'm glad we probably get to leave early now." He tugs at the collar of his shirt, loosening his tie. "This thing is starched to high heaven. It keeps stabbing me whenever I turn my head."

"You aren't mad you don't get to spend more time with your family?" They came such a long way to see him. To meet me and Sam and celebrate with us.

He's silent for a long while, but I don't pressure him to speak before he's ready. If anyone understands what I go through, it's him. "Families like ours are difficult. I think my family always hoped I'd turn out to be an alpha like my father. It took me a long time to realize I'll never live up to their expectations no matter what I do and even longer to decide I shouldn't care. I'm happy with my choices because they were mine. And because they brought me to all of you."

I take the champagne from him and drink, then set it down and lean against him, resting my head on his shoulder. He finds my hand in the folds of my skirts and threads our fingers together.

That's how Sam finds us. He shoves the coats aside and gives me a lopsided, silly grin. "Cozy. I like it." He joins us, sitting on my other side, and tugs the coats back into place.

"How'd you find us?" I ask, handing him the pilfered champagne.

"Coats don't talk. It wasn't hard to figure it out. You okay? I felt whatever happened." He drains the bottle and sets it down.

Okay, as far as hiding places go, maybe it wasn't the most well thought out, but to be fair, I wasn't thinking straight when I darted in here. "I'm fine. We should get back in there." I sigh. I am not looking forward to it. Also, I need to find a mirror and check my face.

"What the fuck for?" Sam shrugs out of his jacket and tosses it onto the floor, then pulls his tie off too. "Oh, that's better. Can we go home now?"

Home. That's what I want. The thought of it fills me with longing. I want to curl up in our nest and cuddle and fall asleep with my pack pressed against me. I'd like to forget how this night ended and only think about the way they looked at me when they saw me walk out. That's what matters.

Tom leans his head against mine, the weight of it comforting. "This wasn't your fault."

My heart squeezes with affection. It means a lot to hear that.

For someone to see it and acknowledge that I tried, and it's okay to be mad at her when she does something like this, even though she's my mother.

I will never make my children feel like my love is conditional.

Squeezing my eyes shut, I sigh and let the breath out slowly, breathing out the pain and frustration until I feel calmer. More centered.

Tom's phone rings, breaking the silence, and he fishes it out of his pocket. "Hello? Yeah. Sam and I have her. Coat closet. No, inside. What do you mean, where? I told you. Inside the coat closet." Tom stands and leans on the rack. He hangs up his phone and tucks it away. "We're leaving, right?"

Marcus's side of the bond is tense until Tom turns around and puts a hand out for me. He pulls me up from the floor, and I smooth my skirts out. Sam joins us, gathering his suit jacket and tie off the floor.

"I'm sorry it took me so long to get to you, sweetheart. I got cornered by a gaggle of grandmothers. You okay?" Marcus asks.

I nod, because the last thing I want to do is talk about right here, right now. He waits for us to slip from the coat closet, then holds his arms out and wraps me into the biggest hug. In the circle of his arms, it feels like nothing can hurt me. Emotion hits me again, and my eyes grow damp once more. I sniff, willing the tears back.

"Do we have to go back in there and say goodbye?" I ask.

Marcus bends down and scoops me into his arms, lifting me up in a bridal carry while Sam runs ahead to call the elevator and Tom grabs our coats. "No, sweetheart. We're going home."

I've never heard three more perfect words.

"But I'll have words with your mother later," Marcus growls.

"Don't." I tighten my arm around his neck while he calls the elevator. I love that he's prepared to wade into battle for me.

Nobody ever has before. But it won't change anything. "She'll only feed off the attention. Take me home."

They bundle me into our limo, and our surprised driver takes us home, not saying a word about how early it is as he slips into traffic. Marcus carries me inside the entire way, even when I insist I can walk and that I'm fine. When it's clear he won't listen, I give in and relax against him. Letting him take care of me satisfies something deep inside me I didn't know needed it.

He peels me gently out of my dress, hanging it up to deal with later, and then he slips me out of my undergarments and presses a kiss to every body part he exposes. The underwear I'm wearing under the smoothing shapewear is sexy. I imagined this evening going a different way. The panties are white lace and crotchless, with a blue bow over the butt. He drags them down my hips without a word, then bundles me into our nest. Sam brings me a wet microfiber cloth, and I scrub the makeup from my face.

Tom nuzzles into my hair, pulling the pins from it until he can run his fingers through it. His fingertips dig into my scalp, massaging it. Sam lies on Marcus's other side, his arm thrown across our alpha's belly to hold mine.

Piled together, with all of them touching me, we sleep. In the morning, they wake me with soft kisses and softer touches, and then we make the nest smell just a little more like pack.

Chapter Twenty-Eight

EMILY

Now that the sun's at its peak, the day is hot, and I shuck my light jacket off and carry it. It's difficult to dress for this weather when the mornings are cold and the days are warm, but New York in the spring is beautiful. All the flowers in Central Park are blooming.

My phone buzzes with a call, but one glance at the screen makes me click the side button to silence it. I send my mother to voicemail. If it's serious, she'll leave a message or text me. I refuse to let her ruin my day today. If she can't apologize for what she did at the ceremony, then I don't want to hear it unless someone's hurt or dying. She doesn't like being put on low-contact. On a day that was supposed to be all about me and my pack, she couldn't help but to try and make it about her. The ceremony made me realize I can't ever make her happy. Nobody can. And that's not my job.

Lindsay sees me coming from her spot in the chained-off patio and she gets up out of her chair and flags me down. "Hey! Wow, this café is packed. I had to order to keep our seats. I hope you don't mind."

I shake my head and duck inside, telling the hostess I'm

joining a friend. Weaving through the crowded tables, I sit and throw my jacket on the back of the chair. "You weren't kidding. We'll have to find a new lunch spot." That's the problem with New York. Something gets popular and then it gets packed and then you have to find the next *it* place and the cycle repeats.

"Nate told me about this cute little sandwich place down in Brooklyn. We should try that one next."

I nod and take a sip of my slightly watery lemonade. "Sure. Tom's new gallery is in Brooklyn." I could bring him lunch and then be his dessert. I duck my head to hide my smile.

"Oh, that's right! His grand opening is tomorrow, isn't it?"

A waitress comes and sets our lunches down. "Thank you." The salad is huge and covered with so many toppings you can barely see the greens underneath. She walks back to the kitchen, and Lindsay and I both eat while we talk. "It is, and he's nervous. The first showing is his own work. Marcus says he always gets like this until he sees what the critics write up in the papers." Like he has anything to be worried about. He's a genius behind the lens. I've never seen anyone capture emotion so flawlessly.

"Wish I could see it," she says. "We tried to get tickets, but it's sold out."

I stab my chicken and cut it into smaller bites. "I thought you couldn't go. Aren't you going upstate to meet Nate's parents this weekend?"

She shakes her head and loads up her fork until things are falling off it. "No. His dad has the flu, so they canceled."

I chew my mouth full and wash it down. "You should come with me. I'm going there now to bring him lunch or he'll work all day and not eat, then come home crabby and wonder why he's so irritated. I'm sure he has some spare tickets set aside."

Lindsay's eyes light up, and we spend the rest of the lunch catching up while I learn all about her new job. When the waitress comes back to take our plates and ask if there's anything else we need, I order Tom's food to go and call for a car from our service.

The Town Car's idling in the taxi zone by the time the restaurant gives me the bagged takeout container. We get in and he takes us to Brooklyn.

"Wow, this is significantly better than the subway." She strokes the leather interior. "I saw a drunk guy pee himself the other day, so now I don't sit on the seats, and holding onto the pole while the car lurches around is a lot harder than it looks."

No wonder Marcus won't let me take public transportation. We head over the bridge, and then we're in Brooklyn and the driver asks if I need him to wait for us. I say yes and tell him we won't be long, and then we stare up at the gallery for a moment, taking it all in.

There's no sign, just letters hand-painted on the glass by an expert tradesman. Beige stone frames large, curved windows, and each window houses one art piece from all the different artists that will be featured here throughout the year. That was my idea, and seeing it implemented in real life leaves me tingly. I love that he valued my input enough to actually implement it.

"Oh, it's so fancy," Lindsay says, craning her head back to take it all in.

"Come on. Let's talk to the front desk." We head in, and a new woman I don't know looks up from her computer. "Hello. I'm here to see Tom. Is he free, or is he stuck in the darkroom?"

She frowns. "I'm sorry, but we're not open to the public yet."

Alicia throws the black curtain that cordons off the actual gallery from the entryway aside. "Mrs. Orello. It's lovely to finally meet you in person. Tom's in the back. He'll be happy to see you. I've been trying to force him to take a break all day."

The receptionist stares at her computer with stiff shoulders as we pass her and follow Tom's personal assistant into the back. Lindsay stops and stares, craning her head back and gawking as we walk through the collection that's technically not on display yet. When people hear that Tom's a photographer, they imagine small framed pictures hanging in their hallway, not five foot tall prints that take up an entire wall. These are show stoppers, art, not family vacation photos.

"Oh. My. God. Is that you?" Lindsay asks, pointing.

It's the one from our mating, a closeup of me crouching over Marcus like a feral thing, his neck a bloody, bitten mess and my lips smeared with it. My hooked fingers dig into his chest like claws and my hair tumbles over my back and shoulders. There's no nudity, just the curve of my breast with most of it hidden by my arm, but it's an intimate shot nonetheless.

I smile as I look at it and remember the moment that everything changed. "It is. They all are, actually."

"Holy shit." Lindsay abandons me to walk around and look at them. "That is intense."

I follow Alicia into the back and leave Lindsay to her meandering. "Can you put two tickets aside for Lindsay and her boyfriend? She's a good friend of mine."

"Of course. Tom! Your mate is here, and she's brought you lunch. Will you stop fussing and let me do my job now?"

Tom turns from where he's looking at five different prints propped against a bunch of stacked prints and paintings against the wall. I edge around crates filled with straw and ceramic statues or glass sculptures. Those are for later showings from other artists.

"What's wrong?" I ask, setting his lunch down on his cluttered desk.

Tom uncrosses his arms and then crosses them again. "I can't decide which one will be the first one they see when they enter. Do I ease them into it, or hit them hard? Shock them?"

I look at the five options and I see what he means. Four of the prints are of sensual closeups that tease without showing much.

They're images of us, but broken into couples. The last is all four of us captured together in the act, my back arching from my perch on top of Tom, his raised knee covering the point of penetration as he takes me in the ass. Marcus is between my thighs, his cock seated deep in my pussy but with him blocking the view. Sam stands behind me, his large hand splayed over my throat as he drags my head back to take him too. Only my breasts and thighs are actually showing, but there's no doubt about what act is being filmed.

I hook my arm around Tom in a sideways hug and lean my head against his chest. "Hang this one."

He hesitates, and that's how I know this is the one he really wants to put up as the front-and-center piece. If he preferred one of the others, he'd be arguing right now. "Are you sure? I don't have to display it if it's too much." He pulls me against him in a hug, his arms coming around my middle to band me against his chest—as if there's anywhere I'd rather be.

It's sweet of him to worry. But I'm not ashamed of being an omega anymore. That voice in the back of my head that sounds like my mother gets fainter every day. I'm not embarrassed that I found my pack and that I love all three of my mates. "I'm sure."

Tom drops a kiss into my hair. "This one, Alicia."

"I'll tag it and have them hang it tonight. Now, I have a million things to do before tomorrow. If you don't need me anymore?" She waits for Tom's dismissal, then walks to the front, her heels clicking on the concrete floor until they fade.

"You brought me lunch?" he asks, his voice dropping low. His hand skims over my belly, then curves down my thighs. He drags the hem of my tight skirt up to mid-thigh and strokes the bare skin there. "That's so sweet, luv. But what if I'm hungry for something else?"

I smile and rub my ass against his front, spreading my thighs to give him better access. "What do you mean?" I ask, playing coy.

"Hmm." He rubs the sheer black thigh-highs I'm wearing, groaning when he inches the skirt higher and realizes they're not pantyhose. He traces the lace-topped edge of them, his thumb brushing against my wet slit. "Luv, you're not wearing any panties."

"I'm not?" I hold back my giggle and bite my lip as he slips a finger through my folds and finds out exactly how wet I am. "I must have forgotten to put them on."

He's hard, his cock poking into my ass while he strokes my clit. I sigh, tilting my pelvis for him. He tuts. "You've gotten so forgetful."

"It's not my fault I've been a little—*mmm*—distracted lately."

His finger dips inside, sinking in past the second knuckle. It makes a wet sucking sound when he pulls it free and pumps it in again. "What's causing it? Is it this?" He glides over my clit again, rubbing it in circles.

"Mmhmm. That's definitely it." I grind against him, my pussy squeezing nothing as he brings me halfway to orgasm, then shoves two fingers into me in a blunt intrusion that makes me gasp.

It takes seconds for him to undo his fly and bend me over the desk, my palms slapping on its surface as he pulls my tight skirt up and bares me for him. "Will this correct it?" he asks as his cock nudges at my entrance. He sinks inside me to the hilt, and I sigh once I'm filled.

"That will definitely—hnng—definitely…" I lose the thread, speech devolving into moans as he fucks me over the desk. I'm not sure who loves doing it in semi-public spaces more, Sam or Tom. The threat of being walked in on, of being watched as he ruts me over his desk, pushes me over that edge quicker than I'd like.

I come, my walls clamping down on him as he fucks me through my release and aftershocks with zero mercy. The desk rattles and shakes as he takes his pleasure, using me until he grunts through his own orgasm. He floods me with cum and leaves me dripping as he pulls out and spreads my cheeks apart so he can watch me work his semen from my body with squeezes.

"That should help you be more forgetful in the future," he says as he tucks himself away and zips his pants.

I turn around and perch on the edge of his desk and pluck his handkerchief from his pocket, using it to clean up. "Don't you mean less forgetful?" I fold it so the messy parts are covered, then fold it up neatly, stand, and tug my skirt down.

Tom arches a brow. "I definitely don't." He grins.

I kiss him, running my hands through his long hair, then nip his bottom lip and dance away from his groping hands before he can talk me into round two. I have plans. "Eat." I point at the food I left on his desk.

"Get up on the desk and I will." His grin is wolfish.

I back away from him, and his head swings as he keeps his eyes trained on me like a predator stalking prey. I keep my steps slow and measured because running only makes him want to chase. "Eat." I arch a brow. "Do I have to call Alicia later to check?"

He chuckles and smoothes the wrinkles from his dress shirt. "No, ma'am."

I give him a sunny smile and turn around, pushing through the heavy black curtain. The receptionist looks over from her computer, her cheeks pink, then ducks her head back down to her work. We weren't all that quiet, I guess.

Lindsay gives me a loaded look when I find her studying the portraits of Tom and Marcus. "All done back there?" She's fighting the urge not to smile, her mouth twitching.

I shove the handkerchief into the purse under my arm. "I got what I came for. Ready to go? I'm headed back uptown, and I can drop you off. They're leaving tickets at the counter for you for tomorrow."

The driver takes us back over the Brooklyn bridge and heads north, and I drop Lindsay off along the way, and then he heads to Marcus's investment firm. My heels click on the tile floor and I tap my foot while I wait for the elevator.

His secretary, a middle-aged woman named Georgene, who runs the office with the efficiency of a drill sergeant, looks up from her computer when I enter. "Mrs. Orello. Mr. Orello is in a meeting. Do you need me to get him?"

"No, thank you. I'll wait in his office for him to finish."

She nods, and I show myself in. They're used to me popping by every once in a while. Marcus's office is imposing, his large desk facing away from the gorgeous view out the wall-to-wall windows behind him. This high up, the people on the sidewalk look like ants. His desk is made from thick, dark wood with curved legs and chunky carvings. It's imposing. Regal and masculine.

I sit in his chair and spin around in slow circles while I wait for his meeting to finish. The door opens, and I stop, my head still spinning a bit as he walks in and sees me there. He pauses, then turns and says something to someone in the hallway and shuts the door.

"Emily. Is everything okay?"

I hop out of the seat and cross the room, smoothing my hands over his big, broad chest. How does he pack all those glorious alpha muscles into such fitted clothes? I tuck the stolen, soiled handkerchief into his pocket, shoving his carefully folded silk one down. His nostrils flare as he catches the first whiff of it.

"Everything's fine. I just had to ask you something."

His dark brow lowers over his eyes. "What is it?"

"For dinner, do you want enchiladas or steak?"

"That's it?" His eyes narrow as he catches onto my game. "You could have called or texted."

I shrug and give him an innocent smile. "I was already out. It wasn't any trouble to stop by and visit you. But I need an answer, because I need to know which meat to thaw."

"Steak," he says, his voice low and rumbly. The sound of it makes my stomach flutter every time, no matter how often I hear it. It'll never get old.

"Great!" I lean up and kiss him, then hike my purse up higher on my shoulder and flounce to the door. I nod at the suited man hovering in the hallway, then wave goodbye to Georgene and take the elevator down. The drive home is quick, the traffic a little thinner at this hour. I thank the driver and tell him I'm done for the day.

"Hello, Bobbie. How are you today?"

Bobbie holds the door open for me. "Great, Mrs. Orello. You have a nice day."

"I already am."

Sam isn't home when I get there, but I find a note on the counter.

Working on the bike :)

I smile and pull the steak out of the freezer, then fill a big bowl with cool water for it to thaw. It's barely two, so there's plenty of time to work on the side dishes later.

It's time to go find my other mate.

Chapter Twenty-Nine

EMILY

I GRAB MY GLASSES FROM THE TABLE BY THE DOOR AND HEAD down into the basement, the elevator not so scary now that I'm used to its creaks and groans. Sam's stripped down to his jeans and white T-shirt, his plaid button-up tied around his waist. I stand there and appreciate the view for a moment while he pulls some rusted part out of the bike and turns it over in his greasy hands.

"Excuse me, sir? I think I'm lost. My car has a flat." I press a hand to my chest and lean into the little fantasy I'm creating. Sam stands from his crouch and wipes his hands clean on the rag that was stuffed in his back pocket. "I'm so glad I saw the sign for your repair shop from the road. There's not much else out here. I had to walk half a mile in the dirt in these heels."

He looks me up and down, taking in the tight black pencil skirt, my white button-up tucked into it. The black thigh highs, their lace topped edges hidden under the hem of my skirt. My heels are high black pumps, and my hair's up in a quick and easy updo that looks more complicated than it is. I adjust the pair of fake glasses on my face, sliding them up my nose from where they've ridden down.

"What's a girl like you doing all the way out here?" he asks, laying a hand on his bike's handlebars.

"I'm headed home. Do you think you can fix my car now? I'd be so grateful."

"Depends," he says, stuffing his rag into his back pocket. "Can you pay?"

I reach for my purse and realize I left it upstairs. "I must have left it in the car. But if you can give me a tow, I can pay. I have my credit card, I promise."

He crosses his arms over his chest. "Card machine's broken. Cash only."

"Oh." I fidget and nibble on my lower lip. "I don't have any cash. Is there… is there any other way I can pay you?"

He runs his tongue over his teeth and pretends to think about it. "Maybe. Suppose you could work for it." Sam reaches for his belt, flicking it open. The metal jingles together as he undoes it, then pops the button on his jeans and drags his zipper down. "I take payment upfront."

I bite my lip harder and glance at the elevator behind me as if I'm thinking about it. As if slick's not creeping down my inner thigh at the thought of sinking down on my knees and swallowing him down. The camera nestled against the ceiling blinks its red dot.

"If that's what it takes," I say, my voice breathy.

I close the distance between us, my heels tapping against the rough concrete, and then I sink down onto my knees. The floor is hard and cold underneath me as I grab the edges of his jeans and tug them apart.

He's hard, his cock straining against the fabric, and I'm not the only one not wearing underwear. I pull him free and work his pants down lower under the curve of his ass, then bring him to my mouth and lick. The bead of pre-cum on his tip bursts with salty musk and the faint taste of oranges and cream on my tongue.

Opening wider, I suck him deeper, my cheeks hollowing until he hits the back of my throat. I fight past the urge to gag and open, swallowing him down. I've been trained well, and I love how much it pleases them.

"That's good," Sam hisses once his cock's buried to the root in my mouth. He tangles his fingers in my hair and holds me there, my nose pressed against his groin. "The minute I saw them, I knew those red lips would look so pretty wrapped around my cock."

He pulls out, letting me breathe, then presses back in, giving me almost no time to recover. "You're good at sucking cock. You city girls always are."

When he draws back, I press a hand to his thighs, so he knows I need a moment. "Do… do you do this sort of thing a lot?"

Sam fists his cock and taps his head against my mouth, smirking when I lick his sensitive underside. I find that familiar vein and trace it with my tongue.

"Only shop around for miles and miles. But if you can talk, then you're not working hard enough." He forces his cock back into my mouth, and I suck him, dropping my hands back to my thighs. He tugs my head down onto his length and my throat bulges with him.

"Goddamn it, that's good. Are you as good of a fuck as you are a dirty cocksucker?" He pulls out of my mouth and palms his cock, jerking it. "Get up. Bend over that bike and lift up your skirt."

I stand, my stockings catching on the rough ground and ripping as I get up and grab fistfuls of my skirt, hiking it up until he can see me. His eyes go right to the juncture of my legs, to my dark thatch of hair and my wet, pink lips peeking out.

"Look at you, you dirty girl. No panties? You knew what you were gonna get when you walked into my shop. Bend over. Ass up, baby. Get ready to pay with that pretty pussy."

I bend over the bike, my palms gripping its leather seat, and wait. He slaps my ass once, then grabs it and pulls the cheek aside so he can see me better as he rubs a finger between my labia and pries them apart.

"So wet. You like this, don't you? You like having my rough, dirty hands all over your pretty, smooth skin?" He sticks a finger in me and pumps it in and out, then adds another. The room fills with wet sounds and the smell of my arousal, and I whine when he pulls his fingers free.

Sam nudges his cock at my opening and slides in. He pumps into me and groans, his hands grabbing onto my hips like they're handles as he tugs me back against his thrusts and adjusts to get a deeper angle. "You're so fucking hot." He grabs me all over like he doesn't know what to touch first. He squeezes my breast through my shirt, then rubs up and down the lace edge of my thigh-highs before slipping his fingers through my folds and fondling my clit.

"Oh, fuck." I moan and slap back against him, taking all of him until we're rocking in rhythm as he circles my clit. He rubs me faster. Harder. Ruts me deeper. "That's so good. Don't stop."

"Yeah? You gonna come on my cock?"

Everything pulls taut as I pant, and the world falls away. It's just us. This moment. We're all that exists. All that matters. I balance on the edge of it and let my head drop forward, the fake glasses sliding down my nose and my hair slipping out of its updo. The ends of it brush against the bike's leather as he bounces me on his cock and rubs my clit 'til I'm panting. "I... I'm gonna come."

"Fucking do it, baby," he says, his hand never stopping even though his cock's slowed its pumping. He fucks me slow and deep and rubs me fast and hard.

I shatter, crying out with my release as my walls clamp down on him. My knees are shaking from the effort of staying upright on these heels as he slides in and out of my wet folds, fucking me through my aftershocks. Breathing fast, I drag in a greedy gulp of air and rock back against him.

Sam puts both hands on my hips again and pumps, bending his knees and nudging me forward until he likes the angle. "You're such a dirty girl, baby, and you're about to get dirtier because I'm gonna fill this pussy with cum."

He grunts, pulling me back on his cock as he fucks me. He uses me, moving me and holding me and taking me, until he moans and his pace slows. Thrusting slowly, his cock pulses as he fills me up and the first lash of semen paints my walls.

"Fuck, baby. That's good. Have all of it. Let's load that pussy up."

When his cock stops twitching, he pulls out with a satisfied groan and spreads my lips wide so he can see how much cream he's filled my hole with. I flex, pushing it out so it drips onto the concrete floor. When I'm done, he drops his dirty rag down to soak it up and steps away. We both right our clothing, and then he tugs me in for a tender kiss.

"Hmm. That was fun."

"It was. Dinner's at seven," I tell him.

Sam presses his forehead against mine and chuckles. "I'll set an alarm so I'm not late."

I smile and slant one last kiss over his mouth, then step out of the circle of his arms and tug my hair out of its holder. "Wash up first too. Tonight's special."

"Okay, baby." He zips his jeans and buttons them, then fixes his belt.

I leave him to finish working on his bike and head back

upstairs, checking on the thawing steak. And then I soak in the bath and shave again before touching up my makeup and dressing in my new outfit. I keep my hair down because that's how they all like it. Marcus and Sam because they think it's pretty and like to stroke it, and Tom because he says it's easier to grab and make a fist.

Once everything's in the oven and cooking, I open the wine and let it breathe while I set the table with our nice china.

The front door slams. "I'm home!" Tom calls.

"In the kitchen!"

Tom sets his things down and wanders in, his jacket off and his sleeves rolled up to his elbows. He looks me up and down, his gaze stuck on my pink knee-length dress and the sheer white silk apron edged in lace ruffles tied over the top of it. He tugs his tie looser and grins.

"Do you like it?" I smooth the apron over my full skirt. It's sheer and absolutely useless for cooking, but that's not the point of it.

"It's almost perfect. Be right back."

What's missing? I check my earlobes to make sure I put the pearl studs in.

Tom comes back holding my pink and white collar in one hand and my rose gold heart-shaped clamps in the other. *Oh, he wants to play.* I lift my hair for him so he can secure the collar around my throat.

"Spread your legs."

I move my legs apart, and he flips my flouncy skirt up, his probing finger finding my clit with expert precision as he tugs the hood back and fits the clamp there. I moan and fidget from the agony and pleasure of it as it pinches, my pulse throbbing between my legs. In a few minutes, it'll go numb. Until they take it off me.

He reaches around me and shoves a hand into the top of my

dress and bra, rubbing my nipples into aching points. One after the other, he fits the clamps there too until all three points are tight and I'm wet again. Everything slips and slides, the clit clamp awkward between my legs as I fidget.

"Satisfied?" I ask him.

Tom threads his fingers into my hair and pulls my head to the side, pressing a kiss to the scars on my throat. "Very."

The front door slams again. "I'm home! Let me just hop in the shower." Sam runs upstairs.

"That's a lot of food," Tom says, gesturing to the spread of pots and pans on the stove. He's still playing with my nipple, his hand moving against the constraints of my bra. "You've been busy."

"Tonight's special."

He stops teasing me and drags his hand up my chest, leaving it there at the base of my throat. "Is all this for my opening tomorrow? You didn't have to."

"Yes, but I also have a surprise."

"A surprise?" He hooks a finger through the ring of my collar and tilts my head to the side. "Do tell."

I smile and shake my head as much as I can with him holding onto me. "That would spoil it."

He grins, and it's a wicked smile that makes my breath hitch. Tom lets his grip on my collar go and flicks my nipple with one long, thin finger. The pain sends a pulse all the way down to my pinched clit, and I'm aching all over.

I grunt and clamp my teeth together until the throbbing fades. "No. You can wait for everyone else."

His eyes narrow, like I've laid down a gauntlet he's all too eager to pick up. Nothing good comes from that look.

The front door slams a third time. "I'm home!" Marcus calls out. He drops his bag at the front, and his keys clink as he puts them in their bowl.

"In the kitchen!" Tom's smile brightens. "And Emily's being a *very* naughty girl. She should be punished. Hard."

My eyes widen, and my mouth drops open in surprise. "Traitor," I hiss at him under my breath, my gaze darting to the kitchen's doorway. Marcus's steps are heavy on the floor, the wooden boards creaking.

"What's that, luv? Didn't hear you." Tom steps away from me and leans against the fridge, his arms folded across his chest. I glare at him.

"Oh, believe me, I know exactly how naughty she's been today," Marcus says. He stands there in the doorway and slips his jacket off, then folds it neatly. "She's been a very bad girl." He takes his tie off next, folding it too and undoing the top button of his shirt. "So bad that she's earned a spanking." He sets them down on a counter and undoes his cufflinks, adding them to the growing pile so he can roll up his sleeves. His veins are already jutting out along his corded forearms.

I back away and bump against the kitchen island, looking between Tom and Marcus and weighing my options. "Tonight is very special. Do you want to ruin dinner?" I wave a hand to the stove so he can see that it's not bullshit. Every single burner on our double oven is simmering.

Marcus stalks to the stove and turns the knobs off one by one, and I swallow, my hands gripping the cold marble counter.

I shouldn't have teased him at work.

The reality of my mistake is settling in. "I'm serious, Marcus."

Marcus stalks around the island, and I try to dart out of reach but Tom corrals me, taking the opportunity to grab a handful of ass while he does so. He lifts me until my feet leave the ground and ignores my squeak of protest.

"So am I."

Marcus pulls out the chair that sits under the small secretary cubby in our kitchen. He sits, and Tom hands me over to our alpha for punishment. The room spins as I'm tossed over Marcus's lap, my skirt flipped up my back. A strong arm bands across my shoulders, keeping me there.

"I take your well being very seriously, now take your spanking like the good girl I know you are or you'll earn double the strokes, later."

Fuck. I don't want doubles. Maybe it's best to get this over with quickly.

Marcus settles a large hand on my bare bottom, rubbing warmth into it, and then he pulls it away and I tense, even though I know it's better not to. I can't help it. It comes back down, slapping me hard with a *crack*.

"Oww!" *God, he hits so much harder than Sam.*

He lifts his hand and ignores my whimper, bringing that palm down again in the exact same spot. The pain doubles as he spanks the sting back into me, his hand heavy.

Crack, crack, crack!

He hits the same spot over and over again until I'm fidgeting on his lap, trying to get free, even though I know it's pointless. I'm trapped.

"Oh, this is so much more fun when you're not the one on the receiving end," Tom says.

I glare up at Tom, my eyes wet from the stinging pain in my rear. Marcus shifts to the other cheek, delivering five hard blows so they match.

"Hmm." Tom tilts his head. "She's still mutinous. Hit her pussy."

"No!" My eyes go wide as the hand pulls back. It comes down on my center, catching both cheeks and the cleft between them. The clamp on my clit bounces, tugging on me, and white hot pain lances deep inside me, mellowing into a warm glow as my pussy spasms and slick makes me wet. "Fuck!" This is way more than the normal twenty swats I earn when I'm naughty. Dinner's gonna be wrecked if they turn this into a long play session.

I wiggle and buck, growling as I hook my fingers into claws and scratch uselessly at Marcus's legs. "Marcus! I'm fucking serious, damnit."

"Beta," Marcus says, ignoring my protests. Tom snaps upright at the dark, thunderous tone. "Plug your omega's filthy mouth."

"With pleasure." Tom unzips and shoves his pants down, stroking his cock to full hardness. He grabs me by the ring on my collar and drags me upright across Marcus's lap, his cock pressing against my lips and surging in to trap my tongue against the floor of my mouth.

"Do you know why you're being punished?" Marcus asks, teasing the seam of my sex until my hips buck. He pulls his hand back and spanks me again, repeating it all over again until my cunt's weeping and my ass is on fire. His pants are going to end up soaked with slick. They're wool. The dry cleaner's gonna kill us.

"You're being punished because I had to sit through three more meetings today with a raging hard on. The only thing saving you from a striping is the fact that they were phone calls with overseas clients."

I mean… he could have just rubbed one out and gotten rid of the handkerchief. It's partially his fault if you think about it. But I can't say anything because Tom's fucking my face, his hands holding my jaw as he moves my head up and down his cock.

"I left work with this hard on. I got into a Town Car with it. Poor Bobbie had to open the door for me. And then do you know what happened? Security stopped me before I got on the elevator. They wanted to ask me if I'd like them to erase your basement footage. *Again*. And I had to stand there and thank them for their courtesy with my rock hard cock shoved down one pants leg and pretend everything was normal and fine."

Oh, shit. I didn't think the security guards would flag him down and mention our little basement show.

Marcus stops rubbing me, and I tense, and then all I know is pain. He spanks me, moving from one cheek to the other, catching my thighs and pussy and the sweet spot between ass and leg that makes my eyes water. It hurts so good. My body is one fire and I'll combust if I don't come, and all thoughts about announcements and openings and dinners fade like mist.

Crack, crack, crack!

They both ignore my whimpering as Tom pulls back so I can suck on his head while Marcus jams a second finger into my pussy and pumps. Each rough thrust pulls at the clamp on my clit and I realize that I'm going to come like this. Draped over his knee, my ass bared and reddened, with Tom fucking my face. Everything pulls taut, and I moan around my mouthful of cock. Marcus pulls his fingers out and brings them down on my pussy.

"And do you know what your punishment is going to be?" he asks.

Tom fucks my mouth while Marcus shoves three fingers into my sloppy wet pussy and pumps. And I'm so close. So fucking close as my clit throbs against that clamp and his fingers cram me full. I need to come. Need it more than fucking air.

"For every hour that you tortured me today," Marcus growls, "that's how many times I'm going to edge you."

I sob around the cock wedged in my mouth. So close. Almost there.

He pulls his hand free and brings it down hard on my pussy, and my world explodes. My walls pulse with my release, the fluttering pulling at the clamp on my clit where it's sandwiched between my slippery thighs. Tom pulls out of my mouth, and I gasp in a breath. He drags my head up higher so I'm straining, my back arched, held up only by the both of them. If they weren't holding me so tightly, I'd be a puddle of limp pleasure on the floor.

"Did you just come without permission? From a spanking?" Tom asks, his tone incredulous and a little awed.

"Is something burning?" Marcus asks, sniffing the air.

"The… the sweet potatoes," I say, panting as I try to catch my breath while my pussy clenches, empty and aching, and my clit throbs. "They're in the oven."

"Oh, oops." Tom holds his pants up as he walks to the stove and shuts the oven off.

I go limp and groan. This dinner was supposed to be special. All that careful timing of the side dishes. Ruined. Everything's going to be cold or burnt and either too hard or too mushy.

"I feel like I missed something," Sam says from the doorway.

"You." Marcus lays his hand on my glowing, red hot ass and rubs until I groan. "You're next."

"Me?" Sam sputters. "What did I do?"

Metal clanks as Tom lifts a pot lid and puts it back down. "We may be ordering takeout tonight."

That cuts through my post-orgasmic bliss like a hot knife through butter. I've been working for hours for this dinner. The after dinner mindblowing sex was supposed to come *after*. I make an unhappy noise in the back of my throat and struggle to get up, and this time Marcus lets me.

"Tonight was supposed to be perfect, and you've ruined it." All the emotions and endorphins brought up by the spanking overwhelm me. My eyes grow hot and tight as tears well and I sniff them back to keep them from falling. The last thing I want to do is cry right now.

These mood swings are ridiculous and getting old fast. I enjoy teasing them and getting spanked, but sometimes I can't help the drop I get after. It's just the release of emotions you get after a good, hard spanking. Rationally, I know all it means is that I need more cuddles, but in the moment, it feels like the world is ending.

"Never mind. It looks fine," Tom says, his eyes wide as he drops another lid onto its pot. "Can't wait to eat it. It smells great."

He's lying. It smells burnt and dry and mushy all at the same time.

Marcus then tugs me onto his lap. I hiss at the contact with my sensitive behind. "Sweetheart, what's wrong? Tom says it's fine. We'll eat it, won't we?"

They murmur unenthusiastic yesses they don't mean. But each one of them would choke it all down and smile and say thank you, regardless of how disgusting it is.

"It's not the food, it's…" I let out a huff and press the heels of my palms into my eyes, willing the tears to go away. When that doesn't work, I try to sniff them back again. My face is thick and congested with them.

"Ah. Got it," Sam says. He pulls the oven door open, and smoke fills the room. He shuts it. "She's fine. Her hormones are just a lot right now while she's adjusting. It's a lot of years to undo."

"Adjusting?" Marcus asks, rubbing my back.

"You gonna tell them, baby? Or do you want me to?" Sam asks.

No, I can do this. It doesn't matter that all of my plans went off the rails because I got horny and stupid. I did this to myself. What we eat doesn't really matter in the grand scheme of things. I sniff and wipe the tears from the corners of my eyes.

"I threw out my birth control."

Marcus goes completely still, his hand stopping mid stroke. "You…"

"I stopped taking it two weeks ago. My heat's due in…" I hesitate and try to count backward.

"Two weeks and three days, give or take," Sam supplies.

Marcus's chest explodes in a purr as he hauls me against his chest and hugs me tight. "Oh, sweetheart. You should have told me. I wouldn't have been so rough."

I don't like to use my safe word unless it's something I really don't enjoy. Yes, I'm mad that dinner's ruined, but he wasn't hurting me in a way I didn't like.

"She liked it, if you couldn't tell," Tom says, leaning on the kitchen island. "I, on the other hand, am still painfully hard and have not yet come."

"Let's fix that," Marcus says, standing and bringing me with him. I throw my arm around his neck and hold on. He carries me toward the stairs and the others follow.

"What about dinner?" I ask, giving the kitchen one last forlorn look.

"Dinner can wait."

"I'm mad at you," I tell Marcus. Sam and I have been working on me expressing myself more. It's scary, but necessary. My confidence grows with each fight that doesn't end with them leaving me. It's hard to let old fears die, even with the mating bites that are as good as a beta marriage. Yeah, dissolved claiming bites can be bitten over, and marriages can end in divorce. Do I think they'll leave me because the sweet potatoes got burnt? No. Fear isn't always rational, but I refuse to let it control my life any longer. I just have to trust them. And I do.

"I know. I'm sorry, sweetheart. I wasn't listening." He nuzzles against my face, then lays me down in the center of our nest and climbs on top of me. Tom and Sam get undressed and climb into the nest, touching one another as they find a spot to settle in.

"No you weren't," I say.

Despite my irritation, his purr rumbles through our points of contact and soothes at something deep inside of me. His scent's no longer spicy like it gets when he's agitated. Now it's all creamy, sweet, and smooth. Each gulp of his pheromones and knocking of his purr loosens my tension and assuages my irritation until I'm mellow. It's impossible to stay mad at him when he's pouring contrition and comfort through our bond.

If this were anyone but Marcus, I'd be scared of how much control his pheromones and our bond has over me and my feelings. Abusive alphas can put an omega through hell, and they'll still want to crawl back to their alpha until they hit the point of breaking. But this is Marcus. He'd never hurt me on purpose.

Now his big body blocks out the string lights hung up above us. "You were wearing your collar. I thought we were playing. I wasn't paying attention to the bond like I should have been. I'm sorry, sweetheart."

He strips down, and then he strips me too, pressing a gentle kiss to every body part he exposes. Marcus unzips the dress and helps me wiggle out of it. He pauses to admire the see-through white bra before unhooking and slipping it off me. My breasts spill out, the clamps tugging at my hard nipples. My heels clatter as he drops them to the floor with a carelessness that's out of character. His eyes eat me up with hungry glances.

"You're so gorgeous, sweetheart. Did you get all dressed up just for us?" he asks.

"Yes. I wanted tonight to be extra special." I wanted to wind them all up so we'd spend the whole night in the nest. To distract Tom from worrying himself sick about his opening.

"Every night with you is extra special."

I roll my eyes, but his corny statement still makes me smile because I know how earnestly he means it. Marcus settles between my legs and his cock slides along the seam of my sex.

"You know I can't get pregnant until my next heat, right?"

"Never hurts to practice." Marcus notches his head to my entrance and pushes inside, seating himself to the root. He covers me, his weight heavy in a way that's comforting. It feels like safety. Protection. Here, in the safety of my nest with my pack and my alpha, I'm untouchable. Marcus grabs my legs and shifts them higher, fucking deeper as he fills me up. My clamps rub against him, and I don't need to reach down between us as he moves, his hips rolling as he fucks me sweet and slow, because the metal tugs at me until I'm panting.

Tom lies beside us, one hand petting me and the other tangled in Sam's unruly hair as it bobs over his length. He toys with my breast, palming its weight, then flicks my nipple. Teasing is his way of saying he cares.

Arching, I come, my walls fluttering on my alpha's cock and then his knot as he plugs me tight and floods me with seed. Practicing. My belly bulges with him and his fountain of cum as he stoppers me full until I'm aching and satisfied, my thoughts no longer worried with things like dinner.

What's one fancy dinner in the wake of a lifetime of these moments?

We're going to make a baby soon.

Me and my pack.

All of us together.

Chapter Thirty

MARCUS

I SNAP THE PAPER TAUT AND SCOUR THE ARTICLES FOR THE ONE I want. After a moment of searching, I find it. It's been three days since Tom's grand opening. "Here it is."

"What's it say?" Tom asks, looking up from his untouched breakfast. "Never mind." He scowls down into his eggs. "I don't want to know. It doesn't matter."

"Are you sure?" I ask, already knowing the answer. "It's good. They loved it."

"Really? Let me see that." Tom snatches the paper from me and reads it for himself.

Sam watches the whole thing with an amused grin when he's not shoveling eggs and bacon and toast into his mouth.

"Slow down," Emily says. "You're gonna choke." She sips her orange juice and nibbles on her slice of buttered toast and watches Tom read. "What's it say?"

Tom clears his throat. "Mr. Orello's collection of portraits and self portraits is a viscerally shocking experience that both tantalizes and amazes. Viewers enter the gallery as if they enter the nest with the lovers in this most intimate of displays. Thirty-four prints display both the harsh and sensual realities of bonding.

Hands grasp and teeth rend, and there is no shying away from the hard, animalistic truth of the moment as blood and other fluids spill."

"Oh, that's good," she says, eating the last of her toast. "Sounds like they really liked it."

I nudge her untouched bowl of fruit closer and smile when she takes a grape and pops it into her mouth, chewing it.

"I can feed myself, you know." She takes another despite her halfhearted protest.

"It's better to get all the vitamins you need from food sources rather than pills. The doctor says they absorb more easily that way."

She rolls her eyes, but takes a strawberry. "I'm not even pregnant yet."

Not yet, but soon. I stroke her hair while she eats and Tom reads the article again, parsing through the words as if he's looking to make sure it's not a trick. Sam clears his plate, then grabs more bacon from the platter.

"How many have you sold?" I ask Tom.

"Four, and another is pending. Is it kind of weird that prints of our naked bodies are going to be hanging up in strangers' houses for them to ogle?"

I laugh. "A little late to worry, don't you think? And no, I don't find it weird." I think my entire pack rather likes the idea. Turns out we're all unapologetic deviants and exhibitionists.

Emily's phone makes a *cha-ching* sound and we all watch her check it, her lips curling in a smile that makes her radiant even with her sleep-rumpled hair. Especially with her mussed hair since it was us that messed it up.

"Another sale? Your online shop is getting busy," Tom says.

She taps on her phone. "Yeah, they really like the Prince of Orange cuttings. I can't keep them stocked. As soon as I get one mature enough to ship it's gone." They share a lingering, sly look.

Sam stops eating long enough to join in, "I saw some pictures of a sweet set up someone has. It's a wooden wall rack that holds a bunch of glass tubes and shit for your plant babies to grow. I was thinking it wouldn't be too hard to make. It would help get the pots and glasses off the dining table. We could hang it on the wall and put up lights or whatever."

One by one they all turn to look at me. I hide my smile behind the rim of my mug. "Sounds like you've got it all figured out.

And it's time to go to work. I smooth my tie and drain my coffee, then kiss them all goodbye and climb into the car. The day passes in a blur of routine. The next one too. For the millionth time, I glance at my calendar and count. A week. Three days. Tomorrow. She's late.

Don't stress. It's not unusual. She says this is normal for her.

Three more days pass. The sun shines through the gauzy curtains in our bedroom, waking me. I kiss Tom on the cheek and he mumbles something like "ten more minutes," so I slide out of the bed, heading upstairs. Emily is curled up in her nest, covered in a mound of blankets, with only her nose visible. I grab the thermometer from the nightstand and sit, smoothing a hand over her bundled form until I find her underneath all those blankets.

She moans and stretches in her sleep, her nostrils flaring as she scents me. Her mouth drops open, and I slide the thermometer in and then we wait. It's funny how quickly new things become routine. After it beeps, I take it out and read the display. Ninety-nine point four. Does that count as a fever? Is it starting? I leave her, and she burrows deeper into her blankets. Outside of Sam's door, I knock and find him already dressing for the day.

"Hey," he says. "I have to go downtown and pick up a part. It came in last night."

I show him the thermometer. "Is this high enough to count?"

He takes it from me and reads the screen, his brow creasing. "Maybe. It could be the start of it. But pre-heat can still take a while. Her cycle's probably going to be less normal even for her. She's coming off birth control after being on it for years."

Despite his casual warning to not get my hopes up yet, that's all I need to hear. I take the thermometer back from him and put a hand on his shoulder. "Call the shop and ask them to deliver the part or hire a courier. From now on until the heat is over, you do not leave her side. Understood?"

Sam nods. "Yes, alpha."

I kiss him on the forehead and leave him to get undressed again, a little envious when he slides back into the nest with her. But work won't wait, and it looks like I have meetings to reschedule.

Georgene's thin lips flatten when I tell her to move all my clients for tomorrow and onward into next week. But she doesn't argue. She may not be the friendliest woman, but she's damn good at her job and she's run this office efficiently since well before I made partner.

Discomfort stabs me through Emily's side of bond, but Sam and Tom's side are both quiet and it keeps me from panicking. *This is normal*, I tell myself. When I head home, I find everyone cuddled on the couch watching a movie. They're sandwiched together, all of them covered with a fuzzy blanket from her nest.

She sees me first and smiles, then winces and lets out a little moan. Tom runs his fingers through her hair.

"Is it time?" I ask.

"Ninety-nine point nine," Sam says. "It might start in the night, or maybe tomorrow."

Tonight. Tomorrow. Soon.

I unbutton my jacket and sit on the couch, joining them. I take her small feet in my hands and rub them until her whimpering stops. There's nothing I can do to ease her symptoms in these early hours. Nothing except to be here and touch her. She relaxes as I slide my hand under the fuzzy blanket and touch the bit of leg that's reachable from where Sam lies on her.

"Do you want me to move?" Sam asks.

"No. Watch your movie. We're going to bed after. We'll eat and sleep in turns from now on." My stomach rumbles, but I ignore it. When the credits roll, they all disentangle from the sofa, and I scoop her into my arms and carry her up to the nest. She's nude already, her skin too sensitive for clothes.

"Alpha," she sighs, wrapping her arms around my neck as if she doesn't want to let go. I hover over her, careful to keep my weight from crushing her as I purr for her until she goes limp. We wrap her in blankets, and Sam volunteers to stay with her while Tom and I go downstairs to eat.

Tom cracks the lid off a bottle of water and downs it until the thin plastic crinkles. He pulls the water bottle from his lips with an exhale. "Gotta stay hydrated. Those weird pills Sam's got me taking to shoot bigger loads make me so bloody thirsty."

I throw leftovers in the microwave and heat them up and grin. "Let's hope they work."

He hums, and when our food's done, we eat. I undress in our bedroom and hang up my dirty suit. There will be a mountain of laundry to take care of when this is all over, but I don't mind. Once Tom is bare, I pull him into a hug and smooth my hands over his back.

"I can't believe we're finally going to do it," he says.

I cup his face in my hands and search his beautiful green eyes. "I love you. Let's go make a baby."

"I love you too." He nods. "Let's go knock her up."

We go upstairs and creep into the nest. Sam slips out to eat and take care of himself while Tom and I get comfortable. Emily's asleep, but she stirs long enough to seek us out as she tries to get cozy again. Another cramp hits her, her bond pulsing with discomfort, but it goes away when I purr and she settles once more.

After Sam joins us, we lie there and sleep until she whimpers and thrashes and the smell of sugary lemon floods my nose. I creep a hand between her thighs and find her soaked. Her side of the bond feels as sharp as splintered glass.

It's time. I exhale, breathing out all the tension from this tiresome waiting.

"Omega."

Her eyelids flutter open, but her eyes don't fully focus. She turns to me in the nest, cuddling close, her nose going instinctively for our mating bond. Reaching down, I palm my cock and stroke. It doesn't take long to work it until it's hard. Fluid beads at my tip, and her nostrils flare, her small hand wandering over my chest. Searching. Seeking for what she knows is her relief.

I take her by the biceps and pull her on top of me, and she sits up on instinct, then rubs when she feels my cock so close to where she wants it. Where she needs it.

Sam and Tom wake and shift in the nest as I grab her by her hips and lift her, ignoring her whimpering, and line us up. She sinks down on me, her head dropping back with a sigh as she stretches and takes me.

I hit the end of her, her little belly pooching where my cockhead hits the entrance to her womb. The womb I'm going to fill with a baby.

Fuck.

Don't come.

Not yet.

She rolls her hips, riding me, and the shattered glass feeling of her side of the bond softens, turning mellow and sweet. "That's it, sweetheart. Take what you need."

I slip my thumb between her folds and stroke her nub, my finger dragging back and forth until her cunt clenches me. She spasms tight, slick dripping down my cock as I fuck her through her orgasm and keep going. I try to hold it back, to delay the inevitable because each edging builds a bigger load of cum in my balls, but her bouncing breasts and little moans and the way she grabs at my chest hair undoes me.

Surging up into her, I press deep and feel my cock pulse. My balls pull up tight and empty into her slick, sweet pussy one shot at a time, my knot swelling behind her pubic bone to tie us together. Knotted, my cock presses tight against her cervix, and I paint it with hot spurts of cum until her belly's so full of me it's bulging. She whimpers, twitching above me, as her labia pull taut around that bulbous plug.

"That's it, sweetheart. Good job. Can you handle a little more?"

Tom and Sam take their cues. They join us, their hands probing as one palms her breasts and plays with her budded nipples while the other rubs her clit. Tom catches my eye and teases over where I'm sunk deep inside her. My cock twitches, and she whimpers, her hips grinding down on my knot. Her writhing is pure ecstasy.

"Oh, fuck. That's good." I get why some alphas love when the omega thrashes. Why they savor working their omegas up to such a frenzy that they're fighting on the knot, tugging at that buried tie. Each twitch of her hips feels like she's sucking the cum right out of my balls.

Tom rubs my head through her belly again while Sam teases her clit and her whimpers turn to moans, and she writhes. Her walls squeeze down tight, fluttering on my knot, and I shoot one more rope of seed into the pool stoppered up tight by her womb.

Emily collapses on top of me, and I purr for her until she's limp and languid. She's snoring when my knot shrinks, and even then I don't move. I stay there under her until my cock softens too much to stay in. It slips out, and she runs with cum and slick. It soaks me, creeping between my thighs to wick into the nest.

Sam drags a blanket over us, and he and Tom settle against us, falling back asleep as we all try to rest.

It's the compulsion to rut that wakes me next. The hard, demanding urge to take. Claim. Breed. My nostrils flare as I drag in the scent of her. *Fertile omega. Mine. Ours.* Sam is licking her cunt while Tom fucks her mouth, and pride hits me, making my chest tight. What good betas they are, taking care of our omega while I rested and made more cum.

They glance up as I stir, Tom's eyes locking once more with mine as he pumps between her lips. He lingers there at the back, his grip on her hair tight as her cheeks pinken. I watch them while I get up on my knees and position myself behind her where she's kneeling over Sam's head.

I guide my cock to her slick-coated hole and press in, my sack hitting Sam's swiping tongue as I fuck into her. If he minds, he doesn't show it. He doesn't stop either. Tom lets her up for air, her cheeks hollowing as she sucks on his head while I thrust into her and rock her against them. I keep it steady, and we find our rhythm.

Tom comes, her throat working to swallow all his seed as he stares at me while he empties inside her mouth with a groan and a curse. He pulls free with a wet pop, collapsing into the nest and tapping out, and I grin at him. They can't keep up with me. Not with the rut coming over me, triggered by her delicious, fertile pheromones. And they don't need to. My sperm won't let them breed her anyway. It's too aggressive in its hunt for her egg. And I aim to fill her to bursting 'til she catches. If we don't get pregnant from this heat, it won't be for lack of trying.

Sam's tongue strokes my balls as I fuck our omega, stretching her cunt and forcing her to take all of me. This position is deeper, and her body strains to fit all of me, but there's no choice. Not for either of us. She's made for this as much as I am.

It starts in my base, that pulsatile feeling. I spread her cheeks wide, watching my cock jerk as I fill her. I shove in deep, lining up with her cervix, and knot her. Sam's lashing tongue swipes across my balls. It flicks at her cunt. It teases over our tie. And she comes as he licks where we're joined, her walls squeezing and milking and begging for more. So more is exactly what I give her, filling her with everything I've got. When I'm done pumping her full, I smooth my hands over her back and the flare of her hips. I purr.

"Omega, thank your beta."

And like the good girl she is, she leans down, sucks Sam's cock into her mouth, and swallows him. They lick one another, her lips wrapping around his tip as she sucks while he strokes our tie. Sam teases one last shot of semen from me, and then I'm spent. He comes, flooding her mouth, and she swallows his load too.

When our tie pops free, I pull off them and watch Sam clean her, his mouth latched to her pussy as he eats my cum from her hole until there's only clean, fresh slick left.

Good. Only the best sperm will make it, the strongest, fastest swimmers. I join Tom, cuddling him to my chest as Sam scoops her up out of the nest and carries her into the bathroom for her first cleaning.

"Is it everything you thought it would be?" Tom asks.

I thread his fingers with mine and squeeze. "It's even better."

We nap. We eat. Sam bullies Emily into drinking when she's more lucid and cooperative, and I shoot sweet, nutritive alpha cum down her throat when she isn't. We fuck.

Tom plucks the crystal-tipped plug from her ass, slicks his cock up in her cunt, then sinks home. She whimpers and thrashes, but he's holding her too tightly against his chest for her to escape him. When she realizes she's caught, she goes limp, letting him fuck her while Sam and I watch. I stroke my cock until I can't stand it anymore, and then I join them.

I climb between both their legs and pump, tapping my head against her hole to dislodge the bead of pre-cum from the tip against her clit. She bucks, Tom's cock sliding in and out of her tight little hole as she wiggles. But she's all smooth, fuzzy edges in the bond and when I notch my dick against her cunt, she goes still and I know it's all play. Tom holds still, buried deep, until we're both fully seated.

"Fuck, why is that always so good?" he asks, moaning.

I surge forward, ignoring her little gasps as her belly bulges with us. My cock slides against his, just a thin wall separating us. I can feel where his shaft meets his head. I slide over that flare of his corona from within her. "Because it feels like I'm fucking you too."

I glance over at Sam, who kneels there, stroking his cock with lazy movements. "Want to join us?" I ask.

"No. When you're done, I want to fuck her pussy while Tom's still in her ass."

Tom groans. "You expect me to last that long? She squeezes like a vice."

I chuckle, reaching down to roll her clit under my thumb as I pump faster. "Tom, you're not allowed to come."

Tom curses under his breath, his neck veins cording as he holds still in her ass while I fuck them both through her thin wall. But he obeys. He's a brat. My brat. But after all these years together, he knows when I'm being serious.

Chasing my pleasure, I come with a grunt and flood her womb, her poor little belly swelling as I fill her up and lock it there. Is she pregnant yet? I rub her clit until her thighs quake and her chest flushes pink. Her cunt flutters, milking me. It sucks the dregs of my semen from me, and she soaks it all up as she comes on my knot.

Tom shifts, his cock jerking in her ass. The pressure of how full she is pushes him out, and he strains to stay there, to bury his cock deep in her guts while my knot keeps all that good alpha cum snug up against her womb where it belongs.

My knot shrinks, and I pull out of her, our fluids dripping all over Tom. He curses again, his hips twitching as he thrusts up into her, his arms banded tight under her breasts.

Sam gets into place, pushing her knees to her chest as he notches his cock at her entrance and sinks into her hot, wet hole.

She twitches, her legs kicking, and whimpers. When I purr, she settles. I watch over Sam's shoulder as he fucks her with all the eagerness and stamina of youth.

"Bloody fucking hell! Can I come now?" Tom begs.

I wait a moment, dragging it out, as Sam batters her cunt, his thick cock gliding in and out, fucking our beta by proxy. The sight of both of them working together to drive her wild fills me with pride. "Yes." Tom moves again. He thrusts five times, and then he comes with a filthy groan that makes Sam follow.

"Thank our omega."

Tom reaches around and rubs her clit until she comes, the fluids dripping out of her. My cum. Sam's too. Her slick. She soaks Tom again, then goes limp. He pulls himself from her ass and rolls them onto their sides, spooning her, while Sam flops down in front, his grin lopsided and proud.

Tom ruffles the boy's hair. "Good job, puppy."

"Are you ever going to let me fuck you for real?" Sam asks, still grinning.

Tom bops him on the nose. "Maybe one day if you're very, very good. But remember, even if I let you fuck me, I'm still the one holding your leash."

"Okay."

I chuckle and walk away, my fatigued cock flopping against my thigh as we take advantage of our brief respite and rehydrate. Taking turns, we slip out of the nest to attend to our needs but all of us return, coming back to the cuddle pile one by one as we lie there in a tangle of limbs and blankets until she stirs again, her insatiable hunger for cock and cum resurfaced.

Sam forces another bottle of her special water down her throat. She clings to him, and he strokes her until her hips rise into the air, her signal that she wants more. That she needs us.

"Looking for a cock, omega?" I ask her.

She whimpers and nods, and I grab her by the hips and roll her onto her belly. She goes up on her knees, her face pressed into the nest and the comfort of our scents. I press my head to her entrance and slide in, her sweet slick coating me once more.

"You feel so good, sweetheart. You're so wet."

She moans. Either from the soft praise or the motions of my cock, I'm not certain, so I give her both.

"So perfect, sweetheart. Gonna breed you just like this, on your knees underneath me where you belong." I roll my hips, sliding in and out of her and tugging her down onto my cock with every thrust against her cervix. "I'm gonna fill this sweet little pussy full of cum and fuck a baby into you."

"Alpha," she whimpers. Her hips rock back to meet me. She wants this. Wants my baby. Wants us to breed her.

"That's right, sweetheart. God, I can smell it. You're so fucking fertile. Smells so good. You like getting rutted raw, don't you? You want this knot?"

Her fingers twist in the sheets, and she clenches on my cock. She nods.

So close. My pelvis tightens with the first twist of seed. I grip both sides of her hips and pin her under me, and then I come, my head dropping to watch my cock jerk as I pump her full and feed it into her. I push deep, the skin at the base swelling as my knot lodges tight. Her pussy stretches, her pink walls gripping my knot and wrapping around it until her labia thins as the base of my cock swells.

Once she's tied and our attachment is secure, I reach under and stroke her clit. "Good girl. Now come on my knot. Suck that seed up deep 'til it's in your womb. Take my baby."

A few strokes of her clit and she comes, her pussy tugging at my knot as it pulses with her pleasure. It pulls another jet of semen from my balls, and I groan as I pump it into her. This time, when the knot shrinks and I pull out of her, I wait for the cum and slick to gush and gather it up. Scooping it up with my fingers, I stuff it back into her, my middle finger brushing up against her cervix as I feed it deep.

"Hold it," I tell her, squeezing her lips together to stem the flow. "Don't waste my seed."

"I didn't know you had such a breeding kink," Tom says from the doorway, his pasta-wrapped fork halfway to his mouth.

I frown at him. "No eating in the nest."

He looks down at his feet and then looks around and gives me a strange look, as if to say, *but I'm not in the nest*. He shoves the huge bite of pasta into his mouth and chews with exaggerated movements. I snort. He's always a brat even when he says nothing.

"Alpha," she whines, her ass still in the air.

I pat her on the hip and climb off her. She sinks onto the mattress, cum and slick dripping out of her as she lies there, panting. Leaning down, I press a kiss to her buttock and get out of the nest.

I look at his pasta with longing. "Is there more?"

Tom nods and finishes eating, and I take his dirty bowl as he climbs into the nest to spoon our sleepy omega while I head down to fetch the giant serving Sam's set aside for me. I kiss him on the cheek and thank him.

"How much longer do you think?" I ask between bites. Rutting is hard work, and I'm starving.

"A day, maybe." He looks down at his untouched food, his thumb moving over the design printed on the bowl.

I set my pasta down, reach over and ruffle his hair, pulling him into me. "You okay, brat? You know that I'm just saving all this cum for her, right? Because we're breeding her? That it doesn't mean anything beyond that and things'll go back to normal once she's pregnant?"

"I know." He presses his cheek against my chest and hugs me back. "I was just thinking how I don't really remember my dad all that much. What if I'm bad at it?"

Fuck. I stroke Sam's hair and rub my fingertips over his back. "You're gonna be great at it. And you know what? I don't know anything about being a dad either. But I know we're all going to figure it out together. Because we love each other, and we're pack, and we're going to love the hell out of this baby. We'll get books and... and read blogs, or something."

He laughs, which was my goal. Sam tips his face up, resting his chin on my chest, and he smiles that beautiful lopsided grin that makes his eyes light up. "Blogs? What is this, two-thousand-and-ten? Who still reads blogs?"

"Shut up, brat." I kiss his bratty mouth and let him go with a smack on his ass, then go back to my pasta. After I wolf it down, I add my bowl to the pile of dishes in the sink. "I love you. Now we'd better get up there. I hear rustling."

We fuck her into complacency again, and then Sam gets her into the bath. When they're done, they join us in the nest and I purr her to sleep against my chest. We get several hours of sleep before the sun wakes us as it streams through the curtains.

Warm and beyond satisfied, I pull Emily tighter against me and lean down to smell her hair. Her perfume is different. It's lost the sticky sweetness of her heat. Now she's all soft, sweet lemons again and my head feels clearer than it has since this started.

I roll her onto her back and sniff her all over, licking her mating bite and the scent gland there to check again. She winds her fingers into my hair as I sniff down her body, giving her pussy a lick to be certain. Her slick's back to normal. She's not pumping out *I'm a fertile omega, breed me* pheromones anymore.

"Hnnng, sore," she moans, throwing an arm over her eyes to shield them from the morning light.

"Your heat's over, sweetheart." I settle between her legs and press a kiss to her belly. It's flat.

For now.

"Am I…" She bites her lip and looks down her body. Emly settles her hand there as if she can feel it. But it's too early for that. One day soon, though, it'll be swollen and we'll all take turns feeling her round belly for baby kicks.

"I'll make a doctor's appointment for us in two weeks," Sam says, rolling onto his side.

Tom gets up on his elbow, looking over the beta. "I bought an at-home testing machine."

Sam glances over his shoulder. "You'll still need like ten days before she can take one."

Emily presses her hand over her belly and smiles.

"I love you," I tell her, purring. I cup my hand over hers and imagine the life we've just made from our pack's love.

"I love you," Sam and Tom both say, reaching over to stroke her as if they can feel it too. Our baby.

After a moment of basking, Sam wiggles out of the nest. "Pancakes?"

"God, yes," Emily says. "I'm starving. I could murder a mountain of pancakes."

I reach up and grab her chin, turning her head so she's looking at me. "You can have one." The last thing we need is a repeat of the restaurant. Especially when she might be in a delicate state. I won't do anything to risk her, to risk our baby. "And if it stays down, we'll negotiate lunch."

Emily gapes at me for a moment, then smiles, her eyes softening so they crinkle at the corners. "Yes, alpha."

Warmth and love unfurls in my chest through our bond, and I feed it back to her, purring, as Sam heads downstairs to cook while Tom flops onto his back and rubs the crust of sleep from his eyes.

My pack.

Mine.

I've never been happier.

Want to keep reading? Join the newsletter and get the bonus epilogue delivered right to your inbox.
https://dl.bookfunnel.com/1jhgqatj9t

Also by Alexis B. Osborne

OMEGAVERSE

Omegas of OAN

(Sci-Fi Omegaverse)

Omega Swipes Right

Omega Revealed

Omega for Rent

Omega Rescued

Heatverse

(Contemporary Why Choose Omegaverse)

Heat Clinic

Rut Bar (Coming 2023)

ALIEN ROMANCE

Outer Limits Quadrant

Engineering Fate

Doctoring Fate

Interpreting Fate (Coming Summer 2023)

Sagittarius Quadrant

Ice Planet Prison

Mate for the Alien P*rn Star

Author's Note

Thank you so much for reading Heat Clinic! I hope that you enjoyed reading it as much as I loved writing it. I started this book with no intentions and zero plan as a way to get the creative juices flowing while I worked through a plot hole with one of my alien romances. Basically I wanted to write a scene I'd been thinking of for a while, a giant glory hole for omegas in heat who wanted relief without the risk of a bite or harm. I thought I'd bang out 20k of smut and then go back to my other book. Instead, I wrote over 120k in 18 days. I have never written a book that fast in my entire life and I probably never will again and that's okay. By the time I was done, my fingers were literally sore and I had a book full of kinky smut, fluff, and feels. Obviously, every good book needs a series, thus the Heatverse was born. I have so many ideas for future books so please let me know what else you'd like to see. If you've made it this far, please consider leaving a review. Reviews are author hugs!

For updates, new release alerts, teasers, sales info, freebies, and bonus content delivered to your inbox about once a month, join my newsletter. To stalk me on social media or visit the shop, you can find that at www.alexisbosborne.com.

-Alexis

About the Author

Alexis lives in New York with her wife and step-son and a small horde of furry beings. She began her love affair with books at an early age, and began writing for fun in High School and College. She fell in insta-love with the strange and unusual at an early age. When she's not reading or writing she can be found painting and making subversive cross-stitch. Her favorite fairy tale will always be Beauty and the Beast. Alexis loves all things fantastical, alien, and weird. She will never forget the gorgeous glory that was the late, great David Bowie.

www.alexisbosborne.com

Printed in Great Britain
by Amazon

51658163R00239